Maizie Albright Star Detective

★ ★ ★ ★

18

CALIBER

★ ★ ★ ★

Wall Street Journal bestselling author

Larissa Reinhart

PRAISE FOR LARISSA REINHART

THE FINLEY GOODHART CRIME CAPER SERIES

"This is as fun a novel as it is moving and at times heart-breaking, never the more so when the final page comes and readers are only left wanting more."

CYNTHIA CHOW, *KING'S RIVER LIFE MAGAZINE* ON THE CUPID CAPER

"Another great mystery by Larissa Reinhart. Con artists, murder, a cast of sinister characters, and some laughs along the way. Loved it."

TERRI L. AUSTIN, AUTHOR OF THE *ROSE STRICKLAND MYSTERIES* ON THE CUPID CAPER

THE MAIZIE ALBRIGHT STAR DETECTIVE SERIES

"Fun characters, a perfect setting, and a mystery that will keep you guessing until the end, this book truly has it all!"

—SHANNON VANBERGEN, USA TODAY BESTSELLING AUTHOR OF THE GLOCK GRANNIES MYSTERIES ON 20 CARATS

"Fans of humorous mysteries like Janet Evanovich's Stephanie Plum and Elle Cosimano's Finlay Donovan should pick up this series. We all need some fun in our reading lives!"

"The banter between Maizie and her besties is witty and always a delight, and the plot moves swiftly along and proves to be extremely grounded and compelling. "

"If you're looking for a fun series that will keep you turning the pages, you've found it here."

"I highly recommend this series and definitely start with Book 1 you won't be sorry! Well written characters and a great mystery."

"The perfect combination of mystery, romance, and laughs."

"This was a fun read—a fast-paced caper that kept me entertained until the end."

TERRY AMBROSE, AUTHOR OF THE
SEASIDE COVE MYSTERIES ON 18 CALIBER

"The mystery and detective cases drive the story, but Larissa Reinhart's characters steal the show every time."

THE GIRL WITH BOOK LUNGS ON NC-17

"Fans of cozy mysteries, southern chick lit, hick lit, crime capers, and humorous mysteries will love it."

JANE READS ON NC-17

"If you love southern settings with plenty of sweet tea and eccentric characters, the meet up of these two heroines is epic."

— BARB TAUB, HUMOR WRITER AND
AUTHOR OF THE *NULL CITY* SERIES ON A
VIEW TO A CHILL

"I encourage readers to delve into this lively, funny, and genuinely satisfying series."

CYNTHIA CHOW, *KINGS RIVER LIFE*
MAGAZINE ON 16 MILLIMETERS

"With visually descriptive narrative, humorous quips, witty repartee and a quirky cast of characters, this was a such a fun book to read."

DRU ANN LOVE, DRU'S BOOK MUSING ON
16 MILLIMETERS

"Sassy, sexy, and fun, 15 Minutes is hours of enjoyment—and a wonderful start to a fun new series from the charmingly Southern-fried Reinhart."

PHOEBE FOX, AUTHOR OF *THE BREAKUP DOCTOR* SERIES ON 15 MINUTES

"Maizie Albright is the kind of fresh, fun, and feisty 'star detective' I love spending time with, a kind of Nancy Drew meets Lucy Ricardo."

PENNY WARNER, AUTHOR OF *DEATH OF A CHOCOLATE CHEATER* AND *THE CODE BUSTERS CLUB* ON 15 MINUTES

"Maizie's my new favorite escape from reality."

— GRETCHEN ARCHER, *USA TODAY* BESTSELLING AUTHOR OF THE *DAVIS WAY CRIME CAPER* SERIES ON 15 MINUTES

THE CHERRY TUCKER MYSTERY SERIES

"Anytime artist Cherry Tucker has what she calls a Matlock moment, can investigating a murder be far behind? A rollicking good time."

TERRIE FARLEY MORAN, AGATHA AWARD-WINNING AUTHOR OF *READ TO DEATH* ON A COMPOSITION IN MURDER

"This is a winning series that continues to grow stronger and never fails to entertain with laughs, a little snark, and a ton of heart."

KINGS RIVER LIFE MAGAZINE ON A COMPOSITION IN MURDER

"Cherry Tucker is a strong, sassy, Southern sleuth who keeps you on the edge of your seat."

TONYA KAPPES, *USA TODAY* BESTSELLING AUTHOR ON THE BODY IN THE LANDSCAPE

"Because of Cherry's experiences, she knows that man has always been the most dangerous game, making her the perfect protagonist for this giggle-inducing, down-home fun."

BETTY WEBB, *MYSTERY SCENE MAGAZINE* ON THE BODY IN THE LANDSCAPE

"The perfect blend of funny, intriguing, and sexy! Another must-read masterpiece from the hilarious Cherry Tucker Mystery Series."

– ANN CHARLES, *USA TODAY* BESTSELLING AUTHOR OF THE *DEADWOOD* AND *JACKRABBIT JUNCTION MYSTERY SERIES* ON DEATH IN PERSPECTIVE

"Reinhart's charming, sweet-tea flavored series keeps getting better!"

GRETCHEN ARCHER, *USA TODAY* BESTSELLING AUTHOR OF THE *DAVIS WAY CRIME CAPER SERIES* ON DEATH IN PERSPECTIVE

"Like front-porch lemonade, Reinhart's cast of characters offer a perfect balance of tart and sweet."

SOPHIE LITTLEFIELD, BESTSELLING AUTHOR OF *A BAD DAY FOR SORRY* ON HIJACK IN ABSTRACT

"Reinhart manages to braid a complicated plot into a tight and funny tale. Cozy fans will love this latest Cherry Tucker mystery."

MARY MARKS, *NEW YORK JOURNAL OF BOOKS* ON HIJACK IN ABSTRACT

"Readers who like a little small-town charm with their mysteries will enjoy Reinhart's series."

DENISE SWANSON, *NEW YORK TIMES* BESTSELLING AUTHOR OF THE *SCUMBLE RIVER MYSTERIES* ON STILL LIFE IN BRUNSWICK STEW

"This mystery keeps you laughing and guessing from the first page to the last. A whole-hearted five stars."

DENISE GROVER SWANK, *NEW YORK TIMES* AND *USA TODAY* BESTSELLING AUTHOR ON STILL LIFE IN BRUNSWICK STEW

"An entertaining mystery full of quirky characters and solid plotting. Highly recommended for anyone who likes their mysteries strong and their mint juleps stronger!"

– JENNIE BENTLEY, *NEW YORK TIMES* BESTSELLING AUTHOR OF *FLIPPED OUT* ON PORTRAIT OF A DEAD GUY

"Reinhart is a truly talented author and this book was one of the best cozy mysteries we reviewed this year."

– *MYSTERY TRIBUNE* ON PORTRAIT OF A DEAD GUY

"It takes a rare talent to successfully portray a beer-and-hormone-addled artist as a sympathetic and worthy heroine, but Reinhart pulls it off with tongue-in-cheek panache."

18 CALIBER, Maizie Albright Star Detective #6

Library of Congress: 2020903483

ASIN: B085HGGBW2

ePub: 978-1-7345638-0-1

Print: 978-1-7345638-1-8

Hardcover: 978-1-7345638-2-5

Past Perfect Press

Author photo by Scott Asano

Original cover design by James of GoOnWrite

https://www.goonwrite.com/

BOOKS BY LARISSA REINHART

MAIZIE ALBRIGHT STAR DETECTIVE SERIES (IN ORDER)

15 MINUTES

16 MILLIMETERS

NC-17

A VIEW TO A CHILL

17.5 CARTRIDGES IN A PEAR TREE

18 CALIBER

18 1/2 DISGUISES

19 CRIMINALS

20 CARATS

21 GUNS

A CHERRY TUCKER MYSTERY SERIES (IN ORDER)

A CHRISTMAS QUICK SKETCH (prequel)

PORTRAIT OF A DEAD GUY

STILL LIFE IN BRUNSWICK STEW

HIJACK IN ABSTRACT

THE VIGILANTE VIGNETTE

DEATH IN PERSPECTIVE

THE BODY IN THE LANDSCAPE

A VIEW TO A CHILL

A COMPOSITION IN MURDER

A MOTHERLODE OF TROUBLE

A FINLEY GOODHART CRIME CAPER SERIES

PIG'N A POKE (prequel, short story)

THE CUPID CAPER

THE PONY PREDICAMENT (coming soon!)

THE HEIR AFFAIR (coming soon!)

———

THE PIG'N A POKE

A Finley Goodhart Crime Caper prequel

When a winter storm traps ex-con Finley at the Pig'N a Poke roadhouse, she finds her criminal past useful in solving a murder.

Free for my VIP Readers!

Join Larissa's email group where she shares exclusive content, news, and giveaways — **www.larissareinhart.com/larissasreaders** — and receive *The Pig'n A Poke* as a gift.

Note: Larissa will not share your email address and you can unsubscribe at any time.

18 CALIBER

A ROMANTIC COMEDY MYSTERY

MAIZIE ALBRIGHT STAR DETECTIVE
BOOK 6

LARISSA REINHART

Past Perfect Press

ACKNOWLEDGMENTS

Thank you, Lord, for unanswered prayers and for inspiring me to write this series. Anything good came from Your blessing.

Ritter Ames, you're an incredible editor, book guru, and a great friend. Thank you for all the help and support. And thank you, especially for your graciousness, understanding, and lightning-fast editing skills!

Terri Austin, thanks for being my beta buddy and for your friendship! I can't wait to read your next book!

The Mystery Minions, know I'm thinking about y'all while writing. You each represent the reason I burn the midnight oil. Thank you so much for your incredible support and friendship!

To my Larissa's Writing Friends on Facebook, and especially to Dru Ann Love, Lori Caswell, Lorie Lewis, and Debby Guisti, thank you for your friendship and guidance. I love the encouragement and support of the writing community. It's a wonderful thing.

To the Funks, Reinharts, and Hoffmans, thanks always for all your love, support, and Facebook shoutouts. Also to my sweet friends (too numerous to name all of you) for your encouragement, especially the Metzler-Concepcions, Schwingshakls, Witzanys (thank you for letting me borrow Maizie's name), and the Benders. Love you! And to all the folks in Andover and surrounds, thank you for your hometown support!

Gina, Bill, Hailey, Lily, Sonja, and Grandma Sally: thank you for beta reading, your encouragement, and generally putting up with me.

Peachtree City, Georgia, thanks for inviting Hollywood to town and giving me the inspiration for this series. And thanks for being such a wonderful place to live and raise my children.

And to Trey, Lu & So, you always have my gratitude and love. xoxo

To my girls
Be proud of your heritage.

ON CHINESE NAMES

Even though I included Chinese citizens in a murder mystery, the characters are human with flaws and foibles, strengths and gifts, as in any of the Americans in my stories. I have a great love for Chinese culture and people. If you didn't know, I have two Chinese daughters. They have Western names, but we also kept their given Chinese names. I used syllables from their names in some of the characters' names as Easter eggs in this book. I thought the information below would help those who struggle with pronunciation or were just curious about the names I chose.

Chinese names are generally ordered as surname first and given name last. In Western writing, the characters of the given name are sometimes written separately. For example, Mao (surname) Zedong (given) can be written as Mao Ze Dong. In the list below, I'm using the Western style of given name first and surname last. I don't separate the syllables to make reading easier. I included the *hanzi*, Chinese characters, and meaning just for fun.

"Chinese given names usually consist of two syllables (though it is also common to only use one). Those syllables can be any of the thousands of Chinese characters, so the combinations are almost limitless. In practice, some characters are chosen more often than others, such as Mei, "beautiful" for girls. Sometimes the first character of the given name is shared by all members of a generation in a family. Chinese parents do not typically name babies after relatives or famous people." [Behind the Name, https://www.behindthename.com/glossary/view/chinese_names]

18 CALIBER NAMES

<u>Shifu</u>

Shīfu 师傅

Master; qualified worker; teacher; respectful form of address for older men.

<u>Lili Liang</u> (lead actress in *Unlucky 18*)

Lì lì 丽丽 Liáng 梁

Lili (sounds like Leelee): beautiful, beautiful.

Liang: also the surname of the scholar in the famous folktale *Butterfly Lovers*, the Chinese version of *Romeo and Juliet*.

<u>Stanley Wu</u> (supporting actor in *Unlucky 18*)

Sī tǎn lì 斯坦利 Wu 吴

Stanley: a popular Western name in China, also a town in Hong Kong originally called Chek Chue.

Wu: tenth most common surnames in China; from the ancient sate of Wu meaning Gateway to Heaven.

<u>Zhihao Zhao</u> (Associate Producer for *Unlucky 18*)

Zhì Háo 志豪 Zhào 赵

Zi (sounds like Gee): will, purpose, ambition.

Hao: heroic, chivalrous.

Zhao (or Chao) (sounds like tch[a]o): from an ancient family line; refers to ancient city-state in now Shanxi province.

<u>Shifu Xiang Xi</u> (Lili Liang's Shaolin kung fu master)

Xiáng翔 Xì 郤

Xiáng (sounds like shaang): Soar, glide.

Xi (sounds like shee): a common surname; also a city around the lower reaches of present-day Quin River in Shanxi province.

Master Kevin Yuan (Maizie's *Kung Fu Kate* kung fu master and Lili's new trainer)

Kè wén 克文 Yuán 园

Kevin: a popular Western name in China.

Surname Yuán: garden, park.

Shiyu Kang (Lili Liang's assistant)

Shí Yù 石玉 Kàng 亢

Shi (sounds like shee): Stone.

Yu: Jade.

Kang: a common surname; one of the 28 constellations; excessive; overbearing; high.

Harvey Lee (Producer for *Unlucky 18*)

Hā luó dé 哈罗德 Lǐ 李

Harvey: a popular Western name in China.

Lee: a common surname (Li); plum

Ning Lee (Producer for *Unlucky 18*)

Níng 宁 Lǐ 李

Ning: Peaceful

Lee (Li): plum

ONE
#EYESPYANOTSODEADGUY

YOU'D THINK with the explosion of DIY home security, Nash Security Solutions would lose a lot of clients. Not so when a celebrity management company acquires your private investigations office. Our clients — rich and posers alike — wanted to hire someone to set up their Ring and Google whatnots. Except for the paranoid few who want their homes to look like a *Mission Impossible* set, most were content with the self-service models, not the high-tech systems we specialized in.

We — Wyatt Nash, a professional PI, and me, Maizie Albright, his apprentice — had gone from private investigations and security specialists to handymen. Or handywoman in my case. Makes me miss cheating spouse surveillance.

Still a paycheck is a paycheck.

"Hand me that screwdriver, Miss Albright. Phillips." His eyes on the door of a trailer, Wyatt Nash held out a hand. A large hand. Calloused. Pocked with a few small scars. But with long, nimble fingers capable of a gentle touch.

A touch that can induce feelings of wondrous and rapturous delight, I might add.

Nash glanced at me. "The one you named Phyllis."

I grabbed the screwdriver from his adorable red metal box

and placed it in the center of his big hand. Then dragged my fingers across his palm before he could close it.

His ice-blue eyes darted to my sea glass greens. "Miss Albright. We're working."

Holding back a pout, I examined the bright blue sky with bare puffs of clouds gliding on the horizon. Winter in the North Georgia mountains was much colder than winters I'd experienced in LA, naturally. But there were days like today, when the sun changed the temperature from chill to brisk. The blue and gold sky lit the tops of the tall Georgia pines, disguising all the dull brown that became more apparent with gray skies.

The sun made me hopeful. I looked back at Nash, who concentrated on screwing in a peephole camera. The tall, muscular body leaned toward the door. The sleeves on his flannel-lined denim jacket straining to accommodate his biceps and chest. Levi's fitting him snugly in all the right places.

I gave into a pensive and mournful sigh. Wyatt Nash was no longer my boss. Officially, I had dibs on him romantically. But he was still the southern gentleman through and through. Which meant a strong division between work and play. Stronger than concrete, steel, or diamonds. And not even flexible-strong like bamboo or spider silk.

He was carbon fiber among men.

And it wasn't just because our boss, Vicki Albright — still-owner of Always Albright Celebrity Management and new-owner of Nash Security Solutions — made clear the rules for our working relationship. No hanky-panky on the job site.

As if.

Nash had been offended she even raised the issue. And I had morals and ethics and all that. Even after growing up in Beverly Hills.

Sort of, anyway. The more time I spent in Georgia, the more I wondered about my prior values.

The real problem lay with Vicki's celebrity connections. We worked non-stop. Which is totally awesome if you're trying to re-establish a foothold in the once slippery position of private investigations and security systems in our town of Black Pine, Georgia. Not so awesome, if you want to date your co-worker and you're working twenty-four-seven-three-sixty-five.

Not that I was working. Not at the moment, anyway. We'd split up the trailers and I had finished my jobs. Yay me for grabbing the electric screwdriver first.

"I'm going to check the special case," I said to Nash. "See what extras were added to the list."

He nodded and continued to screw the camera into the door.

Times like these made me jealous of Phyllis.

I hiked my Golden Goose sneakers across the backlot's pavement. The trailers were rented by a new production — some kind of martial arts action film — and would be hauled to various locations in the mountains when they weren't sitting behind one of the big sound stages that took a large chunk of land on the outskirts of Black Pine. Black Pine Studios was new to the area, although the land had been bought and construction started several years ago. The film industry had recently exploded in Black Pine due to Georgia's generous tax shelters, cheap land, and cheaper labor.

I entered the three-room trailer. Checking the clipboard lying on the table near the door, I noted their security needs. Nothing over-the-top — not like the retinal scanners we'd recently installed in a producer's rented home — but it would need more work than the others. Alarms on all the windows. Emergency button in the bathroom. Scan for hidden cameras and microphones.

I made a quick list of supplies we'd need, then began my walk-through for the alarm count. Like their security feature wish list, the trailer was lavish but not outrageous. The roomy living area had a galley kitchen featuring an eat-in peninsula. Cherry wood and marble. Below a large flatscreen was an inset fireplace. In the mountains, Georgia did get cold this time of year. Large makeup station in the bathroom, complete with Hollywood lighting. King-size bed in the bedroom.

Where a man lay dead.

"Holy Hellsbah," I shrieked and backed out of the room. "Not again."

The dead man rolled over, then sat up.

"Thank God." I slapped a hand over my heart. "You're not dead."

From the doorway, I examined the youngish man. Dressed in (rumpled) trendy clothes with sandy brown hair, he didn't look like a derelict. But if he worked in the business, he would know he shouldn't be in the trailers. "Why are you sleeping here?"

"I was tired." He had an impish smile. "Why did you assume I was dead?"

"Long story but mostly bad luck." I folded my arms. "You can't sleep in these trailers. And you shouldn't be on-set without permission."

Sliding across the bed, he grabbed a lanyard from an end table and held up a plastic badge.

"Then you should know you can't sleep in these trailers." I raised my chin. "Who are you?"

"Jeff Johnson." He grinned. "Who are you? Besides a ginger with a nice...clipboard."

I narrowed my eyes. "What are you? I mean, what do you do?"

"Awesome." He waggled his brows. "And wouldn't you like to know."

"I would. Like to know. Considering I'm installing the security in this trailer."

"No worries, doll." He slid to the edge of the bed.

I wasn't security-security. I was a contractor who screwed in doorbell cams then uploaded the app to the client's phone because they were too busy (lazy) to do it themselves. However, I should report Jeff Johnson. For unofficial napping.

"Before you go, let me see your badge." I used my official

security voice, one I'd developed for a *Julia Pinkerton, Teen Detective* movie that went into production but was abruptly canceled after the producers (and their marketing department) decided the script wasn't pro-STEM enough. Julia had already graduated from high school and the writers decided as a vigilante she'd major in pre-law.

Instead of engineering as the marketing department would have liked.

At the time, I had majored in criminal justice at U Cal Long Beach, so pre-law made all kinds of sense to me. But what did I know about pre-teen demographics? Anyway, I'd had a two-year hiatus from starring in the *Julia Pinkerton, Teen Detective* TV show, and thought for the movie, I could make her more edgy with a scholarly, pandering raspy drawl. I had the college sneer down pretty good, too. Now I used it with on-the-job pests.

I loved finding new uses for old character traits. Recycling always made me feel like a productive citizen.

"Badge," I repeated, extending my hand.

"I'll show you mine, if I can see yours," Jeff Johnson countered to my collegiate sneer with a frat boy smirk. He crooked a finger and deepened the smirk. "Show and tell time."

"Yours first." I'd reverted from collegiate to grammar school.

Jeff chuckled and held out the badge. "Feisty. I like that."

Instead of calling him something that would lower me to his standards (and possibly get me in trouble), I snatched the badge from his hand and examined it.

"You're a visitor for *Unlucky 18*? The martial arts movie? How did you get this?" I handed him the badge. "They haven't started filming. This is pre-production. You shouldn't be here."

"That's an all-access pass. Ask around. Everyone knows me."

"Visitors have restrictions. Someone from the set should be accompanying you."

Looping the lanyard around his neck, he winked. "You know what they say about all work and no play. Are you always this strict, doll?"

"Yes." Not really. Only with this dude. I folded my arms. "These trailers are under surveillance. I'd advise you to find whoever got you the pass and stay with them."

"All right. No harm, no foul, right? Can't blame a guy for trying to find some peace and quiet with all the banging on set." He chuckled and repeated "banging" to himself.

Frat boy humor.

"Just get out of here." It was difficult to nap during pre-production. I'd longed for many a nap on-set. But I wasn't telling him that.

Jeff exited, and I resumed my checklist, then straightened the bed. I didn't want anyone to think we'd been napping on the job. Exiting the bedroom, I heard the trailer door open and scurried into the living area.

Nash glanced around, scowling. But that was his MO. Which made his smiles even sweeter, IMHO. "Did I see a guy exiting this trailer?"

"Jeff Johnson had a visitor badge. I kicked him out. Caught him napping." I pointed to the clipboard. "We're going to need some extra equipment for this one. I guess that's why Vicki told us to do it last."

Nash peered over my shoulder. "They want this swept for bugs? We've not done that before. And a camera on the roof? What the sam hell? Whose trailer is this?"

"Maybe it's for a producer or director. They can get a little paranoid about leaks."

Nash rolled his eyes. "This industry."

"A billion-dollar industry. *Unlucky 18* is a big-budget action movie. Vicki said the production company teamed up with an international consortium. There's a lot of money at stake, so they're just being careful."

"Why do you always defend the dopey decisions these movie people make?"

"I'm explaining their reasoning. It's why they hired us. In their minds, it's important." I shouldn't defend them. The entertainment industry had eaten me up and spit me out like a polar bear on a baby seal. At the same time, this was the work we were given. By Vicki.

I loved polar bears. My favorite animal to watch at the zoo. But on a documentary, I'd seen a polar bear play with a seal before ripping the head off, devouring the meat, and tossing the carcass for fish food. Poor baby seal.

At least its mother hadn't auditioned him for the polar bear.

"And Vicki. You're always making excuses for her." Nash folded his arms. "You don't have to pretend this situation is okay. It sucks. For both of us. You more than me."

"It's not that bad," I pleaded. "We're working."

"On stupid projects. And dealing with obnoxious people."

"We've dealt with obnoxious people before. Most of the people we know are obnoxious."

He picked up the clipboard. "I have a scanner in the truck. I'll see if it picks up any interference from hidden mikes or cameras. Why don't you start installing the sensors?"

I nodded, glad to ignore the elephant — or polar bear — in the room. Nash hadn't wanted an ex-actress as an apprentice. I'd won him over then ruined his career by bringing media attention to a splashy case. Cost him his credibility in the community. He lost jobs, then his company. In that situation, I wasn't exactly the polar bear. But I'd accidentally unleashed the real polar bear on him. Vicki. He said it wasn't my fault. He'd had some bad luck. Also an ex-wife with her own ursine qualities. Grizzly, IMHO. Jolene gladly traded her half of Nash's company to Vicki for a hefty catch. Money not salmon. Although Jolene would have eaten the baby seal if given the chance.

After a lot of good breaks as a child star, I'd had nothing but bad luck as an adult. I couldn't help but feel I'd jinxed Nash. And I only knew one way to make it up to him.

Well, two ways.

But the one I could do at work was to stay positive.

While I attached sticky-backed sensors to the windows and

doors, Nash returned with a hand-held gadget that looked like a TV remote. He moved through the trailer, playing hot and cold, listening to the crackling sounds turn to beeps. It squawked next to a lamp in the living area.

Hidden mike.

We found a pinhole camera inside an empty screw hole in the thermostat panel. And in a wall socket next to the makeup station, another mike.

"Wow." I followed him into the master bedroom where the beeping intensified. He found the bug and a tiny fisheye camera in the overhead ceiling light.

"Nash, that Jeff Johnson. I don't think he was napping." I swallowed hard and sank onto the bed. "Hells. I caught a spy."

"Caught?"

"You're right." I blew out a long, slow breath. "More like let him go."

TWO
#MOTHERFUNDER

AFTER TEARING out tiny cameras and installing new ones, we departed the set. Nash needed to check on a job we'd done yesterday — Vicki's salt grotto manager had issues with app connectivity. Perhaps halo-therapy and security didn't mix. — and I found myself with a little free time. I needed the liberation after the past hour of interrogation in the studio's security office. The *Unlucky 18* staff felt I should've done more to stop Jeff Johnson from leaving the set. Many words were said. Words causing such severe clenching of Nash's jaw, it made me fear for his teeth.

We were going to work all night. Again.

Taking my hour, I ran toward all that was goodness and holy. In my world that was hugs from friends. And a quick blow out. I received both from LA HAIR, my go-to for hair, nails, and emotional guidance.

Pushing through the black and gold crackle-painted glass door, I strode into the oldish shop in an oldish Black Pine strip mall. The layered scents of Aquage, ammonia, and acetone wafted through the space, filling me with soothing ASMR-y vibes. A new water fountain featuring faux bamboo trickled in a corner and a top hits station played through the speakers painted to look like rocks. Bottles of marked-up hair care products and marked-down homemade jewelry lined metal shelves that anchored the row of black vinyl chairs in the waiting area. On the end tables, I would find months-old *People*, *Glamour*, and *Country Living* magazines with pages torn out by customers who felt justified in stealing coupons and recipes.

Although one could not compare LA HAIR with the atmosphere or services given at a Beverly Hills salon, I also never worried about getting stabbed in the back with a pair of gold-plated scissors. LA HAIR — referring to the city or French article, no one knew or cared — had been with me through good times and bad.

Mostly bad since that'd been the luck forcing my move to Georgia in the first place.

"I need the works," I announced to the two women standing behind the black and gold crackle-painted receptionist stand. "But I only have forty-five minutes."

Tiffany and Rhonda were my closest friends in Black Pine as well as LA HAIR's nail esthetician and receptionist. They were Black Pine born and raised whereas I was just born. But in a way, I'd returned to Black Pine to be raised again. Tiffany and Rhonda were part of that movement.

"Girl." Rhonda's right eyebrow edged north and she pursed her full lips.

"Lord," said Tiffany, shaking her blunt, blue-tipped bob.

In Tiff and Rhon-speak, "Girl" and "Lord" both meant, "What now?" They often spoke without speaking. And when they spoke, it could be a teeny bit painful. But no truer words and all that.

"You go first," I said. "Why does Rhonda only have hair extensions on one side?"

"It's a new thing." Rhonda scratched her chin. "Like an angle cut."

"It's what happens when your arms get too tired before you finish your whole head." Tiffany glared at her. "If she'd asked me, I would have done it."

Rhonda pouted. "You said you were busy."

"I was, but if you'd given me a minute, I'd find another day."

"Girl," said Rhonda, ending that conversation. She ushered me toward the row of salon chairs. "What's up with you, Maizie?"

"I found a spy by accident. I interrupted him bugging a movie trailer." Plopping into a chair next to the nail stations, I eyed Shelly at the other end of the salon, washing a customer's hair. Running water blocked the customer's ears, but not Shelly's. I lowered my voice. "In my defense, I didn't know he was a spy when I let him go. Also, deception is kind of the point of being a spy. But I was blamed for his escape anyway."

"What do you mean a spy?" Rhonda draped a black cape over my shoulders. "Like 007? Why would a spy be in Black Pine?"

"Russia isn't infiltrating Black Pine, Rhon. It's a movie thing." Tiffany spun my chair to face her. "Why would anyone spy on a movie when they could spy on something important?"

"This film is in pre-production and it's a big picture. It could be an industrial spy from another studio, but he also might be some creeper who's stalking one of the stars. Gross. And to think I let Jeff Johnson walk out of that trailer." I scowled. "That's what bothers me. How could I fall for such a fake name? His visitor badge looked real, but you don't even need Photoshop to fake something like that anymore."

"Maizie, get over it. You're not going to get fired and your boss will cover your ass. That's the best thing about working for someone else—passing the buck." Tiffany picked up my hand to study the nails. "But you're ruining your manicure with all this doorbell camera business."

"Your hair, too." Rhonda lifted a lank of my strawberry blonde tresses. "Your ends are stressed."

"Maybe just hair today. I have to be at the office in an hour. Do what you can." I smiled graciously, then caught myself. This smile was for the Beverly Hills salon. Hells, Rhonda and Tiffany didn't deserve that smile. "Thanks, girls. I'd be a mess without you."

"I like you having money," said Tiffany. "I don't have to turn you down like I did when you weren't making anything."

"True," said Rhonda. "Working for Vicki can't be all bad. I could use a raise and benefits package. I wish she'd take over LA HAIR."

"Money comes with a price," I said, misery tingeing my voice.

"It's called a paycheck," said Tiffany. "You work and they pay you. And that's how you pay us."

"Truth," I said, although the implication hurt. I'd worked since the age of two. Just not conventionally. "Although she is ruining my relationship with Nash. Mainly because I keep reminding him of the paycheck."

"You're caught in the middle," said Rhonda. "Happens all the time. I got caught between Tiffany and her ex. But I held my ground by reminding her, it doesn't matter what gifts he does or doesn't bring, they're most likely stolen anyway."

"Damn right," said Tiffany. "That weasel was always trying to buy me off."

"It'd be nice if you'd remember this before taking it out on me." Rhonda rapped Tiffany's shoulder with a brush.

"And you'd best remember smacking me gets the underside of my collar hot." Tiffany glared at her. "And when my temper's up, my fist tends to react."

"Huh," said Rhonda. "Your probation officer told you that's no excuse. See Maizie, I'm still getting caught in Tiffany's relationships."

"Um, yeah," I drew out the word to give Tiffany time to cool off. "Nash thinks I defend Vicki too much. But she is my, you know." I shrugged.

"Mother?" said Tiffany.

"Actually, I understand her better as an ex-manager. And the decisions she makes in taking clients as related to the entertainment industry. That's where Nash struggles. He doesn't get the movie business. He finds everything 'hinky' or 'stupid.'" I slunk down in my chair, fearing the reality of our real dilemma. "Between Vicki pushing us around and me having to explain the industry all the time, it just reminds him how different we are."

Rhonda's brush smacked my arm. I straightened, and she continued yanking out my tangles. "Maybe he needs reminding that marrying, divorcing, and ticking Jolene off good and plenty — before and after — also made for a broke ass business."

"That doesn't make me feel better." Mostly worse. His ex-wife always made me feel worse.

"Keepin' it real, hon'," said Tiffany. "We're just pointing out it's not all about you."

"Right. Thanks."

Rhonda led me to the sink without further comment. For the next thirty minutes, they washed, conditioned, trimmed, and styled. And I convinced myself DIY doorbell cameras were better than the alternative. Which, for me, was reality show hell, unemployment, or prison. For Nash, working for Vicki was better than staying married to the Wicked Witch of Black Pine or Chapter 11.

I'd imagined my so-called new life differently, but different doesn't always mean better.

Of course, not better could also mean worse.

In Nash's case, maybe that's how he saw his current predicament.

Rhonda spun me around so I could examine my smooth and shiny blowout. I nodded but couldn't stop a tear from traveling down the side of my nose.

"Girl," said Rhonda.

"Lord," said Tiffany.

"It's nothing." I held up a hand. "But I am troubled."

"We can see," said Tiffany. "It's called crying."

"You don't like the blowout?" said Rhonda.

"The blowout is wonderful. I couldn't have done it better myself." Which was true. I was not a professional stylist. "I've ruined Nash's life by trying to make mine better."

Tiffany sucked and rolled her lips. "I hate to say it, kid—"

"Maybe, don't." I held up a hand. "I get your point."

"Maizie." Rhonda clasped her hands in mine. "Remember, you've got two sides to your DNA."

"Do you mean two strands? Because I think they store the same information—"

"No, she means you've got a mother and a father, and even if you didn't live with your daddy until now, he has been involved in your life," said Tiffany. "Remind Nash of your Black Pine roots. Get Boomer to invite him to dinner. Or watch a football game or go fishing. Men like Boomer and Nash bond over that shit."

"OMG. Genius." I brightened then dimmed. "But Vicki…"

"You've got to stop letting her boss you around," said Tiffany.

Kind of hard when she was my boss. "Her management company is growing. She has a lot more clients."

"More than just you is a good thing," said Rhonda.

"Yes," I said, although I hadn't reconciled my feelings to that yet. My ex-therapist Renata used to say, "One issue at a time, like one day at a time."

My now-therapist didn't say much because he was in jail. I tried a session on visiting day, but he needed more counseling than me. "I had thought that once her entertainment roster grew, she'd be distracted from remembering she owned a PI firm. I thought this buy-out of Nash's business would be a temporary thing. And although she is distracted, she doesn't seem to have any interest in relinquishing the company."

"You thought Vicki Albright would just give up the reins?" Tiffany laughed.

"As her ex-client and—" I shifted in my seat.

"Daughter," prompted Rhonda.

"Yes, our relationship being…familial, she might let this go, seeing I hadn't changed my mind about changing my career."

Tiffany snorted. "Unbelievable. You still think Vicki might take your side?"

"She's not evil. She's just—"

"Greedy?" said Rhonda. "Backstabby?"

"Selfish?" said Tiffany. "Bitchy?"

"Jelly," I said. "I'm wondering if she's holding on because she is jealous. You know, now I have Nash. Sort of. And Daddy's been with Carol Lynn all these years. It used to be just Vicki and me. Giulio's not there for her. I mean, Giulio's not there mentally or emotionally for anyone. Not even himself. But I can't seem to reach Vicki. I've been trying despite… things."

"Like, despite Vicki skimming off your acting job trust, forcing you into a reality show you didn't want to do, driving you into substance abuse, then letting you take the fall when your boyfriend was busted for selling Oxy?" Rhonda shrugged. "Just quoting *Entertainment Weekly*."

"What about following you to Georgia?" Tiffany fisted her hands on her hips. "When she couldn't trick you into going back on her reality show, she bought the place where you work and now has you working for movie star peeps. Your probation states you're supposed to stay away from the entertainment industry. That's just crazy."

"I mean…" I felt the pinch between my eyes and blinked to ward off the tears. "She is my mother. I'm sure she at least *thinks* she has my best interests at heart."

"I think Nash made a deal with the devil when he let Vicki buy him out." Tiffany cocked her hip and shook her head. "Y'all were broke, but there is worse than being broke."

"But you said it's good to have a steady paycheck."

"Girl, I was talking about myself and you paying me."

"Here's what I think, Maizie," said Rhonda. "If you leave Nash Security, Vicki will leave Nash Security. And dig her nails into wherever you go next. What does that say to you? Does it sound like something a mom should do?"

"Did you consider the spy might be Vicki?" said Tiffany. "Keeping an eye on you and Nash?"

"Okay, wow," said Rhonda. "That's evil."

"She wouldn't," I said.

But would she?

THREE
#WEDGIEDINLOVE

ON THE WAY to the office, I tried not to think about the possibility of Vicki nanny-camming us. Why would she do it? It couldn't be the work. The clients were happy. I was way too old to be helicoptered. Although she didn't approve of our relationship, I didn't think she'd do hanky-panky surveillance. She didn't have the time.

Unless she hired someone else to watch us. And considering we were an investigations firm that seemed an unnecessary expense.

I parked my dirt bike, Lucky, in front of Dixie Kreme Donuts by habit. Inhaled to absorb the intoxicatingly sweet scent of fried dough. The neon red "hot and fresh" sign had been turned off. Too late for a donut break. I gazed longingly at the office windows at the top of the old brick-front building, then forced myself to walk two blocks to our new location.

Albright Security Solutions was located on Black Pine's turn-of-the-century town square, where a building had been torn down and rebuilt to look exactly like the original brick store-front. Still quaint and vintage-y, complete with the name hand-lettered on the plate glass window. But the Disneyfication of the building unsettled me. Our work felt as faux as the building. As dusty and scruffy as our old office was, it was still ours. Including the donut smell.

Which I really missed.

Plus, Lamar, Dixie Kreme's owner and Nash's silent partner, couldn't drop by as he did before. Even if the drop-in was meant for a mid-day nap. Lamar still held ownership rights to Nash Security Solutions, but the percentage meant he didn't have much sway. Vicki held Nash's half and Jolene's percent. I was still training. Georgia said I couldn't become a licensed PI for two years. And I had no money for ownership anyway. A two-year apprenticeship didn't feel long working for Nash.

Chained to Vicki felt like the prison sentence I thought I'd escaped by moving to Black Pine.

The shop chime rang as I walked through the front door. I tossed my shearling coat on a chair and passed through the shiplap and (faux) brick and plaster waiting room and into the inner sanctum that had once looked like Sam Spade's office until Nash had tossed the staged stuff. The room now resembled *The Maltese Falcon* meets *Minority Report*. We had all the cutting-edge technology needed for investigations and security. With none of the heart.

Not that taking candid photos of husbands' strip club trysts had a lot of heart. But you know what I mean.

"You look…different." Nash squinted at me from behind a Sam Spade desk covered in gadgetry.

"I went to LA HAIR. How was the meeting with the salt cave guy?"

Nash rolled his eyes. "He forgot his password. And his sign in."

"Hope it didn't take long." I strolled to the desk. Shimmied my hip onto the edge. A stapler clattered to the floor. Ignoring the stapler, I dialed my voice to sultry. "Do we have a minute?"

He licked his lips. Pulled in a breath. His eyes traveled from my hair to the top snaps in my RE/DONE Henley bodysuit.

Purposefully — but tastefully — unsnapped for a hint of cleavage. And hopefully, a hint of heaven.

"A minute?" he rasped. He cleared his throat. "Miss Albright…Maizie."

I gave my hair a small toss, wafting Biolage Freeze Fix toward him. To be honest, Rhonda was a teensy too smitten with extra hold, but it did have a nice scent. I parted my lips and slid an inch closer.

His hand crept toward my hip.

"A minute," I said in a slow exhale, "is all I need." Bending forward, I trailed my fingers up his arm. His chair scooted closer. I leaned toward him. Felt the strain of fabric against skin. Caught my breath, then bent forward. The fabric bit into my skin. I jerked back.

Stupid too-small bodysuit.

I slid off the desk. Backed toward our other desk and angled my butt against the corner.

"What are you doing?"

Trying to casually undo the massive wedgie I had created. "I'm sorry. I know how you feel about mixing work and… pleasure."

Nash stood, knocking his chair into the file cabinet behind his desk. "It's after hours," he said, then glanced at the wall clock. "Seven fifteen. Definitely after hours."

"Overtime." I straightened. "We have to debug the trailers."

"We have a minute. What I meant to say earlier…you look pretty. Pretty damn amazing, actually. With the…" He waved a hand. "…hair. And all."

My heart pounding, I moistened my lips and smiled. Then took three flying steps toward Nash, who'd already bounded around the corner of the desk. Our bodies smacked together like clashing symbols — with less of a percussive sound and more of a dull thud — and our lips met with the same urgency I normally applied toward breakfast.

"I—" I couldn't form words. Partly because my brain had

short-circuited. And partly because my mouth was too busy devouring Nash's. His hand had slid onto my nape, then twisted into my hair. Undoing the effects of my blowout, but I hardly cared. His other hand skimmed the length of my body, then gripped my hip to pull me against him.

The front door chimed.

Nash tore his hands from my body, then his lips from my mouth.

"Shiplap," I hissed. "Shiplap, shiplap, shiplap."

"Just a—" Nash cleared his throat and his voice returned to his normal octave. "Be with you in a minute."

He exited the room. I finger-combed my hair, then followed.

Vicki's driver, Misty, stood in the reception area. With her hands behind her back and a driver's cap cocked jauntily on her head, Misty had an expectant look. Like we should be glad to see her. By now, Misty should know we wouldn't see her arrival as good news. Misty was eternally pleasant and existentially phlegmatic.

And possibly a teeny bit sadistic.

Nash glanced over his shoulder. "We've been summoned."

"Why?" I marched around Nash's wide (and irritated) stance to address Misty. "Why did she send you? Why can't she just call like a normal person?"

Misty pressed her lips together and moved her gaze to the window. The questions were rhetorical anyway. I could answer them better than Misty. With the help of my therapist.

"She said it's an emergency," said Misty. "And she's having a dinner. And she doesn't want the police involved because of her guests. And she'll compensate you well. And to hurry."

"What's the emergency?" said Nash.

"She'll tell you when you arrive."

"Police?"

"She'll explain when you get there."

I folded my arms. And snorted for Misty's benefit. Even if it wasn't Misty's fault.

"Ms. Albright also said you can eat while you're there. She had the dinner catered by YEAH! Burger in Atlanta for her guests."

"Oh, well then." I stepped forward.

Nash put a hand on my arm. "It's after hours. And we're working anyway."

"And she'll offer points toward your future contract negotiation. But it's an emergency. She's frantic in a way I've not seen before."

Nash clenched his jaw. And unclenched. "I'll drive myself. And Miss Albright."

Misty shrugged. Nash always drove himself. And Miss Albright. I actually preferred Vicki's Escalade as opposed to Nash's old pickup, but it was the principle of the thing and all that.

"I'll tell her you're on your way." Misty spun around and held open the door for us. "Miss Albright, she also said to tell you it's unfortunate you don't have time to change, but she understands. Although if you could use your travel time to freshen up, you'll appreciate her advice."

"Of all the nerve." I glowered, then glanced at my Henley. I snapped the top two buttons. Just in case.

In Nash's truck, we tossed around ideas for emergencies. Vicki wasn't one to use the word emergency unnecessarily. "Crisis" was her favored call-to-arms.

"At a party?" Nash said. "Maybe she ran out of booze."

"She'd send Misty for more. Or have it flown in by drone," I said. "It's got to be one of her guests. Something she didn't want to say on the phone or in front of Misty."

"I don't like it," said Nash. "Not wanting the police involved? The mention of police. Sounds…"

"Hinky?"

"Illegal." Nash scowled, then patted my leg. Like that would make me feel better.

It did.

FOUR
#NEMODOESIT

MISTY LED the way in the Escalade. We wound through the streets of downtown Black Pine and up the town's namesake mountain. Vicki's stone monstrosity was somewhat secluded, built on a ridge chosen for the view of Black Pine Lake.

Possibly also due to her preference for being above people.

Once the summer home of a late nineteenth-century peanut baron, the mansion had been remodeled several times since—although the home still retained its original marbled oak trim. And marbled marble.

Black Pine had always been a resort town for rich Southerners and rich carpetbaggers to escape Georgia's heat. At some point in the late nineteenth century, building castle-like homes in the mountains had trended. Mountain palaces made for great views and free air conditioning. Vanderbilt's Biltmore mansion was just a couple hours north in Asheville. Lookout Mountain had the Krystal mansion.

The Peanut Mansion was no exception. Maybe it had been the rule.

Misty took a split to follow the path to the lower parking garage. Nash kept to the front circular drive and parked his Silverado before the granite walkway to the house. After shooing off the valet, he shoved his keys into his pocket and opened my door. I bounded out and we hoofed it to the front door where, surprisingly, Vicki answered.

In an ankle-length, black and white silk dress with an attached asymmetrical cape, she was dressed more for a red carpet run than an at-home gathering. Her makeup was flawless and professional. Her blonde, shoulder-length hair pulled back into an elaborate twist.

"Valentino?" I said. "I thought you were serving burgers."

"Yes. We finished eating, so don't worry about how you look, Maizie. I'm sure they'll understand."

"I wasn't—" I wasn't until now.

We stepped through the massive wooden door and onto the parquet fitted to look like a giant peanut vine. And halted. An eight-foot-wide columnar aquarium stretched from the floor to the second-story balcony overlooking the foyer.

"This is…new." My gaze followed a school of clownfish flitting from a coral sculpture to a life-size treasure chest that opened and shut with a burst of bubbles. Exposing what appeared to be a booty of gold coins and pearls.

I gasped. "Are those real?"

"Really, Maizie. Costume jewelry?" Vicki crossed the parquet to point at the bottom of the coral reef tank. "Look."

"I can't not look." A parrotfish flashed by followed by a butterflyfish.

"What's the emergency?" Nash folded his arms. "Misty said you were frantic."

"I am." Vicki's eyebrow rose fractionally. Which was all the Botox could afford her. "Positively."

Spying a school of angelfish, I scooted to the edge of the tank.

"Don't put your hands on the glass, Maizie," said Vicki. "And stop goggling the fish."

"Goggling?" I said. "But that's what an aquarium—"

"Look." Her Dior *Passion* red nail flicked out and pointed to something on the gravel floor. "There's a bullet in my coral reef tank."

Nash crossed the foyer and squatted to study Vicki's find.

I leaned over him. "That's not a bullet. It's a casing."

"Nine-millimeter by the look of it," said Nash. "But that's not a Luger. Odd."

"My beautiful dragon fish pushed it up with his nose. Charles might try to eat the bullet," said Vicki. "Do you know what that could do to a fish?"

"This is the emergency?" Nash rose and turned to face Vicki.

"You named a fish Charles?" I said.

Vicki waved at the tank, billowing her cape. "Charles is a super red Arowana dragon fish. They're the Fabergé of the fish world. Get it out before he eats it."

Something buzzed through the treasure chest's bubbles and I followed it around to the side of the tank. "It's Dory." I flicked a glance at Vicki. "You didn't get the rights to the real Dory? That's not a thing, right?"

"Aren't you wondering how a bullet casing got in your fish tank?" Nash strode to the oak and marble staircase that wrapped around the foyer.

"I'm wondering." I watched Nash bound up the stairs and cross the gallery to stand above us. "Also, I'm wondering who's at this dinner party?"

"Just my house guests and a few of their associates from *Unlucky 18*. Producer, director, and stars. They wanted to eat American food." She shrugged.

"A dinner with burgers, Valentino, and gunplay?"

"Of course not, Maizie. Who do I know that has a gun?"

"Me," I said. "Nash. Daddy. Daddy's wife. And you live in Georgia now, so probably your neighbors."

"I mean *know* know." Vicki rolled her eyes. "It's ludicrous. No one I associate with would drop a bullet casing in my fish tank."

"Unless they were trying to shoot your fish."

"Why would someone do that?" Vicki sucked in a breath. "Oh

my God, Charles. They could've broken the glass. Killed my precious babies. My historic parquet would have been ruined. Who would do such a thing?"

"It does seem pretty ridiculous." I narrowed my eyes, searching for this red fish. Feeling ridiculously put out by her theatrics, I added a dash of *Julia Pinkerton* snark. "But you never know. Does *Charles* have any enemies?"

"This tank is open at the top." Nash leaned over. "Doesn't it have a cover?"

"A cover would ruin the effect of looking into it from the balcony," said Vicki.

"It's always uncovered."

"Obviously." She turned back to me. "Really, Maizie."

"Any water on the floor or the sides of the tank?" said Nash.

I circled the tank and examined the sides. "No."

Nash held his arms over the tank like he was aiming a gun, then moved them to point at the tank and other areas in the room. I backed up to watch him, then glanced over my shoulder. I pivoted and walked to the doorway, squinting. Then gasped.

"Someone wasn't trying to shoot your fish." I rose on my toes and pointed at a spot where the thick wood had splintered near the top hinge. "They were trying to shoot your door."

"Or trying to shoot someone standing in your foyer," Nash said, bounding down the stairs. He stopped next to me and laid a hand on my shoulder but turned his burning blue gaze on Vicki. "You better hope they missed."

FIVE
#SHUTTHESHOTDOOR

"I THINK you need to tell us more about this dinner," said Nash. "A list of guests and where they're staying would be helpful, too."

"It couldn't have happened during dinner. We would have heard the gunshot." Vicki peered at the hole in her door. "This door is walnut and an antique."

Indignation burned inside me. I couldn't contain it. Used to Vicki's callousness, the new hostility I felt troubled me. My ex-therapist Renata would advise a quick listing of Vicki's positive qualities and a gratitude check. I couldn't think of any positive qualities except for the way she could carry off a Valentino on a Thursday. And that didn't seem to help my anger.

"Maybe you could have someone from special effects make it look like an old bullet hole." I used Julia Pinkerton snark instead of screaming. "You could tell a story of some old family feud from yonder days to explain it."

"Do you think the National Trust people would believe it?" Rising to her toes, she fingered the splintered wood. "There might be someone who specializes in forgeries, who could replace the bullet with something vintage."

"What?" I gaped. "I meant for cocktail chat, not to dupe your insurance company."

"Maizie, if you understood the preservation laws on these old homes, you wouldn't be so glib."

Nash sighed. "Vicki, aren't you concerned someone shot a firearm in your home?"

"Of course." Her face strained to scowl. "I'm appalled."

"Appalled? That someone had the effrontery to shoot your door?" My hands landed on my hips. "Or a guest could have been killed in your foyer by an unknown assailant?"

Vicki nodded.

I eyed her, then glanced at Nash. He rubbed the scar on his chin, which told me the same thought likely ran through his mind. This smelled like the Santa Monica Pier. And not just due to the mega-aquarium.

"Do you have any idea when this might have happened?" said Nash.

She shrugged. "Charles found the bullet. That reminds me. I'd like you to install some kind of motion detectors on the tank, so this doesn't happen again." She pursed her lips. "Poor Charles."

"Motion detectors on an aquarium? You do realize, they are always swimming." I pinched the bridge of my nose. "Oh, sure. We'll just add it to our list. After everything else."

"Do that."

Nash pointed at an unobtrusive panel near the door. "It looks like your alarm system isn't engaged."

"Not inside the house. I have guests staying and I can't always be turning the alarms on and off. They come and go as they please. The outside security is enough."

Nash's nostrils flared. "You've spent more than a million on a security system you're not using? You had the walls reinforced, put in steel doors, and painted your art thingamajigs with your DNA, for cripe's sake."

"Which is why I feel perfectly safe not to have the inside alarms on. Aren't the radars and whatnots outside enough?" Vicki pivoted. Her skirt and cape flared out. "I must get back to my guests."

"We'll talk to them in a minute," said Nash. "I need to confer with Miss Albright."

"Confer." Vicki snorted. She glanced over her shoulder, her eyes traveling from me to Nash. "We'll be on the patio. But don't mention the bullet. No interrogations. No questions. Just meet and greet and gone."

I narrowed my eyes, wondering if there was a hidden nanny-cam reference in that snort. "How do you expect us to investigate this and not ask your guests about the bullet? We need to get a frame of reference for the time. One of them might have noticed the hole in your door or the casing in your tank. Or might have tried to shoot someone."

"My guests include Lili Liang, Stanley Wu, and Van Vorling. Firearms are most likely illegal in their countries. The only guns they've handled are movie props." Her green eyes glittered. "Stanley, Lili, and her entourage are staying with me while they make *Unlucky 18*. I'll not have you frightening her while she's visiting. The news stories they get overseas about the US are scary enough."

Dismissing us with a flick of her wrist, Vicki traipsed across the foyer. A contrail of Chanel No. 5 wafted behind her.

The nonexistent dinner in my stomach curdled. "This is not good."

"Yep," said Nash. "An entryway shooting has all kinds of possibilities and none are good. The best-case scenario is some idiot played with a handgun and accidentally shot the door."

"We need to interview all her staff. Vet them against gun registrations. But I doubt Vicki would hire anyone who carries." I frowned at the aquarium. "Maybe one of them did want to kill her fish."

"No one wants to kill her fish. The casing would have dropped on the floor upstairs if they were aiming at the fish."

"What is with the fish anyway? Since when is she into fish?" I fought the hysteria tinging my voice. "Didn't she seem overly emotional about Charles?"

"You're talking about Vicki. Emotional doesn't come to mind."

"Believe me." I hiked my chin to look him in the eye. "She's emotional. The last time I saw her like this was when they canceled *Julia Pinkerton* and we were between contracts."

"You mean *you* didn't have a contract," Nash's voice dropped to a growl. "And it's better if you don't remind me of your days of child labor guised as acting while I'm working for Vicki."

My mouth rounded and I snapped it shut. "Wow. I was more upset that I wasn't allowed to have a pet and now she's got Charles. And Dory. And the rest of the cast of the Nemo movies."

Nash's brows squeezed together. His hand fumbled in the air, then patted my shoulder. "I didn't know you liked fish so much."

"Never mind." My voice trembled. "She's acting weird. Do you think Vicki's capable of covering something up?"

"Without knowing what happened, it's hard to know how someone would react," Nash said, keeping his voice neutral. "People aren't always what they seem. Even someone you know well, like a family member, could have hidden depths within their personality you've never come across."

Flustered, I squinted at the door, then turned to take in the large foyer. "It's too bad there aren't cameras inside the house. We can check the outside footage."

Nash looked relieved we were back into the comfortable world of door violence. "They might have used a silencer. But if it happened tonight, they still would have heard it at dinner."

"It's not silent?"

"Sounds like far away gunfire. Or fireworks in the distance. Pops or cracks. Definitely not silent, but not anything as loud as real gunfire." He folded his arms. "The walls are thick, but Vicki must know more than she's letting on."

"In that case, why call us in?"

"Better us than the police."

"Do you think someone was shot?"

"Only if the shooter let off more than one round." He stuck his finger in the hole. "That's buried pretty deep."

His focus on the wood paneling, Nash moved along the foyer's walls, searching for evidence. I walked across the peanut floor to the tank and faced a group of tiny white and red basslets.

"Maybe there are more casings in there. They could've fallen in the treasure chest."

"Dammit. I hope not." Nash grimaced. "I'm not getting in that tank."

SIX
#LOVELYLILI

AFTER CALLING the aquarium cleaner to search for bullet casings — they had a scuba suit and we didn't — we hustled out to the patio. Basking in the glow of antique gas torch lights, Vicki and an Asian woman sipped from sherry glasses, both in wraps and gowns. A handsome Asian man, wearing trendy glasses and a cashmere houndstooth that had to be a Kiton, stood with them. At the stone wall edging the patio, a middle-aged, Nordic-looking man and a tall, broad-shouldered Chinese man — both in Italian suits — gazed out at the lake while speaking in hushed tones.

Vicki glanced over her shoulder and turned to face us. "Meet Lili Liang and Stanley Wu. Lili and Stanley are starring in *Unlucky 18* with Chey Tyrone." Tipping her head toward the stone wall, she indicated the men standing there. "Van Vorling is directing. Zidong Zhao is the associate producer. He knows the Lees."

Without recognition or interest, the dropped names thudded at Nash's feet. He nodded and proceeded to eyeball the guests. No doubt looking for tell-tale signs of gunpowder or fish scales on their ten thousand-dollar suits.

"I admire both of your work very much." I held out my hand

to Lili and Stanley. "And I know Chey from my time in California." From a short stay at a Malibu facility, but when it came to networking, rehab had become LA's cocktail party.

Without the cocktails, of course.

While Mr. Zhou hung back, Van Vorling strode across the stone patio to shake my hand. "A pleasure," he said in a Germanic accent. "It is my first American-Chinese film. The burgers were delicious. You should be proud of your work."

"Um, thank you?" I slid my hand from his hearty shake and snuck it behind my back to rub the blood back into my fingers.

"Maizie isn't the caterer, Van," said Vicki. "She's…in security."

"Private investigation," said Nash.

"I'm also Vicki's daughter." I smiled, knowing I was getting the same look Vicki had just flashed at Nash. "And I used to be an actress. Vicki was my manager."

"Wonderful," Lili intoned in a deep, posh British accent. "I love your look. Cédric Charlier?"

"You got it." I grinned at Lili. My shearling cropped jacket seemed out of place with the cashmere and long gowns. I appreciated her graciousness. "Is that Lisa Perry?"

She beamed, smoothing the pink silk crepe. "I like New York designers."

"You have a good eye," said Stanley in an accent matching Lili's. "Your mother has exquisite style. The Lees were impressed."

"The Lees?" said Nash, who wasn't much on niceties, small talk, or designers. He palmed a small notebook. "A couple? And who else was here?"

"Harvey and Ning Lee did a Facetime appearance," said Stanley. "They're still in Shanghai. Coming over soon."

"Is something wrong?" said Lili. "Why are you taking notes?"

"Everything's fine," I said. "It's just an issue with a fish."

"Fish?" said Stanley. "Not Charles, I hope."

"You know about Charles?" My voice sounded high and reedy. I clamped off the whine.

Laughter rippled through the group. I didn't get the joke, but I managed a smile. Nash had that irritated look he often got when dealing with clients. I slipped a hand down his arm, snagged the notebook, and slid it into my pocket.

"Charles is fine. Of course, he's fine." Vicki played off the tension in her voice by stroking her wrap. "Maizie and Nash were just checking on him. And now they're going."

"After I ask if anyone heard a—"

"Mr. Nash." Vicki trilled a laugh that made it obvious why I had become the actress in the family. "No one heard anything other than the wonderful conversation between new friends. And the small jazz quartet I'd hired for our dinner."

"Band's name?" Nash's pen clicked and he reached for the notebook in my pocket.

I swatted his hand away. "Sounds like a delightful evening. And I hope you did enjoy the burgers." I also hoped there were leftovers as promised.

Nash shot me a look. "We need words with the staff before going."

"Your mother offered to allow me and my people to stay at her beautiful home," said Lili. "I hope to see you during the shoot."

I nodded. "And where is everyone else staying?"

"Black Pine Resort, obviously." Behind Lili, Vicki's hand waved, shooing us. "Who else in this small town could give these esteemed international visitors the kind of hospitality they're used to?"

"I'm sure we'd be fine anywhere." Slipping an arm through mine, Lili strolled to the edge of the patio, taking me with her. "Let me borrow Maizie for a moment, Vicki."

"Of course," said Vicki, although her words didn't match the sentiment.

"Mr. Vorling, was it?" said Nash behind us. "Do you have an interest in handguns?"

I glanced over my shoulder to see Vorling's reaction, but Lili pulled my attention away from the group. "Tell me honestly, Maizie. Is it security or detective work that brings you here tonight?"

"A little of both," I said.

Lili dropped my arm to place her hands on the stone wall and lean forward. A breeze lifted her long hair, ruffling it. She turned to cast me with a wry smile. "I'm also in need of a little of both."

"Both what?" I shoved my hands in my pockets. The wind blowing off the lake had a bite.

"Security and detective work." She glanced across the patio, then quickly looked away. She pulled me further down the walk.

I glanced behind me and spotted Mr. Zhou watching us. The tall, quiet associate producer.

"My shifu — my kung fu master — is missing," Lili whispered. "Vanished. Last seen here at Vicki's and now gone. I can't understand what happened. I haven't told anyone, though, because I don't want him to get in trouble."

"Oh no," I said, but my thoughts ran in another direction. Like to the bullet in the front door.

I yanked a hand from my coat to chew on a nail, realized what I was about to do, and shoved it back inside the pocket. Why did I go there first? Who would want to shoot a kung fu coach?

"Are you sure the last time you saw him was here? When was this?"

"Yes. On Saturday." She turned to face me. "Rather peculiar. We had tea with Vicki. I had a cast meeting with the producers and director, so I left them to finish tea by themselves. When I returned for the party, he was gone. Vicki was the only one home, but she hadn't seen him leave either."

"What about his things?"

"Still here." She shook her head and a tear trickled down her cheek. "Shifu Xi's healthy and speaks English. He had a lucrative contract to help me with this movie. I don't understand how he could just vanish."

"That is peculiar." I gazed out at Black Pine lake. The very deep Black Pine lake. "Did he say anything that might indicate he'd take off?"

"Of course not." Her tone was as crisp as the air. "Shifu Xi was completely reliable. He would not have been hired as my trainer if he wasn't."

"Anyone else at the tea besides Vicki and Master Xi?"

Lili shook her head. "Just the three of us. My boyfriend picked me up to take me to the meeting."

"You don't use Vicki's driver?" I looked up from my notebook. "Misty?"

"I don't want to leave Vicki stranded. She's been so lovely. A car hired by the movie drives me sometimes, too."

"Who was at the party?"

"The cast and crew were invited." She stared out at the lake. "I could make you a list, but perhaps it would be easier to get the guests from Vicki's assistant."

"Master Xi wasn't at the party?"

"I didn't see him. And when I asked, other people hadn't either." Her brows pushed together. "It's been five days and I can't wait any longer. Vicki knows a trainer from your days on a kiddy show. He arrives tomorrow from California to help me."

"Jerry?" I muttered. "Shizzles."

I had to avoid Jerry at all costs. Squats would be the least of my worries. All his work on making my body a temple had teetered and collapsed since moving to Georgia. Jerry was all about solid structures. He'd want me to rebuild, starting with clearing of the rubble. Which would mean some God-awful cleanse-of-the-month.

"Jerry? No, that must be someone else. Master Kevin Yuan," said Lili. "Is he good? You look worried."

I let out a breath that had held unchecked accountability and a multitude of excuses. "Master Kevin? He's awesome. Such a sweetie. Yep, he did all my training for *Kung Fu Kate*. I haven't seen him since I was about thirteen or fourteen, though."

"I'm relieved." She lowered her voice. "I'm ecstatic about this part. Even though *Unlucky 18* has the action I'm known for, it's a serious period drama. I'll be able to stretch in this role. As a principally US film, I'll be up for awards here. You have no idea what that could do for my career."

"Master Kevin's worked with the best in Hollywood. I got lucky landing him for *Kung Fu Kate*." More like Vicki somehow finagled me into his classes and brokered a deal for the show. "He works exclusively with film stars. He'll be a great asset for you."

"And Shifu Xi? Can you find him? I'm very worried. It's his first time out of our home country." Lili reached into the pocket of her cashmere wrap and pulled out a business card case. "That's all my contact information for the US."

Taking the card, I bowed. "Thanks. Let's talk tomorrow. But shouldn't the studio have taken care of him?"

"I haven't told the studio he's missing. It hasn't been long, and we haven't started the choreography." Pain flickered across Lili's features. "One minute he was here and the next he was just gone. Disappeared."

Not good. Kind of a like not good in a mysterious entry shooting sort of way.

SEVEN
#GONEFISHING

AFTER SPEAKING to the staff and caterers, I reconvened with Nash. While he finished his study of the door — With a tape measure. Grunting about trajectory. — I made mental notes about the fish. But in truth, more of an accounting.

"I don't even see a red fish," I said. "Maybe someone did shoot her baby."

"Baby?" Nash didn't look up from his notebook.

"Pet. You know how people call their pets their children?"

"We're an entirely different species. There are specific names for juvenile animals."

"Forget it." I scooted across the peanut parquet and stood next to him. "Do you think any of the staff were covering for Vicki? Not a single one had any idea."

Nash shoved his notebook in his pocket and turned to face me. "Do you think anyone working for Vicki would want to cover for her on something like this?"

"They could lose their jobs. We know more than anyone how well she pays."

"Would you cover for her?"

I opened my mouth, then shut it. "Not for money."

"What's that look? What happened?"

"Lili wants us to look for her missing kung fu trainer." I showed him the business card I'd shoved in my pocket. "They came over from China together and he disappeared soon after."

Nash's gaze traveled from the business card to the bullet hole.

"My first thought, too. But what's the likelihood of someone shooting a kung fu trainer in Vicki's house?"

"I don't want to guess." Nash stroked the scar on his chin. "Anyway, we don't have a motive."

"Vicki arranged for my old trainer in California to replace Master Xi."

"Is there any reason to believe Vicki would have an ulterior motive for bringing on a new coach?"

"Like scoring points with the producers and talent? That's always helpful for networking but hardly worth shooting someone over." I bit my lip. "Wait, a minute. What am I saying? Why are we considering this?

"We don't even know if more shots were fired. I'm just spitballing." Nash shrugged.

"But it's Vicki's house. The bullet's in her door. I don't think it happened tonight. The staff doesn't know anything about it, nor did they hear a gunshot. No reported break-ins."

His jaw clenched. "Except she's not using the security. And she doesn't want the police involved."

"Vicki's a lot of things, but she's not—" I placed my hands on my hips. Then folded them under my arms to hug myself. "I mean, she wouldn't— Maybe by accident and then to cover— What am I saying? You don't think Vicki would—"

"Look," said Nash. "We don't have much information yet. We shouldn't draw any conclusions. We need to treat these as separate investigations. But we're going to have to study the homeowner. She's a common thread in both circumstances."

"The homeowner." My shoulders sagged. "I've got to treat my manager — I mean mother — as the homeowner."

"In these cases, it's best to create some distance." Nash gave my shoulder another awkward pat.

I thought back to the camera and mikes in the trailer we'd found that morning. "Did Vicki ask for the extra security sweep for the *Unlucky 18* trailer? Or did someone else ask for it and she just assigned it to us?"

"I was wondering the same thing. Kind of hinky." He squatted, eyeing the floor.

"Are you doing what I think you're doing?"

He looked up. "These pieces by the door. They're a slightly different shade than the others."

"There are a lot of different shades. It's parquet." My voice hitched. "Like a wood mosaic."

"Shade like new versus old. These pieces aren't original. Although it looks like they've been banged up and stained to look older."

"Like they had to be replaced because of blood splatter?" I whispered. "This can't be happening."

Investigate Vicki. It was like I didn't even know my own mother. How is that possible? We lived together all my life until my return to Black Pine. I turned away from the door and its bullet hole. And the parquet and its suspicious arrangement of new and old wood tiles. A large red fish watched us.

Charles. My eyes narrowed and lip curled.

OMG. What's wrong with me?

I smoothed my features but still felt the bite behind my eyes. Clenching the business card, I pinched the skin next to my thumb to stop any tears from forming. "How could Vicki do this?"

"Do what? I thought we weren't jumping to conclusions." Nash glanced up. His brows squeezed together. "Are you okay?"

I'd spent years of therapy examining Vicki's motives and my responses to them. Although some of her behavior seemed malicious, none we studied had anything to do with bullets. Why would the assumption seem so easy for me to make?

"Wait," I said. "Giulio. Where's Giulio?"

"Is he still—Are they still together?" said Nash. "I haven't seen Belloni for a while. Not that I'm complaining."

"As far as I know they're still engaged." As disgusting as that was. Giulio Belloni was another nail in Vicki's ethics coffin.

"You think he bolted?" Nash's eyes lit with spiteful glee. Not-a-Giulio-fan only scratched the surface of how Nash felt about the tall, dark, and hunky Italian soap star. "Another suspect. Should make you feel better."

It didn't. "Even with Giulio's shortcomings, he's still a friend."

"He's also your ex-fiancé." Nash's brow lifted. "And your potential stepfather."

"Don't." I grimaced. "Makes it even ickier. Besides both were for *All is Albright*. They do fake engagements on reality shows all the time."

"When you were engaged, you were the only one who didn't know the proposal was orchestrated." Nash folded his arms.

"As a professional actor, Giulio takes the ratings seriously."

"Why are you defending them? I know how you actually feel."

I hugged myself. "I don't know. I can't go down that road."

"The road where Vicki lives with your ex-fiancé? You already traveled there."

"I meant the road ending in a bullet in Vicki's door and new wood for her floor. Why didn't she didn't mention the floor?"

"Don't go down that road yet either. Why would she show us the bullet casing? She's not stupid." Nash strode across the foyer to the stairs. "Come on. While she's busy, let's take a look in her rooms."

"She's not stupid, but she is wily. Think of all the questions the aquarium cleaner asked us about the bullet casing." Still clutching the business card, I ran to catch up. "Like 'why is there a bullet casing in your tank?' And 'how did it get in there?' And when we said, 'we don't know, just get it out' they were still all up in our business about it."

"Vicki could have easily lied to the aquarium cleaner as to us."

"Hells." On the second story landing, I gripped Nash's arm and he stopped. "That's why she wanted us to get the casing out of the tank."

"Or so she wouldn't have to pay someone else. She asks us to do her dirty work all the time." He scowled at the tank. "But getting in a giant fishbowl? Big no."

"Can't you swim?" There were still many mysteries about Nash I'd yet to discover. Mostly because he wasn't much of a talker. Or a sharer. I sucked in a breath. "Are you scared of fish?" There went my plans for Nash and Daddy bonding over fishing.

He glanced at me askance. "Are you kidding? Who's scared of fish?"

"You seem put off by the idea."

"Of getting in an aquarium and scooping through a fish litter box to look for bullet casings?" He grabbed the railing and peered into the tank. "Besides I've never done scuba. You'd have to wear oxygen for a tank of this size."

"When you put it like that." I shrugged. "I've done some diving, but I always forget to breathe. Which is kind of the point of scuba. And snorkeling. Plus, there's a lot of stuff in the water once you get down there. That's a little freaky. Safe to say, someone could be scared of fish. Just look at sharks. They're pretty scary."

"So, no scuba in our future." Nash turned from the rail to continue down the hall.

I froze, staring into the tank. My heart had stopped. For a millisecond. Then jumpstarted. And almost popped out of my chest.

Nash said "our" and "future." Together. In the same sentence.

He was kidding about the "no scuba." But still.

I clasped my hands together, clutching Lili's card against my chest and willing my heart to resume a normal, safer pace. While

I waited, the crimson fish with large scales circled up the column. His mouth popped above the water, gulping.

Charles.

He swam near the top, lapping the top of the tank, making quick turns. His body undulated, rippling back and forth. Like a dragon in a Chinese New Year's parade.

"Sorry, Charlie. We're not getting in there with you."

I leaned over the railing to watch him. The dangling card slipped from my hand and plopped into the water. Charles sped across the tank and scooped the card into his massive mouth. His tail jerked to the side. Water splashed the railing, I held back a shriek, and Charles zipped to the lower realms of the tank, disappearing.

Pretty safe to say someone can be scared of fish.

EIGHT
#SIGNSPOINTTONOTGOOD

I FOUND Nash in Vicki's office. Instead of the oaky vintage-mansion vibe of the foyer and patio, she'd had her office retrofitted with blond wood accents and modern furniture. Framed posters from my TV shows and movies hung on the walls. My awards lined a bookshelf. A smallish conference table had been parked across from the awards. A desk anchored the other end, holding only a blotter and pen cup.

An attractive and efficient room. Not too showy but with evident success. Just like Vicki.

With his hands clasped behind him and legs shoulder-width apart, Nash studied a poster. Intently, it seemed. A made-for-tv movie called *The Black Rose*, a noir-ish Hollywood murder mystery. The pulp-like cover featured me leaning over to adjust the line in my stocking. My long strawberry blonde locks — tinted flame-red — hid my face. Above me, a revolver edged into view. However, my butt, legs, and hair took up most of the visual space.

My nineteen-year-old butt, legs, and hair.

More than slightly embarrassing.

"Um, so yeah." I moved toward Vicki's desk. "I'll just look around. And what are we looking for?"

Nash swung around and aimed a thumb at the poster. "There she is."

I felt a flash burn hit my cheeks and travel down my neck to my chest. "Yeah, that one was panned. Super low on Rotten Tomatoes. I don't know why Vicki hung it in here. They were hoping to move me from teen detective to something more adult. But it was kind of more *adult* than adult if you know what I mean?"

"No idea." Nash frowned. "I was talking about the .38 in the picture."

"Oh, right." Heat shot back into my cheeks. "They thought it looked like a gangster's gun."

"Cops and gangsters used them back in the day. But you know…" Nash raised an eyebrow.

This time, I had no idea. I raised my brows along with my shoulders.

"We both have a .38 Special."

I nodded.

"That's kind of romantic, right?" He gave me an inscrutable look.

Not really. "Sure."

What was this? He thought we bonded over handguns? Did he even know me? I rarely carried mine. When I did, I preferred it unloaded. It was also pink. Who takes a pink gun seriously? My .38 had been a sixteenth birthday present from Daddy. When I had wanted a car.

Right now, I could use a car. Not a dirt bike (my fifteenth birthday present) and definitely not a pink .38 Special.

Nash cleared his throat. "Anyway, I'm not sure what we're looking for. I just figured while we're here…"

"Yeah," I drug the word out for lack of a better comment. Pulled on a desk drawer. And yanked again. Something heavy moved inside.

"What's the matter?" Nash strode to the desk.

"Locked."

"Maybe there's a key in a drawer. People do that all the time."

I slid the top drawer open. "Boxes of fountain pens. Unopened Post-it notes. A box of paperclips. Does she use this desk? Hang on. On *Julia Pinkerton, Teen Detective* they were always hiding desk keys and lost letters under desk drawers." I felt beneath the drawer. "Wait, there's something here."

Nash reached inside the drawer and tossed the unopened boxes on the desk. "Flip it over."

"It's sticky." I yanked out the drawer and flipped it over. Two rectangular patches of gluey residue remained on the bottom side of the drawer. Tiny bits of black fuzz stuck to the substance.

"Velcro. Vicki had a Velcro strap beneath her desk." I looked up at Nash. "That's weird, right?"

Nash leaned against me and studied the drawer over my shoulder. "It held something flush against the bottom of the drawer. Something not too heavy."

"Smaller than a breadbox. Hand-sized."

Nash straightened, lowered his brows, and pulled a grimace. "Shiplap."

"Does she even use this room?" said Nash. "Who has access?"

"I'm not sure. I've never met her in here. She likes lunch meetings because they're more productive. But I think that's because she doesn't actually eat."

He opened the other drawers, jiggled the locked one. "I wonder what's sliding around in there. Sounds metal, anyway."

The office door swung open. Vicki's stopped just inside the frame. She took her time to scan the room, seeming to consider our hover over the desk. She did noir much better than me. Silhouetted by the bright hallway in the gown and with the effectual pause…you couldn't get more L.A. noir. Like the reincarnation of Rita Hayworth playing Elsa Bannister in *The Lady From Shanghai.*

Not how one would want to consider their mother.

"What are you doing in my office?" Her eyes flickered over

the posters, stopping on *The Black Rose*. "Showing off your high school trophies?"

I felt it best to get to the point. "Vicki, why did you have a Velcro strap beneath your desk?"

She strode across the room. "Velcro? I abhor it on shoes."

"Not talking about Reeboks. It was under your desk."

"Do you use this office often?" said Nash. "What about the desk?"

"I don't call it an office," said Vicki. "I believe offices will soon be passé, and I want to get ahead of the trend."

We blinked at her.

"We'll try again. This room with the desk and the conference table, that's not an office," I said. "Do you use it for meetings and such?"

"Much like Mark Cuban, Jeff Bezos, and Elon Musk, I find meetings terribly unproductive. Instead, I collaborate. Collaboration is key to good business, not meetings. This desk is only meant for contract signings. And that's not a meeting. And we don't need a desk for contract signings, just a flat surface."

She frowned. "Maybe I should have Lydia get rid of my desk. No wait, it holds contracts. Never mind."

Nash and I looked at each other. This is what Nash called, "trying his patience." It was what I called, "the ever-evolving world of Vicki." The language might be foreign, but it was always in vogue.

"More to the point," said Nash. Through gritted teeth. "Is this room locked?"

"Of course it's not locked. My guests might need a meeting room." She paused. "For collaborations."

"Great." Nash rolled his eyes.

She beamed at me. "Imagine saying to award-winning international film stars, '*mi casa es su casa.*' And I did. And I meant it."

"I hope your guests know Spanish."

"Lili's popularity in Asia morphs any star here." She sighed.

"If only we had 4.5 billion people on our continent. Think of the fame a star could achieve."

"Yes," I said. "One could only hope for that sort of popularity. Just the sheer number of bodyguards one could employ boggles the mind. In other words, anyone can come in here at any time?"

"I said that," she snapped. "I'm just pointing out, in America we cannot begin to fathom the impact a megastar has in Asia."

"If only you had raised me in China." My *Julia Pinkerton* snark had returned. "Vicki, we're trying to understand why there's evidence someone might have strapped a handgun under your desk."

"Don't be ridiculous."

"Someone did shoot your door. We don't know if they stored the weapon in here, but it's possible."

She shrugged. "It couldn't have been one of my guests."

"Perhaps a hobo wandered off the street to collaborate in your non-office, hid his handgun in here, and then shot your door." I folded my arms. "Is that a possibility?"

She tried to pull her eyebrows together. "Are there hobos in Black Pine?"

"You're making it worse, Miss Albright," muttered Nash. "And I can't take much more."

"Let me try something easier. Vicki, do you have a key to the desk? One of the drawers is locked. And please don't say locks are passé."

"Why would I lock the desk? I don't even use it. Except for the contracts. Is that the locked drawer?"

I shook my head. "But the key?"

"Why are you so worried about the desk?" Vicki ran a finger across the edge and examined it for dust. "You can't tell who shot the door from the bullet, can you? Maizie never did a police procedural show, so I don't know much about bullets and Velcro."

Nash and I glanced at each other.

"You could determine the type of weapon by the rifling and

size of the bullet, but you'd need the actual weapon for comparison." Nash replaced the drawer, squatted, and peered at eye-level. He sat in the desk chair, leaned forward, and mimicked grabbing the handgun. Shook his head. "You'd need to do ballistic tests. Get the bullet out of the door first, of course."

"You have my permission if you need it."

"Vicki," I said. "We don't do ballistic tests. We'd need to call the police. And they'd need to call the GBI to do the tests. They're like the FBI but in Georgia."

"No police." She waved her hand and strode toward the door. "I'm not going to press charges anyway, so there's no reason to involve the police. And certainly not a government organization. Everyone knows not to trust them."

Nash rose. "Who exactly would you press charges against?"

"Whoever shot my door, of course. They put a bullet in history." She stopped in the doorway to stare at him. "You're going to figure it out, right? I expect this to top your to-do list. Get the bullet and casing out of my house. Such an inconvenience." She shook her head. "And Maizie, Master Kevin Yuan will be here tomorrow. He's working with Lili and he'll want to see you."

She breezed out the door and into the hall, her cape and gown billowing out behind her.

I hugged my arms against my chest, pressed my lips together, and held in a silent scream.

"It's like she has people firing guns in her house every day." Nash shook his head. "Like this is normal."

"Nothing is normal about Vicki." I felt sick. "And she gets less normal every day. Or I get less tolerant. Or her non-normalcy is more apparent in Georgia. I'm confused."

"Stand in front of the desk and reach under it."

"Kinky." I winked and stretched my hand under the desk. "I feel the sticky spot." I turned to face the door, reached behind my back, and felt again. "It's easy to reach here. And hidden by the decorative piece in front."

"Not meant for someone sitting behind the desk," he agreed. "But if the desk is just a storage piece, it makes sense."

Using his phone, Nash took pictures of the desk and drawer. Pulled out the drawer again for more pictures.

"Are you going to show those to Detective Mowry?"

"We don't know a crime's been committed. And if she's not interested in pursuing the person who shot her door, there's no point in talking to the police. They'd have to do paperwork without taking action and they hate paperwork. I'll hang on to these in case something turns up."

"We'll get the casing from the aquarium dudes. We need an antique specialist for the door. That'll be fun to explain. Maybe the housekeeper knows where the key to the drawer is." I jiggled the handle again and heard the thunk. "Are you thinking what I am about what's in this drawer?"

"Could you tell if she's lying about her knowledge of the shooting?"

"Too difficult to say. But she does abhor Velcro, so there's that." I sighed. "More importantly, does she think we're stupid enough to retrieve the bullet and not ask questions?"

Nash shook his head. "I don't think so. Vicki knows we'd look into it."

"Because she owns us? She knows I need two more years training and I won't leave you—" I swallowed. A little too hard. I paused for a coughing fit. "I won't leave the shop without you. And you won't leave because I need to be apprenticed."

"Possibly." Nash pursed his lips. "But she's got to realize, if we found anything we'd go to the police."

"We won't find anything. Or if we do, it can't be related to Vicki."

He swung back to look at the poster for *The Black Rose*. "At least the bullet wasn't from a .38. That's a good sign."

A good sign of what? We had a missing man, a mysterious shooting, and a bullet in a door. If Nash was looking for signs on the health of our relationship, placing his confidence in a weapon seemed like a bad sign to me.

NINE
#MOTHERCOVERUP

IN NASH'S TRUCK, he looked at me. "There's one possibility we haven't considered."

Relief flooded through me. "Thank goodness. I thought someone had borrowed a prop gun, played around but didn't realize it was a real gun, and shot Vicki's door. And maybe shot the kung fu trainer, too. And they decided to cover up by dropping him in the lake."

"That's a little different than the possibilities I came up with."

"Let's hear it." Because anything was better than an accidental shooting with a body in a lake.

Pretty much. Unless it was worse. I chewed my lip, no longer feeling relieved.

"Vicki bought a gun for protection, and she's lying to us. Although it's hard to believe she'd leave it in the desk drawer. Her bedroom didn't turn up anything, but tomorrow we should comb the house more thoroughly."

"Protection?"

Nash cast me a glance. "Do you know who Vicki's enemies are?"

"Enemies?" I shifted in my seat. "Not off the top of my head. But I mean, everyone has enemies, right?"

"Do you have enemies?"

"Of course, not. There are people who don't like me." Like his ex-wife, Jolene. My ex-probation officer. My ex-fiancé. Not Giulio. The other one. Ones. The fiancé list was a little too long. "Antagonists would be a better description. Frenemies."

"Exactly my point. Not everyone has enemies." He reflected. "But antagonists, certainly."

"Who is your antagonist?"

"Vicki."

I'd hoped he'd say, Jolene. "Right."

"But as soon as I have enough money saved, that issue will be resolved. I'm paying down my medical expenses now, then I'll buy back the shop. When it's profitable, Lamar can afford to invest more and buy out what was Jolene's share from Vicki. Then the only adversary I'll have is the IRS." His smile was quick but filled with hope.

Mine was less hopeful and more forced. He'd forgotten about me in this scenario. Not just where I fit into his plans — and I'd be lying if that didn't sting — but Tiffany and Rhonda were right. Vicki had only invested in the office because I was working there. Vicki wouldn't allow him a buyout unless I wasn't in the equation. In fact, she'd heavily invested in equipment — all the fancy gadgetry littering his desk — and overhead, like the new office.

Nash suffered from delusions if he thought he could walk back to his old office above the donut shop without Vicki raising the price tag. She was Queen of Contracts and Negotiations. Every investment she made paid off. Except for her last one. With me. But she was making up for it now.

Which one of us was Mephistopheles in the equation?

I didn't want to bring up Nash's predicament. Maybe after we were married with children. One could always hope.

I changed the subject instead. "You think Vicki bought a gun to defend herself from her enemies? Doesn't make sense. She'd rather hire bodyguards. In fact, she'd love the excuse. Someone else to order around. And dress."

"You have to admit she's acting cagier than usual."

"Yes…"

"And erratic when it comes to 'get rid of the bullet but don't tell anyone.'"

"Er…"

"Vicki acts like she has no idea about any of this, but she obviously does." Nash leaned forward, eyes on the windshield as we wound down the mountain road. "Maybe it isn't her gun. But how did it end up under her desk? Or in her desk, if that's what we heard thumping?"

"Giulio?"

"Do you think Belloni has enemies?"

"I'm not sure. He immigrated from Italy. Maybe he got in trouble with the mafia?"

"On a soap opera?"

"We call them daytime dramas now. I'm not sure what they're called in Italy. Telenovela is Spanish…"

"The point, Miss Albright," Nash gritted his teeth, "is whether Giulio Belloni would have planted or left a handgun at Vicki's."

"If I can find him, I'll ask. He'd tell me the truth. He doesn't deliberately obfuscate. Unless it has to do with his career. And extra-curricular female interests."

"And what if the gun involves one of those two things?"

"Actually," I said breezily, "that can't be Giulio's gun. I've seen him with a stage gun. He couldn't have hit the door if his life depended on it."

"What if he wasn't aiming at the door." It wasn't a question.

"I see your point."

"You're doing it again. Defending them both. This is serious, Maizie. We need to find out if a crime happened, for our own protection."

"What do you mean?"

"We're working for Vicki. She's basically asking us to cover this up." He let that thought sink in.

I pinched my thumb and slunk in my seat.

"Whether she was directly involved or not, Vicki knows something. But anything we find —like a gun in a locked drawer — she'd want us to think it our own discovery."

"Why?"

"Life is a chess game for her. She doesn't care about the means but the end. Her ethics are her own. But you know Vicki better than anyone. What do you think?"

"She's not a good mother. I've come to terms with that. Sort of. Not really. But whatevs. But Vicki having enemies? Not just frenemies? Like 'I literally want to kill you, so I need to buy a gun to shoot you first' enemies?" I rubbed my forehead, then covered my face in my hands. "I mean…I guess it's possible. She's pissed off a lot of people in Hollywood. And some are just a tad…extreme. Lots of moms whose daughter's dreams of stardom were crushed because of Vicki."

I swallowed hard and dropped my hands to look at Nash. "Oh, shizzles. In Texas, a cheerleader's mom hired a hitman. Remember, Holly Hunter played her in *The Positively True Adventures of the Alleged Texas Cheerleader-Murdering Mom?* That was just cheer. The mothers we knew were clawing their kids' way into Disney and Nickelodeon. We're talking huge contracts, paving the way for huge careers. A lot of money was on the table. Vicki showed no mercy."

Nash's brow creased. Sympathetically but it made my stomach flip. Like he should feel sorry for me because I had the type of mother who gave people motive for murder.

"Is my mother…I mean, do you think Vicki is evil?"

Saying it out loud was worse than keeping those thoughts in my head.

Nash cut his eyes away and back to me. "Evil's a strong word. Manipulative. Deceptive. Self-serving. Vain. Greedy—"

"Her industry-self. It goes without saying. Dog eat dog and all that."

"Do all parents of actors become their manager so they can bill their children?"

"It was a percentage not a bill." I shook my head. "The largest percentage that's legal. But we lived on it. My money was put into a trust. And the trust's gone. The trust had a stipulation stating if I ever got into legal or financial trouble, I would pay the fines and fees from the trust. But after my financial obligations were taken care of, I had to give the rest to charity. I loved that idea. When the trust was set up, I was seven and obsessed with Madeline, so I left all my money to an orphanage in France. I had no idea Madeline wasn't even an orphan."

"All your money went to an orphanage in France?"

"Vicki thought it would be a good PR move, so it'd be easier to get jobs again. Little did she know I would quit. And face a judge who'd make me quit."

"Who managed the philanthropical part of your trust?"

"Vicki." I sucked in a breath, then moaned. "Oh, those poor orphans."

"It was like she knew you'd get into legal trouble." Nash winced, then placed his palm on my thigh and squeezed. "Don't worry about it. We'll figure this out."

And by that he meant we were going to investigate my mother.

TEN
#CONSTRUCTIONONTHEROAD
#TODESTRUCTION

THE PART of my night not spent debugging the studio was plagued with thoughts about Vicki's gun. Or the gun that wasn't Vicki's. Luckily, the scent of sizzling breakfast foods woke me, refreshing my mind. And soul.

Presumably not my arteries, but you can't have everything.

A tiny knock preceded the slam of my door against the wall. My six-year-old half-sister strutted into my room and climbed into bed. A crown jammed into her silky brown hair caught me in the neck. The cowboy boots she wore over her footed pajamas thwacked my shins. Toothpaste dribbling from the corner of her mouth smeared against my arm. Three seconds later, six Jack Russell terriers lunged through the door and leaped onto the bed.

Yapping, the pack circled our bodies. Little paws stepped on my limbs and clawed my skin, climbing over and under. Finding no enemies, two flopped on their sides to sleep while the other four proceeded to dig into the blankets and pillows. In case a chipmunk hid under my covers. Or treats. A possibility with Remi in my bed.

"Are you awake?" she said.

"I am now." I hugged her, angling my chin away from the

crown and legs from her boots that had probably tromped outside before coming into my bedroom. There were worse things about moving in with your father when one was in her mid-twenties. Getting to know my little sister was not one of them. Privacy and clean sheets, maybe. "What's for breakfast?"

"Sausage and cheese grits." Remi stuck out her tongue and wiggled into a sitting position. A dog stuck his nose in her armpit, and she waved him away.

I smiled and sat up. The smallest Jack Russell, Teeney, climbed into my lap, and I scratched under her ears.

"When's he coming?" Remi meant Nash.

"He's not." I lifted Teeney off my lap and rose from the bed. "I'm going to Vicki's today, so I'm taking Lucky."

"Momma said she's surprised you haven't had a dirt bike accident yet. She said it'd be better for you to get a vehicle with doors and a roof before you end up with a face full of gravel."

"She's right. Tell her I could use a cosigner on a loan for my safety."

"Don't go to Miss Vicki's. Stay with me." Remi tugged on my t-shirt. "Daddy says y'all made a pact with the devil working for Miss Vicki."

"He's probably right."

"It's ba-ad," she bleated. Liking the sound of the bleat, she tried it again, setting off a howling fit among the dogs. Remi placed a finger before her mouth. "Hush."

They quieted.

That never worked for me.

"I'm getting up," I said. "Why don't you mosey your boots over to breakfast?"

Remi grabbed my hand and pulled me back onto the bed. "Daddy's fixing to hire you away, even with all y'all's nepa-isms. What's that? A germ?"

I thought for a minute. "Nepotism. It means he doesn't like to hire family because it might not be fair. And so there are no hard feelings when he fires them."

Remi angled her chin up and pursed her lips. "He's never fired me."

"I guess you're pretty good." I winked. Her words hit me. "He wants to hire me? To do what?"

She shrugged.

"I have a job. And I need to keep it for two years until my apprenticeship is done."

"He don't think you'll make it."

"What?" The words hit me low in my abdomen. I hugged my stomach and blinked off my shock for Remi's sake.

Remi folded her arms over her PJs. "He thinks y'all are making a big mistake. And Mr. Nash 'don't think with his big head' with you around and that's a 'damn shame.'" Her tiny face tipped to the side. "Where does Mr. Nash keep all those heads? Is he like Bluebeard?"

"Never mind." My cheeks warmed. "How do you know about Bluebeard?"

"TV." Having finished tearing through my sheets, the dogs climbed on Remi. She fell over giggling.

"I'm going to shower, Remi-sita. Save me a bowl of grits." I trudged toward the bathroom, bowing under the weight of the monkey who no longer clung but danced on my back.

Remi popped back up. "One more thing."

I groaned. But listened anyway. It was like biting a hangnail.

"Mr. Nash is following you down the path of 'struction just like he did with Miss Jolene. What are y'all building?"

Path of 'struction? "Destruction." I sighed. "Daddy thinks I'm going to destroy Mr. Nash."

Remi's eyes rounded and she hooted.

"You shouldn't spy on people, Remi. I know you're trying to help me, but—"

My words were drowned out by a cacophony of dogs who had caught on to Remi's hoots. I leaned against the wall, sagging under the idea of me as Jolene's doppelgänger. Jolene 2.0. Jolene, the second coming.

My father thought I was going to destroy the man I loved.

Daddy would know. Boomer Spayberry had been married to Vicki.

Until she tossed me in a baby seat and took off to LA to become rich and famous.

HAVING LATHERED with Ouidad and scrubbed with St. Ives, I cleared my head along with my complexion. If Daddy was seriously worried, he'd have words with me. Boomer Spayberry did not hold back his thoughts and opinions. Unfortunately.

Remi couldn't deliver tone or nuance. He could have been joking, after all. Remi eavesdropped on a private conversation with his wife about his daughter. Didn't parents view their kids in exaggerated terms?

I loved Nash. How could I destroy him?

Let's see, Maizie, said my brain. *Nash sold his business to Vicki and continued to work for her because of you.*

But only because he was broke. Because we couldn't get clients. Due to misunderstandings the media aired, ruining his reputation in town. Which wouldn't have happened if my celebrity hadn't brought attention to him.

OMG. I was destroying him. At least his business. I hoped not his heart.

But what was all that about kismet through .38 Specials?

I called Rhonda. "I'm destroying Nash."

She moaned. "Do you know what time it is? Why are you up this early?" A clunk drowned out her mutterings.

The mutterings stopped.

"Rhon?"

"You killed Mr. Nash? Oh Lord, is he dead? I knew this would happen, I just didn't think so soon."

"He's not dead." I paused, her words taking hold. "Wait. What? You thought I would kill him?"

"Girl, don't be calling me before I'm awake and expecting me to be sensible." Rhonda cleared her throat. "Start over. What did you do? Set fire to his office? Blow up his truck? He doesn't have anything else to destroy, does he?"

"It's much worse." I sighed. "My father thinks I'm going to destroy him like Jolene did. My father doesn't believe in me."

"You don't believe in you either. You told us the same thing yourself yesterday."

"I was speaking of Nash's career, not his heart."

"There's a difference? Okay. Let me think." Water ran in the background. Two clatters and a muffled curse later, Rhonda returned. "Everyone knows Boomer Spayberry is a serious man."

"What do you mean?"

"What you and Nash have…it's…I don't know. But maybe Boomer is overestimating your relationship. I wouldn't worry about it."

That sounded even worse. "You think we don't have enough of a relationship to worry about destroying?"

"Girl, it doesn't matter what I think, does it? It only matters what you think. But you're always bitch— explaining how y'all never have time to do anything remotely couple-ish."

"You think Daddy doesn't see me as serious. I'm stringing Nash along or something?"

"Haven't you had like twenty engagements? How many times has Boomer Spayberry thought he'd have to pay for a wedding?"

"Only twice. Well, three times. Four, but I don't count that one. Not really." I tapped my chin. "I see. I need to show Daddy, Nash is not a flavor of the week for me."

Rhonda yawned. "Yeah, maybe."

"Thanks, Rhon. You're a lifesaver."

She wrapped her goodbye in a yawn. I considered her earlier advice. Boomer and Nash needed to bond, but not over fishing or football. They needed to bond over me. And I needed to be there to show my earnest intentions.

ELEVEN
#RESISTANTREASSESS

I FOUND Daddy in the kitchen, studying the newspaper over a cup of coffee. Even sitting, he appeared as tall and sturdy as the pine he'd felled to build the table and chair where he sat. Dressed for work in a camouflage-print blazer and dark khaki slacks — that thankfully didn't smell like the deer-scented products his company sold to hunters — his style spoke more Paul Bunyan than Fortune 500. He'd always been a bit of both.

He stroked his thick auburn beard, looked up, and caught me studying him. "Morning darlin'. You eating?"

Considering I rarely passed up an opportunity to partake in Carol Lynn's cooking, I took his words as an invitation for breakfast conversation. I grabbed a place setting and a cup of coffee then sat on the bench near his end of the table. A covered bowl and plate of sausage rested in the middle of the table.

I sipped coffee, mulling ways to broach the topic of my relationship with Nash. And perceived a golden opportunity to gain some important information. I could warm Daddy by broaching a worse subject in his eyes: Vicki. "Daddy, when you were married to Vicki…"

He froze, spoon stuck in midair. A thick eyebrow rose.

"Was she interested in guns at all? Did you shoot things together?"

"Things? You mean like targets?"

"Sure." Targets. Doors. People. "Knowing you, I'm sure you must have introduced her to hunting and shooting or whatever. Or gave her a weapon of some kind?"

He set the spoon down. "She grew up around hunting, of course. It's recreational and for consumption around here. Pretends like she's all city, but we met in high school. Back in the day, I'd go turkey hunting before school. The boys and I would—"

"Did Vicki have a gun back then?" I said before he took a trip down the wrong memory lane. "Or did her family?"

His eyes traveled to a distant place and time. A faint smile slid across his lips, quickly replaced with a scowl. "I don't believe so."

Relieved, I grabbed the bowl of grits and began spooning the sticky mash into my bowl. The savory scent of pepper and cheese enveloped me, and I took a deep breath, gaining courage from its goodness. "I also wanted to talk to you about Nash. And my work."

"I agree." He smoothed the paper on the table. "Baby girl, it's time to re-evaluate your accomplishments since moving here."

"I—" wasn't expecting that. Grinning, I took a bite of sausage. This was going to be better than I thought. I swallowed. "Alrighty. I obtained and kept a job in private investigations, just like I dreamed. Although it hasn't been that dreamy. Except for Nash." I cleared my throat. "But working with him has been… educational and edifying."

"I believe those mean the same things." A ginger eyebrow rose.

"Well, I have learned a lot. Which brings me to my point. Why don't we have Nash over for dinner? A dinner where we can get to know each other better. And see each other in, perhaps, a new light. A light where one might—"

"I meant let's re-evaluate who you're working for now. You've gone full circle since moving here from California. And considering that's what got you in all the trouble, I think you need to reassess this particular situation."

"Um. Reassess what?" Sometimes it took a moment to get on the same dialogue page with Daddy.

He pointed with his coffee mug. "You ain't working for Wyatt Nash anymore, baby. A sad but true fact. Not matter how edifying it has been. You're back to working for your mother which may look like a primrose path covered in money, but it's still the primrose path."

"I'm not sure about flowers? And as for the path, I'm still driving the dirt bike you gave me?"

"Exactly. Now, I've been thinking." He set his mug on the table. "We can start you off in security since it seems to be your thing. And if the business appeals to you, we might move you into management. Eventually. First, you need to learn things from the ground up. Maybe do some tours of duty in the stores. Have you ever worked in retail, honey?"

I shook my head. "I've worked in acting with a bit of modeling on the side. And now private investigations. With a side of security installation."

He knew this. Wait, was this a job interview?

"Daddy—"

"No matter." He waved his hand and pushed out of his chair. "I'm sure you can learn the ropes. It may take some time, but the tutor said you were bright. Although, you just never know."

"Thank you?"

"When you're paying for a private tutor, they'll say things to flatter the parents. How do I really know how smart you are?" He folded the paper, stuck it under his arm, and grabbed his coffee mug. "Which's why Remi's getting a public education. It was good enough for me and for her mother. I want to see a report card with actual letter grades on it, not that 'affable learner' mumbo jumbo."

He strode to the sink and set the coffee mug down. "Just see HR and they'll figure it out. And don't go using your real last name. This is the kind of situation where stage names might work better. You don't want deferential treatment."

"I don't? Wait. HR?"

His long legs carried him down the hall where the pack of Jack Russells surrounded him, barking and bouncing around his feet.

I stood to call after him. "What about asking Nash to dinner? And my real name is Albright. Vicki had it legally changed when I turned eighteen."

Vicki. I'd vowed to not let her control my life anymore and here she was, driving it from the backseat of my dirt bike. Daddy was right. I had come full circle.

Hells.

How did I let this happen? Because of Nash? Shizzles, I'd gone full circle with men, too. No, wait. I needed my apprentice-ship. I had no choice but to join forces with Nash. Stick by his side.

Stand by my man? OMG. Were we even supposed to do that anymore?

The man who wanted us to investigate my mother. Because she might have shot a kung fu trainer.

Or just her door.

Here I was jumping to conclusions again.

I paced the kitchen. A crown full of light brown hair poked up from under the table followed by two brown eyes. The eyes followed my track along the pine boards.

The lack of privacy in this house.

I stopped my pace, squatted, and spied Teeney curled on the floor, licking her muzzle. Remi slid out from under the table, carrying an empty bowl.

"You didn't eat your grits, did you?"

Remi shot me an impish smirk and set the bowl in the sink. "We have to hide from the other Jacks when we eat."

"Teeney should stick to dog food. It's better for him. Grits are for growing girls."

"Teeney is a girl." She eyed the waistline of my Alo yoga pants. "Are you still growing, too?"

"Never mind me." I tied my hoodie around my waist. "Stop listening in on conversations. It's going to get you in trouble."

She rolled her eyes. "You want me to get Momma to ask Mr. Nash to dinner?"

"Thank you, Remi. That'd be lovely."

"I got your back, sister."

I grinned and held out a hand for a high five.

Remi squeezed one eye shut and stuck out her tongue. "But y'all kiss too much."

I gasped. "Stop spying. Or I'm going to tell Daddy."

"No," screamed Remi. She leaped around me and bolted from the room. Teeney popped from under the table, yipped, and ran out of the kitchen, barking. A cacophony of howls erupted in the back of the house, followed by the slamming of a door.

As soon as my probation was up, I seriously needed to get my own place. Or a cloaking device.

The doorbell rang. A minute later, Carol Lynn beckoned me to the foyer.

"Misty." I halted. "I didn't know you were picking me up."

Misty smiled.

I often didn't know she was picking me up, and I think she enjoyed that fact.

"Are you ready?"

"I was going to drive Lucky. Can I just meet you there?"

"That seems like a waste of time and gas and it's cold. Anyway, I thought you didn't like driving up the mountain on a dirt bike. You said it almost made you 'tinkle from fear.'"

My skin heated. "I said that to Nash, not you."

Misty shrugged. "I can't always remember what's told to me or what I overhear."

What was with all the eavesdropping? But she was right. I

didn't want to arrive with wet pants at Vicki's of all places. "You can drive me, but I need you to take me back to the office when I'm ready to leave. I don't want to get stranded."

She tugged the brim of her chauffeur's cap, which I took as some sort of salute. Although I wasn't sure if that was confirmation or Misty's form of sarcasm.

Free transportation comes at a price.

TWELVE
#KUNGFUPAPA

MISTY LEANED AGAINST THE ESCALADE, staring up at the DeerNose cabin. The logs to build Daddy's home had also been taken from his property, like the pine table, pine floors, and the dead animals decorating the walls. Daddy felt his cabin was modest. But his property stretched from the shores of Black Pine Lake through the forest to DeerNose headquarters. Some two thousand acres.

One couldn't help being impressed with Boomer Spayberry's property. Much like the impression made by Vicki's peanut baron mansion. Across the lake, Black Pine Mountain rose, the peak ensconced in mist. I suspected Vicki chose her home across the lake from Daddy's property so she could look down on him, but I was full of negative thoughts about my mother these days. The suspension of familial ties made for a slack line. Caught between my parents, I hung at the bottom between their heights.

"Does she make you wear that hat?" I said to Misty. A chauffeur's cap seemed cliché for Vicki.

"Does he make you hunt?" said Misty, opening the car door for me.

"God, no," I said. "Daddy does try to get me to fish. Mainly, I sit on our dock and chat until he tells me the vibrations from my voice disturb the fish, and I can thankfully go inside."

We drove along the lake, skirting the town, toward Black Pine Mountain.

"How do you like working for Vicki?" I watched Misty's face in the rearview mirror.

"I like driving." Misty didn't flinch or wrinkle her nose. "It's all right. I could do worse."

I wasn't sure about that. "Did you happen to take Master Xiáng Xi anywhere? He's one of the Chinese guests. Lili Liang's martial arts coach."

She shook her head. "I've driven Lili and her entourage back and forth to the studio a few times, but I don't remember a Master Xi. I picked up Kevin Yuan at the airport. He said he's Lili's coach. Do you think Kevin's his real name?" She sounded suspicious.

"He legally changed his name to Kevin when he immigrated. He said Americans couldn't pronounce his real name. Kevin's a popular Western name in China." I smiled. "I'm seeing Master Kevin today. I can't wait. He's a sweetheart."

"He didn't say much."

"Master Kevin's not super extroverted. And he can be intense during workouts. A real taskmaster. He's got high expectations for his students that are sometimes hard to meet."

"Sounds like a real sweetheart," Misty dosed her tone with extra sarcasm.

"Master Kevin actually helped me through a lot when I was shooting *Kung Fu Kate*. We were together for five seasons. I was young and needed a friend."

"You didn't have friends your own age?"

Vicki saw peers as competition, so I didn't do a lot of sleepovers. I kept that to myself, not knowing the strength of Misty's loyalty to Vicki. "It's hard for child actors to have a normal life."

We pulled off the mountain road and drove through the brick pillars marking Vicki's drive. Ornamental trees and bushes lined the approach. The topiary had been cut into the shape of various fish. Charles' green leaf tail whipped behind him.

"When did she do this?"

"The gardeners were here this morning." Misty parked in front of the house.

"It's still morning."

Misty shrugged and opened her door. Slipping out of the Escalade, she hurried around to my door.

"That's not necessary." I slid from the backseat and strode toward the porch. Misty hustled past me to open the front door. Next time I vowed to move faster.

I wanted to race my mother's chauffeur. What was wrong with me?

Inside, I checked on the bullet hole — still there — and casing in the tank — not there. Chanel No. 5 wafted into the room. My stomach clenched.

"Good morning, Maizie." Vicki's voice was brisk and irritated. More so than usual. "The aquarium cleaner arrived earlier. Where have you been?"

"It's barely past ten. Do you have the bullet casing?"

"Why would I keep the casing?"

"As evidence..." Evidence you'd want to be rid of if you felt guilty. Or Vicki no longer cared about the gunshot now that her precious fish were safe. I turned back to scan the tank for Charles.

"We lost a clownfish."

"Huh?"

"A clownfish is gone. The cleaner counted for me and one is gone."

"Your list of missing is growing. You're also missing a Chinese visitor and your fiancé." I studied her face. Her Botox prevented me from noticing any suspicious movements. Except for her eyes. Which rolled.

"Oh, him."

"Which him?"

"I don't want to get into that right now," said Vicki. "Master Kevin asked for you. He and Lili are in the gym."

"Don't want to get into what? Did you and Giulio break up?"

"We're on hiatus."

"You and Giulio?"

"No, the show. Really, Maizie." She scoffed and traced a finger down the side of the tank, following an angelfish. "Hello, precious."

I'd forgotten *All is Albright* — the reality show Vicki created as a vehicle to put me back on the celebrity map after one of my (several) falls from grace — wasn't taping. Which made it easier to visit my mother as I wasn't supposed to be involved in anything related to the industry. Except for screwing in door cameras for celebrity clients, finding missing kung fu movie trainers, and solving mysterious door shootings.

"But where is he?" I persisted.

"Giulio? He's doing work on another reality show. They're in some cabin up there." She gestured toward her ceiling, which I took to mean north, not heaven. "Twenty men and one woman, I believe."

"Is that safe?" Hang on. "Is he doing some kind of bachelor show? When he's engaged to you?"

She shrugged. "He can film what he likes while he's on hiatus. I gave him those terms in his contract."

Alrighty then. So romantic. But at least that meant Giulio was not involved in the front door shooting.

"There you are," she said, ignoring me.

I glanced at the tank and saw the scarlet fish churning through the water toward Vicki. His tail oscillated and body curved. Vicki held open her palms to the glass, and Charles swished past, made a turn, and returned.

Scowling, I narrowed my eyes before I realized what I was doing. I took a calming breath, reality-checked as per my ex-therapist Renata's instructions, and forced myself to feel happy for

Vicki. At least she could give unconditional love to something. That the something was a fish saddened me.

Pity was a better feeling than anger, right?

Leaving Vicki with her beloved Charles, I shlepped toward the gym. Inside, Lili sparred with Master Kevin Yuan. It'd been at least ten years since I last saw him. His thick hair was more salt than pepper, but his body was as lithe and strong as ever.

He and Lili crossed the wooden floor, moving with grace and precision. Calling out moves, he directed her kicks and punches. In tight-fitting leggings and sports bra, Lili's muscles rippled and flexed. Master Kevin wore the traditional kung fu *gi* — pants gathered at the ankle, a jacket with frog buttons, and flexible shoes. His movements were quick and responsive. When they finished their set, he bowed to Lili, then turned to me.

"Maizie, honey. Good to see you after all these years." He strode toward me, arms open, and I rushed to meet his hug. Releasing me, he held me by my shoulders and examined me. "All grown up. You're a beautiful woman now. That baby fat has given you a nice figure."

"And surprisingly, your hair is not as white as it could be." I burst into a fit of giggles.

He laughed with me. Master Kevin gave me my first lessons in trash-talking, but they'd been more art than putdown. He'd pointed out the back-handed compliment, a linguistic staple in LA, and taught me how to dodge them. The big-boned euphemisms can be confusing when you're ten and not allowed to gain weight. We had practiced parrying and thrusting with words while we did stage combat on the mats.

On the side of the room, Lili toweled off and watched us. Master Kevin pointed at her. "This one is very good. She doesn't need a trainer, only a practice partner."

Lili smiled and responded in Chinese.

Kevin shook his head and laughed. "You are the master and I am the student today."

Lili snorted, grabbed her water bottle, and moved toward a bench on the far side of the gym.

"I hope this picture does well for Lili Liang," said Kevin, watching her. "And I hope in her next picture, she doesn't do martial arts and is even more successful."

"Don't you want martial arts films to be popular?"

He sighed. "Of course, but I'd like Americans to see another side of Chinese life in their films. It is the easiest way to introduce a culture, in my humble opinion."

"Lili's very talented, isn't she?"

"I've watched her Chinese movies. Some lack the finesse of American production, but she's consistently good. She has strong chi. If they don't allow her to do serious drama, maybe she could still become a household name, the next Jackie Chan or Jet Li. Bigger than Michelle Yeoh, even."

"That would be cool." I studied him. "Did she tell you about the trainer who followed her from Shanghai? What do you think happened?"

Kevin's look darkened. "It's hard for me to say. I know very few facts."

"Lili wants me to find him. I work in private investigations and security." I expected him to laugh at the thought of me as a PI, but his eyes drew tight and his mouth thinned.

"I have heard." He pivoted slowly to place his back to Lili. He lowered his voice. "You work for Vicki?"

I followed his unhurried movements to stand alongside him. "Not intentionally. She bought the PI office where I apprentice. I only work for her peripherally."

"I suggest you go to another company." His eyebrows drew together. "This is very bad."

"Why?" I pinched my thumb skin, not because tears threatened, but at the surprise I didn't want to show. "There is no other private investigation office in Black Pine."

"It's unfortunate, but for the best, if you leave. If you can't move, perhaps you can find another line of work."

I'd struggled to get and keep the job I now had so I could get my PI license. Best of intentions and all that, but it was disheartening when the two father figures in my life wanted me to quit. "I don't want another line of work. I studied criminal justice. I like it. Despite its sometimes icky side."

"You won't change your mind." It was not a question. "It's disappointing."

"Why is private investigations so bad?"

"As you said, there is an icky side. And I fear the icky side may be dangerous for you."

Before I could ask what he meant, he tensed. The drift of Chanel No. 5 arrived before Vicki. She spotted Kevin and me in our huddle. Opened her mouth then closed it.

Kevin gave her a short bow, then turned his back on her. Not the slow deferential pivot he gave Lili. A quick jerk, so I now stood alongside his left side instead of his right.

I still faced Vicki and caught the look of surprise in her eyes. The shock didn't flare to annoyance but to fear. She edged backward, and her lip caught between her teeth. A response I'd never seen her do.

"Keep your eyes open, Maizie," Kevin whispered. "I'll do what I can to help."

THIRTEEN
#TOMMYBAHAMAGONER

RATTLED, I left Master Kevin and Lili. To avoid Vicki, I snuck through the kitchen to the backstairs. Besides a giant fish tank and gym, the Peanut Mansion also had a wing of guest bedrooms. After asking a maid who had what room, I strolled the second floor. Judge's paneling and chinoiserie silk wallpaper lined the hall. A hand-tufted rug ran the length. The Peanut Mansion didn't do wall-to-wall carpeting. Each door had a small plaque. The missing Xiáng Xi had stayed in the Green room. I ducked inside, closing the door behind me. Vicki had kept the old-world vibe in this room. Forest green damask drapery. Fluffy duvets. Antique-ish furniture.

Her housekeeper had attended to this room, despite Xi's disappearance. Or because of his disappearance. His four-poster bed had been made. Trash chucked (unfortunately). Bathroom cleaned. Otherwise, everything seemed to have remained intact. I rummaged his drawers, finding clothes neatly folded. His empty suitcase rested in the closet. A Tommy Bahama catalog was still on the bedside table. The bedside table had empty candy wrappers the maid hadn't seen. I sniffed the bits of wax paper but left them in the drawer.

In the small desk, I found his passport, wallet with credit

cards, and a Chinese identity card — my guess, since it was written in Chinese. Also, an employment card likely issued by the Chinese government for work abroad — not a guess, since it was written in English. I took pictures of everything and returned them.

Everything he'd need to travel or stay in the United States was here. Except for a cell phone and a laptop. Perhaps a martial arts master didn't use electronics. Perhaps he read paperback books and didn't play Words with Friends. Maybe he didn't email, text, or Facetime.

Or someone had removed them because they might have information related to his disappearance.

I sank onto the bench positioned at the end of the bed and scanned the room slowly. Then crawled under the desk and found the USB charger (minus the cord) he would have used for his phone. I found the laptop case in the zippered front of his suitcase.

That left me with three options. Master Xiáng Xi had taken his phone and computer and skedaddled for an unknown reason. Master Xiáng Xi had skedaddled and, after the fact, someone else took his phone and laptop.

Or someone had forcibly skedaddled Master Xiáng Xi and rid themselves of the evidence.

I EASED out of Master Xi's bedroom and slunk down the hall to Lili's room, the Cherokee Rose suite. I knocked on her door. When no one answered, I turned the knob and poked my head inside.

"Lili?" I called. "It's Maizie."

Her suite was larger than Master Xi's with more modern decor. Half-closed pocket doors separated her sitting room from the bed and bathrooms. A sofa and a pair of leather chairs faced a flatscreen above the fireplace. Perfect for viewing dailies or relaxing with her entourage.

Or relaxing with her honey. A framed picture sat on the end table, and I picked it up, spying Lili in a red carpet-worthy dress. Giambattista Valli, if I had to guess. Focused on the dress, I almost overlooked the man standing next to her. She gazed at him, not disguising her adoration. His arm was around her waist. Laughing at the camera.

No. He was smirking at the camera.

I knew that smirk. My eyes narrowed, and I felt my lips tighten. Jeff Johnson. The frat boy-wannabe-possible-spy from Lili's trailer. What in the hellz was he doing with Lili? I studied the backdrop behind them. The Toronto International Film Festival?

"What are you doing in here?"

The frame slipped in my hands, but I caught it before it fell. Looking up, a small, slender woman stood in the open pocket doors. Her thick, dark hair fell to her shoulders in a blunt cut. She peered at me through chic, blue frames, her dark eyes widened with surprise.

"I'm Maizie Albright. Vicki's daughter. I was just looking for Lili." I set the frame on the table.

The young woman's shoulders relaxed with her sigh. "Hello. It's nice to meet you." She strode forward, holding out her hand. "Shiyu Kang. I am Lili's assistant."

I smiled, shaking her hand. "Did you travel with her from Shanghai?"

Shiyu nodded.

"Then you know Master Xi," my voice rose in anticipation. "Lili hired me to find him."

Behind the glasses, her gaze darted away then rested on her feet. "Yes, he's been gone for almost a week, although I don't think we realized it until Monday when he missed practice with Lili."

"Did you see him leave on Saturday?"

She shook her head. "Lili had to go to the studio in the afternoon, but she didn't need me, so I decided to do some sightseeing. Misty took me to Atlanta. It was her day off, too. We thought it would be fun."

"Misty? Fun?" I shook off my surprise and refocused. "When was the last time you saw Master Xi?"

"Breakfast on Saturday morning."

"What about the party that night? Was he there?" I hoped Shiyu liked to gossip. "Big turnout?"

"I didn't want to go to the party." She shrugged.

I guessed she didn't gossip. Or she didn't like parties.

Looking up, she sighed and moved across the room. I gestured at the couch, hoping we could talk more comfortably, but she ignored me and opened the door to the hall.

"I'll tell Lili you're looking for her," said Shiyu.

Hells. I'd thought I was good at making friends with…

Hang on, maybe this was the problem. I still categorized people as those whom one "worked with" and those who "worked for" us. This could be why Misty didn't like me. I gave off "upstairs" vibes. Vicki did, too, but she didn't care. While I wanted friends, Vicki wanted efficiency.

But I also needed efficiency. Standing inside the doorway, I switched tactics. "Did you have fun in Atlanta?"

Her face brightened. "Oh, yes. Misty took me to the outlet mall in Dalton. We went to the World of Coke and the Georgia Aquarium. I ate fried chicken at Aunt Pitty Pat's Porch."

I filed away a compliment for the next time I saw Misty. And wondered if she would take me to the outlet mall. I'd never been to an outlet mall. Aunt Pitty Pat's also sounded delightful.

"Do you think Xiáng might have done something similar? Gone sightseeing?" Without his wallet. But I kept that comment to myself not knowing if it was common knowledge he had disappeared without his important documents. It looked like Vicki only had the room cleaned, leaving things for his return. "Maybe he went to visit sights, and something happened to him?"

Her mouth tightened. "I don't know."

"Is it possible he decided to quit and go back to China?"

"Shifu Xi wanted to come to America. Xi is very responsible. Why would he return to China without finishing the work? It makes no sense." Her gaze flitted into the hall and she retreated a step.

She didn't know he'd left his passport, then. Something wasn't right. It wasn't just me. I watched her gaze comb the hall. "If he didn't return to China, maybe he quit and went someplace else."

"His home is in Shanghai." Her features darkened. "I don't want to be here either, but Lili needs me. We will return when we finish the picture."

Either? "But if Xiáng didn't return to China or go sightseeing, what happened to him?" I paused to check my tone. "Could something have happened to him here? In Black Pine? Or in this house?"

Please don't say, "I think your mother shot him and tossed him in Black Pine Lake because she wanted to hire your martial arts coach for reasons we can't fathom but will become evident in a month or two when she makes another million."

Shiyu took a deep breath that appeared more painful than cleansing. She glanced into the hall again. "Even if this is a mistake, Shifu Xi should not leave."

"What's a mistake? The movie? You think *Unlucky 18* isn't good for Lili's career?" Even Kevin wanted Lili to do the movie. Why wouldn't Lili's assistant want her to become an international hit?

"These people are bad for her career," Shiyu muttered and yanked the door closed.

I stumbled forward, barely missing the not-so-proverbial door hitting my backside. And found Vicki and Kevin standing in the hall, watching me.

Did Shiyu mean Vicki and Kevin were bad for Lili's career?

"What are you doing in the guest wing?" asked Vicki.

"What are you doing in the guest wing?" I countered. Which

was stupid. Repeating the same question made me sound defensive. And suspicious.

"Really, Maizie," said Vicki. "I hope you're not bothering my guests."

Kevin studied me. I gave him a short bow he returned.

"What's going on?" I said. "What are the two of you doing?"

Vicki inched from Kevin and glanced away. "Nothing."

"If you're free, we could chat, Maizie," said Kevin. "I'd like to catch up with my old student."

Before I could answer, Vicki moved around him, blocking me. "Actually, Master Kevin, I'd like to talk with you." She glanced over her shoulder. "I think you have a project in the front hall, Maizie?"

"Front hall?"

"Isn't someone coming to fix the door?" she said sharply.

Kevin glanced from me to Vicki. "I'll catch up with you later, Maizie."

"Do you know where Lili is?" I wanted to know what she was doing with Jeff Johnson, napper and possible spy. I also had more questions about Master Xi.

"Conditioning. I gave her homework," said Kevin. "She's still in the gym."

"Don't bother her," said Vicki, waving her hand behind her back. Waving me off. "Door."

I watched them walked away. Master Kevin had a Shaolin school in Chinatown. Students. Teachers who worked for him. Contracts as a consultant on TV shows and movies. Yet with all those responsibilities, my old coach flew to Georgia a few days after Lili's coach vanished.

It was like Vicki knew Xi would disappear.

FOURTEEN
#ALLABOUTMYFAKEFATHER

I SAT in the backseat of the Escalade, allowing Misty to fulfill her chauffeuring dreams. As we zipped down Black Pine Mountain, I called Nash and explained the strange conversation I'd had with Master Kevin.

"Why would Vicki be scared of Kevin?" I said. "She looked shocked. She knew he was there and sent me to talk to him. It doesn't make sense."

"Did you see his expression?"

"He turned his back on Vicki after bowing to her. There wasn't an opportunity to give her a death glare or anything."

"Are you sure you can trust him? There might be something between the two of them you don't know."

I played with the zipper pull on my coat. "He was like a second father to me."

Nash didn't know anything about Master Kevin, and Nash was suspicious by nature. I couldn't blame him for questioning Kevin's motives. My past baggage kept turning up, but we hadn't explored the good parts of my backstory, like my relationship with Kevin Yuan. To be honest, I didn't know much about Nash's past either. Except what I witnessed when we were around Jolene. Who, thankfully, we hadn't seen in awhile.

"Kevin's a good guy," I said. "Just trust me."

"All right," said Nash in a surprisingly soothing tone. "Maybe it wasn't Kevin who surprised her. Anyone else in the room?"

"Lili, but Vicki knew she was practicing with Master Kevin. I don't get it. I've never seen Vicki act like that."

"Do you think seeing you and Kevin together made Vicki think of something?" There was an edge to Nash's voice that made me feel a little squeamish. A dose of pity.

My stomach rolled, and I turned to Julia Pinkerton's teenage snark for help. "Like Vicki suddenly remembering she hadn't buried the body of the kung fu trainer properly?"

I bit my lip, then checked Misty's reaction in the rearview mirror. Misty's eyes were on the road. Hopefully, her ears were, too.

"We have no motive or evidence of that, but you might have a point. Not about burying a body, but she was reminded of something. We'll set it aside for now. Did you find anything out about the missing Chinese man?"

Using my chin, I held the phone against my shoulder and covered my mouth and phone with my hands. "Everything is still in his room, except his laptop and phone. I spoke to Lili's assistant. Shiyu doesn't believe he'd return to China or leave the project. She wasn't home on Saturday and didn't go to the party, so she can't pinpoint any better than Lili when he disappeared."

"Why would he take the phone and laptop and not anything else?"

"Unless whoever got rid of him took the phone and laptop."

"No motive or body, Miss Albright. A bullet in a door doesn't make for either."

"Kevin might have some suspicions, but he says he doesn't know enough to comment."

"That's a weird thing to say."

"I know, mysterious much?" I forced a laugh and caught Misty's eyes in the rearview. "But that's just like Kevin. The

Asian mystique is part of the role he's played in Hollywood for so long he's probably forgotten how to speak normally."

"Speaking of normal, Carol Lynn Spayberry called and invited me to dinner."

"That's nice, right?" Remi was true to her word. Or trying to get on my good side so I didn't tattle. "Dinner when?"

"This weekend. Where are you headed?"

"Back to the office. How do you feel about coming to dinner?"

"Carol Lynn is a great cook. I'm sure it'll be a great dinner."

Great and great. Totally not what I meant, but fine.

"Our office or the other office?"

My heart pattered at the word *our*. "Other. I'm going to start an internet search on our missing kung fu trainer. What are you doing?"

"Hoping to find a similar-sized key for the locked desk drawer. A pistol might not be in there, but I want to be sure. I'd also like to know if Vicki is purposefully obtuse or just clueless." Nash sighed. "We have so many unanswered questions, it's hard telling in which direction to go."

"We need to get the bullet out of the door before she gets rid of it. She tossed the casing after the aquarium dude grabbed it for her."

"Lord. It's really like she's working against us. Did the cleaner find any more casings?"

"I don't think so."

"You forgot to ask?"

"I was distracted." By Charles. I feared I needed professional help with this jealousy issue. I never had this problem with Remi. Maybe I just had ichthyophobia.

"I know a carpenter. I'll handle the door," said Nash. "It's going to be difficult to track an international visitor. If Xi returned to China, Homeland Security isn't going to help us much. But if his passport is still here, we'll focus locally, then spread out our feelers."

"Got it."

"You sound happy."

"I'm excited. We're doing investigation work that doesn't involve a screwdriver."

"I might have to use a screwdriver on Vicki's door." I could hear his snigger. "But you're right. I'm a little excited, too. It feels good to do real work."

"Except it still involves Vicki."

"That will change. She won't always own the business. We'll get rid of her one of these days."

But Vicki would always be my mother. And if my relationship with Nash went anywhere, he'd be stuck with her, too.

Vicki and I had been through so much together. Putting aside her maternal failures, as a manager, I always thought she had protected me from an even bigger Hollywood meltdown. Saved me from fates worse than rehab and jail.

No matter what she did, I couldn't abandon her.

Although it felt like she was driving me toward an ultimatum I didn't want to face.

FIFTEEN
#23ANDVICKI

BACK AT THE NEW OFFICE, I used our databases to research Xi, then scoured social media sites. He hadn't been in the US long enough to make much of a ripple. I typed up the information I'd found, uploaded the photos I'd taken, and thought about motives for an ex-pat who'd recently moved overseas to disappear.

Maybe we were looking at a *White Knights*-styled defection. In that case, Nash and I were over our heads.

The bell on the front door rang. I rose from my chair and peeked around the corner. And smiled.

Nash strode through the shiplap and brick waiting room, met me in the doorway, and gazed down at me.

"A real job," he murmured.

"We get to put away your toolbox." I rose on my toes and circled my arms around his neck. "I'll miss Phyllis. But only a little bit." I placed a tiny kiss on his scar.

"A real job still means we're on the job." He handed me a ring of desk keys. "Distract yourself with these."

Sighing, I lowered my heels and examined the small keys. "For the desk?"

"Hopefully one will work. I want to know if she's got a

firearm in there. Why she would lie about shooting her own door? Just bugs the crap out of me. If someone else did it, why be mysterious?"

"And if someone else did it and she doesn't know?"

"Then she's got a bigger problem than a hole in her door." Nash brushed a hair from my face then cupped my cheek with his hand. "I've been doing some research at our office. I didn't want it to be on the servers here."

"Oh?" I knew he meant he'd been researching Vicki. A prickly feeling stole over me.

His thumb stroked the side of my face. The ice-blue eyes had warmed. But looked sad. Bending forward, he kissed my forehead. He patted my shoulder. And strolled to the window to stare at the street.

OMG, what did he find? That was the kind of tenderness you gave someone after finding out their mother had Ebola. Or their ancestry test showed their spit matched Ivan the Terrible's. Or my Ivan the Terrible genes had given me Ebola.

Maybe the emotional equivalent of Ebola.

I shook it off. If Nash found something nasty in Vicki's past, he would share. It wasn't like I didn't know Vicki's crown was tarnished.

Unless the news proved she had horns.

How could I think such things about my own mother?

Change of subject needed. Stat.

"I couldn't find much about Master Xi online. He has a series of training regimens on YouTube, so we have a good physical identification for him. He founded a Shaolin school in China, but it looks like it's not around anymore."

Nash turned, appearing relieved I hadn't asked him about his finds. "Could be working for Miss Liang is more profitable."

I nodded. "I've got his address in China. Couldn't find much else on social media, unless there's a Chinese site that's blocked. And all his consumer credit information is in China. It doesn't look like he's applied for anything here."

"You ran him through the IRB?"

"All our databases. I did find pictures of him online. With Lili and some other actors. *Variety* type stuff plus local entertainment news. Also some pictures with him and a government official, but Google Translate garbled the English. I couldn't understand what it meant, but it didn't look significant. He received an award for something. That's about it."

"Good work, Miss Albright. Have you talked to Miss Liang yet? Maybe she'll shed some light."

"She had training this morning. I'm supposed to meet her later. Earlier, I was distracted by Kevin and Vicki and forgot to mention this, but I did see a photo of Jeff Johnson, our possible spy, in Lili's room. A red carpet photo of him with Lili."

"Hinky." Nash rocked back on his heels. "Makes more sense that he'd be in her trailer."

"Makes even less sense if he's bugging her trailer, though. I'm going to ask Lili about him." I looked at the keys. "I'll do some research with these, too."

"I'll drop you off at the Peanut Mansion, then be over later. I have a lead on someone who might retrieve the bullet without damaging the door."

"What if Master Xi defected?"

"Crossed my mind, too," said Nash. "In that case, it's no longer our case."

Which made me wonder if the spy devices in Lili's trailer weren't meant for her at all.

I FOUND Lili on a recliner facing Vicki's infinity pool. While the sun shone, a breeze charged with mountain-y frostiness blew across the space, making me shiver in my sweatshirt.

"Aren't you cold?" I turned on an overhead heater, dragged a chair to sit beneath it, and used my backpack as additional coverage.

"Although I live in Shanghai now, I'm from Beijing in

northern China." Her British accent was as crisp as the air, but the tone much warmer. "This time of year, it's frigid. I find this Georgia temperature pleasantly bracing."

"I'm from Black Pine, but I've lived in Southern California most of my life. Although it's nice to truly enjoy boots and sweater weather, this mountain winter is getting long."

"I love boots and sweater weather, too," said Lili. "Did you see Alïa's spring collection? Their flared coats are adorable this year."

"Totally," I lied. Unfortunately, my financial situation prevented me from scouring the lookbooks. I could've checked out the new spring lines, but the thought of all the beauty I couldn't afford made me feel squinchy. Not that I regretted my decision to give up that part of my life. Some things were just harder to face than others. Like wearing t-shirts and jeans every day. And gun holsters.

Mostly the gun holsters, because I did not like guns.

"About Master Xi. Any names and numbers you could give me would be helpful. If I could speak to some of his family or friends, it might help me to understand where he went. Or..." I hesitated, "if he returned to China."

"He could not have returned. His passport is still here."

They had searched his room. Because why wouldn't they? As an employee, possibly Shiyu wasn't in the know.

"You have to find him quickly," said Lili. "Master Kevin can do the fight choreography and he's a wonderful trainer, but I'm frightened for Shifu Xi. I can't believe this is happening to me. First Shifu and now Jeff."

Now Jeff? "Speaking of Jeff, did you give him an all-access set pass?"

"Yes." Lili smiled. "Sweet Jeff. We met online, which sounds ridiculous, I know, but..."

Sweet Jeff?

"I saw your picture. You looked smitten." And he flirted with me in your trailer. But this I kept to myself. Those remarks generally backfired. Lili was a client. And soon-to-be international film star. "What did you mean by 'now Jeff?'"

She leaned her head against the lounge's cushion. "I don't know what scares me more. Shifu Xi's missing, and I can't get a hold of Jeff. He went to look for Shifu for me and now Jeff's missing, too."

Shiplap. Shiplap. Shiplap.

SIXTEEN
#SLEEPINGWITHTHEENEMIES

"WE HAVE ANOTHER SITUATION," I hissed into my phone.

After excusing myself from Lili, I'd slipped around the side of the house to call Nash. Unfortunately, this side of the house was shaded. The gentle mountain breeze felt more like wind, and my skin was quickly chapping.

"Please don't tell me you found another bullet in a door. The carpenter has a backlog of work and I'm having trouble convincing him it's urgent."

"No bullet. A boyfriend."

"I can barely hear you," said Nash. "Are you in a tunnel?"

"Wind tunnel." I turned my back on the breeze and the wind whipped my hair forward into my face. "Jeff Johnson, the possible spy, is Lili's boyfriend like we thought. And now he's missing, too."

Nash didn't say anything.

"Did you hear me?"

"I heard you."

"What does this mean?"

"We don't have enough information to know if it means

anything." He paused. "Sumbitch. What's with Lili and men disappearing on her?"

"Maybe Jeff was spying on Lili. He's so sketchy. How can someone as nice and wonderful as Lili date a creeper like him?"

"A lot of women date pigs. Let's focus on the 'he's missing' part of the equation."

"True," I said. "But he's scammy. I can tell."

"We don't know anything about him except you caught him napping in her trailer and she thinks he's missing. When did he go missing?"

"A trailer that was bugged, remember." I knew he remembered. But sometimes a girl needed to make a point. "She hasn't heard from him since yesterday. Just after we saw him. Jeff Johnson was looking for Xiáng Xi, too. Why would Lili hire us and send her boyfriend to look for the same man?"

"Hinky."

Nash was a man of a few words. Literally.

"Maybe Jeff and Xi ran away together," I exclaimed. "That'd be sad for Lili. I knew Jeff Johnson was a scoundrel. I just thought him another kind of scoundrel."

"Xi's been gone since Saturday and we saw this Johnson guy yesterday. Why would she think he disappeared?"

"He could have ghosted her."

"I don't know what that means." Before I could explain — and knowing I'd want to explain — Nash continued, "And I don't know how Jeff Johnson fits with our current problems. Other than he's supposedly looking for Xiáng Xi, too. Maybe Miss Liang is feeling paranoid about her boyfriend."

I'd be, too, if my boyfriend flirted with other women. But this I also kept to myself.

In the background, a voice called out. Nash murmured a "can do" to the voice, then spoke to me. "I'll be there soon. Talk to Vicki's people about the day Xi went missing. See if you can get any other details from Vicki. Focus on Xi. Leave the Jeff Johnson thing for now."

I crossed my fingers behind my back. "Um, sure."

I SAILED through the French doors and slammed into Stanley Wu, the charming Hong Kong rom-com star.

"Excuse me," Stanley laughed, but with his delicious British accent. "You look positively fetching except your hair appears to have gone a jet ski trip without your permission."

"Stanley, I'm glad to run into you. Although not literally." I smoothed my hair. "Lili's outside if you're headed to see her, but can I steal you for a few minutes?"

"Always." He followed me to a pair of club chairs.

"How long have you known Lili?"

"Forever." He grinned. "Lili and I attended the same performing arts school in Beijing, but I moved back to Hong Kong while she went to Shanghai. Our careers have taken different paths, but we stayed in touch. She did action and I did romantic comedies, but now we get to try our hand at something a bit more challenging."

"I'm excited for you both. Particularly if this movie is an international success. It can do wonders for everyone's career."

He tugged the collar of his shirt and winked. "Don't I know it."

"Did you know Xiáng Xi? Lili's shifu?"

"Not well. Of course, I've met him. He's staying right down the hall. And I thought I'd be training with him. We sparred a bit in the gym last week."

"You know he's not been heard from since Saturday?"

"Yes." Stanley's friendly countenance turned serious. "Disturbing, isn't it? Particularly for a Chinese national."

"The political implications are a little terrifying. Any reason for Xi to, you know," I flicked my fingers, "Poof?"

"Politically?" Stanley's face tightened. "Maizie, I'm a citizen of Hong Kong. Draw your own conclusions."

I hurriedly moved on. "When was the last time you remember seeing him?"

"Let me think." Stanley's gaze drifted toward the French doors, then snapped back to me. "I think breakfast on Saturday morning. I went to Atlanta with Chey. Did a little shopping. Can't remember seeing Xi later."

"You were at the party here on Saturday night?"

"Of course." Stanley smiled. "Director's orders. Make a potential investor happy."

"Vicki's a potential investor?" I stumbled on the words. "I thought your producers and studio were all squared for *Unlucky 18*."

"Darling, you know a picture like this can always use more money. Who'd turn down a check even at this late stage?"

Certain behaviors began to make sense. Vicki would love to have a big movie notched onto her belt. She'd always felt her TV producing titles didn't lend her enough legitimacy in the industry. Chasing dreams never stopped in the entertainment world. They just got bigger.

"Now the party." Stanley leaned forward. "I'd love to dish."

"Go." I scooted forward in my chair.

"Lili's man and our famed director had a tussle. Certain accusations were tossed about."

"About Jeff Johnson?"

"About Vorling. He spends quite a bit of time in Macau." Stanley grinned. "But don't we all?"

"Vorling gambles?" I cocked my head. "How did Vorling's last movie do?"

"An indie project. I believe it won some awards." Stanley shrugged. "He hasn't done a blockbuster for quite some time. Rumor has it the AP, Mr. Zhou, tossed him in rehab to clean him up for this project. The execs wanted him for *Unlucky*."

"The executive producers wanted a semi-washed up director with a gambling problem?"

"That's the story. But his earlier films were big. German action movies, so you might not know them. Did quite well in the foreign markets. Outside America, of course."

"You know a lot, Stanley."

He shrugged. "I pay attention."

"I'm looking into Master Xi's disappearance. But it seems Jeff Johnson has flown the coop, too."

"Ah, well." Stanley rolled his eyes.

"Cheater?" I said.

"Possibly." Stanley pursed his lips. "He does pop out quite a bit."

"What does she see in him?"

"Have you seen him? You're not into the whole hunky Anglo look?"

"He smirks too much. Like a frat boy at a social mixer." I bit my lip. "Probably shouldn't have said anything."

Stanley whooped. "Darling, that's delicious. I love it."

"Seriously, though. Is Jeff Johnson particularly jealous? You said he got into a fight with Vorling. Would Jeff stoop to spying on Lili?"

"Interesting comment. I thought—" Stanley shook his head. "Never mind. That can't be right."

"What?"

"This is how rumors get started. The argument he had with Vorling, the innuendo was Johnson knew something about Vorling. And planned to use it against him. Or perhaps the other way around? I'm not sure. It's all muddled in my head now. Too many martinis. All around."

Too many loose threads all the way around. And not one leading to a missing man.

SEVENTEEN
#THENEUROTICPSYCHOPATH

VICKI'S PEOPLE — her housekeeper, gardener, and virtual assistant (who was virtually no help) — confirmed Lili's story. Master Xi had been at tea and not seen since. Nobody knew much about Lili's boyfriend, Jeff Johnson, either. He'd stayed at the house. He was funny and nice.

Obviously, they didn't know him well.

Uber and the other local ride services didn't report any pickups at Vicki's. Xi would need his passport as identification to fly, bus, or train it anywhere in the US. As excited as I was to have a real case, I was also a little bummed. If Xi had somehow obtained fake identification, we might be SOL when it came to finding him.

But if someone had shot Xiáng Xi in Vicki's house…

In the foyer, I chewed my nail, thinking. And watched for Charles in the super tank.

"Maizie, do you even care about your manicure anymore?" said Vicki.

I jumped. Normally Chanel No. 5 gave me a warning to Vicki's whereabouts. I sniffed and detected something lighter. Hermès? No, Armani Beautiful. Vicki had worn Chanel No. 5 as long as I could remember smelling her. What in the Hades was happening to Vicki?

"What are you doing here, standing around, biting your nails?" she said.

"Wondering what happened to Master Xiáng Xi." Partially true. It would not behoove me to let Vicki know I might be scared of Charles. Who was behind the glass. And a fish. "And wondering if his disappearance had anything to do with the bullet in your door."

"Of course they had nothing to do with each other."

"How do you know?" I pressed on, using Julia Pinkerton's sharp interrogation-style voice which had served me well in past cases. Or so I thought. "Then what happened to your door? The floor's obviously been fixed. And why would Master Xi leave without telling anyone?"

"I don't know." Vicki's eyes darted to the floor, then to the door. She crossed her arms. "Why should I?"

"Because your house is where both things happened?"

"Yes, well." Vicki shrugged. "Stranger things."

"What does that mean? Don't you see how this looks?"

"I'm very concerned about how things look. Which is why I'm hosting a party here this weekend." She lifted her chin. "I assume you're free."

"I'm not." But I was bewildered why a party changed the fact there was a mysterious bullet in her door, new parquet mysteriously made to look old, and a mysterious man missing from her afternoon tea. The man wasn't mysterious, but the fact he vanished was.

It was all *Scooby Doo*-ish.

"Why are you not free?" demanded Vicki. "I'll give you the time off."

"It's the weekend—" The problem with working for someone who didn't keep regular office hours. "Nash and I have been invited to dinner by Carol Lynn."

"Who?"

"Daddy's wife."

"Oh, yes. Her. Why?"

"Why is she Daddy's wife? I think they have a lot in comm—"

"No, 'why' refers to the dinner. You often eat there because you live there. What makes this so special you'd miss a party here?"

I fought my befuddlement. "Well, because Nash and I...Well, it's the first time Nash has been invited...in conjunction with me. And Daddy...it'd be nice if they would have a more personal relationship because of...you know."

"Really, Maizie. You're making absolutely no sense." She narrowed her eyes. "I thought you and Nash are just—"

"Please, don't say it."

"Lovers."

Gah. I hated that word. It made me think of hot tubs and bad movies from the seventies. And eighties. And bad jokes from the nineties.

"Not really," I spoke quickly, my voice high and reedy. "We are in a relationship of sorts. One in which mutual respect and companionship are paramount. One in which we are not seeing other people."

At least I didn't think we would. Exclusivity had not been discussed, only assumed. Relationship discussions weren't Nash's strong suit. He preferred the nonverbal use of his mouth. But this wasn't something I'd share with Vicki.

"I don't care what you are," said Vicki. "As long as it doesn't interfere with your work. For the record, when you start speaking of yourself in the third person and using words with more than two syllables, it means you're lying."

Hells. This was the problem with interrogating your ex-manager, still-mother.

"I'm not lying," I said. "Nash is invited to dinner. In a formal way. Because we are in a semi-formal relationship of sorts."

Vicki pursed her lips. "What kind of dinner?"

"It's hard to say. But Carol Lynn will likely make something delicious. Like fried chicken. Or chicken pot pie. Or chicken and dumplings." I reflected on the past month's dinners. "It's a good bet that it will involve chicken."

"I don't mean the food." Vicki rolled her eyes. "Only you would think I meant food."

"Isn't the word dinner generally associated with food?"

"Who is going to be there, Maizie? It's the who that matters, not the what."

The 'what' did matter to me, but she had a point. People should be placed above experiences.

Even fried chicken.

"Daddy's family. Nash. Me." I tapped my chin. "Sometimes Carol Lynn's parents visit. They're super nice. But I don't know if they'll come. They live all the way down in—"

"Stop," said Vicki. "Obviously, this is a casual sort of event. You'll cancel and take a rain check."

"No, I won't." I crossed my arms. "And you need to tell me everything you remember about Xiáng Xi. You're a suspect."

She blew out a forced laugh. "I'm what? Suspect in what?"

"OMG. Haven't you been listening? In the disappearance of Xiáng Xi. And the strange case of the bullet in your door." Which sounded more *Nancy Drew* than *Scooby Doo*. Which was also not much better. But whatever. "But mostly Xiáng Xi. You are the last person to see him. Alive."

"He's dead?" she said.

That was a very good question I couldn't answer. I kept my features still, deciding to play it as mysterious as her bullet. "How did Master Xi seem to you at the tea last Saturday?"

"Really, Maizie." Vicki sighed and strode across the parquet.

I followed her into the living room. It had retained its old-world vibe, like the foyer — minus the coral reef — and was also oak and stone with a carved marble fireplace. A beautiful room, now looking slightly sinister considering it was possibly the scene of the tea where the disappearance of Xiáng Xi had happened.

"Was this where you had tea?" I said, looking around for a tea cart. The only drinking substances were cut-glass bottles of alcohol on a credenza in the corner. Which was actually more Vicki than tea things. "How was he?"

"Yes, this is where we had tea." She sat on the edge of the sofa and picked up a magazine from the coffee table. "Do I need a lawyer?"

"To answer a question about what Xiáng Xi was like at tea?" I flopped onto the sofa next to her. "What is wrong with you? You've been acting weird all week."

"If he's truly gone and dead, I might need a lawyer. He was staying at my house, after all," she snapped.

"This is true." I watched her rifle through the magazine. "Why can't you just answer my questions?"

"He was fine," said Vicki. "We drank tea and ate little biscuits. It was horribly boring. The conversation was about the movie and the kind of choreography they wanted to do. Nothing terribly interesting. In fact, the conversation was stilted. But most conversations are when it's just small talk. She's better off with Master Kevin. Kevin understands how things work here."

After seeing how she reacted to Kevin, I found her defense of him slightly odd. But everything was odd these days. "What happened after Lili left?"

Vicki tossed the magazine on the coffee table. "I don't know. I made some excuse about needing to make a call, so I left. He remained in here sipping tea, I suppose."

"Was the alarm system on? Would it alert anyone if he left the property?"

"Of course not. I have people coming and going all day. I'm fully staffed. We turn it on after I've gone to bed. But not since— Anyway, just at night."

"'Not since' what?"

"Nothing." She leaned back on the sofa. "There's no reason to have it on during the day. If he left the property, which he must have, no one noticed."

"It bothers you."

"I think it's rude for a guest to leave without telling his host, yes." She looked at me. "Any more questions?"

"Aren't you worried about what happened to him?"

"He's a grown man. He should be able to look after himself. But like most grown men, it wouldn't surprise me if he can't."

"I talked to Giulio." Called him while at the office. Just to get his take on Vicki and guns and bullets in doors. And learned nothing new about Vicki, but everything new about Giulio.

His new reality show sounded like a mashup between *The Bachelorette* and *American Ninja Warrior*. Except on a snowy *Wipeout*-styled course at a Blue Ridge cabin. Which was odd, since Black Pine was only forty-five minutes away and didn't have snow. But not the oddest part of the conversation, which had been about a hot tub. And then I had hung up before losing my lunch.

She sat up, eyeing me warily. "You went to the *Sporting Love* set?"

"I called him. Do you want to know how Giulio's doing?"

"I imagine he's doing his best to win that contest," she said drily. "It'll mean a lot of talk shows and magazine covers. And I imagine he's enjoying the competition."

"Yes. But I didn't say what he's doing, I asked if you wanted to know *how* he's doing. Don't you miss him?"

"Yes, well." She waved a hand dismissively. "We're both very busy."

I leaned toward her. "You had a party for the *Unlucky 18* cast and crew the same night as the tea when Xiáng Xi disappeared."

"And I'm having another one this weekend. I highly suggest you ditch your dinner with dad. You're too young to settle..." She trailed off deliberately.

I ignored the dig. Particularly because I didn't know if "settle" referred to Daddy's family, Nash's social status, or my relation-ship wishes. "Was Xiáng Xi invited to that party? Did you see him at the party?"

"Yes, he's in the crew. No, I didn't see him. But I don't talk to… I spent most of my time with the producer and lead actors. I don't see what that has to do with his disappearance."

Neither did I, other than Vicki was a snob. But that was old news. "A carpenter is coming to take the bullet from the door."

She steeled her voice. "I don't like this kind of ramrodding from you, Maizie."

"Get used to it, Vicki. Remember you're a suspect."

"I thought I was your mother."

I internally winced. My ex-therapist Renata had many theories about my need to please my mother and father. She said it was healthier than the alternative, not caring what they thought. Neurotic trumped sociopathic.

At least I had that going for me.

"And as your employer," continued Vicki. "I am asking you to stop seeing me as a suspect."

"Can't—"

"I'm now hiring you to find Xiáng Xi, as well as discover who shot my door."

"But—"

"Or I will fire Nash. And without a licensed employee, I'll be forced to shut down the office. Which means you'll also be out of a job."

My neuroses felt a little sociopathic. So I left.

EIGHTEEN
#MONSTERINLAW

WITH SLIGHTLY SOCIOPATHIC feelings and my last therapist in jail, I couldn't wait for Nash. Leaving the peanut nuthouse was imperative.

I had Misty drive me to LA HAIR. Unlike paid therapy, Tiffany and Rhonda's advice was not gentled like a calm, objective professional's. Truthfully, the advice was often harsh and stinging. But it was given with hugs, which I could not get from a therapist. Or at least, not from Dr. Trident.

You're not allowed to hug someone in jail if it's not a family visit.

Misty dropped me at the nineties-era strip mall holding LA HAIR and the other shops frequented by the older residents of Black Pine. I pushed through the door. The bell tinkled. Rhonda looked up from the receptionist desk. A broad smile beamed from her cherubic face. Then it dimmed.

She lowered her chin to give me the eye. "What happened? Is it Nash?"

"She killed him?" Tiffany popped from behind the styling room wall. "You owe me twenty, Rhon."

"Very funny." I peeked around the wall, seeking a free chair. "Can you do my nails today?"

"I'll fit you in." Tiffany strode to the shelf of enamels and picked up a bottle of taupe OPI polish. "Does 'Berlin Done That' suit you?"

"Pretty much." I sighed.

At Ashley's station, a woman jerked her head from a magazine. Head covered in rows of folded foil, she looked ready for a space odyssey. Or full highlights. "I thought you were gonna do my nails next, Miss Tiffany."

"Janice has twenty minutes until I rinse her," said Ashley.

"Keep your pants on, Janice." Tiffany strolled to her nail station. "If I don't start this one, she'll lose her shit. We don't want tears in the salon today."

"Thank you, Janice, and I apologize." I sniffed. "But Tiffany's right. I find getting my nails done very soothing. My ex-therapist—"

"Maizie's been gnawing on her nails something awful," said Rhonda. "Janice, it just won't do. Everyone in town knows Maizie Albright comes to LA HAIR to get herself done up. It's all over social media."

"It is?" said Tiffany.

"I take her picture every time she's in here, and I post it on my Instaface thingy," said Rhonda. "I'm branding us as a salon good enough for ex-celebrities."

"You do?" I said, feeling uncomfortable. "You are?"

Tiffany pointed at the chair before her nail station. "Sit down and tell us what happened."

"Go on, Maizie." Rhonda scooted a chair next to me and plopped into it. "Just to clarify — for Tiffany — Nash is not in the hospital or a morgue. But you're still seeing him."

While Tiffany removed my old polish and filed, I explained Vicki, the bullet in the door, the unused office with the Velcro strap imprint, missing Xiáng Xi, and the also missing, slightly stalky Jeff Johnson. "And Vicki has a new aquarium. She has a fish named Charles, who hates my guts."

Rhonda leaned forward. "Fish are like that."

Tiffany shot her a look from across the table, then picked up my left hand and began painting. "Vicki's blackmailing you, in a way. Means she's feeling guilty about something."

"It's very confusing." I laid my left hand on the table and gave Tiffany my right. "At first Vicki wanted us to get the bullet casing. But denied anything happened. Then told us to 'sort-of' look into it. Then officially hired us. But Nash had already decided to investigate the bullet and Vicki, to make sure we don't get into trouble. And I was already hired by Lili to find Master Xi and now her boyfriend, Jeff the schemer."

"You're confused about who will pay you," said Rhonda in her soothing, faux-therapist voice.

"No, I'm confused why Vicki would hire us if we think she's a suspect. Particularly since we're already working for her."

"To prove her innocence." Tiffany inspected my right hand's nails. "You'll be reporting to her. That way, she can cover her steps more easily."

"Oh, I think I saw this in a movie." Rhonda tapped her chin.

"It's kind of like you want Vicki to be guilty," I said.

"Not kind of." Tiffany glanced up, the little polish brush unwavering. "That woman is a monster. I hope she gets tossed in the can."

The idea of Vicki in jail caused my chest to burn. And not in a good way.

"The thing is, she's not really a monster," I stumbled over my words to get them out. "She's a product of Hollywooding, just like me. I knew a lot of people like her. It's all business for them. She's Machiavellian and Sun Tzu-ish. It's how you succeed there. That's why I couldn't. I don't have the killer instinct."

Rhonda patted my shoulder. "It's hard to be a poodle in a pit bull world."

"Sounds like Vicki might have a literal killer instinct." Tiffany pursed her lips, cranked a brow, and placed a manicure fan over my fingers.

"The thing is, I want to find Master Xi for Lili. Even if I don't like her boyfriend, I need to find him, too." I gave them a hard look. "But I don't want to learn Vicki's guilty of something more than being a ruthless businessperson."

"And a horrible mother," said Tiffany. "Because you already know that, right?"

"Yes. I've accepted it." At least, I thought I had. "You just don't want to learn your horrible mother is—"

"A stone cold killer?" said Rhonda and took my picture.

I forgot to smile for the camera.

NASH PICKED me up from LA HAIR. I slid into the passenger seat and refrained from reaching for him — I was never sure when we were on the clock — even though I could have used another hug. Instead of a hug, he handed me a bullet with a flattened head and scored sides.

"Evidence from the door," he said. "But evidence of what, we don't know. It's a nine-by-eighteen millimeter, just like the casing we found. Interesting."

"Why interesting?"

"A nine millimeter bullet is common. A nine-by-eighteen? Not as common. Although not uncommon."

"I don't get it."

"It's eighteen caliber."

"Okay." I still didn't get it, but ready to move on. "Now we can guess what gun shot Xiáng Xi in the foyer."

"We don't know if anyone shot Xiáng Xi in the foyer, period. Someone shot an eighteen caliber pistol. At what or why we don't know. Other than it hit the door."

"And they had to replace the floor."

"Maybe. I was looking at the realtor reports. The wood might have been replaced before she moved in, and we never noticed it." Nash's jaw tensed. "Vicki's flat refusal of police intervention is not a good sign, though. Most people would be horrified a weapon was fired in their home."

"I told her she's a suspect and she didn't like it. She threatened to fire you if we didn't solve this case. Although she might have threatened to fire you only because we consider her a suspect."

"Fire me?"

"The girls think she's a monster. Do you think Vicki is a monster?"

Nash studied me, then looked away. "I think there's something hinky going on, but we don't have nearly enough facts to piece together the what or how hinky."

I adjusted my seat belt strap to lean against his arm. "Thank you."

"I wouldn't want someone calling my mother a monster either." He patted my thigh. "Even if she was."

I pulled back. "Was she?"

"No." He put the truck in reverse and backed out of the parking space, conveniently keeping his eyes on the rear view and side mirrors. "But she wasn't perfect. She made some bad choices."

This was the most I'd ever heard about Nash's family life. I was afraid to ask for more. But I wanted more so badly it made my teeth hurt. "Bad choices in what?"

"Men mostly." He shifted into drive. "Let's see Lamar and see what he has to say about the bullet."

I placed a hand on Nash's arm, slid it over his deliciously large bicep, and slipped my hand in his. "Thank you."

"For what?" He glanced at me. His brow was pinched and the scar on his chin stretched tight due to the clenching of his jaw.

"For telling me about your mother. No matter her faults, she produced a wonderful son."

"She did her best, I guess. I didn't help her much." The clenched jaw and pinch between his eyes eased. "You know what I like best about you?"

"What?" I asked a little too quickly.

"You don't want your mother to be a monster." He braked at

the four-way and looked at me. "Most people would write Vicki off and never speak to her again, even if it still ate at them. It'd be easier, not having to deal with her. Despite everything, you still try."

He leaned over to kiss my cheek then accelerated through the four-way.

Tears pricked my eyes. "You know what I like best about you?"

He slid a look over to me.

"You would tell me that." I sniffled. "Thank you."

NINETEEN

#MULEKICKER

NASH PARKED in front of the Dixie Kreme Donuts Shop, hopped from the truck, and came around to open my door. I placed my hands on his shoulders, slid out, and squeezed against him.

We stood in the open doorway, holding each other. I gazed at him, wanting to spill all my complicated, gushy feelings. He studied me, then leaned down. My gushy feelings exploded into a hot rush of desire. I grabbed his head, pulled him to me, and locked on.

The scent of donuts, mixed with the special Nash blend of male and Acqua di Selva, is one heady combination.

After a long, hot minute, Nash broke our volcanic lip lock. "I guess Lamar's waiting for us." His hands slid up and down my sides. His icy blue eyes had become warm blue pools. Tots McDreamy. He pulled me against him. "But we've got another minute."

I glanced at the shop, then back to Nash. "Lamar's employees are using us for their coffee break entertainment."

Nash dropped his hands and stepped back. "I can't believe I'm mauling you in public. You make me a little crazy, Maizie."

"Crazy bad or crazy good?"

Please say good. Please say good. Please say good.

With nary a glance at me, he shut the truck door but took my hand. We gazed up at the Dixie Kreme building, then walked to the second floor entrance stoop.

"I miss this old place." I sniffed, inhaling donut. A shot of that scent was better than any drug for soothing my feelings, IMHO.

"We'll get it back someday."

There was that word *we* again. Vicki could pulverize the word in an instant. How could he forgive me if she fired him from his own business? Or if she took her money, closed the shop, and left him with his debt and no way to start again?

He had begun figuring me into a future, not knowing the path we tread was littered with land mines.

OMG. Tiffany and Rhonda were right. I might blow him up.

Nash dropped my hand to open the door, then followed me up the dusty, worn stairs. Bitterness, resentment, and despair shoved up against all my gushy, warm feelings and trampled them, leaving me cold. Making my heart and stomach cramp. I pinched the base of my thumb to stop myself from crying, then stopped before the old-timey door. The stenciled glass used to say "Nash Security Solutions" before Vicki made Nash take it off under threat of litigation.

The first time I opened this door, I had caught Nash half-dressed. It was still a favorite memory to replay at night when I couldn't sleep.

Oblivious to my flight of sentimentality, Nash reached around me to turn the knob. "Hey, Lamar," he shouted. "We're here."

"Sweet Jesus, you scared the tater out of me, Nash." Even exasperated, Lamar's voice was honey to my ears. If Morgan Freeman had a voice twin, Lamar was it. His soothing tone and rhythm calmed my nerves and shot me full of hope. This was why Black Pine was good for me, despite my worsening luck. If

Nash was a balm to my heart, Lamar, my LA HAIR besties, and Remi were each a balm to my soul.

"Hey, Lamar." I abandoned my issues for his sake. And for Nash, who was oblivious to the Maizie-cloud-of-doom hanging over his head.

"Come here, gorgeous." In the brown corduroy La-Z-Boy, Lamar eased from the horizontal to vertical. After his retirement from the Black Pine police, Lamar had taken over his father's donut shop (as a cop, the joke was not lost on him). Lamar often caught naps in the La-Z-boy. For him, life literally revolved around "time to make the donuts." Since Lamar had been a father figure for Nash, Nash opened his private investigations office above Lamar's shop where they could both keep an eye on one another.

Which made Vicki's new office venue an even greater pill to swallow.

"Thanks for sticking around to see us." I rushed past Nash to hug Lamar. "I miss you."

"Miss you, too, honey. You taking good care of my boy?"

"She is."

I glanced over my shoulder at Nash. His stern features had eased into a smile that turned my innards into goo. A hot glorious mess of goo. I had to bite my lip as well as pinch my thumb.

Nash moved around me to clap the squashed bullet into Lamar's hand. "What kind of gun are we looking for? Pretty sure the casing was nine-by-eighteen, too, but we couldn't get a good look at it to check the stamp."

Lamar held it up, squinting at the bullet. "Dollars to dough-nuts, a Makarov. We'd need to have forensics examine the mark-ings to determine the rifling."

"Makarov was what I was thinking."

"Wait a minute," I said. "The Russian gang in *Julia Pinkerton*, Season Four, used Makarovs."

"Makarovs are Russian designed semi-automatics," said Lamar. "Don't make them anymore. But Russia exported them here. At least until the mid-90s, I think. They gave the license to other countries for manufacturing, too. Mostly in Eastern Europe. There are a lot of Bulgarian Maks in the US because they didn't stop exporting until the early 2000s. I believe they all have the Red Star logo on the grip."

"I don't think Vicki knows many Russians."

"I don't think Russians have anything to do with this," said Nash.

"My first centerfire pistol was a Polish Makarov. A P-64," said Lamar. "Damn thing kicked like a mule. The first time I shot it, felt like I broke a bone in my hand. Stiff recoil. The thing is, since the barrel was stationary and welded to the frame, it was a sharpshooter. Incredibly accurate."

"Not so much for whoever shot the door." I smirked.

"I'm putting this in our safe." Nash tossed the bullet between his hands. "The casing is gone. Vicki got rid of it. She might have the gun in a locked drawer."

"I forgot to check the drawer," I said. "I was waylaid by Vicki again. But it does look like the gun might have been strapped under her desk."

"But anyone can get into the office. She doesn't use it."

"That's not good." Lamar squeezed his chin. "What's the deal with the missing Chinese man?"

"The trail is pretty cold." Nash looked at me.

"He was last seen at Vicki's having tea. Then disappeared. Without any of his things, including wallet and passport, although his phone and laptop are missing. The same night there was a party and possibly, the door was shot then. Nobody noticed or said anything until Vicki's fish nosed up the casing."

"That's not good either," said Lamar.

"Hinky," agreed Nash.

"If we assume Xiáng Xi wasn't shot and dropped in Black Pine Lake—"

"We're not assuming that," said Nash. "We don't have a motive."

"Then how would he leave Vicki's if he doesn't have a passport or driver's license? He's a foreigner in a foreign land. No Ubers, taxis, or hired cars came to the house to get him. He wasn't at the party according to Lili." I slapped my forehead. "Unless he waited until the party started and caught a ride to town when someone was dropped off. Most of the partiers are staying at Black Pine Resort."

"Good thinking," said Nash. "The resort might have sent them together in a car. That's easy to check."

"Does your missing person have money?" said Lamar. "Money's all he needs. He can buy a fake ID, passport, all kinds of stuff. He could have gotten fake papers before leaving China."

"What about used car lots?" I said. "With cash, it wouldn't be hard to buy a car and take off. If he paid well enough, the dealer might overlook things like insurance and a driver's license."

"Good idea," said Nash. "I'll call the used car dealers. Particularly the mom-and-pop outfits."

"Lili's boyfriend is also missing," I said. "She said he went to look for Xi. Except yesterday I found him napping in her on-set trailer. A trailer full of spy equipment. I don't think he was napping. I think he was bugging the trailer."

"Why would he bug her trailer?" asked Lamar.

"He's a creeper," I said. "Or an industry spy."

"It was a lot of tech for a creeper," said Nash. "But we now know Jeff Johnson's stayed at Vicki's. We need to get our equipment over to the Peanut Mansion."

I turned toward Nash. "Why?"

"Vicki's house could be bugged, too."

"The party," I said a tad bit excitedly, judging by their expressions. "It'll be perfect. We can 007 our way into the party."

Lamar looked at Nash. "What is she talking about?"

Nash shrugged.

"Vicki is having another party tomorrow night and she

invited me. Mostly the same guests since she has a captive audience. Literally. Lili and her entourage plus Stanley Wu, are staying at Vicki's."

"But we're having dinner at Boomer's," said Nash.

"*You're* having dinner at the DeerNose cabin?" said Lamar.

"Carol Lynn invited me," said Nash.

"Dinner with the parents?"

"I know." Nash shrugged.

"What's the big deal?" I said. "Daddy's family eats early. We'll go to the party after dinner. While I distract Vicki and the guests, you can hunt for spy stuff. I can interview the guests from last Saturday on the sly. Total 007. We can recon behind the aquarium."

"Why would anyone recon behind a fish tank?" said Nash. "You can see through it."

"I've been trying to get you to come over for years," said Lamar. "Olivia will be hurt."

"Don't tell her," said Nash. "I didn't mean to hurt her feelings. I just…you know."

"What is going on?" I glanced from Nash to Lamar.

"Nothing," said Nash.

"Who's Olivia?"

"Lamar's wife. You knew that."

It's strange the things I don't know after six months with these men.

Lamar shook his head, leaned back in the recliner, and closed his eyes. "*Women.*"

"What women? Do you mean me? Why am I getting a 'women?' You're the ones who never told me about Olivia. How do you not mention your wife? More like 'men.'" I folded my arms. "*Men.*"

"You knew I was married," protested Lamar. "You've seen pictures of my kids."

"I assume nothing and I'm too polite to ask. And he," I jerked my thumb toward Nash, "is even more closed-mouthed than you about personal stuff." I narrowed my eyes at Nash.

"We'll go to the party," said Nash in an obvious rush to change the subject. "After dinner with your dad. But I'm not wearing a tux."

"That's perfectly fine. You're going to be sneaking around anyway." I winked. "I'll be wearing the tux."

TWENTY
#DINNERWITHTHESPAYBERRYS

ALL SATURDAY, my emotions popped and fizzed like a newly opened bottle of Armand de Brignac. I did miss industry parties. Or, more truthfully, I missed dressing up for the parties. Getting the blowout and style. Choosing my outfit and accessories. All the primping and fuss.

As much as I wanted to completely adapt and adopt to my new role of small-ish town, private investigator, I couldn't escape my shallower side. I loved fashion. Looking good made me feel good. It was a much prettier, more glamorous side of business than the kind that screwed in doorbell cameras, took photos of cheaters, and served subpoenas. And it smelled better, too.

I inhaled the mix of Oribe, Ouai, and Ormaie. *Intoxicating.*

Smoothing a hand down the satin tuxedo stripe of my wool-mohair trousers, I grinned. *Luxurious.*

I puckered for the mirror and dabbed on Nars lipgloss. *Sexy Time.*

The name, not the event.

Smiling, I floated from the bathroom, down the hall, and through the kitchen where Carol Lynn lifted a dish from the oven. More heavenly smells. The doorbell chimed and Remi raced past me, sliding in her cowboy boots on the tile floor. My black, patent leather, ankle-strap pumps tapped a pleasing staccato on the tiles as I hurried my float to get to the door before Remi. Then I stopped, because she would beat me anyway and why ruin a good float? Nothing could spoil my mood.

Nash and I were really doing this. Dinner with the family. And infiltrating a party with major Hollywood hitters. It was like a scene in *Mr. And Mrs. Smith*. Before they tried to kill each other. Life could not be sweeter.

"What in the hell are you wearing?" boomed a voice behind me.

I turned and almost slipped on the tiles. "Saint Laurent. Head-to-toe." I tapped a toe. "Even my kicks. Aren't they awesome? The stilettos are four-and-a-half inches. I can't remember the last time I wore stilettos—"

"I can see through your top." Daddy pushed air through his nose. "Why aren't you wearing an undershirt?"

"Undershirt? I don't have—"

"My Lord, girl." His face grew mottled. "A man's coming to dinner. And your sister. And Carol Lynn. And me."

"Daddy, nobody wears a bra under something like this. A bra would show. And it's not Italian. This is semi-sheer, not sheer. Oh wait, Anthony Vaccarello designed it for Laurent. Guess it sort-of is Italian." I grinned and twirled. "Besides I'm wearing a vest. And pasties. Nothing is showing."

"Your nothing leaves little to the imagination."

"If it bothers you that much, I'll button it." I quickly did the buttons meeting below the lapels. At my midriff. Making a plunging neckline. Which was why I wore the georgette blouse beneath the vest. I looked up at Daddy.

His nostrils flared. "Not helping," he choked.

"What in the hell are you wearing?" said a voice behind me.

"Not you, too." I spun around. Remi hopped on one foot next to Nash. His eyes flashed between me and my father, seemingly not able to decide where to land. "This is my version of a tux."

Nash's jaw tensed. "It doesn't look like any kind of tux I've ever seen."

"I like them shoes." Remi crouched to examine the heels. "You could use them for all sorts of things."

I slid my foot back and made a mental note to hide my stilettos. And all shoes featuring a heel.

"You can't go out in public like that," said Nash. "Someone will see you."

"It's not public. It's a party. But I went out in public like this all the time in California," I said. "This is not a big deal. You can't see anything."

"I can imagine a lot," said Nash.

Daddy's eyes narrowed. "I'd advise you to do your imagining with someone else." He turned to me, growled, "Put some clothes on," and stomped from the room.

"Honestly. I finally get the chance to look hip and hot." I sighed and shook my head. "Fathers."

"I thought this party was for you to do recon and for me to sweep for bugs." Nash stared past me, watching Daddy disappear down the hall. "You're not helping."

"I am helping. A lot. I'll blend. I don't have anything new, but this is classic. It's Saint Laurent, chic, and sexy as hellz."

"I know it's sexy. That's the problem. A big problem." Nash clenched his jaw and his scar whitened. "And I meant helping with your father. You can't be sexy for me in front of your father. Don't you know anything?"

"I'm not doing it for you. I'm doing it for Lili."

"Then we have a whole different issue."

I rolled my eyes. "Don't worry about Daddy. How can he not love you? You're both from Black Pine. You have a job. And you fish." I leaned toward him. "You do fish, don't you? Or hunt? Or whatever else falls into those categories?"

Nash shook his head. "I shoot targets, mainly."

I raised a shoulder. "I'm sure that counts for something."

"Maizie," Nash sighed. "I'm not the kind of guy parents like to meet. This is probably a mistake."

I laughed. "Don't be silly. Daddy's met my other boyfriends. You're exactly the kind of guy my parent would like to meet."

HALFWAY THROUGH CAROL LYNN'S excellent dinner — chicken fried steak. Not actually chicken but still in the title — I began to think Nash might be right. Not about my outfit. Although I did agree to put a hoodie over my top through dinner. It was a practical consideration. When it came to gravy, there would be splatter and I was wearing silk.

But Nash might have been a teensy right about being the type of guy parents didn't like to meet. Which I didn't get at all. Nash wasn't like any of my other boyfriends or fiancés. He was Black Pine, not Southern Cal. A working man, not an actor. What was the issue?

"How about the baseball?" I said after a long silence broken only by the scrabbling of paws beneath the table. A pack of dogs vied for not-so-secret forkfuls of chicken fried steak fed to them by Remi. We'd spent much of the dinner moving our feet as dogs bumped into our legs and sat on our toes.

"The baseball?" Nash looked at me. "What do you mean?"

I waved a hand. "The, um, Braves? Don't you follow them?"

"Season hasn't started. Still spring training." Nash cocked his head. "I didn't think you followed baseball."

I stared at Nash, then glanced at my dad.

Nash blinked. "Do you follow the Braves, sir?"

"Football. Georgia?" Daddy scooped mashed potatoes into his mouth and eyed Nash.

"Alabama."

"What?" Daddy spluttered, then coughed. Carol Lynn reached to pound on his back and Remi sprang from her seat to help. He shooed them off. "How?"

"My grandparents were from Alabama."

Daddy shook his head.

"Guns," I said. "Show him your .38, Nash."

"I don't generally carry it to dinner, Maizie." Nash quirked a brow at me.

"I carry to dinner," said Remi, pulling a Daisy from beneath the bench.

"Remington Marie, put the gun away," barked Daddy. "We don't carry weapons to dinner."

"Never heard that one before." She shrugged and hopped from her seat. Twenty-four paws scrabbled beneath the table, ready to follow their alpha. "See y'all later."

"You didn't eat your dinner," said Daddy. "I saw you feeding the Jacks."

"Chicken fried steak is their favorite," said Remi.

"Sit down and eat."

"What about my gun? We don't carry weapons to dinner, remember?" Remi fluttered her lashes. "I should put it away, don'cha think?"

Daddy sighed and eyed Carol Lynn. She took the air rifle and carried it to the garage. He swung his gaze back to Nash. "What are your long-term plans since your business is sunk?"

I sucked in a breath. None of my old boyfriends got this kind of grilling. They mostly got ignored. Easier to do in California, admittedly.

"I don't consider it sunk," said Nash. "Just in a holding pattern until I save enough cash to buy Vicki out."

"I'll tell you something." Daddy pointed his fork at Nash. "If *that woman* is holding the keys to your office, it's sunk. I'm trying to understand what kind of man would let Vicki buy his business and stay to work for her."

A muscle jumped in Nash's jaw.

I glanced at the clock. "Well, look at the time."

"Carol Lynn made dessert. Hold your horses." Daddy glowered at Nash. "My daughter shouldn't be working for *that woman* either. Has she explained to you the rules of her probation?"

"Now, Daddy," I said. "This has nothing to do with Nash."

"I find that difficult to believe, honey. In fact, I imagine Wyatt Nash, here, doesn't believe it for a minute either. Do you?"

Nash forked a piece of steak and chewed.

"Way I see it," continued Daddy. "Maizie can get herself into some real trouble with this new business of her mother's. Heard all the clients are with the movie industry. And I'm pretty sure working in entertainment's against the rules of her probation. Maizie's a lot of things, but stupid ain't one of them."

I was glad to hear this, although I wondered what the other things were. Without really wanting to know.

"She is a fool when it comes to men, though." Daddy stared at me, then slid a look at Nash.

I gasped. "Daddy."

"I'm sorry, honey, but it's true. How many idiots have you been engaged to now? I'm saying this for your own good. Wyatt Nash needs to know where I stand and so do you."

"Well, I stand on my own two feet, Daddy." I glared at him. "And I might have made poor choices in the past, but I was younger and living a whole different life. I know what I'm doing. We're working for Vicki so Nash can continue mentoring me for my private investigator's license. I've told you it takes two years. And Nash agreed to work for Vicki *for me*. He's making a sacrifice for me. Isn't that honorable?"

"You may think you're standing on your own feet, Maizie Marlin Spayberry, but you're standing in your mother's shoes. You know it. Wyatt Nash here knows it. And I know it. You both need to get the hell out of this situation. And you may think it's honorable, but Wyatt Nash here's not using the good sense God gave him because you have clouded his judgement."

Pronouncement made, Daddy pushed back from the table, stood, and began gathering plates. "I'll do the dishes, Carol Lynn, if you get the dessert."

"How about those Dawgs, sir?" Nash pushed the words

through a tightly drawn mouth. "Hoping they'll make the play-offs again?"

The doorbell chimed.

Daddy turned, a stack of plates in one hand. "Who would that be?"

"I'll get it," Remi and I chimed together.

"I'll get it," said Daddy. "Both of y'all, sit."

He set the plates in the sink and strode toward the foyer. Carol Lynn smiled calmly and pleasantly, gathered the rest of the dishes, and walked them to the sink.

I looked at Nash and winced. His shoulders were drawn back, spine erect, mouth firmed in a tight line, and ears red. "I'm so sorry," I mouthed to him.

"Sorry for what?" Remi ducked beneath the table and returned with a cleaned plate.

I shook my head at Remi and turned on the bench to face the kitchen doorway. Daddy's boots rung on the tile and a moment later he returned to the kitchen with Misty. He jerked a thumb at her. "She said she's here to pick up Maizie for a party."

"Misty," I said. "I don't need a ride. Nash will take me."

"Vicki said I was to pick you up." Misty sniffed. "Smells like chicken fried steak."

"Would you like a plate?" asked Carol Lynn. "Or dessert? I made lemon pudding cake."

"Can I just have a popsicle?" said Remi.

"You won't have anything until you eat your momma's dinner, Remington Marie," said Daddy. "Maizie Marlin, you want to tell me why this woman says she's taking you to Vicki's when Carol Lynn invited Mr. Nash to dinner? My wife made chicken fried steak and lemon pudding cake for him and you're leaving to go to a party?"

I chewed my lip and tasted Sexy Time.

It couldn't be farther from the truth.

TWENTY-ONE
#DADDYDAUGHTERDANCEOFF

"HANG ON A MINUTE, DADDY," I said, jumping from my seat. I grabbed Misty's elbow and pulled her into the hallway. "Listen, Misty, you need to go back to Vicki's. Now."

"It's a wasted trip."

"I. Don't. Care. Tell Vicki I'm coming later."

"I don't believe Mr. Nash is invited," said Misty. "Which is why Vicki asked me to pick you up."

I sucked in a deep breath and blew it out through my nose. "Leave. Now."

"You don't have to get so uppity with me. Just because I'm a chauffeur, doesn't mean you can speak to me like this."

Striding to the front door, I yanked it open and pointed outside.

Misty strolled to the doorway and stopped. "You're a lot like your mother, you know?"

Wincing, I closed the door gently behind her and hustled back to the kitchen. Nash shook Carol Lynn's hand while Remi clung to his leg. Daddy stood behind them, arms folded and scowling.

"It's just work," I told Daddy. "We're infiltrating a party because we're looking for a missing man."

"He's hidden in your mother's house?"

"Really, Daddy." I pulled off my hoodie, folded it over my arm, and grabbed my clutch. "Let's go, Nash."

Nash cast me a strange look, then moved his gaze to Remi and ruffled her hair. "We'll take you another time. You need to eat your dinner."

"If I eat, will you take me?" pleaded Remi.

"No," said Daddy. "Don't even think about it, Remington Marie."

"It's an adult party," I gentled my voice to oppose Daddy's angry bellow. "You'll be bored."

"I'm never bored with Mr. Nash," exclaimed Remi. "He's so exciting."

I knew how she felt. I often wanted to cling to his leg while gazing adoringly at his strangely dangerous yet handsome features. Which was totally not with the times.

"Maybe that's the issue," muttered Daddy.

Could Daddy read my mind? I patted my cheeks, then spluttered, "I can't believe you. I'm twenty-five. Nash is one hundred percent better than anyone I've ever dated in my life. And as for his business, he's trying his best to make it work."

"Your math, as well as your life choices, needs work. We'll talk about this when you come home."

I narrowed my eyes. "Maybe I won't come home."

Daddy pulled in air through his nose and tightened his lips.

"I think we better go." Nash pulled Remi off his leg, placed a hand on the small of my back, and walked me out of the kitchen. "Where's your coat?"

"I don't need one," I fumed. "I've got a friggin' hoodie. Unbelievable."

Nash spun around the foyer. "You must have a coat somewhere. You're going to get cold in that outfit."

"You know what?" I shouted toward the kitchen hall. "I think I will move out. I think it's better for our relationship to go back to the way we were. I'll see you in the summer, Daddy."

Nash pinched the bridge of his nose, yanked open the front door, and pulled me outside. "You're right. You don't need a coat. You need to cool off."

WE RODE to Vicki's in silence, where I pretended not to notice Nash's clenched jaw. I also feigned not feeling cold nor needing the hoodie (I needed a coat). I couldn't fake moving out of the cabin was an option that would go over with my probation officer. Judge Ellis expected me to live there.

Growing angrier, I replayed the scene at Daddy's and kept my eyes on the passing scenery, so I didn't have to look at Nash's clenched jaw. The fish topiaries signaled our arrival. Nash drove around the circular drive to park before the front door. Lights beamed inside and outside the mansion.

A valet rushed forward, but Nash waved him off to open my door. The faint strains of jazz drifted from somewhere inside or from the patio. I sniffed and took in another breath. Plumeria scented the air. At her parties, Vicki often had fragrance pumped out the entrance to set the mood. However, neither jazz nor exotic blossoms helped the funk. Neither of us felt the rhythm of the night (in the true DeBarge sense).

Nash extended a hand to help me out. Which I took because of the stilettos.

For some reason, I felt a teensy peeved with Nash, too. For reasons I couldn't fathom. Possibly due to leftover anger with my father. And my mother. And the universe for dealing me a crappy hand of cards in the real game of Life.

If your sort-of-boyfriend was investigating your mother in a missing person's (and mysterious bullet) case, shouldn't your father *not* pick now — of all times — to act like an ass?

Closing the truck door behind me, Nash glanced over his shoulder at the valet before looking at me. "It's not too late," he murmured. "Boomer knows your words were said in anger."

"I can't handle two parents who insist on acting like the world should be governed by their rules alone."

"Better than no parents." Nash arched a brow.

I set that thought into my mental Nash box to examine at a time when peace reigned. Which might take a while. "It's not fair."

"He's your father. He's trying to protect you."

"I'm not a kid."

"Then don't act like one."

I felt my face get squinchy, but before I could smooth it, my bottom lip trembled. Jerking my chin up, I created a new character for myself, Maizie the pissed-off-daughter-ready-to-conquer-the-world (or-possibly-just-her-hometown). I used a helping of *Julia Pinkerton*, a dash of *Kung Fu Kate*, and a smidge of the hooker with a heart of gold (and a lot of moxie) from *The Black Rose*.

Only because her mother had sold her out, too. But, like, literally.

Nash sighed. "Listen, Maizie. We're rushing things. Our relationship is new, and we're stressed out about the business. Put your issues with Boomer aside for a time. Focus on the case."

"Right. Focus on the case to prove to him we're not totally incompetent," I seethed. "And in the meantime, I'll move in with Vicki."

"What?"

The words had surprised me, too, but my new character seemed to be okay with the idea. "It makes sense. I could watch her and stay on top of the case."

He expelled a gush of air. "I thought you wanted to move in with me."

"Oh." I stared up at him. "Did you want me to move in with you?"

"No." His scar flexed with the gritting of his teeth, but he grabbed my hand and patted it. A little roughly, but I could tell he meant well. "I mean, we're not ready for anything like that.

It's what I meant by rushing. Moving in together can ruin a relationship. Especially a relationship under pressure. Like ours."

"I wasn't thinking of moving in with you anyway," I stammered.

At least he had used "relationship" several times. And "ours." That was a plus.

Maybe.

"Since we're working for Vicki and making more money, you could get your own place, if your probation officer will let you." Nash eyed me. "Have you ever lived on your own?"

I shook my head. "Only because I was doing *All is Albright* and we filmed at home. And I got into trouble, so I stayed at home. Then the judge said I had to move in with Daddy. But I'd also never wanted my own place. A house and staff felt like too much responsibility for my early twenties."

"A house and staff?" He shook his head. "What about an apartment?"

I shrugged. "I mean, I could have…"

"Sometimes I forget how young you are."

"I'm not that young."

"We have a few years between us."

I felt my nerves sizzle. "Like seven. It's not a big deal."

"You might not think so now—"

"I should go to the party." I turned from him to re-center my awareness on something other than rejection. I focused on my new character, placed my mission forefront in my mind, and pivoted back to face Nash. "Are you going in through the servants' entrance?"

Nash gave me an incomprehensible look. "I'll meet up with you later, Miss Albright."

"Okay?" Had I offended Nash by not wanting to live with him? He slept in the old office. I wasn't sure if there was even room for one of my suitcases. Certainly not enough room for all my shoe boxes. And besides the shoe logistics (and the bathroom in the outside hall which was a total no-go), there was the lack of a bed. Unless you counted a lumpy couch and Lamar's recliner. "Where should we meet?"

"We'll figure it out." Nash waved the valet over. "She's ready to go in. I'm pulling around back. To the servants' entrance."

"Did you mean the kitchen?" said the valet.

"Is that what they're calling it now?" Nash took the hoodie from my arm and walked around the truck to climb in. "Good luck, Miss Albright."

"You, too, Mr. Nash."

Shizzles, I'd just upstaired my boyfriend. No wonder he didn't want to live with me.

TWENTY-TWO
#LOVEGEOMETRY

I FOLLOWED the valet up the stone walk. As he swung the front door open, I scanned the barely recognizable wooden plug that replaced the bullet hole. Then glanced at the floor with its new (old) parquet, before fixing my gaze on the coral reef tank. An Asian couple stood behind it, speaking in low voices while watching the fish zip in and out of the plants. Through the wavy glass, I recognized the producer, Zhao, whom I'd seen at Vicki's burger dinner. His smile appeared mischievous and I wondered if he flirted with the woman in the little black dress and blue glasses. I studied the woman and realized she was Lili's assistant, Shiyu.

Not surprised because she's an assistant. Shiyu didn't like parties. Or at least, that's what I thought. Or surmised?

Was I being classist? Or racist? Or just reeling from Daddy's dinner ambush and Nash's you're-too-young-for-me and I-don't-want-to-live-with-you speech.

I gave myself a mental shake, then my hair a real shake. Striding across the parquet, I forced myself to enjoy the sound of my heels, the scent of plumeria, and the icy air seeping through my silk, semi-sheer georgette blouse.

I may be freezing, but I looked good. Dammit.

Rounding the side of the tank (with an eye out for Charles), I stopped before Zhao and Shiyu. Shiyu jerked away from their huddle.

"Nice to see you again," I said. "How's the party?"

"Good evening." Zhao's articulation wasn't like the other three. His English was clipped and quick with a stronger Chinese accent.

"Hello, Miss Albright," she said in her crisp British accent. "The party is lovely."

"Yes." Zhao rocked back on his heels and shoved his hands in the pockets of his suit jacket. "Food is good. Music is okay. The movie is on track, so everything's great."

Pleasantries done, I focused on my mission. "And how does this party compare to the last one?"

"The last one had the small trouble," said Zhao. "Remember, Miss Kang? Lili's American friend...Oh, you didn't attend the last party."

"No." Shiyu folded her arms. "I was in Atlanta. I don't know what happened at the last party."

"What was the trouble at the last party, Mr. Zhao?" I said, knowing the answer after my conversation with Stanley.

"Mr. Zhao doesn't like Lili's boyfriend." Shiyu glared up at Zhao.

Zhao smirked. "The producer does not like the star to be distracted. You sound jealous, Miss Kang."

"Jealous?" Shiyu's mouth opened and snapped shut.

"Do you mean Jeff Johnson?" I had a feeling a love triangle, possibly quadrangle, had happened between them. I didn't want to interfere — or change the destiny of geometry — but I couldn't help myself. I didn't trust Jeff Johnson. "It's true you don't like him?"

"No." Zhao snorted. "I don't see him tonight, which is good."

"According to Lili, he's missing, too," I said. "Do you think he ghosted Lili?"

"A ghost?" Shiyu's eyes widened. "What do you mean?"

"Not literally," I said quickly. "Like he dumped her and didn't tell her."

"Ghosted." Zhao doubled over with laughter. Shiyu stomped away. Wiping his eyes, Zhao watched her cross the parquet. "I like this *ghosted*."

"It's a newish expression. Do you know what happened to him?"

Zhao's eyes remained on Shiyu's fleeting figure. Laughter and chattering voices drifted from the living room. He seemed to take his time, pondering my question. "It's curious, yes."

"Lili wants me to find him."

Zhao's face darkened, but he regained his amused expression before turning to face me. "I shouldn't be surprised Lili asks this of you. You are also looking for Xi, her coach, right? He broke a contract."

"I hope not purposefully," I said. "But I also hope nothing happened to him."

"Do you have any news about Xi?"

"Not really. But we're working on a new lead." I paused. "Do you have any issues with Master Xi? I can't seem to understand a motive for him disappearing."

"Me either." Zhao shoved his hands back in his pocket. "If you find that bitch, tell him he broke his contract. He owes the movie money."

"What if something happened to him?"

"Xi? Why would anything happen to him?" Zhao snorted. "What about Jeff Johnson?"

"I saw him on the set two days ago."

Zhao's eyebrows rose. "Where?"

"Lili's trailer. Taking a nap."

"A nap?" Zhao snickered. "What an asshole."

I had a feeling something was lost in translation. "Lili said Jeff went in search of Master Xi, but she can't get ahold of him."

"Lili is better off without him."

"Why?" I hesitated, but pushed on with my train of thought,

hoping Zhao would tell me more about Jeff. "I know she met him online. That's odd for a film star. At least, here."

"She hid her true self on the dating site." Zhao shook his head. "Lili can be crazy like that. She's too famous in Asia. She can't trust the men she meets. Because of her beauty, she went to live at a performing arts school at a very young age. For this reason, she does not have a strong attachment to her family. They were poor, so they don't have the right connections for a good match anyway."

"Why did she want to meet an American?" I said. "I'm assuming Jeff Johnson's American, anyway."

Zhao rolled his eyes. "Who knows? She wants to star in American movies. Maybe she thought Johnson would help her. He's nobody. He's done nothing. He's using *her*. Who is making her the big star? Me. With the Lees' money. She should stay in China." His gaze drifted to the aquarium. "But then again, I like America. It's easier here."

"You admire Lili."

"Lili's very talented."

"It's not the first time a producer fell in love with his ingenue."

He cut his eyes back to the fish tank. He'd lost his swagger. Evidently, I was correct in my geometrical theories.

"What happened with Jeff Johnson at the last party?"

"Too much alcohol." He swiveled his gaze back to me. "I need to speak to Vorling, the director. Excuse me." I nodded and stepped back to let him pass.

Instead of following Zhou, I walked around the aquarium and fled up the stairs. 007 time. Inside my Bendetta Bruzziches' clutch was the ring of desk keys. I wanted to make up for my previous mistake, letting Vicki distract me from my mission. The party seemed the perfect opportunity to check the locked desk drawer. She'd be preoccupied with the party. As would everyone else.

Upstairs, the hall lighting had been dimmed to set off the

LED lighting showcasing the coral reef tank. Perfect for a little clandestine snooping. At the top of the stairs, I glanced down at the backstairs, then checked the short flight leading up to the guest wing. Not seeing anyone, I stole across the gallery to the office.

The door swung open silently. I left the lights off and hurried across the room to the desk. I felt beneath the top middle drawer. Still sticky, but no Velcro. Moved around to the side drawers. The bottom still thumped when jiggled. I opened my clutch, pulled out the small keys, and began trying them in the lock. The sixth key in, the blade slipped inside. I wiggled the key and caught the tumblers. Yanked the drawer open.

Bingo.

But no pistol. A small laptop and smartphone were inside. Chinese models, guessing by the names.

Vicki had Xiáng Xi's things. She'd brushed off our questioning with her whole "I don't do meetings" nonsense. And she thought a simple lock on a drawer would keep her secret hidden?

"Oh, Vicki, what the fleep?"

I slipped the phone into my trouser pocket, placed the laptop on the floor, and opened the clamshell. Tapped on the power. The screen brightened. I pulled off my stilettos and crouched on the floor behind the desk.

Password protected, of course. I chewed my thumb and thought about obvious passwords. Although what was obvious to an American, might not be for a Chinese citizen. I slipped my phone from my clutch, ready to call Nash with the news.

In the hallway, someone giggled, then a man spoke. I shut the laptop and waited. Dim lighting spilled into the office. I ducked behind the desk, shoved my phone into my purse, and gathered my shoes. Rustling and more giggling followed. I peeked over the desk. Spotted two figures plastered together. Groping one another against the wall.

Great. This was what happened when you declared your office open to the public for collaborations.

Several options presented themselves for escaping before the couple got too hot and heavy. None where I could walk out with a computer. Other than popping up from behind the desk with a, "Hey dudes, excuse me for hiding in here when the rest of the Peanut Mansion is partying. Except for you two. Who appear to be doing the vertical version of the horizontal mambo. Just let me stroll out of here with a stolen computer, 'aight?"

Slipping the laptop into the desk, I gently closed the drawer and locked it. Peeked over the desk again.

Wonderful. They'd moved their collaboration to the conference table.

No way would I wait for their big finish. I needed to get to the party before I lost my dinner. I grabbed my clutch and shoes and began to crawl toward the door. Slipping through the door, I rose. I collapsed against the outside wall, trying to quell my churning stomach.

I wasn't sure what made me more queasy. The couple or Vicki's secret.

Down the hall, a door creaked. I smoothed my clothes, adjusted my parts, and slipped Xi's phone into my clutch.

At least I carried half the evidence of my mother's nefarious activities.

I wasn't sure how I felt about that either.

TWENTY-THREE
#ASHOTATCHIC

GUESTS STOOD in clusters in the oak-paneled room. On the opposite side, the French doors to the patio stood open. Outside, gaslights flickered, and heat lamps bathed the partiers in a cheery orange glow. The jazz quartet played somewhere on the patio. Hopefully under heat lamps.

People from a variety of nations and cultures gathered here. Assumably most spoke industry business (gossip) over their martinis, whiskey, and wine. For a moment, I felt proud to be part of this chic global event. I tossed my hair back, curled my lips into my best party smile, and checked my vest for peekage.

Wait, I wasn't a real guest. I had a mission. I had a stolen phone in my clutch. A stolen laptop resided in Vicki's desk. And somewhere upstairs, my partner snuck around, seeking spy devices.

I made my way into the throng of guests, hunting for insiders who would know Xiáng Xi and Jeff Johnson. Zhao had cornered Vorling, the director, and seemed to be introducing him to two more Asian men in fashionable suits. Passing them, I found Stanley Wu and Chey Tyrone, Lili's other co-star in *Unlucky 18*.

"Hey boys," I said. "When do you start filming?"

Chey gave me his famous smile that changed his somewhat

delicate features from finely urbane to roguish sensualism. "Hey Maizie, haven't seen you in a while. How you've been? The film crew is taking a trip out to examine the location shoots next week. I was just telling Stanley I'd like to go with them, to get some visuals in my head."

"Maizie, how do you know Chey?" Stanley grinned. "Film or TV? Are there stories? Do tell."

"A few years ago, we were staying at the same place in Malibu and got to know each other." I glanced at Chey and bit my lip.

Chey shrugged. "The media outed me already. We met at rehab."

"Oh my," said Stanley. "Sorry, I asked."

"No worries," said Chey. "Gambling was my vice of choice, but I was also working through some other related issues."

"Our treatment facility was comprehensive," I explained. "I'm so happy you're doing well, Chey."

"Thanks, Maizie. How about you?"

"I'm sure you heard about my fall from grace, but I'm working through it with a new career." My eyes drifted to the ceiling where the other half of my career snuck around. "You know me. I'm my own worst enemy."

"I wouldn't say that." Chey's eyes moved past me. "Sometimes we're set up to fail. You've got to recognize the traps."

Following Chey's gaze, I glanced around. Vicki had spotted me.

"I hope the weather holds for your location trip," I said, eager to get back to my mission. "Chey, were you also using Xiáng Xi for rehearsing combat scenes?"

"No, my character's weapon of choice is a Winchester." Chey's grin sobered. "I heard Mr. Xi vanished."

"Lili asked me to look for him. It's strange. No clues. Unless you've heard something?"

Behind his stylish glasses, Stanley's eyes closed, then opened. "I didn't mention this earlier, but I recall Shifu Xi once telling me about a distant cousin living in the US. She took him to Disney World, I believe." Stanley shuddered. "Disney. Give me Happy Valley any day."

"Those are fighting words in the US, my friend. Don't diss the mouse." Chey elbowed Stanley and laughed.

"Does Xiáng Xi's cousin live in Florida, Stanley?" I said.

"I have no idea. Maybe Lili knows?"

"I wonder why she didn't tell me Xiáng had a cousin living here. That would have been the first place we'd check." I turned to look for Lili and realized Van Vorling and Zhao had moved in behind us.

"Van," said Chey. "Do you know Maizie?"

"We met briefly the other night. A pleasure." Vorling grasped my hand. "Sorry, darling, I must go."

We watched him stride away with a hurried wave to Vicki before rushing out the door.

"What was that about?" said Stanley.

"Who knows?" Zhao lifted his shoulders. "Stanley, I want to talk to you. I did some rewrites to the script."

I drifted away, presumably to let Zhao and Stanley speak, when I wanted to find Lili. How did she fail to mention the cousin? Why would Stanley know and not Lili? I moved to the bar for a glass of sparkling water. Chey followed me.

"I know he's got the big connections..." Chey muttered, rolling his eyes. "Zhao's supposed to be an associate producer, but he can't leave anything alone."

"Does he know scriptwriting?"

"Not that I can tell. He knows the co-producers, the Lees. Zhao's supposed to be watching the production for them, but now he's getting over-involved in everything. Pretty soon he'll start cooking for craft services."

"Mr. Zhao's just excited. It's his first movie, isn't it?"

"Lili needs to reign him in. This is her baby."

"Speaking of producers, Vicki isn't involved in this movie, is she?"

"She's not listed," said Chey. "I think she's working it to get in with the Lees. I bet she's hoping they'll finance future stuff and she won't need an associate, like Zhao."

"Did she get paid for bringing in Master Kevin?"

"Not that I know of. But you know Vicki. She's likely banking favors." Chey grimaced. "The Lees are arriving from China tomorrow. I hate performing for the money people. I don't even know how they're getting around the new film financing laws in China. You know they're staying here?"

"The Lees are staying at Vicki's?" It was my turn to roll my eyes. "Could she be more obvious?"

"Hello, Maizie. I'm glad you could join us." Vicki stepped into our huddle, forcing Chey to slide down the bar. "Chey, lovely to see you again. Glad you could make it. I heard you've sunk your teeth into this character."

"Thanks," said Chey. "I don't know if I'd call it that, but I've got some good scenes. Nice to play a leading man for once."

Vicki's smile flickered. "More of a supporting role, isn't it? I thought Lili was the lead. But I'm sure this job will serve for even greater parts."

"Of course. Excuse me. I spotted someone I need to speak to." He nodded at me. "Maizie, so good to see you again."

"I never liked him," said Vicki, watching Chey stride toward the patio. "He walked away from a feature they were considering you for. What was it? That superhero film."

Vicki never forgot a title. Or a name. She was prompting me to remember a slight. "Wasn't that when Chey was ill?"

"Is that what they call it in rehab?"

"That's what we called it when I was in rehab. With Chey." I crossed my arms, felt my neckline gape, and uncrossed them. "Chey's a nice guy and talented. He's going to be great in this picture, and if you had any consideration for Lili, you wouldn't say things like that to him. You're messing with his head and Lili needs his A-game."

"He'll get over it." Vicki waved a hand, then snapped a finger at the bartender. "We don't want him stealing Lili's thunder. Really, Maizie. Do you want Chey front and center, when Lili can do much more for diversity in the industry?"

"Stop making this political. You're just being petty." I counted to ten. Found my center and lasered in on the mission. "What's in your office desk drawer?"

"We already discussed this. I don't know. Didn't Lydia find the key for you?" Vicki took a glass of seltzer from the bartender and glanced at me. "Have you found Lili's boyfriend yet?"

"She told you I'm looking for him?"

"She's better off letting that one go. Don't look too hard." Vicki sipped her seltzer. "Do you know those two men who were talking to Zhao?"

"No. It looked like Zhao was introducing them to Vorling. I figured them for investors or somebody else related to the picture."

"You should mingle." Vicki sipped her drink, her eyes on the two Asian men standing near the bookcase. "We'll speak later."

"Try not to be so obvious," I hissed. "Everyone sees through it."

"I never hide my intentions, Maizie. That's why people do business with me. They know exactly what they're getting." Vicki raised a brow. "I don't play a role. I just play to win. In this industry, one might call it refreshing."

"I heard the Lees are staying here, too. I hope you have an extra room because I'm planning on doing the same."

"Your room has been ready since the day I moved in." Vicki placed a hand on my cheek. "Do try to keep up, sweetie."

TWENTY-FOUR
#MISSIONTOTALLYIMPOSSIBLE

I STALKED toward the French doors. Stepping onto the patio, the heat from my anger vaporized as an icy breeze swept through my thin blouse. I moved from heater to heater, seeking Lili and trying not to hug my arms across my chest. Vicki's ruthless scheming had become myopic. Not that I had enjoyed being the focus of her goals, but she seemed to be wandering into dangerous territory. Bullets, stolen evidence, and missing people literally littered her home, and she only cared about furthering her empire.

Had I unintentionally caused this dangerous path because she had lost her sole focus —cultivating my career?

Worse, did I even care?

I spotted Lili, by the pool again, the breeze whipping her long hair behind her. She sat on a lounge, a plush cashmere throw tossed around her shoulders. Stanley had squeezed in next to her, elegantly draped along the back while avoiding her flying hair.

"Stella?" I said, admiring her jade, crepe satin jumpsuit.

"Carolina Ritzler," she replied, flipping the cashmere back to expose her single bared shoulder. "Phillip Lim and Jay Godfrey are also doing satin jumpsuits, but this is a fall design."

"Satin jumpsuits," said Stanley. "Has disco returned, too?"

"Stanley's upset over his lines." Lili leaned against him. "He'll get over it. Did you meet everyone, Maizie?"

"I'm doing the rounds," I said. "Stanley tells me Master Xi had a cousin in the US."

"Oh, I forgot about that." She sat up. "I don't know the cousin's name. But I doubt Shifu Xi went there."

"Why? If he left, that would be the most likely place."

"Shifu Xi and I were close. I think he would have mentioned visiting his cousin."

"In any case, if you know the cousin's name and where they live, that'd be helpful."

"No idea, darling." She smiled up at me. "And what about Jeff? Any news there?"

Shivering, I shook my head. "Mr. Zhao said something happened between Mr. Vorling and Jeff at the last party."

"Zhao?" Lili's smile faltered. "I'm not sure…"

"This is what happens when you play one against the other, dear," said Stanley. "I warned you."

She shook her head. "Don't be ridiculous, Stanley. That's not my game. I've been honest with Zhao."

Shivering, I hugged my arms, no longer caring about the gape in my blouse. Maybe Zhao had chased off Jeff Johnson. Although, Jeff seemed pretty comfortable in her trailer. There was something I was missing.

"Did Jeff have an issue with your director?"

"I don't think so." Lili folded her arms. "I'm a little chilly. Perhaps we should go inside, Stanley."

"Are you not telling me something, Lili?" I said.

"I'm worried about both of them. Why would I hide something? Please find them." She flipped her hair into the breeze, letting it flutter down her back as she traipsed toward the house.

Stanley watched Lili cross the patio.

"I think Lili's lucky to have you in this picture," I said.

"I'm glad for *Unlucky 18* despite the eccentricities of our production team."

"I thought you weren't happy with the rewrites."

"Oh, my dear, if I don't draw lines, I risk getting pushed from the sandbox." He laughed. "I'm happy with my lot, but I have to stand up for myself from time-to-time."

"That's a novel approach to life." I smiled at Stanley and glanced up at the house. "I just don't understand why Lili won't give me more information about Master Xi and Jeff Johnson if she wants me to find them."

"Lili might be in trouble herself. I think she hired you to help her, not the missing men."

"But—"

Stanley shook his head. "Just a hunch. I can't answer your questions any more than that."

The more answers I received, the more questions I had. I stared up at the house, wondering how Nash did with his bug hunt. And realized someone was missing from the party.

"Have you seen Master Kevin?" I glanced around the party. "I was hoping he'd be here tonight."

Stanley gave me a smug smile. "I think I caught him canoodling with your mother."

"What?"

"Perhaps not canoodling, but Kevin and Vicki certainly weren't happy when I walked in. Although I might have misread the situation. Perhaps they're not happy with each other. Angry in a familiar way, though. While Vicki ordered me a martini, Kevin tore off to the guest wing."

"Excuse me Stanley. I need to speak to my old friend."

I SCURRIED ALONG THE PATIO, bypassing the open French doors for another set at the far end of the mansion. Inside, I stole to the back stairway. At the top, I veered right, up the short flight to the guest wing and darted down the hall toward Kevin's room. Before I could knock, a hand gripped my shoulder and spun me around.

Holding my arms up at right angles, I stepped back, ready to block an attack. And realized it was Nash. I lowered my arms.

"What in the hell was that?" said Nash.

"I thought you were Kevin. He used to surprise me so I'd stay sharp. Kind of like Cato in the *Pink Panther*."

"Weren't you nine?"

"Good preparation for life." I lifted a shoulder. "Did you find any hidden cameras?"

Nash flipped open a notebook and showed the running tally of transmitters and cameras throughout the house. "I took them down," he murmured.

I curled my lip. "That's low even for Vicki. Violations of all kinds of privacy."

"Don't think it was Vicki. They were in her wing and her office, too," he whispered.

"Look what I found." I opened my clutch and pointed to Xi's phone. "The locked drawer had Xi's laptop and phone. I got trapped and left the laptop."

"Trapped?"

"Seems everyone does know the office is unlocked and accessible. Perfect for a rendezvous."

"Gotcha." He lifted the phone and inspected it. "This could be helpful. We'll grab the laptop as we leave. We should go now."

"I need to talk to Master Kevin," I said. "This is his room."

"Later." Nash's eyes gleamed, but he kept his voice low. "Lamar got a hit. Xiáng Xi didn't buy a car. He bought a used camper."

"Oh, thank God. Vicki didn't kill him."

"That was never a reasonable explanation—"

"But a camper?" I placed a hand on Nash's arm and glanced down the hall toward the Green Room. "The taffy. And Tommy Bahama. Disney."

Nash squinted at me. "What are you doing?"

"Xiáng Xi's gone to Florida." I danced. "We figured it out. I'll find Lili to tell her."

"Hang on, Nancy Drew." A smile flickered on his rugged features. "Even if he did go to Florida, that's a whole state to explore. We've still got to track Mr. Xi down. And we don't know why he bought a camper. He's supposed to be working. This could become a State Department issue if he's running."

"Defecting?" My voice rose from a whisper and I clamped a hand over my mouth.

"Could be. But someone is helping him."

He pulled out his phone and began texting.

"Are you telling Lamar about my Florida hunch?" I tried to read upside down. "You are. I'm taking the Nancy Drew remark as a compliment."

"Do that." He looked up. "Are we okay?"

"I'm okay." I clasped my hands against my semi-sheer silk georgette to prevent my heart from (almost) slamming through my chest and falling with a slurpy thwack onto the carpet runner. "Are you okay?"

Nodding, he pulled me toward him. "Boomer's more het up about us working for Vicki than he is anything else."

"I know." I snuggled against him, staring up into the clear, blue eyes. "And he's forced to deal with an adult daughter who's lived a whole different life than he's used to. If you haven't noticed both of my parents are high achievers. Although one tends more toward authoritarianism and the other toward opportunism. Neither can deal with marching to someone else's beat. I can forgive and be flexible, but I don't have to conform."

"You're something else, kid." He ran his hands up my arms, warming the gooseflesh beneath my blouse.

"I paid attention in therapy. And I'm not a kid."

"Don't I know it." He pressed his lips against my forehead. "We'll figure it out."

Before I could ask what the "it" was — our relationship, how to get Vicki off our backs, how to win Daddy's approval, the mystery of Xiáng Xi, why Vicki had bullets littering her door, or perhaps all of the above — the door behind us cracked, then opened.

"Maizie?" said Kevin.

"We were not getting busy in the hall." I stepped away from Nash. "And even if we were, I'm an adult."

"It's not my business. But I did notice you," Kevin nodded at Nash, "taking down the camera in the hall. Did you find them all?"

Nash studied Kevin a moment, then answered in his low tone. "I hope so. I couldn't check the private rooms. When did you notice the camera?"

"Soon after I arrived." Kevin stepped back from the door. "Come inside."

We followed him into a room similar to Master Xi's. "Master Kevin, this is Wyatt Nash, my..." I paused, wondering if my familiarity with Kevin meant I could divulge our relationship status. Of which, I still was a little unclear.

"Business partner," finished Nash, shaking Kevin's hand. "We do private investigations and security."

"Maizie told me." Kevin folded his arms. "But you work for Vicki."

"At present," said Nash. "Why didn't you tell Maizie about the camera?"

"I don't like to speak about something until I'm sure. Besides, I've been in many celebrity homes. It's not unusual to have additional security. As long as my privacy isn't violated, it's their house to do as they please." Kevin shrugged. "But it seems you have reason to believe Vicki didn't have these installed."

Nash glanced at me, flickering a warning in his eyes.

"We haven't spoken to Vicki about it yet," I hedged. "We're doing some other work for her."

"Maizie, I warned you to step away from this work." Kevin dropped his arms. "It's not too late. Mr. Nash should also heed my advice."

"Why do you want us to stop investigating?" said Nash. "We need information. And it sounds like you know more than you're letting on."

"I don't know all the facts."

"That's not helpful."

"In the past, Vicki made business decisions that could have jeopardized her career. But Maizie's talent — and frankly, Maizie's earnest and conscientious attitude — saved their ruin."

"Tell me something I haven't already figured out," said Nash.

I inched closer to Nash and placed a hand on his arm. Kevin was careful. Of course Kevin would voice an opinion, but he'd never tell me something untrue. He didn't like gossip. He worked with too many high profiles to speak out of turn. Nash didn't always grasp the politicking that accompanied celebrities. Nor did Nash sympathize with it. But I understood both sides. I could bridge the middle.

"Look," said Kevin. "I think Vicki's getting in over her head with the Lees. And Lili may be, too, but for entirely different reasons."

"Do you think Lili is willing to compromise creative control on the picture over money?" I said. "I know Mr. Zhao's been messing with the script. The director Vorling didn't seem happy, either."

"Possibly," said Kevin. "But you need to tell Vicki to back away from this slowly. She can't uninvite people like the Lees. But after they leave and the picture is finished, she needs to have nothing more to do with them."

"They're powerful," I said. "How far above Vicki's level?"

"Way above. All this pretension," Kevin waved his hand around the room, "the mansion and accoutrements? It's nothing to people like them."

"*Crazy Rich Asians*?"

"You watch too many movies." Kevin snorted. "An entertaining book, but Americans wouldn't get the real thing. The

Lees gave her that dragonfish as a thank you gift. An illegal, ten-thousand-dollar fish"

"Charles?" I hissed. "Is that why she's so attached to him?"

"Ten-thousand dollars?" said Nash. "For a fish?"

"Listen, I don't know the Lees," said Kevin. "I have no idea who they are. I'm asking around, and when I find out, I'll tell you. But I have some suspicions and Vicki will not listen to me."

"Vicki doesn't trust you," said Nash.

Kevin bowed his head and shrugged.

"I bet you know too many things," said Nash. "I'm on a steep learning curve and it's not pretty."

Leaving Kevin, we crossed the intersection of the staircases, hurried across the balcony, and pushed open the door of the office.

"Hello?" I called, entering the room. "The couple is gone, thank goodness."

Nash strode to the desk. Leaning over, he grasped the drawer handle.

I opened my clutch and took out the keys. "It's the sixth key. Just a minute."

"Don't bother," said Nash.

"What do you mean?"

He joggled the drawer handle. "No thumping. The damn thing is empty. Someone else got to the computer first."

TWENTY-FIVE
#WHENAMANLOVESAWOMAN

IN NASH'S TRUCK, I put on my hoodie and felt glad to see the topiary flash by in the side view mirror. Our 007 mission had ended badly. And it was my fault.

"At least you got the phone," said Nash. "I don't have the right equipment to decrypt it. Or knowledge. I think we should take it to the police."

"But Vicki…"

"Is in a lot of trouble."

"We need to tell her about the spy devices you found," I said.

"Foremost is finding Xiáng Xi. That's what we were hired to do." He glanced at me. "We'll go with your gut first. Start calling campgrounds and RV parks in Florida. Then surrounding states. But your gut feels right to me, too. Florida's far enough, but not too far away."

"Will they be open this time of night?"

"It's going to take some time to gather the information, so we can call first thing in the morning." His face hardened. "I didn't get the chance to tell you. Lamar told me the RV seller said Xi had a driver's license, obviously faked, and was going by the name, Tang Lung. Someone helped him get the fake ID. Here or in China. Of course, you can order a fake ID on the internet pretty easily."

"Tang Lung." I stared out the window, thinking. "*The Way of the Dragon*. One of Bruce Lee's last movies."

"How do you remember that stuff?"

"Movie trivia is my superpower."

"Even if we find Xiáng Xi, which I hope we do as quickly as possible, there's this other problem. Someone's bugged Vicki's house. And someone at the party took the computer. This is some serious espionage. We may be in over our heads. I say, we locate Xi, if we can, then turn this over to the police with the phone."

"You think he defected."

"That makes the most sense. But I don't know why someone would go to the trouble of spying on a kung fu coach."

He laid a hand on my thigh, and I slipped my hand in his.

He squeezed my hand. "Kevin hinted about Vicki's relationship to the Lees. Like they're…I don't know, connected?"

"Connected, connected? Like the mob?" I scoffed. "I thought he meant Vicki's reaching too high. Jumping from TV to a Big Five-quality film is quite a leap. She's brown-nosing the mega-rich."

"Are we sure we can rely on Kevin? You said he's acting differently. You haven't seen him in a long time."

"I'd trust him with my life. He's always treated me like a daughter."

"What about Vicki's life?"

I slipped my hand from his and played with the string on my hoodie. "He knows stuff about her. But I don't think he'd do anything that would hurt me."

"All right. We still haven't found the gun, maybe she's telling the truth about her ignorance of the bullet." Nash squeezed my thigh, then patted it.

I bit my lip. "Do you think Xiáng Xi saw something he

shouldn't have and taken off? Like someone shot in Vicki's house? Maybe he's not defecting, just hiding."

"Could be. But we're going off on tangents again. We need to approach this like two entirely different cases. First Xiáng Xi. The computer and the phone in her desk are directly related. The bullet in the door, I'm not so sure. And the spy gadgets?"

"I still need to find Jeff Johnson, but I think Mr. Zhao might have scared him away."

"Mr. Zhao would scare anyone away."

"Mr. Zhao's in love with Lili, and he might ruin *Unlucky 18* as a result."

"Wouldn't be the first time a man ruins his career over a woman."

That remark felt a little too close to home for me to say anything, so I kept my mouth shut and hoped he didn't feel the same about us.

AFTER POURING over maps of RV parks and campgrounds in Florida, we slept at the office — Nash on Lamar's La-Z-Boy, I took the couch — until the parks opened. While Nash ran downstairs to speak to Lamar, I freshened up, then glanced at the list we had compiled the night before.

There were a hella lot of RV parks in Florida. Nash thought we should focus on those near popular tourist destinations, like Orlando, Daytona, and Pensacola.

I frowned, thinking of Master Xi's Tommy Bahama catalogs and saltwater taffy. And started a new Google search.

In the front room, the doorknob jiggled, and the glass pane rattled. I looked up from the spreadsheet listing the parks. Nash stood in the doorway of the inner office, holding two large coffees in each big fist and a bag of donuts clenched under his arm. Looking more delicious than the coffee and donuts was the grin that made his pale blue eyes gleam and chiseled features soften. A hint of a dimple peeked above the scar.

When my heart restarted, I smiled back. "Good morning."

"I couldn't ask for a better one, seeing you in my t-shirt and sweats, frowning over the state of Florida." He set the coffee and donuts on the desk. "I might have to rethink the living together thing."

My heart popped out of my chest and landed somewhere on the state of Florida. But my head shouted, *Slow your roll*.

After a night at the office, I agreed with my head.

His shower looked like it had been rigged by a twelve-year-old Boy Scout on his first camping trip. The single jet had taken off a layer of my skin more vigorously than any scrub. And the couch? The princess from *Once Upon a Mattress* had nothing on me.

"Actually, what we need to rethink is our plan of attacking Florida's RV parks," I said, forcing a laugh. Which likely fooled neither of us. (Didn't fool me, anyway.) "Instead of Pensacola or Daytona, why not Clearwater?"

"Clearwater? I don't know anyone who goes to Clearwater."

"Exactly. But Chinese tourists go to Clearwater. Clearwater is number one on the list of best beaches in the US. Therefore, that's where the bulk of tourists go, particularly foreign tourists."

"But Xiáng Xi's not a tourist."

"He's also not American and certainly not from Black Pine. We have no idea where his cousin lives, but if Master Xi's running, that's the first place anyone would look. He can't go to his cousin's. But Florida's the preferred destination for Chinese tourists. Clearwater is logical."

"Makes sense." Nash set the coffee and donuts down, rounded the desk, and pulled me from the chair. "We have a minute before we start calling the Clearwater RV parks."

I wiggled closer. His large hands made my hips feel small. And even though his style of living was undesirable, the man who lived it certainly wasn't.

Maybe I could get used to slimy showers and lumpy couches.

No, I couldn't.

Did that make me shallow or just realistic? To thine own self be true, yadda? If I was willing to die for this man, shouldn't I be willing to adjust to a lower standard of hygiene?

"Darling, you got something on your mind?" Nash murmured against my neck. "I can tell it's not on me."

I snapped out of my interior monologue and focused on the man whose face was mashed against my own. I gave him a quick kiss on his softened lips. Pulling back, I changed topics in my head from icky bathrooms to the case. For both our sakes.

"I'm thinking of Xiáng Xi. I'd like to tell Lili I found him. She's super worried about him. And maybe that will help with finding Jeff Johnson, too."

His eyes studied mine for a moment. "You're right. I'm not focused on work and we're on the clock. What am I thinking?"

"Not that we shouldn't take breaks from the clock," I said quickly. "Breaks are good. I didn't even punch in. Technically, we haven't started working yet."

"I promised Vicki that I'd keep my—we'd keep things professional while working. And I should abide by my word." He pulled back and glanced around the room. "Besides, I haven't checked this office for bugs. You never know."

I hopped back. "You don't think?"

"Actually, I don't think. If they'd bug any office, it'd be the new one on Palmetto. This isn't an official office." His eyes narrowed. "At least the person spying on Lili and Vicki wouldn't think so."

"You think they're spying on Lili and Vicki?"

"Lili's trailer and Vicki's house, so far. Maybe just Lili, but they did plant listening wires and cameras in Vicki's wing, too."

"But why Lili?"

"I'm hoping Xiáng Xi's got an answer for that. Let's get to work." Nash tapped on the map of Florida. "Lamar's got a buddy who's retired from Black Pine PD. I think he lives in St. Pete's or thereabouts. He might help us locate Xiáng Xi."

"I'll call the RV parks, and you talk to Lamar." I gave him a push and pulled out the desk chair.

"Miss Albright?" When I looked up from the computer screen, Nash smiled down at me. Except it was the pitying smile that made my stomach clench. "I think you need to consider whether we tell Vicki her place is bugged."

"Why wouldn't I?"

He grimaced. "I hate to say this…"

"In case she already knows?" My stomach unclenched and dove toward my feet.

Nash jerked his head in a quick nod. "More importantly, we need to proceed from now on like somebody's always listening."

TWENTY-SIX
#FLORIDADREAMING

FINDING XIÁNG XI was a lot easier than expected. Once we knew where to look, anyway.

After twenty phone calls, we located Tang Lung at the Happy Campers RV Park in Clearwater. Lamar's cop buddy agreed to do a stakeout until we could arrive. Nash booked two flights and a rental car in Tampa. As our search became a road trip and the office was found clear of bugs, I danced down the stairs of the Dixie Kreme building, bad showers and lumpy couches forgotten.

"I understand telling Lili, as the client, we're going to Florida," said Nash. "But why did you tell Vicki?"

"Vicki thinks she's our client, too. Or we're working for her, anyway. If we're inaccessible, she needs to know." Truthfully, I was afraid she'd fire Nash if we didn't tell her where we'd gone. Or that we had a hard lead. "I only left Vicki a message. Lili was excited to hear our news, though."

"Something about this feels hinky." He ran a hand over his head. "Actually, everything feels hinky. But I can't complain about a quick trip to Florida. I'll take you to Boomer's so you can change. I don't want to be late for our flight."

. . .

AT THE DEERNOSE CABIN, my Louis Vuittons had been placed in the foyer. Next to the suitcases, stood six plastic tubs filled with shoe boxes. Nine boxes for hanging clothes. And three big tubs of toiletries and other beauty products.

Nash blanched. "This is all yours?"

"This is just the stuff from your room," said Remi. "Daddy said, he's gonna clear out the storage unit tomorrow."

"He didn't put my Birkins in a plastic tub, did he? OMG, the leather—" Then bit my tongue. Nash looked queasy. "Maybe you should wait in the truck. I'll handle this."

"I can't believe he's kicking you out," said Nash.

"You said you didn't want to live with us no more. Soon as y'all left, Daddy called some packers. And at breakfast, when Daddy saw you didn't come home last night, he turned a funny shade of purple and told Momma, 'she always had to learn the hard way.'" Remi crossed her spindly arms across her tiny chest. "You're in for it this time. He usually says that about me."

I sighed. "Looks like I do have to move in with Vicki. I don't even know if my probation officer will approve a move."

Remi flung herself at me and wrapped her arms around my hips. "I want you to live with me. You can't live with a witch. Remember *The Wizard of Oz*?"

"Witch?" I peeled her off my torso and realized Daddy had likely used another term to describe Vicki. "You need to stop listening in on private conversations between Daddy and your momma. Daddy's just teaching me a lesson, Remi. It's not forever. It won't be like it was before. California is far away, and I'll just be on the other side of town."

"I solved that problem." Remi pointed to a small plastic suitcase decorated with Minion characters. A sand pail had been tied to the handle. "I'm coming with y'all. And I'm bringing my bucket to protect you from the witch."

"No, honey. You can't. You have to go to school and it'd make Carol Lynn sad if you didn't live at home. Besides, Nash and I are on our way to Florida."

"But living in sin sounds funner than school," Remi's voice rose on a wail. "You get to do all the good stuff."

I unclenched my jaw from the snap it'd just experienced and hugged her. "We're going to Florida on a case. We won't even be there long. Like an afternoon. But I'll get you something while I'm there."

"A gator?" She sucked in her breath and her words ran out in one long wheedling stream of air, "Please bring me a gator. A real one, not one of those plastic ones. I'll take real good care of him. He can live in the lake. I'll feed him whatever the Jacks catch. And I'll name him Teeth."

"I doubt Black Pine's Wildlife and Game would approve of an alligator living in the lake. How about a hermit crab?"

"I don't think crabs got teeth."

"You could paint teeth on his shell house."

"That's about the dumbest thing I ever heard." Her tiny lips squeezed together in a pout then slid into a sly smile. "Alright. I'll take a hermit crab."

"Don't worry about anything, Remi. I won't be gone long." I squeezed her goodbye. Choosing the smallest suitcase, I carried it to the door. "Bye, honey."

She looked up from her musing. "Do ya think a hermit crab can be trained to fight a raccoon?"

"You know, I forgot, I'm not allowed to bring live animals on airplanes. I'll get you a stuffed Mickey." And before she could argue, I fled.

WHEN WE FLEW from Black Pine, the temperature had been in the forties. A gray mist shrouded the mountains, and, except for the deep green tops of lanky pines, the landscape appeared a mottled brown. We found Tampa in the low eighties with sun-kissed palms and neon-bright flowers. California dreaming, I rejoiced to be back in a non-winter wonderland.

Nash tossed my suitcase in the trunk of the rental. I opened the passenger window and sucked in warm air. And exhaust. But still left the window open, reveling in the sun on my skin. Nash climbed in to begin our drive to Clearwater and also opened his window.

"Too bad we couldn't get a convertible," I shouted over the noise of traffic and wind.

"You must miss your Jaguar."

I shrugged. I did. But my little blue Jag was a part of my old life. "I miss having a real vehicle. Lucky isn't great in the winter."

"I don't get Boomer." Nash's jaw clenched. "He wants you to live independently from Vicki, but he knows you're broke. Instead of giving you a real vehicle or even cosigning for a loan, he makes you take your old motorized Huffy. That damn bike is dangerous in good weather."

"Daddy's the original OG. You pay for everything in cash and if you can't afford it, you go without."

"If you get hurt on that dirt bike, I'll kill him." Nash's scar flashed white. He glanced at me and patted my thigh. "I'm sure he thinks you're perfectly safe."

"I know." I sighed. "I should take Vicki up on her offer of giving me a company car. I didn't say no to a company iPhone and credit card."

"Boomer will love that."

"I don't like relying on you and Misty for rides. And it's too cold for Lucky. What else can I do?"

"Get your own vehicle?" Nash arched an eyebrow. "You've got a steady paycheck. You can get a loan without a cosigner."

I chewed my lip. Of course, Nash was right. I wasn't sure what kind of loan my credit rating would allow, not to mention my legal issues. And it felt shallow, but I feared what my meager savings could afford. Lucky felt temporary. Buying my own car felt permanent. Or at least a longer kind of permanency than the two-year luxury leases I had grown used to in California. "I'll look into it when I return to Black Pine."

"Speaking of that, I'll help you move when we get back." He

gave me that awful look. The one of pity mixed with embarrassment. "It won't take long with my truck. Maybe we can talk Boomer into letting you keep your stuff in the storage unit. Because that was a lot of…stuff."

Oh, God. Move into the office or Vicki's? Both made me feel nauseous for entirely different reasons. Getting my own place would require a background check, and with my history, I'd likely be disqualified from renting. Life was humbling.

No, I'd humbled myself.

I folded my arms across my stomach and watched Florida flash by my window. And prayed for a change in fortune.

TWENTY-SEVEN
#NOTSOHAPPYCAMPING

THE DRIVE to Happy Camper RV Park only took forty-five minutes from Tampa. After a quick exchange with Joe Fortunato, Lamar's retired cop friend, we learned Xiáng Xi was in his little Winnebago. Along with a woman who danced at a local club.

Nash and I exchanged looks.

"She's very friendly," Joe winked. "And he looks particularly pleased with himself."

"How nice," I said, relieved we wouldn't have to deal with an angry stripper. I'd had my fair share during cheating husband surveillance.

"Not how I meant it. But she's friendly like that, too."

"How do you think he's going to react if we knock?" said Nash. "I didn't want the hassle of flying with a firearm."

Joe gave Nash an understanding nod. "He's not taking many precautions to hide. Why'd he run?"

"We don't have a motive," said Nash. "Could be defecting."

"You'd think he'd run himself to an embassy and asked for asylum or something," said Joe.

"I don't think he's covered for asylum," said Nash. "He's not political. Neither his country nor his job warrant asylum. At least, I wouldn't think."

"Homeland Security won't take too kindly to an expired work visa shacking up with a stripper."

"I wonder if Lili knew about the dancer," I said. "Maybe that's why she was so worried about Master Xi."

"They hooked up soon after he got down here, from what I heard. Your Xi got 'lucky.'" Joe liberally applied air quotes. "According to the neighbors. Who are real friendly, too."

"That's nice."

"You're too literal for this kind of work." Joe laughed. "I meant friendly, like they watch each other's business and gossip. If Mr. Lung means to keep himself to himself, he picked the wrong RV park. They're all snowbirds from Michigan. Got nothing better to do."

"Thanks, Joe." Nash handed Joe an envelope and shook his hand. "Appreciate it."

"Tell Lamar I want him to come down. Good fishing in these parts." Joe ambled back to his truck.

We turned to face Happy Campers. "Nice amenities," I said. "A pool, pickleball, and HBO. And only a ten-minute walk to the beach."

"Hopefully, Xi wants to enjoy those amenities. We can take photos of him and send them to Lili, showing where he is. If we get this done quickly, we'll have time to enjoy the beach ourselves. Smell that salt air." Nash grinned, raising his face to the sun.

"I thought we were going to talk to Xi," I said. "There are a lot of questions he might help us answer."

Nash lowered his chin. "Technically, we just needed to find him."

"He might know about Jeff Johnson and we're supposed to find him, too."

"Talking to him might set him on the lam again."

"Or help him to realize he needs to speak with Lili, his student and friend, who is worried."

"You're something else." He slung an arm around my shoulders and kissed the side of my head. "I've got a good feeling about this. Xi's not being cautious. He's hooked up with a stripper. The man obviously thinks he's got the world on a string."

I leaned into him. "And then we'll enjoy the beach. I promise."

TWO FOLDING camp chairs sat outside the door of Xiáng Xi's (aka Tang Lung) Winnebago. We knocked on his door and a moment later, a woman answered. Looking somewhere between thirty-five and fifty-five, she wore a ponytail and a bikini beneath her tank top and cutoffs. The lines on her face were made more visible by a generous helping of makeup, but her smile was genuine. She also seemed oblivious to the fact Xiáng shouldn't be introduced to any yahoo knocking on his camper door.

"Hey Tang," said Xi's lady friend. "Folks here to see you."

Nash and I exchanged a look.

A moment later, a Chinese man of indeterminable age in Tommy Bahama apparel appeared. He looked extremely fit and not at all nervous or anxious. Which I would be if I had skipped out on a contract to work in a foreign country.

"Xiáng Xi?" said Nash.

His face hardened and his body language changed from relaxed to poised. I recognized the potential lethality in his slight muscular frame.

"Lili sent us." I smiled to ease his nerves.

Instead of softening his stance, he pulled his weight back onto his back leg. His right foot barely rested on the ball. The Shaolin kung fu cat stance. He was ready for action.

I placed a hand lightly on Nash's arm to warn him. "We just want to talk. We're private investigators, but I'm also a friend of Lili's."

"Miss Liang is worried about you." Nash held up a hand. "She hired us to find you."

Xi leaned out, glanced around, and flattened himself against the wall while holding the door. "Come in."

I eased past him, while Nash waited for Xi to follow me up the steps and into the sitting area. We took seats on the bench at the tiny kitchen table.

"June," said Xi to his lady friend in a crisp British accent. "This is about my work. Would you excuse us?"

"Nice to meet y'all." Seemingly unconcerned at our arrival, June leaned forward to peck Xi on the cheek. "I need to go anyway. I'll come over after my shift ends."

Xi waited for June to leave, then sighed. "I'm sorry I had to leave Lili in this way, but I saw no other choice. I'm not going back."

"It's not our business whether you break your contract or not," said Nash. "We just told Miss Liang that we'd find you."

"Can't you call her? She's so worried," I said.

"Calling her will make it worse." Xi folded his hands on top of the table. "I'd rather you say nothing at all. It will make things more difficult for Lili."

"I'm no expert, but I believe you're in violation of your visa status," said Nash. "You can't stay here."

Xi smiled weakly. "I know. I plan to return to China before my visa expires."

I internally sighed. Xi would soon be on the run again. "Lili sent her boyfriend, Jeff Johnson, to find you. Have you seen him, or has he contacted you?"

Xi shook his head. His eyes betrayed his distrust of Jeff Johnson, though.

"She hasn't heard from him either. Any idea why he'd volunteer to look for you and not answer her calls?"

"I can't say. I didn't know him well."

"Did you ever notice anyone with a firearm in the house where you stayed?" said Nash.

"I am not aware of this."

"We've also noticed there's been some electronic surveillance on Miss Liang," said Nash. "We found it in her trailer on set. What's that about?"

"I have no idea." His eyes cut to the trailer door.

Nash hadn't mentioned the hidden equipment he'd found in the mansion. Maybe Xiáng Xi needed a greater jolt to spill the beans. If he had any feelings for Lili, he'd want to help.

"Someone shot Vicki's front door," I said. "Soon after you left."

"The door?" His eyes rounded.

"Do you see how distressing this is? Your replacement, Master Kevin Yuan, believes Lili could be in trouble," I said. "Can you help us to understand why?"

"My replacement as Lili's shifu?" The knuckles on Xi's folded hands reddened and turned white. He slipped his hands beneath the table. "Don't trust him. Don't trust any of them."

TWENTY-EIGHT
#TWOTICKETSTOPARADISE

"I CAN'T BELIEVE we found Xi," I said, walking back to the rental car. "It feels too easy. And disturbing, at the same time. I don't like his implications about Master Kevin."

"We need to think about how to handle this," said Nash. "Obviously, we work for Miss Liang and should tell her what we've learned, despite his objections. This is why I don't like talking to the individual under surveillance."

"What about Vicki? She hired us, too."

Nash rolled his eyes. "In case she was implicated in Mr. Xi's disappearance. I wish he'd tell us the real reason why he didn't want Miss Liang to know where he was."

"You don't trust Kevin, do you?"

"I don't trust many people. Don't take it personally." Nash tucked my hand in his and squeezed.

"You trust me, don't you?"

"Of course." He squeezed my hand again. "What if we only tell Miss Liang we found Xi, then hand the case over to the state department? Xi's not a citizen. He's working for a Chinese film company. It's an international incident. Above our pay grade."

"I don't want to report him. At least not yet. I want to know more about what's happened. It doesn't make any sense. There's June to think about, too."

"The stripper?"

"Exotic dancer. Maybe they'll get married so he can get a green card or whatever. It happens all the time in movies. Didn't you see *The Proposal*?"

Our walk halted at the rental car. Nash opened my door for me but kept his hand in mine. "Miss Albright, Xiáng Xi bailed on his contract. He took money he didn't earn. He stole from the producers. He has a fake identity. And his exotic dancer girl-friend thinks he's living here legally. She doesn't even know his real name. Is that fair to her?"

"I can't help it, I liked him." I sighed. "They seemed happy together."

"Honeymoon period. Wait until the truth leaks out."

"Are we still in our honeymoon period?" The words were out before I could take them back.

"Us? I don't know. We've known each other longer than a week unlike Xi and June, the exotic stripper." Nash stroked the side of my face, then tucked a stray strand of hair behind my ear. "But these months have been intense. I'm not sure if we even qualify for one."

"What does that mean?"

"We haven't been given a chance to have a real honeymoon period." He leaned in to kiss me, then pulled back to give me a long look. "Speaking of honeymoons, I booked a hotel room on the beach."

Somewhere inside of me, a rocket launched. Heat blazed, stars scattered, and comets whizzed beneath my skin, making me feel fizzy and prickly. "Don't we need to get back to Black Pine? Deal with Vicki and tell Lili what happened?"

"The case is closed. We'll make a call to Miss Liang. You're probably right about her boyfriend bailing on her. If you want to spend our time productively, our hotel has internet." He waggled his brows. "We can run Jeff Johnson's credit report and address checks while we enjoy the view."

Nash was willing to work and be off the clock for me. My heart pounded. "I didn't want to tell you, but I've had sixteen messages from Vicki. And twenty unanswered calls."

"Me, too." He pecked my cheek. "I don't care. We're in Florida. It's Sunday. We came all this way and I'm not leaving without two things. A beer on the beach."

"What's the other?"

The blue eyes gleamed and a dimple marked his grin. "You in that hotel room on the beach."

SPOTTING A CUBAN SANDWICH SHOP, Nash pulled into the parking lot of a strip mall. My phone pulsed in my hand. Another text from Vicki. Nash popped the car door latch.

I turned the phone over in my lap. "I feel like we're playing hooky."

"Can't we enjoy an easy missing persons case for once?" said Nash. "Look at that sun and the palm trees. Beats gray skies and dead leaves, doesn't it? I haven't felt this good in a long while. Something about Florida makes all the pressure lift off my shoulders."

"But don't you feel like we missed something with Xi?"

"Xi definitely knows more than he told us. But our job was to find him. We found him."

"I forgot to ask him about Mr. Zhao's feelings for Lili. It might be why Jeff Johnson took off."

"I'll grab lunch," said Nash. "Stay here. Find out what Vicki wants. And if it'll make you feel better, after we eat sandwiches on the beach, we'll return to Happy Campers. You can ask Xi about Mr. Zhao and Kevin. Then we'll go to our hotel. Sound like a plan?"

My nerves crackled and a flash of heat scalded my cheeks. "Okay."

"Florida looks good on you." He leaned forward to brush a kiss against my lips. "Cubano? They might have fried plantains, too."

I nodded.

"Don't tell Vicki our plan. She doesn't need to know we found Xi yet. We'll tell Miss Liang first. At the hotel." Nash hopped from the car, leaned back in to kiss me again, then ambled to the sandwich shop. He whistled as he walked. I'd never seen him do that before. Didn't even know he could whistle.

I turned my phone over, ready to call Vicki. Nash's "don't tell Vicki" and "don't trust Vicki" made me uncomfortable. However, Nash never suspected Vicki killed Xi for professional advancement.

That would be me.

Sure, Vicki snowplowed my acting career. But she never Wanda Holloway-ed for me. And she didn't bribe anyone to get me into college. (Then again, she also didn't see college as beneficial for getting me bigger roles.) Why did I jump to the conclusion Vicki had something to do with the bullet in her door as soon as I heard Xi was missing?

It distressed me more that *I wasn't sure* what Vicki would do to ensure the path to success. Particularly since she had her eyes set on Lili. Lili's star would shine much greater than mine ever could. I never had half of her gumption and talent. And if Vicki could sign Lili now, as her star rose? That's a lot of power, prestige, and money.

Hells. It wasn't Nash's distrust that made me uncomfortable. It was me. I didn't trust Vicki.

Which made me a bad daughter.

It also made me a bad girlfriend. Because this woman — my mother — stood in the way of Wyatt Nash's happiness. Clearly evident in the enjoyment of this short time away from her. I knew it wasn't just the balmy weather, scent of coconut oil, and Coronas. He let Vicki treat him horribly. For me.

The girls were right. Vicki would not let me go. And Nash

would put up with her until I finished my two-year apprentice-ship. Or longer, if this hotel room on the beach thing became more permanent in his mind.

I flipped the visor down and studied my reflection in the mirror. Thought about the hotel room on the beach. Smiled and applied lip gloss.

Then frowned.

In the past, I'd receive some piece of commemorative jewelry conveying permanency before agreeing to something like this.

OMG. Not only was I a horrible daughter and girlfriend, I was also a serial fiancée.

My ex-therapist Renata would think I sought stability through men instead of relying on myself. She'd blame my parents, of course. Didn't Nash deserve a hotel room for all he'd withstood for me?

But damn it, I was also a fan of Beyoncé. I knew I was worth the promise of permanency, at the very least. Yet again, I also knew Nash. Until he dug his way out of the financial hole he faced, he wasn't going to offer what he couldn't deliver. And he thought I needed more than he could currently offer.

And if I was honest, I wanted more than he could currently offer.

God, I was an awful girlfriend. Responsible adulting was so friggin' hard.

I shoved my phone in my pocket. Vicki could wait. The afternoon was proving to be complicated enough. I reached for the visor, glanced in the mirror, and spotted a familiar pair of cutoffs in the parking lot behind our car.

Xi's exotic dancer friend leaned into an open window of a rented car with tinted windows. She spoke to the driver inside, gesturing in the direction we'd just driven. Turning around in my seat, I peered through the rear window to watch her. Reaching inside the car, she retrieved a wad of cash and shoved it in the back pocket of her cutoffs.

Ew. I wrinkled my nose and took back my thoughts of future happiness for Xi and June. He deserved better.

I also determined I was a Beyoncé kind of woman. Nash didn't need to put a ring on it now, but I needed some confirmation…

I stopped my train of thought. June walked away, swinging her cutoffs along the sidewalk. The car pulled from the curb, zipping the tinted glass up as they drove away. I couldn't register a face. Only the flash of sunglasses. But there was something familiar that made me uneasy.

And made me worried for Master Xi.

TWENTY-NINE
#NOCUBANOSFORYOU

THE CAR DOOR OPENED. Nash slid inside, handing me two grease-slicked paper bags and a Styrofoam cup. I inhaled the scent of toasted bread, pork, and hot oil and told myself an exotic dancer's payoff was not a reliable reason to dash this man's dreams of Cubanos on the beach.

I sipped the tea he'd bought me and tried not to imagine the car speeding toward Xi's Winnebego. "I could get used to this."

"Florida?"

"You bearing heavenly-smelling paper bags."

He winked and started the car.

"Nash," I said. "I'm sorry. I can't do this."

He moved the gearshift to park and turned toward me. "Can't do what?"

"I just saw June speaking to somebody in a rental car. The car drove in the direction of the RV park. Something about the inter-action felt hinky. I'm worried about Master Xi. "

"You're right." Sighing, he patted my leg. "Mr. Xi, then the beach."

We munched on fries and fried plantains during the short trip to Happy Campers. Parked before the Winnebago. Nash banged on the door.

No answer.

"Dammit," said Nash. "We weren't gone for more than twenty minutes."

"I didn't see the rental car in the parking lot. Maybe Xi's still hiding from whoever that was." Turning the knob, the door swung open. I stepped on the landing. "It's just us, Master Xi. We have Cubanos."

"You're giving him our Cubanos?" muttered Nash.

"I'm trying to draw him out."

"He's not a cat."

"Mr. Xi, I just have one question I forgot to ask you," I called, mounting the stairs. Reaching the top, I pulled in a breath, choked, and backed down the stairs. On the bottom stair, my back slammed into Nash's chest.

"What are you doing?" said Nash.

"Out. Out. Out." I shuddered, pushing my shoulders against Nash. My skin flashed cold and hot, prickling all over. My stomach had flipped upside down. Limp as overcooked pasta, my legs buckled, and I slid down Nash's body.

"Maizie, what's the matter?" Grabbing me, Nash turned me to face him. "You're white as a sheet."

"Wrong trailer." I gulped.

"This is his Winnebago. What do you mean 'wrong trailer'?"

"When I'd entered Lili's trailer, I thought Jeff Johnson was dead. He wasn't."

"Maizie. Darling. Breathe."

He was right. I couldn't breathe. I gulped again. "In Lili's trailer, Jeff was asleep. Pretending to be asleep. But Master Xi. Still sitting at the table. He's—" I shook my head. "He's not asleep."

"Shit." Nash's eyes widened. He pulled me against his chest and folded his arms around me. "Are you sure?"

"Pretty sure," I said against his chest. "There's a hole where his forehead used to be."

.   .   .

"ALL THIS TIME, I assumed Master Xi was dead, and now he is." I stared at Nash from the camp chair outside the Winnebago. "Do you think I did—"

"No, of course not." Nash kneeled in front of me and took my hands. "You've had a shock—"

"A big shock."

"You were right. We missed something. A big something."

Nash looked over his shoulder, watching a deputy exit the trailer. He turned back to me and squeezed my hands. He lowered his voice, "I heard something when I was speaking to the cops. The bullet casing they retrieved is eighteen caliber."

"What?" I leaned forward and Nash gave his head a quick shake.

"Obviously," he murmured, "they'll have to wait for the physical examination of the victim to determine the bullet."

"Bullet in his head." I licked my lips and felt a raw cold flash through me despite the warmth of the setting sun. "It's the same kind of bullet as the one in Vicki's door."

"Most likely." He pressed my hands together and rubbed them.

"Do you think someone followed us? Or they found Xi like we did?"

"I don't know. I should've been watching more carefully. Damn." Pulling my hands to his lips, he kissed them. "I'm sending you back."

"Can I even go? I'm a witness."

"I'll stay. They have your testimony and information. I'm the acting private investigator in the case. You're my assistant. Besides, I told the deputy your probation officer only gave you a two-day leave. You're in the system."

"Oh. Right."

"And they're eventually going to want to talk to Miss Liang. Vicki, too. You should tell them in person."

"Sucktastic."

"Exactly." He blew out a long breath. "I screwed up. Focused on my own stuff and I didn't take this seriously enough."

His guilt shook me out of my shock. I slid my arms around his thick neck. "This isn't your fault. We couldn't find a motive. Or a connection between Vicki's bullet and Master Xi leaving."

He bowed his head. "We have one now."

THIRTY
#IDREAMEDOFMANDALAY

AT THE TAMPA AIRPORT, I found my boarding gate and (reluctantly) checked my messages.

"Your room is ready for you," said Vicki's voicemail voice. "It's in my wing, not the guest wing. Lydia can show you. I thought you were staying last night, but I was obviously mistaken. Misty found your bags at your father's, abandoned as it seemed, and took them to your room."

Delete.

"Mr. Nash is also not answering his phone. This is terribly irresponsible of you both."

Delete.

"Lili would also like to speak to you."

Delete.

"This is intolerable."

Delete

"Master Kevin would also like to speak to you. I'm not a message delivery service. Really, Maizie."

Delete.

"Time is money, Maizie. I thought you enjoyed a paycheck. Perhaps I'm mistaken."

Delete.

"I suppose you don't want the suite I've offered. It makes no difference to me. As it seems you can no longer live with your father, I assume you'll live in your car. Wait, you don't own a car. You drive a motorbike. Or have you decided to actually *slum* it? I know you, Maizie. You were never one for camping. Camping would be more comfortable than living in that godawful office."

I scowled. My finger was growing a delete callus.

"Don't waste your future on this kind of heartbreak, Maizie. I'm forwarding Mr. Nash's last tax statement filing and credit score by email. Or maybe you'd like a testimonial by his ex-wife? She's done well for herself. Since leaving him."

I shoved my phone into my backpack, fearing I might throw it across the boarding area. Counted to twenty. Did a quick sun salutation in the corner and practiced a cooling breath position. Hopped up from the floor after realizing I was drawing attention. The floor was not the cleanest either. I moved to a seat in the corner and yanked my phone from the backpack.

Lili and Kevin wanted to speak to me. That was easier than speaking to Vicki. I tried Kevin first and left a message on his voicemail. Nibbling the side of my thumb, I thought about Xi's warning before he died. Not to trust Kevin or "any of them." Did that include Vicki and Lili? Did he even know Master Kevin?

Poor Master Xi. He was right not to trust anyone. The hole in his head proved it.

I pulled my thumb from my teeth and pinched the V between my pointer finger and thumb to ward off the influx of tears I felt coming.

What had Xi done to warrant his murder? There was nothing in his background pointing toward anything illegal. Except breaking his contract and running. But who would murder him for that? A lawsuit would be a lot less messy and illegal.

Had he heard or seen something at Vicki's house, as I thought?

Kevin was worried about Lili and didn't trust Vicki. Lili's

trainer and boyfriend both disappeared. The entirety of her entourage. Except for Shiyu.

But Shiyu didn't trust anyone either.

Would she disappear next? And what about Kevin?

Was this some sort of macabre retelling of *And Then There Were None*?

Shizzles.

What was going on in that house? Maybe Lili had heard from Jeff. I dialed her number, Shiyu answered, and I relayed Vicki's message.

"Lili is not available," said Shiyu in her crisp British tones. "I don't know why Lili wanted to speak to you."

"Is Master Kevin there?"

"No, we're not at the house. We left for Mandalay this morning."

"Manderley? The house in *Rebecca*? Wait…what? Why?"

"The Lees have the condo on the Mandalay. I don't know Rebecca, but perhaps she lives in the same building?" Shiyu paused, and I realized her accent had confused my interpretation. "Is that correct? The address names here are so confusing."

I blinked. "Mandalay like Mandalay Bay? In Las Vegas?"

"Not Las Vegas. The Lees want to be on the best beach. They bought a penthouse facing the Gulf of Mexico. They looked for the most expensive flat on the best beach for their winter vacation." Shiyu spoke in Chinese. Without understanding, I got her gist. Shiyu didn't care much for "most expensive and best." Or she didn't care much for the Lees. Or it was American addresses she had an issue with. "Just a moment. They gave Lili the address."

"Gulf side beach? Could be Florida." My heart hammered in my chest. I prayed for an Alabama or Mississippi address — Louisiana or Texas would work, too — but from the little I knew of the Lees, I didn't think my prayers would be heard.

A moment later, Shiyu spoke. "613 on Mandalay Avenue."

"What city?" But I knew before she said, "Clearwater."

Of course, the Lees would be in Clearwater. For the same reason we tracked Xiáng Xi to Clearwater. The most popular beach destination for Chinese tourists.

Both statistically probable and extraordinarily coincidental.

"Vicki is in Clearwater?" My voice grew shrill. "She's been there since this morning?"

"There was a private plane for the brunch."

"Brunch? Vicki hosted a party last night." I sucked in a breath. "What happened at the party after I left?"

"I don't know. I went to my room. I don't like—"

"Right, you don't like parties." My stomach had flipped upside down. I breathed through my nose. "You didn't hear any, like, gunfire last night, did you? Is anyone missing this morning? Notice any stray bullets in the aquarium?"

"I'm sorry? You asked if I heard—"

"Never mind." I pinched the bridge of my nose. "Tell the staff I'll be moving in shortly. That will be all."

I ARRIVED BACK in the land of gray skies and chilly temperatures, making me miss my California winters even more. Walking out of the airport, I found Misty parked in front. Next to my Uber driver. Although I wanted to eschew Misty for Uber, I wanted information more. I tipped and five-starred my Uber driver as an apology, then climbed into the front passenger seat next to Misty.

"How did you know I was at the airport?"

She glanced at me. "I feel more comfortable with you riding in back."

"I'd feel more comfortable if I knew how you're aware of my location."

"Look, *Miss Albright*, I'm just the driver."

"Look, *Misty*, I just came from a crime scene. Blood splatter and everything. How did Vicki know I'd be arriving at the airport?"

"Ask her yourself." Misty kept her eyes on the road and accelerated out of the airport.

"She's in Florida."

"She's home."

I massaged my temples. I couldn't keep up with these people. "When did she get home?"

"About ten minutes ago. Private plane. She saw you exiting your airplane and the Lees had already arranged for a driver. She went home with them and told me to wait for you."

"Was that so hard? Why can't you just answer my questions?" I slumped in my seat. I was hoping to speak to Kevin and Lili and arrange my thoughts before confronting Vicki.

"Because I'm not paid to answer your questions. I'm just paid to drive you."

"You could still—"

"Why don't you have a car?" ranted Misty. "Or rent one? How are you twenty-five years old and still don't have a vehicle?"

"I have a—"

"I know what you have. A dirt bike. And that's ridiculous, by the way. Aren't you ashamed of yourself? Making other people drive you around when you're capable?"

My cheeks heated. The bitter bile of humiliation blazed in my chest. But it wasn't the first time I'd had this heartburn. "You drive Vicki."

"She pays me." She shook her head. "Rich people."

I sucked a breath in through my nose, counted to ten, and exploded, nonetheless. Humility was good for the soul, but sometimes my pride needed airing out. "My last car was repossessed. Upon arriving in Black Pine, actually. When I refused to sign my last reality show contract, my manager stopped paying the lease and didn't tell me. I used all my savings on legal fees and college and paying off other debt I wasn't even aware I had. Therefore, I have horrible credit, but my parents won't cosign a loan. I can't afford anything better than a dirt bike." I pinched my thumb. "And I'm on a DNR list for rentals."

Misty glanced at me and relaxed her jaw. "Do not resuscitate?"

"Do not rent." I rolled my eyes. "I'm sure you heard about my life in California. If you rent a car and break the law, rental agencies won't rent to you anymore."

"What'd you do?"

"Friends drove my rental to Vegas, parked illegally, and while trying to break the boot on the wheel, the driver was arrested for drug possession, vandalism, and contempt. The rest got drunk and disorderlies. When it comes to my legal trouble, not everything that happens in Vegas stays in Vegas."

"Where were you?"

"Passed out in a hotel room. They left without me."

"And your manager, the one who didn't tell you she stopped paying your lease? Vicki?"

I nodded. "I have issues. A lot of issues. I've made a lot of mistakes. I was a rich kid who took things for granted. Now I'm a poor woman who has no clue how to operate in the real world with horrible credit and a semi-criminal record."

Misty cut her eyes toward me. "I wouldn't say you're totally clueless."

"Thanks." I sighed. "But this isn't my pressing concern."

"What is?"

"What in the Hades is going on at Vicki's. Did you know someone shot her door?"

"I heard."

"Any ideas?"

She shook her head. "That's the front of the house. I'm either in a car or in the back of the house."

"Right, the servan—" I cut myself off. "Kitchen. What's the staff think about all the stuff going on? Xiáng Xi and Jeff Johnson disappearing. Bullet in the door. There must be suspicions."

"We're not paid to gossip." Her jaw hardened.

And here I thought I was getting somewhere with Misty. "Surely you hear things?"

"I'm paid not to hear things."

We drove up the long drive past the fish topiary. Charles the topiary was blooming with red flowers. "How did she get the bush to bloom right when the Lees arrived? It's not spring."

"Camellias bloom in the winter," said Misty, stopping before the front door. "But to be honest, I think Vicki had the gardener do something."

"You know who else did that?" I seethed. "The Queen of Hearts in *Alice in Wonderland*."

"Funny."

Misty hopped from the car to open my door, but I'd already rushed out and marched up the front stairs. It wasn't funny to me. Not the least little bit. My mother had become the mad queen.

"Holy shmizzles," I muttered. "Off with their heads. Like literally in Xiáng Xi's case."

THIRTY-ONE
#DELIVERINGBADNEWSANDFRUIT

I DARTED through the hall and down the corridor to the guest wing before anyone (Vicki) could notice I entered. Heading upstairs, I zipped toward Kevin's room. I wanted to give Lili the news about Xi first, but I needed help. Kevin had been working closely with Lili this week. He admired her and wanted her to succeed. He was already suspicious of the goings-on. And even though Master Xi had thrown shade at Kevin, I still trusted him.

I just wish he trusted me. It had to be the reason why he wouldn't tell what he really thought was happening at Casa Vicki.

I knocked on his door and announced myself. "I was in Florida," I said once inside and safe from prying ears. "We found Master Xi. But I have bad news."

Kevin nodded and motioned for me to sit down. "Vicki was also in Florida. Collecting the Lees with the others. They gave a brunch."

"I heard." I sat on the loveseat pushed against the end of his bed. "Before I tell you the bad news, I need you to be honest with me. I know you don't want to misrepresent anybody or anything, but I need to know what you think about this situation."

"Situation?"

"The Vicki situation, namely. You can't tell me to quit my job without giving me a good reason why. I need more than hints."

Kevin sighed and perched on the loveseat next to me. "Vicki cares more about her position than anything else. Her ego and ambition are driving her to make decisions that are dangerous for you."

"Sort of always been the case. But I've had some good therapists—"

"There's more. Your mother is making powerful friends."

"The Lees?"

"I told you they are far beyond her league. You know the expectations of producers from working in this business. I found out Vorling is gambling all he has to make *Unlucky 18* a box office success." Kevin dropped his voice. "And I'm quite literal in my meaning. I did not want to say anything, because I don't know this for sure, but I believe Vorling owes the Lees money."

"I heard he has a problem with gambling. Do you mean the Lees covered his losses?"

"I learned they own casinos in Macau."

"They're not just crazy rich." I closed my eyes. "Vicki wouldn't know the protocol for mega-rich. You're afraid she might offend them."

"Of course, she will offend them," he said bitterly. "And these are people you should never offend."

"I thought this was Lili's movie. Did the Lees find the script?"

"No, it is Lili's project. Somehow, she connected with the Lees and they acquired Vorling for her. I don't know Zhao's reputation, but I have a feeling he learned of Lili's script and he convinced the Lees to finance the production for her."

"That makes sense. He's listed as the associate producer and the Lees are co-producers." I let out a breath. "And I think he's sweet on Lili."

"Too bad for Lili."

"Too bad for Zhao, because I don't think she's interested.

She's still hung up on Jeff Johnson." Who was still missing. Which brought me back to my current predicament. "Kevin, I need your help. Xiáng Xi's dead. He was shot. I've got to tell Lili."

"His family." Kevin closed his eyes. "His body is here, and they are in China. This is very bad."

"Because they can't grieve him properly?"

"Because he was murdered, Maizie." Kevin opened his eyes. "Your mother should not have the Lees here. This house is very unlucky."

LILI HADN'T ARRIVED home and Shiyu wasn't around either. Kevin returned to his room and I went in search of mine. I plodded past the Magnolia room where one of Vicki's people hurried out, carrying a potted flower.

"Is that where the Lees are staying?" I said.

She nodded, calling over her shoulder. "Sorry, I'm in a hurry. I have the wrong kind of orchid."

I watched her rush down the hall, then peeked inside the door. This suite was bigger than Lili's but similarly arranged with a sitting area separated from the bedroom with pocket doors. I slipped inside and shut the door. A basket of fruit and a bouquet of yellow roses rested on a table by the door. No cards. I moved to the pocket doors, cracked them open, then entered.

The bespoke leather and brass luggage rested empty in the closet. Savile Row suits and haute couture dresses hung above them. Silks and linens were placed tidily in the cedar-lined dresser. A large wall safe in the closet was locked. The desk held a password-protected laptop and charging iPhone. The alligator briefcase held papers written in Chinese.

The only thing I could surmise from the Lees' room was they were indeed mega-rich.

The handle on the bedroom door jiggled. I stood to the side of the pocket doors, hoping it was just the maid with a quick orchid swap. A moment later, an older Asian woman in a Chanel suit walked past the pocket door. Ignoring me, she entered through the next door, closing it firmly behind her. I shot out of the bedroom and halted in the sitting area as a Chinese man stepped through the door. I gave him a short bow. He handed me the fruit basket.

I left with the fruit and thanked my lucky stars that the Lees were so wealthy, they were used to finding strangers in their room.

Passing Lili's room, I noticed the door stood slightly open. Lili or Shiyu had returned. Or I had happened on another orchid turn-out. I adjusted the fruit basket and raised my fist to knock. Heard voices and lowered my fist.

"You can't just rewrite the script. It affects the integrity of the film," ranted Lili.

"But Lili, I am trying to help you. The scene was pivotal and as it was written, Stanley threatened to steal the emotional value from your character." Zhao remained calm in the brunt of Lili's ire, but his heavy accent and low voice forced me to strain to understand him. I moved closer to the crack in the door.

"I don't care why you were doing it," Lili clipped her words. "You have no business touching the script."

"You know I'm a fast learner, Lili. I'm smart. Smarter than the Lees give me credit. You should trust me more. I have a lot of scripts for you. Projects that will make you the bigger star here in America. I'm not going back to China. After *Unlucky 18* wraps, I will stay here. And I know you want to do the same."

"I don't care," she said icily. "I wanted this picture made and then we're done. That was the deal. And whatever you heard about Vorling isn't true."

"It better not be."

"Leave it alone."

Zhou cleared his throat. "We don't have to use the Lees in the future. I am talking to Vicki Albright about financing future films."

I caught my forehead before it thudded against the door. *Frigarendous.* Vicki had gone too far this time. Stealing an associate producer to get to the star? She didn't have the kind of money co-producers needed to make major films. Did Mr. Zhao even know her actual net worth? How would she pull that off? Rob a bank?

Lili and Zhao had continued their argument. I placed thoughts of Vicki's diabolical schemes on hold to focus.

"Zhao, you cannot profess your love when I am who I am. You act too familiar with me."

Shizzles, I'd missed a profession of love. I loved a romantic love profession. Which I hadn't literally gotten from Nash—

I shook my head and refocused.

"Because you are in love with this Jeff Johnson?" Zhao exploded. "You don't even know who he really is. Where is he anyway? That investigator found hidden cameras—"

"Get out," she screamed.

Hold up. How did Zhao know—

The door jerked open. I looked up at Zhao. As my eyes widened, his eyes narrowed. "What do you want?"

"Fruit delivery." I shoved the basket at him. "Congratulations on the film."

He studied me. "You bring me fruit?"

"I need to talk to Lili," I said. "It's important."

"I was leaving." He glanced over his shoulder. "Miss Liang, Maizie Albright is here for you."

"Maizie, dear, please come in," Lili's voice sounded overly bright.

Zhao moved around me, carrying the fruit basket under one arm. I scuttled inside and shut Lili's door. She dabbed at her eyes, forced a smile, and waved at her club chairs. "Please. Would you like some tea? I've already turned the kettle on."

"Let me make the tea," I said, moving to the electric pot on the wet bar. "I think you should sit down. Where's Shiyu?"

Nodding primly, Lili sat on the edge of her small sofa. "I gave her the day off."

"I'm afraid it's bad news."

"At least one of us has good news." She sniffed. "I heard from Jeff."

I whipped around. The teacup flew out of my hand and bounced on the carpet. I bent to pick it up and fixed my expression before rising. "I'm so glad to hear that. Was he still looking for Master Xi?"

"Yes, but Jeff couldn't find him." Lili's grim expression studied mine. "But I guess you did."

"We did. Nash and I." I poured the water into the teapot and carried the tray to set in front of her. "Master Xi was in Clearwater, Florida. Under a new identity and living in an RV."

"RV?"

"Recreational vehicle. Like an on-set trailer." I cleared my throat. "Doesn't matter."

"Go on." Lili leaned forward to pour her tea. Her hands shook. She pulled back and fisted her hands in her lap.

"We spoke to Mr. Xi," I said, thinking carefully about my words. "He was sorry he left you the way he did."

She clutched her hands against her chest. "He's okay? I thought—"

"We spoke to him, then left." I took a deep breath. "When we returned, Xi…had been shot. Fatally. I'm so sorry, Lili."

"I don't understand. He was alive?"

I nodded. "Someone arrived after we did."

"Do they know who did it?" Tears coursed down her cheeks. She grabbed a napkin and dabbed at her eyes.

"Nash is still in Clearwater, working with the police. Do you need me to tell your producers and director?"

She sucked in a small breath. "No. That's not necessary. Thank you."

"Is there anything I can do for you?" When she shook her head, I hesitated. I wanted to ask about Jeff, but I didn't want to get all Lizzo on her. For one, she was hurting over Xi's death. For another, I could tell she didn't want to hear it. And to be honest, Lili was a major star. There was something in the swag power of a major star that was cowing to us minor stars.

But at the same time, Jeff disappeared, Xi was murdered, and now Jeff was back?

Although why Jeff would want Xi dead was a mystery, but then why anyone would want Xiáng Xi dead was a puzzle.

Which meant Jeff's ghosting and reappearing was on the table.

"I'm glad to hear about Jeff. At least he can give you some comfort." I patted her shoulder. "Where was he? Did he also learn Master Xi was in Florida?"

"He didn't say, but following a false lead, evidently." She waved a hand. "Doesn't matter now. I'll see him tonight. He's driving up from Atlanta now."

Which meant he could be driving from the airport in Atlanta. My inner detective rubbed her hands gleefully.

Or not.

"Lili, you almost seem like you were expecting bad news. Was there something you didn't tell us about Master Xi? It could help the police solve the crime."

"He was innocent." She shut her eyes and fat tears squeezed out. "Unhappy but innocent. He didn't want to come here, and I coerced him. I'm afraid I'm the one who should be blamed for his death."

THIRTY-TWO
#ALIFELYFT

INSTEAD OF HIDING in my room (from Vicki whom I dreaded talking about Xi's death and her involvement), I decided I needed a dose of clarity. Which meant getting a Lyft to see my LA HAIR BFFs for dinner. Vicki's housekeeper hadn't planned on me anyway. While waiting for the driver, I called Nash.

"The bullet that shot Xi was a nine-by-eighteen," said Nash. "Waiting on ballistics but most likely he was shot by a 9mm Makarov. If I had Vicki's bullet with me, I'd let them compare the two, but I bet it's the same firearm."

"Did you give the police Master Xi's phone?"

"Yes, and they appreciated it. He had nothing else connected to his old identity. Forensics has already gone through the trailer. We're the break in the case for the Clearwater police. I'm getting to know the lead detective, giving him all the information we know, and he's reciprocating, somewhat. He told me if Xiáng Xi was defecting, he was not seeking political asylum. Looked like a professional hit to him."

"A hit? Like by a hitman?"

"Could be organized crime. Could have been mixed up in something illegal back in China."

"But Lili said he was innocent. She said it was her fault he was murdered because she forced him to come here."

"Then she's lying about something. Quitting your job isn't a motive for murder. And he didn't just quit, he created a whole new identity."

"Maybe she feels guilty because she made him come to America on this job and then he was murdered."

"Don't let your feelings confuse the facts. Investigators need to divest themselves of their emotions as best they can."

If that was the case, I was an investigating failure.

"Xiáng Xi had been planning this disappearance," said Nash. "You need to put the pressure on Miss Liang to explain herself. She knows something."

"Jeff Johnson suddenly reappeared. She wouldn't say or didn't know where Jeff was except, he'd been looking for Xiáng Xi. She passed it off like Jeff had been on the wrong track."

"Hinky," said Nash. "Could be true, but why didn't he contact her? I don't trust Miss Liang."

"Vicki and the Lees were in Clearwater today," I said abruptly. "Everyone was, including Lili. The Lees had a brunch." Not that I was anxious to move the conversation away from Jeff. But because the fact had been swelling like an overinflated balloon and I needed to leak the information before my head exploded.

"Dammit," said Nash. "I'll tell the police."

"I also learned Vicki's cozying up to Mr. Zhao so he'll let her produce his next projects with Lili."

"Shouldn't surprise you."

"I thought she'd just want to manage Lili. She doesn't have the kind of money or connections for big movies. At least, I don't think she does."

"Looks like she's got a lot of money to me."

"There's money and then there's money."

"Is Vicki still in Clearwater?" By the tone of his voice, I knew he wanted to question her himself.

"No," I said quickly. "She returned to Black Pine right before I did."

His silence implied more than any words could.

Misty pulled up in front of the steps. I waved her on. She opened the door and walked around to the passenger side.

"I have a car coming," I shouted at Misty. "A blue Toyota driven by a woman named Shirley."

"They turned her away at the gate." Misty flapped her hand toward the backseat. "Hurry up."

I stared at the sky, then looked back at Misty. "I am trying to be a responsible adult who is adulting her own ride."

"What in the hell does that mean?" said Nash.

"I'm talking to Misty," I said to Nash. "Vicki won't let me hire my own driver."

"Dammit, I forgot to give you my truck keys," said Nash. "I'm sorry. I'll keep you posted on anything new. And I'll tell the detective about Jeff Johnson."

I sighed and climbed into the backseat of the Escalade. "Everything feels wrong."

"We'll figure it out." He paused and his voice deepened. "Our hotel room has a view of the ocean."

"That doesn't make me feel better."

"Doesn't make me feel better either. I tell you what *would* make me feel good."

"What?"

"You in this hotel room with me."

I grinned, then scowled at Misty. "Nash, ixnay on the Ickivay in Earwaterclay."

"You're breaking up."

"Don't say anything about Vicki being in Clearwater to the police," I whispered. "At least not yet."

"Maizie, we can't protect her from this."

"I know. It's just—I'm not ready to…I can't deal…" I caught my breath. "I haven't told Vicki yet about Xiáng Xi's murder."

"Do you want me to do it?" he said with more eagerness than I wanted to hear.

"No. I need to do it." I heaved a sigh.

"Listen, if she has nothing to hide, then there's no issue. But you know the police will eventually figure it out. Tomorrow I'm meeting with the detective after they've finished canvassing the Happy Campers. We'll talk before then."

Which meant I needed to interrogate Vicki before the night became tomorrow. But first I needed nourishment. In food and friends.

THIRTY MINUTES LATER, Tiffany, Rhonda, and I were seated at Casa de Ray's, a local Black Pine establishment not yet (maybe never) discovered by industry peeps. When I'd called the girls, I told them I needed some help sorting my current hot mess.

Rhonda had said, "If you can't have alcohol, you're going to need something fried."

Sundays at the Casa were two-for-one night. Margaritas. Tacos were on Tuesdays, naturally. Rhonda and Tiffany volunteered to drink my margarita for me.

I'd explained the finding of Xiáng Xi. And Vicki's machinations in becoming the next Jerry Bruckheimer. "Vicki is somehow involved with a murder," I said. "I'm afraid she's somewhere between a witness and an accessory."

"What about an accomplice?" said Tiffany.

"Why do you always want to go worst-case scenario with Vicki?"

"Worse-case would mean she committed the murder."

The waiter brought three plates of steaming and sizzling food with fist-sized dollops of sour cream. I took in a deep breath of cheesy enchilada sauce and said a prayer of thanks for Southern-style Mexican food. And as long as I ate plenty of guacamole, it was all good, because avocado was a healthy fat.

Everyone knew that.

"Vicki's a lot of things, but she wouldn't shoot someone in the head," I said when the waiter left.

"Are we talking close range?" said Rhonda. "Because I'd agree with you when it comes to distance. That's tricky."

I sawed off a hunk of chimichanga, dipped it in sour cream, and chewed. "If Vicki's involved, it's because she's protecting someone. My guess would be Lili Liang because signing Lili into Vicki's management company would be a huge coup."

Rhonda gasped. "Lili Liang murdered her kung fu master?"

"No, he was murdered by a professional. But Lili blames herself for his death." I set my fork down. "Stanley Wu thinks Lili hired me to help her, not the missing men. Although now her boyfriend isn't missing. We found her martial arts trainer and the police have taken over that case. I don't know how else to help her."

"Pray for her," said Rhonda. "Then you've covered your bases."

"I just hope y'all still get paid," said Tiffany. "Does it count if your missing person dies right when you find them?"

I sighed. "I was supposed to be in a hotel room in Florida tonight."

"You're right," said Rhonda. "We should've done a girl's weekend."

"A hotel room with Nash," I added. "I've been kicked out of Casa de Spayberry. Your whole thing about Daddy bonding with Nash? Epic failure. Turns out Nash roots for the wrong football team or something. Nash works for Vicki, and I guess that's an unforgivable offense in Boomer Spayberry's mind. I got angry and said some things Daddy took literally."

"What things?"

"Like I didn't want to live with him anymore."

"Damn," said Tiffany. "So where are you living?"

"Don't worry." I speared another hunk of fried tortilla covered in sauce and sour cream. "I'm staying at Vicki's. Better to keep an eye on her."

"Good thinking," said Rhonda. "They say you should keep your enemies close. That'll do the trick."

"Vicki's more Nash's enemy right now," said Tiffany. Focused on piling her tortilla with fajita meat, Tiffany missed my wince.

Rhonda spotted it and patted my arm. "Why don't we say frenemy? It sounds less scary."

"No, Tiff's right," I said. "I've been letting Vicki take advantage of Nash because I want him to continue mentoring me. He would have lost the company if Vicki hadn't bought him out, but he'd probably be a lot happier doing something else. Maybe it's better for Nash if I give up on my dream of becoming a private investigator."

"Give up your dream?" Rhonda sucked in her breath. "They always say to never give up on your dream. How can you give up on a dream?"

"By getting a real job," said Tiffany. "A job that pays real money so she can get her own place and her own car. Putting a roof over your head and being responsible for your life is a good reason to give up on a dream. Because, by definition, dreams are not real."

The idea of a real job and lost dreams did not sit well with the mix of fried tortilla, cheese sauce, and avocado. I slapped a hand over my mouth until my stomach stopped gurgling.

But Tiffany was right.

"OMG, I'm still not truly adulting." Tears pricked my eyes. I dropped my fork to pinch my thumb. "All those stories about Millennials are true. I'm just another fulfilled stereotype."

Rhonda threw her arms around me. "Honey, it's not because you're Millennial. It's because you've grown up privileged. Plenty of Millennials grew up with no money and became adults. Just look at me and Tiffany."

Tiffany waved her fork. "Already got a job, my own place, and an ex-husband."

I hugged Rhonda, then straightened in my chair. "I am going to change. I'll quit working for Vicki and get another job." I tilted my chin. "Not just to help Nash but also to help myself, of course. Fierce goddess within and all."

However, I couldn't bring myself to tell them before the realization of my fierce goddess, I needed to first figure out how Vicki was connected to this murder. Kevin thought she was in over her head and I agreed.

Before I helped Nash, I had to help my mother.

THIRTY-THREE
#BLACKKNIGHTED

AT VICKI'S, I marched through the foyer — not even giving Charles a glance — and looked for Vicki and the Lees in the living room. Then the conservatory. The sunroom. The game room. The rear parlor. The terrace, in case the Lees liked "the bracing chill" like Lili. But they were from Macau and not Beijing, so I didn't find them there either.

The staff had gone home for the night, except for a housekeeper, but she was locked in her room with the TV blaring. Although I had gained the gumption to speak to Vicki, I didn't have the wherewithal to interrupt Vicki's housekeeper, because God knew after working for Vicki all day, she deserved her Netflix and Chill.

Digesting enchiladas had burned up my spare energy and I lost my mettle. I slunk up the backstairs and crept along the hall toward my suite. Not only did I need to confront my mother, but I also needed to face my father. I missed Remi and Carol Lynn and the Jack Russells and even the big man himself. Daddy needed to know I understood how difficult it was to have your adult daughter move in, particularly when her life didn't mesh with his. Especially when we'd not had more than extended visits over the last twenty years.

But he also needed to know these life lessons were especially painful *because* we'd not had more than extended visits over the last twenty years. He needed to stop punishing me for Vicki's transgressions.

Parenting my parents proved extremely precarious.

Passing Vicki's study, I heard the thud of a drawer or door closing. I took a moment to find my fortitude and apply it to "wronged-child mixed with wily private investigator" — a new character I was working on.

Time to confront Vicki.

No. Time to confront my mother. The possible felon.

I nudged the door open. "Vicki, we need to talk about your involvement in this movie. I think you're in serious trouble."

A light blinked off, shrouding the room in darkness.

"Don't pretend you're not here. I'm not waiting until morning. The police are going to want to talk to you tomorrow and we need to hash this out." I felt along the wall for the switch, then stopped and sniffed.

No Chanel No. 5. Nor Armani Beautiful. I had also spoken several sentences without interruption.

This was not Vicki.

"Who's in here?"

My hand slid along the wall, and I touched the edge of the plate. Before I could flip the switch, my fingers were pried back. A figure stood before me, then whipped behind me as they forced my arm around. I couldn't think or react. Bent backward, my fingers felt like they'd break. I hissed. The applied pressure extended to my wrist. Then my elbow. My knees bent, then slammed into the carpet.

Someone howled.

Holy shizzles, that sound came out of me.

My face smashed against the carpet. My chest crashed next. My right arm remained suspended by the vicious puppeteer who used my bent fingers as strings. The joints blazed and my wrist felt close to snapping. Yanked overhead but pulled down by my weight, my shoulder seemed unsure whether to stay connected to my arm or collapse against the floor.

A searing pain told me a decision would be made soon.

Fat tears bled onto the carpet and I inhaled them with a copious amount of snot pooling around my mouth.

Something thwacked the carpet. I blinked through the haze of tears and turned my head. My right hand lay next to my head.

"Oh my God, my arm," I sobbed. "You pulled off my arm."

I stared at my hand. It lay like a fish that had been tossed ashore. No longer flopping.

Someone screamed.

Oh, right. That was me.

THIRTY-FOUR
#NONCOMPLIANCED

I WOKE, took a beat to figure out why my lips were glued to the carpet and jerked upright. Thankfully, my arm accompanied my body. I gingerly flexed my aching, stiff fingers. My wrist felt swollen and my shoulder numb. However, everything was attached and unbroken. I wrapped the bottom of my t-shirt around my arm as a makeshift sling and shook off my daze.

"Holy frijoles. Who was that?" Clambering to my feet, I dashed out the door. Vicki's private rooms and my suite were down the hall to my left. The front and back staircases were past the gallery to my right. Where to look first?

Vicki.

I sped toward her room and stopped myself from pounding on the door. Slipped inside. Shot through the sitting room, then her real office — a laptop, iPad docking station, and a massive Kate Spade planner on a coffee table — and stopped before her bedroom door. Laying my ear against the door, I heard her speaking and I sighed.

I hustled back to the hall, checked my bedroom. Ran in the opposite direction and gazed out over the foyer. Beneath me, Charles circled the top of the tank. Wall sconces bathed the vestibule in low amber light, but no one lurked in the shadows.

Holding my arm, I zipped down the stairs and dashed through the first-floor rooms, then sped up the backstairs to the guest wing. All was quiet. Eerily quiet.

I stood in the guest wing, wondering if I should hit the panic button on the alarm. Thereby freaking out all within, including the Lees and Lili Liang.

This was an issue with the rich and powerful. You constantly walked on eggshells around them. Would they be offended I woke them to announce I'd been ninja-attacked? Or would they want to be woken to hear how I'd been ninja-attacked? In a house they deemed safe…

Vicki would kill me if I woke them.

Not that I cared.

But I hadn't been seriously injured. Just put in a pain compliance hold.

One that made me pass out for a minute.

But they obviously knew what they were doing and could've truly hurt me. And didn't.

I mentally facepalmed. Now was not the time to deal with coping strategies. Now was the time to find out why someone had been rifling through Vicki's desk. The phone and computer were gone. What else could there be?

I hurried back to the study and flipped on the overhead light.

The drawers in Vicki's desk were closed, but someone had been searching through them. The leather blotter sat askew. A crystal dish of paperclips had been overturned. Vicki fired maids over presentation. I couldn't tell if anything was missing.

The Velcro. I slipped my hand beneath the desk. The underside of the drawer was no longer sticky. The Velcro strap had been replaced and hung loose.

I yanked my phone from my back pocket. Luckily, I had face planted and my body hadn't crushed the phone. Silver linings. "Nash," I said breathlessly. "Are you awake? I need you."

After a moment of silence, his voice purred in my ear, rough and deep. "Alright, darlin'. I hadn't expected this, but let's give it a whirl."

I blinked. "Give what a whirl?"

He cleared his throat. "What exactly did you need?"

"Someone snuck into Vicki's office and attacked me. They were going through her desk."

"Attacked you? Are you hurt?"

"I'll recover. It's not why I'm calling—"

"Recover from what?"

"I'm fine. It should never have happened."

"Maizie, what shouldn't have happened? What did they do to you?"

"Never mind. The Velcro strap—"

"Miss Albright, I need to know you're okay and you don't sound okay. You are ten hours away and it's driving me bonkers."

Who used the word *bonkers*? Certainly not big, brawny men like Nash.

But he just did. My heart fluttered.

"Bonkers?"

"Bonkers," he repeated. "I'm in a damn hotel room meant for you. There's a hot tub. A private balcony overlooking the beach. Fluffy robes. Room service. They even have all the girly shower stuff you like."

My heart melted, leaked into my feet, and made my toes curl. "That is so sweet."

"It's not meant to be sweet," he snarled. "There's nothing sweet about it. And I should be with you when you're attacked."

"Next time, I promise," I said.

"Not funny," he growled. "What did they do to you? How did they hurt you?"

"It's so embarrassing. I've been training for surprise attacks since I was ten. And they only used my fingers."

"Your fingers?" he said slowly.

"Applied pressure backward to completely disable me."

"They bent your fingers backward and that disabled you?"

"My entire arm is out of commission at the moment." I adjusted my tone to one less defensive. "Nothing is broken. I'll be okay. Small joint manipulation is extremely effective. It's a pain compliance strategy and illegal in most martial arts."

"This was a kung fu thing?"

"Not necessarily, but—" I stopped. I didn't like his implication, but he was right. I needed to approach this without emotion. Whoever had attacked me had known what they were doing. "With the right training in any kind of martial arts, small joint manipulation can allow a weaker person to take advantage of someone much stronger and bigger."

"Which means a woman could have done this to you," said Nash. "Narrow it down to the kung fu club staying at Vicki's house."

"Master Kevin or Lili? I think Stanley only knows stage stuff." I couldn't believe either Kevin or Lili would snoop in Vicki's office, let alone attack me. "What if it was someone who's not staying here? It's ridiculously easy to get into this house. I walked in and through the house without tripping any alarm."

"If I said it once, I've said it a hundred times, there's no point in state-of-the-art security if you don't—"

"I can handle this," I said, interrupting his rant. And he had said it at least one hundred times. I forced my tone to cheery. "You should learn what you can about Xiáng Xi's murder. I'm fine. They could've seriously hurt me, but they didn't. It's all good."

"Whoever assaulted you was looking for something in the office? An office Vicki doesn't use?"

"Hells." I sucked in a breath. "They were coming back for the gun. That's why the strap is back."

Nash's curses plagued my ear. "The shooter attacked you?"

"Seems logical," I whispered. "Unless you have another theory?"

"Darlin'..." His tone had gentled and accent thickened, caressing my raw nerves.

"Yes?"

"Do something for me tonight." His voice deepened, low and intimate. "Before you get ready to bed down."

"Yes?"

"Sleep in the office. I know it's not the most comfortable. Or cleanest. But it's a lot safer than Vicki's."

"But I was on my way to tell Vicki about Xi's murder."

"There's only one murder I'm worried about. The one you just came close to experiencing."

I POUNDED on Vicki's bedroom door and let myself in. I felt a Nash-like rant about the pointlessness of personal security when not in use, but I ignored it to focus on other feelings. The lack of any in my arm, for one. And the growing trepidation that not only could one be ninja-attacked in this house without raising an alarm, but the possibility of a gun being fired without being heard.

An issue with well-built mansions, I supposed.

Or perhaps more to do with people who look the other way. Without turning their cheek.

Vicki had to know something.

I stalked through the outer rooms, knocked on her bedroom door, and opened when I didn't hear a protest. Vicki was not in her California King but reclining on a tufted chaise before the fireplace and skimming her thumb over her phone. She waved her hand to shoo me from the room, but I ignored it, determined to demonstrate my fierce goddess within. Who vaguely resembled Julia Pinkerton with a touch of Vicki.

I opened my mouth to speak. She held up a hand and pointed at the white plastic emerging from her ear.

"I can't talk. Maizie's here," she said and paused. "I don't know why."

She shot me her own fierce goddess look, one mixed with the combative narrowing of eyes used by managers and mothers universally.

"What part of 'I can't talk' did you not understand?" she spat and touched her right ear. "What do you want? It's late."

Her brows rose when I didn't answer.

"Me?" My goddess fumbled. "I wasn't sure—"

"Really, Maizie." She tossed her phone on the chaise, ripped the Airpod from her ear, and stood. "What happened to your arm?"

I glanced at my makeshift sling. "You've been invaded."

"Invaded?"

"Maybe burgled. And I was attacked. In your office."

"What would they burgle in the office? I don't use it for anything but meetings. I mean, collaborations."

"I'll be fine, thanks," said my goddess with as much sarcasm as she could muster. "Merely a flesh wound."

"What is that? A Monty Python reference?"

"Why aren't you concerned? You should be calling the police."

Her eyes rounded and she took a step back. "No police."

"Why not?" I barked before I could wince from her seeming lack of empathy. "You don't even know if they stole something. At this moment, they could be burgling the entire house."

"You're in security. Why didn't you trip the alarm?"

Shizzles. Vicki knew why I didn't trip the alarm. I didn't want to literally alarm her guests. Nor did she.

"I checked the house and looked in all the rooms that weren't locked." I was losing this argument. My goddess had returned to her celestial palace and left me to fend off the gaslights.

"I figured as much. And you ran around the house like that." She waved at me.

I wasn't sure if she meant my arm in the makeshift sling or just my state of dress in general.

"I don't have time for this," she continued. "I've got to go."

"Where are you going at this time of night? You're in your pajamas."

She stalked toward her closets. "I need to go the hospital."

I bounded toward her and touched her arm. "Are you sick?"

She reared back, scrunching her perfectly crafted nose. "Do I look sick?"

"Why are you going to the hospital this time of night?"

"Van Vorling was taken to the ER. I don't have time to talk to you." She reached for her closet door. "This is much more important."

"What happened to him?"

"That's why I'm going to the hospital." She slammed the door behind her. "To find out."

THIRTY-FIVE
#WANNABEADULTING

AS THE SLAM of the closet door reverberated, I ran to the chaise and grabbed Vicki's phone. The light had dimmed, but I touched the screen, lighting it up. Her habit of clearing text messages had continued. Nothing to read. But tapping the phone icon for "Recents," I noted the caller. Kevin Yuan.

Why was Vicki speaking to Master Kevin? Lili's number was beneath Master Kevin's. She'd spoken to Vicki just before Kevin.

Both had had time to attack me and call Vicki. I needed both to have an alibi, mainly because of feelings. Which as an investigator, I wasn't supposed to have.

I pressed Kevin's number.

"Vicki, I don't appreciate being hung up on," said Kevin. "Are you ready to talk or do I need to explain what will happen again?"

"What will happen?" I said.

Master Kevin drew in a breath. "Who is this?"

"Maizie." I hesitated but focused on my inner goddess for strength. "Are you threatening Vicki?"

"Why are you on her phone? Is Vicki there?"

"Did you tell her about Vorling?"

"Vorling? The director?" Kevin's voice deepened. "What about Vorling?"

"What's going on between you and Vicki? Why is she scared of you?"

"Look, Maizie, I don't want to involve you in this." Gone was the gentle, patient tones of my teacher. Hostility sharpened his voice. "I told you to stay out of this mess. Don't get pulled into this web."

"Web?" I'd used that word in conjunction with Vicki before, but I didn't like other people flinging it about. Metaphorically or literally. "Explain this web to me, Mr. Yuan. And specifically, how you're connected to it. Or are you also stuck?"

"It's Mr. Yuan now? This is how you treat your old master?"

"How should I treat you? You're suddenly coaching a martial arts mega-star who wants to make movies in America. The value of such a gift is massive, both financially and for your reputation. Vicki brought you here just a few days after Xiáng Xi disappeared. That's more than convenient. Don't you have students and other actors back in LA? How did you get here so quickly?"

"What are you saying, Maizie? You think I have something to do with Xi's death in order to further my career?"

"Don't you mean his murder? I don't know, Mr. Yuan. You tell me." I blinked and two fat tears plopped onto my arm. My goddess didn't approve of crying, so she ignored the little cutting pains in my chest and continued her rant. "I've always trusted you and you don't trust me. What are you doing with my mother?"

Across the room, a door shut. I turned. Dressed for business, Vicki stared at me. "Is that my phone?" She crossed the room and pulled it from my hand. "What happened to your phone? I thought the office was paying those bills. Is this why you didn't call me back today?"

She tapped the speaker icon on the phone. "Is this Mr. Nash? Where are you? Did you not pay the phone bill this month?" She glanced at the phone. "He hung up. Really, Maizie. He's a Neanderthal. I don't understand what you see in him."

"Wasn't Nash," I hissed. "It was Kevin Yuan."

Her eyes widened. "Kevin? What did he want? Why did you answer my phone?"

"I called him."

"At this time of night?"

"You were just talking to him. About what?"

Vicki sniffed. "That is not your concern."

"Argh," I shrieked. "Why won't anyone tell me what's going on?"

"You're a little old for a tantrum." Vicki rolled her eyes. "Honestly, I don't know if you should live with me if you can't respect my privacy."

She spun toward the door with the phone in her hand.

"Visiting hours are over," I called.

"If you enter through the ER, you can visit at any time." She spoke over her shoulder, thumbing through her phone.

"I'm coming with you," I said.

"Fine, Misty's not answering her phone, so I need a driver. Honestly, it's so hard to get help these days."

"Twenty-four-hour availability is unreasonable."

"Uber manages." She glanced over her shoulder to catch my eye. Her sea glass green to mine. "Really, Maizie. Try to keep up with the times."

DRIVING the Escalade took most of my goddess's focus, so she was no help with Vicki. In fact, I had a lot of doubts about the whole inner goddess thing. My people came from Ireland, so who exactly was my goddess? A fairy? Katy Perry's was an Egyptian Aphrodite in "Dark Horse." And Beyonce's goddess was Indian. Or did Coldplay choose hers?

Paganism was so confusing.

While reversing — and trying not to scrape the sides of the

Escalade against the garage door walls — I told (blurted) Vicki that Xiáng Xi had been murdered. Vicki responded by not responding. I had screamed in frustration. She put in both Airpods and ignored me. Therefore, allowing all my concentration to remain on driving — silver lining — but leaving me angry and confused about her lack of interest in all things criminal.

And now we stood in line at the ER desk, for God knew what reason.

Actually, God and Vicki knew. I did not. Which frustrated me even more.

"Why are you sulking?" said Vicki.

"Why aren't you upset about the person who attacked me in your office?" I said when I should've returned to the whole Xiáng Xi murder issue. All the gods had abandoned me and I was stuck with Maizie Albright, slighted child — not adultish enough to truly adult, despite her age.

"There's nothing in that office I'm worried about."

"What about me? I was in the office."

"You said you were fine."

"I said, I'll be fine." I pointed toward my arm. "They used small joint manipulation on my fingers and almost pulled my arm out of its socket."

"Next." The nurse looked up from her computer. "How can I help you?"

"Her arm was almost pulled out of its socket and something about her fingers," said Vicki. "She has health insurance but is presumably not carrying her card. While she's filling out the paperwork, I'm here to see Van Vorling. He came in an hour or two ago after an accident."

The nurse glanced from me to Vicki. "Your daughter is hurt, and you're here to see someone else?"

"Yes." Vicki's eyes narrowed. "Why do you assume she's my daughter?"

"You look alike."

Vicki scoffed.

I reared back. "Are you kidding me? I mean you're blonde and I'm a ginger, but other than that— This better not be about my weight. Your bird-bone DNA did not get passed to me, I got Daddy's big bones—"

"My new skin treatment is supposed to make me look younger, not older. Obviously, I need a word with my esthetician." Vicki shook her head. "Anyway, where's Mr. Vorling?"

The nurse dropped her eyes to her computer, but her mouth played with a smirk. "Let me admit your daughter first."

"I'm fine," I said. "I want to see Mr. Vorling, too. I got put in a compliance hold and it's just going to take a minute for the feeling to come back in my right arm."

"How long has it been numb?" said the nurse.

"You heard her," snapped Vicki. "Mr. Vorling's room number?"

VORLING WAS ASLEEP, as anyone should be at two in the morning. Particularly someone in the hospital with a concussion, multiple contusions, and broken ribs. After I had spoken to the night shift RN, I found Vicki in the waiting room.

"He'll be out in the morning," I told Vicki. "The nurse said he didn't need a room, but Mr. Zhao insisted."

"I should be here when he wakes up." Despite the steel in Vicki's voice, her eyes flitted around the room, betraying her fear.

"You're not involved in this movie. He's not staying at your house. Why are you fretting over Vorling when you should be worried about the actual people staying in your home? Like Xiáng Xi."

Nor worried about me, I thought, but we'd already covered that.

"Master Xi wasn't at my home when he was murdered. I'm

sorry for his family's loss, but he was in Florida. He shouldn't have defected."

"We don't know he defected. If he did, that's still not a reason to be murdered. And by the way, you were also in Florida when he was murdered."

She tilted her chin. "I was brunching with the cast and escorting the Lees to my house."

"Your brunch was twenty-five minutes from Happy Campers RV park where Mr. Xi was killed. The police will take note of that. Don't you see how this looks?"

"If the police think I murdered Xiáng Xi, they're crazy. And I'll have my attorney prove it."

"Your lawyer will prove the Clearwater police are crazy?" I shook my head. "Vicki, it's so obvious you're hiding something or protecting somebody. That's what the police will be after. Why don't you just come clean now before you're indicted as an accomplice?"

"Accomplice? To murder?" She snorted. "Really, Maizie. I have much bigger things to worry about."

"Like what?"

"Van Vorling quit *Unlucky 18*. I have to convince him to return."

"Why? They'll get another director. They haven't started filming."

"It's like you've never spent time in the business." She sighed. "They're rehearsing for God's sake. If they get a new director, it will slow down everything. Pre-production will start over, costing tens, maybe hundreds of thousands if the new director wants major changes. Besides, Vorling is perfect for this picture. He's amazing. Somebody has to protect Lili's interests."

"Again, why you? Let the producers hash this out."

"The Lees asked for my help." She took my hand and patted it. "Perhaps this will be hard to hear, despite your protestations otherwise. I've signed Lili. I'm managing her career. You see, it has to be me."

THIRTY-SIX
#SOPRANOSATDOWNTON

IN MY FOUR-POSTER KING — snuggled between a fluffy duvet and down mattress topper — I stopped debating the time and called Nash.

"Shot?" he barked. "Coming. Now."

"Who was shot?" I sat up, pulling the soft duvet with me.

Rustling and heavy breathing rumbled in my ear. "Albright? I was dreaming—"

"Yes, I'm sorry about the time. I've just come from the hospital—"

"What?"

I flinched at his roar. "Not me. The feeling's come back in my arm and except for the stiffness, I'll be fine. Van Vorling, the director, was hurt. That's why I'm calling, I need help sorting this out."

The heavy breathing slowed. "It couldn't wait?"

"Vorling quit. It's not professional."

"I assume there's more to the story."

"Vicki signed Lili."

"Not surprising." He paused and his voice gentled, "Oh, I get it. I'm sorry, darlin', it must—"

"No, that's not what bothers me. I called Detective Mowry—"

"You called Mowry? At..." He shifted in his bed. "Three in the morning? Over this?"

"It was two, now it's three. And Ian said I could call him anytime."

"I bet he did." Nash cleared his throat. "Why did you call Mowry?"

"Vicki and I assumed Vorling was in a car accident. Everyone was using a driver, but I supposed he might have rented a car. He's German or whatever. They like to drive, I think."

"But he wasn't in a car accident."

"The night nurse said something about his 'fight.' At the time, I was more focused on dealing with Vicki. But now I've had time to process it. Another fight?"

"He's one of those movie-types who gets into fights?"

"That's mostly tabloid-fodder stuff," I said. "But he did fight with Jeff Johnson at the first party. I thought Stanley meant an argument, not fisticuffs."

"Fisticuffs? What century do you live in? If he's in the hospital, someone pounded him, not boxed him."

"You say hinky— Never mind. If he did get in a fight, it wouldn't be hard to understand why the story's been spun into an accident. Vorling quit, though..."

"You think he was made to quit? To not put a bad slant on the movie?"

"That's how I would've interpreted it, except the Lees asked Vicki to convince him to return."

"They're the producers? They call the shots?" More rustling sounded on his end, and I pictured him getting out of bed to pace the room, his processing habit. Although we were five hundred miles apart, it felt comforting to know he'd pace for me, despite the time. "Did Mowry find out what happened? Any reports of bar fights, domestic disputes, or whatever that could have involved Vorling?"

"According to Ian, it's been a quiet night. A DUI and some domestics but just the regulars."

"A quiet night except at the Peanut Mansion, you mean."

"Vorling's not staying there, he's at the Black Pine Resort. I called there, too. And the studio. Nothing to report." I released a deep breath. "I know, hinky, right?"

"Most fights aren't reported or disruptive enough to be called in. Just look at Vicki and her refusal to call the police over a shot to her door," he scoffed. "Why is this disturbing you from your beauty sleep?"

"Vorling's one more person related to *Unlucky 18* who's run into bad luck."

"The second person, Jeff Johnson returned."

"But Vicki was too insistent on speaking to Vorling."

"Insistent is her M.O."

"Like frightened insistent. Not just demanding to make sure Lili's picture is safe. Something is going on."

"There's been a murder. That's a pretty big something."

"But she doesn't care about the murder."

"What kind of person doesn't care about murder? Oh, right, this is Vicki we're talking about."

I ignored the jab, although he had a point. But one for my therapist, not for this conversation. "And there's still the spy issue. And the gun and bullet issue."

He exhaled. "Since you're up, go into my office and I'll walk you through plugging the password into the—"

"I'm not at the office." I flounced against the fluffy pillows and sank further into downy softness. "I convinced Vicki to return to the house. Vorling was asleep—"

"Miss Albright, that house is obviously not safe—"

"Which is why I need to be here. I locked my door." I made a kissing sound. "Thanks for talking me through this. Go back to sleep, we'll talk in the morning."

BREAKFAST HAD A *DOWNTON ABBEY* VIBE — if the Crawley family had hosted Chinese dignitaries. One of Vicki's staff, dressed in traditional black with a white apron, flitted around, pouring coffee and tea. On the buffet, silver chafing dishes held eggs, sausage, and bacon, along with noodles, steamed dumplings, and a kettle of rice congee. The guests had gathered at a long dining table in the large room anchored with a fireplace. Above the fireplace hung an oil painting. Vicki seated regally. I posed before her in a Christian Dior gown.

At eight, it was a little much.

And at any age, it was a little much.

"Where's Vicki?" I said to the server. "Is she coming down?"

"I believe she's still in her room. She said she has a brunch meeting at Black Pine Resort."

Giving me time to eat before I tried to reason with her again. I needed the sustenance for that task.

After generously filling my plate — I was not only a lover of breakfast but a global citizen and felt it my duty to partake in all offerings (or so I told myself) — I surveyed the guests before choosing a seat. On one end, Stanley Wu studied a script while sipping tea. In the middle, Lili thumbed an iPad while Shiyu spoke to her softly, pointing at items on the device. Jeff Johnson, very much alive and not lost, sat next to Lili. At the far end, Master Kevin's gaze flickered to the painting and back. He scowled, then turned to his bowl of congee. I chose a seat as far from Master Kevin as possible. It was too early for faux-father-figure fighting. The Lees were not present. I had a feeling they did room service.

Actually, breakfast was more *Gosford Park* than *Downton Abbey*. Everyone was a suspect I could analyze while they noshed.

Jeff Johnson smirked at me across the table. "Imagine meeting you here. Do you need to check my badge, doll?"

I scowled and he grinned.

"You're Vicki's daughter, Maizie Albright." He winked. "Didn't introduce yourself properly last time. You should've said."

Lili looked up from her iPad. "Have you met Maizie, Jeff? She's rather lovely. Maizie's been a great help to me."

He draped an arm over the back of Lili's chair. "Rather lovely?"

"She found poor Shifu Xi. I'm so sorry for her."

Jeff's eyebrow rose. "Did she now? I'm sorry for her, too."

"All in a day's work," I said, then bit my lip at my callousness. "Under very unfortunate circumstances, though. I was sorry to deliver the news. I'd hoped for a happier report."

"Lili said he was murdered," said Jeff.

Stanley looked up from his script. Shiyu's eyes rounded behind her glasses. Master Kevin rolled his.

I narrowed mine on Jeff. "Yes, he was murdered almost immediately after we talked to him."

"He was killed because you'd talked to him, then?" Jeff cocked his head. "That is terrible."

"Maybe because he was speaking to us, yes," I used Julia Pinkerton's sharp, flinty "I'm coming for you, you obnoxious creep and possible killer" voice. "Or someone didn't want him talking."

"Must have been an interesting conversation, then."

"We shouldn't be speaking about Shifu Xi like this," said Shiyu.

"No worries." Jeff stood and deposited a kiss on the top of Lili's head. "I'm going to work out."

Lili gazed up at Jeff and captured his hand in hers. "I'll be up soon. Master Kevin's choreographing some stage combat for Stanley and me."

"Cool. Maybe I can follow your moves."

"You also do martial arts, Jeff?" I said, shoving his name higher on my mental "highly suspicious" list. "Do you know compliance holds?"

"Shaolin training is something we have in common," said Lili. "Jeff's a great sparring partner."

"Interesting." I studied Jeff, wishing I had gotten a visual on my attacker.

"You want to spar with me?" Jeff smirked. "Or was your kung fu just for show?"

"She was a moderately successful student." Master Kevin's eyebrows rose as he shot me a look.

"Gee, thanks," I said.

"You're welcome to join us, Maizie," said Lili. "Today, we will brainstorm choreography. Mr. Vorling was going to watch so he can block it later."

"Yes, let's meet in thirty minutes," said Master Kevin. "We will talk about the scene first so our breakfast can settle."

"Speaking of Mr. Vorling, has anyone heard how he's doing?" I stared at Jeff. "Has the police spoken to anyone about his *accident*?"

"He recuperates for a few days," said a deep voice behind me. "Then he will return."

I turned in my chair. Mr. Zhao stood in the doorway. He spoke to the room, but his eyes were on Jeff Johnson, who still hovered behind Lili.

"Vorling's back to directing?" I said. "Vicki already spoke to him? That's good news."

"He never left *Unlucky 18*." Zhao's gaze dropped to Lili. "I made sure of it. We need to talk."

Shiyu narrowed her eyes at Zhao. "Lili's very busy."

"That is true. Mr. Zhao, if you need to speak to me, you can make an appointment through Shiyu." Standing up, Lili grabbed Jeff's hand. "We'll leave you to your breakfast, Maizie."

"I need also need to warm up. My abilities are far from moderately successful and they're all staged," said Stanley, pushing back from the table. "Adieu, all."

Zhao stepped backward as the five filed from the room.

"Coffee?" asked the maid, and he nodded.

Taking the delicate cup and saucer, Zhao moved toward the

door, then stopped and returned to the table. "Vicki Albright is your mother."

I bobbed my head.

"How well does she know the Lees?"

"Honestly, I'm not sure. Vicki doesn't talk to me about business. Why?"

Taking his time, Zhao sipped his coffee, set it carefully on the saucer, and placed his hands on the table to lean toward me. "As her daughter, perhaps you can advise her anyway. If the Lees know she has made the contract to manage Lili, they will want to negotiate their own contract."

"To produce Lili's future films?"

He nodded. "Ms. Albright should not make any agreements with the Lees. She doesn't understand who they are."

"I don't understand. Can you be clearer? Just who are the Lees?"

Zhao's dark eyes flickered to the door and back to me. "Important people. Powerful people."

"Like Big Five studio powerful? Or like streaming service powerful? Because Netflix and Amazon are almost as big as Paramount and—"

"Different powerful." He muttered in Chinese, casting his gaze once again to the door, then looked back at me. "Just tell her to not make the deal with the Lees."

"I don't get it. You're the associate producer. You brought the Lees on for this picture."

He shrugged. "They have the money. And in China, the laws for financing foreign films have changed. With the Lees, we can work around."

"Workaround?"

"They can get the…how do you say?" He glanced up at the ceiling. "Legal loopholes for this picture."

When playing with millions of dollars in the film industry, legal loopholes were necessary. I understood that. I also had no clue as to the rules and laws of Chinese foreign funding, other than it had essentially dried up in Hollywood. I thought they had gotten the "workaround" by creating a US-Chinese partnership.

But the legal loophole he implied felt more...criminal than that.

The Lees owned casinos. So did mobsters. Or at least they did in the 50s. Images of Warren Beatty in *Bugsy* flashed through my mind. Did Bugsy Siegel back movies or had he just been friends with the movie stars?

Holy shiplap, Vicki. If the Lees were in a crime family, what was she doing with them in her house?

Maybe befriending mobsters was trending. It had during the Golden Age. George Raft grew up with Bugsy Siegel. Many studio actors and producers — Clark Gable, Gary Cooper, Cary Grant, Louis B. Mayer, Jack Warner — had been buddies with him. Sinatra and the Rat Pack, too. And what about in the 70s? Had there been a Hollywood story in Scorsese's *Casino*?

I briefly closed my eyes, trying to remember.

Master Xi had chosen the name of Bruce Lee's character in *The Way of the Dragon*. And Tang Lung had been fighting the mob. Xi could have used the name Tang Lung as a call for help.

My lids flew open. Or Master Xi had just been a Bruce Lee fan. Why was I trying to guess at the Lees' legal loopholes through mobster movies?

But if organized crime was Hollywood cool again, of course, they'd flock to foreign syndicates. American crime would be too pedestrian. *The Sopranos* had made the mafia too American, unfortunately. And everyone knew not to mess with the Latino gangs, thanks to *Narcos*.

Now a Korean crime organization would do well, what with the current popularity of K-pop and K-dramas. Korean movies were hot.

I wondered if Korea had organized crime. Japan had the yakuza, surely...

I blinked, realizing Mr. Zhao had continued talking.

"I try to prevent Lili from doing more films with the Lees. But *Unlucky 18*?" He shrugged. "The Lees are happy. They'll have their names attached to a famous movie. It's good for them. Then they need to be finished with Hollywood. At least with Lili, anyway."

"Do the Lees know how you feel?" I chewed my lip. Wasn't Mr. Zhao worried?

I was jumping to conclusions. I did that. Organized crime was a big conclusion from which to jump, and I had a fondness for Scorsese and Guy Ritchie.

"It doesn't matter how I feel. I'm supporting Lili now, but I want to protect her future." Zhao shrugged. "I don't like this new management with Albright. I will work with her but only without the Lees. Can Vicki Albright finance future projects?"

"Who knows?" I said bitterly. "I have no idea what she's capable of."

A squeak sounded from the hall. We flinched and turned toward the door. The parquet near the threshold had been fitted too tightly and sang when someone stepped on it. I pushed away from the table, but Mr. Zhao moved to the door before I could stand. He leaned toward the edge of the doorway, held out a coffee spoon, and angled it back and forth.

He looked back at me. "Too many people in this house. We say '*Géqiángyou'er,*' the walls have ears." Winking, he tossed me the spoon, then sped out of the room.

And didn't he tell Lili the walls literally had ears until Nash removed the bugs?

Too many people indeed. People I didn't know and didn't trust.

Including Mr. Zhao who knew how to check around corners using a spoon.

THIRTY-SEVEN
#HEAVYMETALMELTDOWN

I LEFT THE DINING ROOM, seeking Vicki, while keeping my eye out for whoever had been listening to our conversation. Vicki's scheming had always stayed within a gray zone of ethics but had not crossed the line into illegalities. That I knew of. But still, consorting with powerful people who owned casinos slid her Manolo Blahnik-clad toe over that fuzzy line. For what?

Okay, for a chance to get involved in major-motion-picture-superstardom-money.

Something that would tempt many a toe to slide.

I hurried through the foyer past the aquarium — ignored Charles — and up the grand stairway toward Vicki's wing. I halted on the gallery overlooking the foyer, then glanced behind me. Someone stood half-hidden behind a gallery pillar close to the guest wing stairs.

Jeff Johnson.

Watching or reading something on his phone. Had he been the ears outside the dining room? He was our number one suspect for bugging the trailer and the house. Even Mr. Zhou thought so. Nothing came up in our reports about him. It was almost like his history had been wiped clean. Even his pre-Lili Facebook posts appeared fake. To me, anyway.

Looking up, Jeff spotted Lili and Stanley traipsing down the stairs. Shoving his phone in his pocket, he joined their descent. All dressed for the gym.

Shiyu wasn't with them, but likely did business in her room or Lili's. Zhao had disappeared. Master Kevin had gone to the gym already. The Lees had yet to appear.

I followed them, keeping my distance.

They disappeared inside, and I stood at the door, hesitating and wondering what I could learn from watching them practice. Behind me, hearing a noise, I turned.

Shiyu rounded the corner and stopped, placing a hand on her chest. She was also dressed to work out. "What are you doing?"

"Deciding if I should go in and warm up with everyone." I shrugged. "I'm out of shape and unmotivated to do something about it. But hearing everyone at breakfast inspired me. I miss my old practices with Master Kevin."

Not a total lie.

She smiled. "Wushu strengthens your mind and body. It's a great sport but requires a lot of discipline."

"Do you also train? You know kung fu?"

"Lili wanted an assistant with whom she could also spar. It was important to her." Shiyu cast her eyes to her sneakers. "Of course, I'm not nearly as good."

"Did you train with Master Xi?"

"Sometimes."

"You must miss him. It's horrible what's happened. Lili seems glad to have Jeff back to comfort her, but it must be hard for you, too." I watched her shoulders droop. "So odd how everyone was in Florida when it happened. Was Jeff also with Lili then?"

"At the Lees' condo?" Her eyes widened. "No."

"Did he mention where he went when he disappeared?"

"No."

"I take it from your tone, there was something odd about his disappearance?"

She pressed her lips together but seemed to grudgingly relent. "I don't think he was looking for Master Xi."

"What do you think he was doing?" I murmured.

"Meeting with someone." She dodged a glance behind her. "Maybe. I don't know."

"Another woman?"

She shrugged.

"Has he been spying on Lili?"

She blinked at me behind her glasses. "Why would you say that?"

"Because of the equipment we've found. At the trailer. And in the house. Don't worry, we removed it."

"Do you think I should tell Lili?" She twisted her hands together, winced, and slipped her hands to her sides.

I thought about Zhou and Lili's argument. "She might already know. Although she doesn't want to believe it. How could she? To suspect her boyfriend is..." I deliberately paused, waiting to see if Shiyu would fill in the blank.

She didn't.

"Cheating," I finished lamely.

"Do you know something about him?" she said. "You're an investigator, right?"

"I'm going to find out." I held out my right hand. "Thanks, Shiyu."

She held out her left, keeping her right hand close to her side. I awkwardly switched to my left, wondering if I had made a cultural mistake, and gingerly shook her hand. Then bowed just to be safe.

I opened the gym door, peeking inside. Master Kevin swiveled around and caught my gaze. He gave me the "watching you" horns. I stumbled back and waved for Shiyu to move around me.

"You're not coming in?"

"Not today. I've got to see..." Was there a point in speaking to

Vicki? "Van Vorling. Check on his recovery. Tell Lili I'll give him her best."

I closed the door after her and moved down the hall. Talking to Van Vorling was a good idea. I could thank Shiyu for prompting me to that action. Maybe he'd reveal what had happened to him.

What was the point in trying to talk to Vicki? She wouldn't tell me if the Lees were tied to criminal activity. I'd need an interpreter to question the Lees. The little research I'd done had mostly been translated magazine articles and websites. Their casinos were beautiful as were their homes, cars, yachts, and private planes. Unless Nash knew someone in law enforcement who might tip us, I wasn't finding any dirt on them.

But if the Lees were criminals, did I want to tip law enforcement toward Vicki? What if she were innocent? What if they were innocent and I'd completely misconstrued Zhao's comments? His English wasn't great. I had been speculating based on movie portrayals of casino owners.

But Xiáng Xi had been murdered. And the Clearwater police said it looked like a professional hit. I'd seen the hole in his forehead.

That hole haunted the little sleep I'd had last night.

I should relay my conversation with Mr. Zhao to Nash so he could tell Clearwater police. But I needed real evidence, not gossip. We'd hit a dead-end in research. But our resident spy had given me an idea about how to learn more about Vicki's guests.

Even if she were guilty, I had to protect Vicki. The Lees would be a means to an end for her. She would look the other way if it meant getting a leg up from producing cable-TV movies to big pictures. I didn't need Kevin Yuan breaking my heart by telling me what I'd already recognized. But I knew Vicki wasn't evil, just weak despite her strong resolve. It wasn't the fame or even the money that attracted her to the industry now. Outside politics, finance, and tech, the most powerful women in the world congregated in entertainment. She wanted on that list.

And I no longer held her back from moving up those ladders.

I didn't have the talent or ambition to drive her further in the industry. If I'd remained an actress, Vicki might have been content managing my career and producing my B-movies and TV shows. In some ways, this was my fault. I'd turned my back on her, leaving her at her own career crossroads. Without me holding her back, there was now a path toward greater opportunities in entertainment. Ironically, following me to Black Pine had helped shine a light on a new inroad. More movies were now made in Georgia than in California or New York.

And it seemed, even in the tough terrain of entertainment, she might have found a thorny fast track. Possibly one paved in dirty money.

IN THE BACK of the Escalade, I kept my hand cupped around the speaker, hoping Misty couldn't hear me. "Have you met with the Clearwater detective yet?"

"What's all that noise?" said Nash.

"I asked Misty to play the satellite radio's heavy metal channel so she couldn't listen in on my conversation," I whispered. "I'm on the way to the office to pick up some tech."

"I thought I recognized Ozzy," said Nash. "It looks like I'll be staying longer. The detective wants me to accompany him in an attempt to get a search warrant for the Peanut Mansion."

Anxiety gnawed at my chest. "All the way in Georgia? Can Clearwater police do that?"

"If the detective can show probable cause he can find evidence for Xi's murder, you bet." Nash paused. "There's a federal agent on the case now, too, so I don't think we'll have trouble with warrants."

"Is the FBI going to investigate Vicki?" I gasped. Had they already figured out an organized crime connection?

"They're investigating the death of a Chinese citizen in the US. One who stayed at Vicki's a week before he was murdered."

"It is possible," I whispered, "the Lees are connected to organized crime."

I waited for Nash (and Ozzy) to stop shouting. "The detective knows they have a condo in Clearwater," I continued. "But why would they put out a hit on a kung fu trainer?"

"Crime bosses?" said Nash. "In Vicki's house? Sumbitch, this is some murky pond she's wallowing in."

"Mr. Zhao didn't say they're crime bosses. They used legal loopholes for funding. They own a casino. I put two-and-two together with the murder looking like a professional hit."

Nash quieted. Or I couldn't hear him. Korn had replaced Ozzy.

"Did you hear me?"

"Okay, it's conjecture." He paused. "What tech?"

"Do we have night vision camera kits and an NVR for continuous recording?"

"A client wants that installed? Can it wait until I get back?"

"Not really."

"Miss Albright?"

"I want to plant hidden cameras all over the Peanut Mansion. These people won't tell me what I need to know, but they could be talking amongst themselves. Or at least I might catch something shady. Maybe Vicki doesn't know—"

"That's illegal. We're professional. We don't break laws. Besides, spy cameras in a house that might hold organized crime figures? Are you nuts? Do you want to get whacked?"

"Remember we don't know they're mobsters. You said it's conjecture."

I switched ears as my right had lost its hearing due to Nash and Korn.

"And I have the legal issue covered," I continued. "I'm going to get Vicki to sign a waiver for the cameras under a new security agreement. If Vicki's distracted, I can get her to sign without thinking."

"Also illegal," he snarled. "How did you think you were going to install all that without anyone seeing you?"

"Get the girls to help me."

"The girls?"

"Tiffany and Rhonda. I thought they could act as a lookout. Create a diversion if needed. We did that in *Julia Pinkerton, Teen Detective*. Season Five, Episode Three, 'To Catch Some Thieves.' Julia and friends were after a black-market ring—"

"These Hollywood people are making you crazy. That is the dumbest—" He cut off his words. I could feel the irritation rolling off him. He was pacing again.

"Miss Albright." He was more than irritated. I could probably kiss ocean-view hotel rooms goodbye. At least for the immediate future. "Move out of that house. Your safety concerns me more than Vicki's. She's made her bed. And the last thing you need is to get busted for hidden camera charges."

"Look at that, we've arrived at the office," I jabbered. "I'll have to get back to you later? And looks like we have a customer."

"Did you hear me?" he yelled.

I held the phone up to the speaker and let Slipknot thrash in his ear. "Can't hear you very well. Gotta go."

THIRTY-EIGHT
#BLACKPINECONFIDENTIAL

A PERHAPS-CUSTOMER DID STAND in front of the Albright Security Solutions office. A youngish woman with her dark hair pulled into a ponytail. Not the usual look of our clientele with her jeans and ski jacket. She glanced over her shoulder, spotted me, and turned to wait. I rushed to the door to unlock it, tossing apologies and introductions as the bell chimed.

"What can I do for you?" I said. "We're out in the field today. Normally we take appointments rather than walk-ins. I'm glad you caught me."

"I'm Annie." She held out her hand for me to shake. "I wanted to look around."

"Okay?"

"Go on about your business." She waved me forward. "I just wanted to see inside. Every time I've come by it's been locked."

A frown puckered my eyebrows and I quickly smoothed it. "You don't need anything?"

"I'm good." She smiled.

"I just need to get something from the back room. I'll be right out." Was it safe to leave her alone? Was she some sort of reporter? Private investigator-stalker? "If you've wondered what a PI office looks like, it's not as exciting as the movies."

She laughed. "No kidding."

"Okay, then." I zipped into our back office and gathered equipment. No night vision kits. Only doorbell cameras. I grabbed as many as could fit in a duffel bag and tossed several laptops in my backpack. Seized our tool kit and shot out the door.

Annie stood gazing out the front window. "Seems kind of slow."

"Depends. We do a lot of entertainment-related cases now." I bounced on my toes. "Anything else I can do for you?"

"It was nice to meet you." Annie bobbed her head. "I can see you're busy."

"Sorry, but I really am." I opened the front door and ushered her out. Locking up, I glanced back. Annie climbed into a Jeep. Waving, I hurried to the Escalade and climbed in.

Weird, but weird was not unusual for me. "Misty, I need to go to Black Pine Resort. Would you mind dropping this stuff off at the house?"

"I'm not a pack mule, just a driver," said Misty.

"Not an ask, more of an order," I snapped. Then blushed. And began mentally preparing for my meeting with Van Vorling.

CHEY TYRONE, Lili's costar, also stayed at Black Pine Resort. Only knowing Van Vorling peripherally, I asked Chey to accompany me on my "sick visit." One in which I hoped Mr. Vorling would explain how he received his injuries.

Black Pine Resort was for local business people what Chateau Marmont was for Hollywood insiders. Besides having a highly rated hotel with cottages and fine dining, the grounds also held Black Pine's social club hosting two golf courses, pools, tennis, a yacht club, and private dining. Wheeling and dealing happened in all parts of the club from the links to the pool bar. Black Pine Club and Resort occupied a major share of the town's lakefront property (Daddy's property took another share which irked some of the newer residents since private docks were few and far between.).

Now that the entertainment industry had moved to town, the resort's hotel had become a hot spot. A business lunch in the vicinity of a possible celebrity sighting always helped sales. Parking was becoming an issue. Misty stopped before the sprawling hotel's stone and oak portico.

"I've got to take the Lees to the studio and wait for them there," said Misty. "You're on your own."

"No worries," I said. "I'm perfectly capable of ordering a ride."

"I wasn't worried." Misty rolled down the window and gunned the motor. I hopped onto the curb before she flattened my toes.

The glass front doors swished open. I strolled through and waited for Chey before the massive stone fireplace, enjoying the heat against the day's chill. My phone chirped. Nash had texted to apologize for getting angry and wanted me to call him. I glanced up, spotted Chey carrying paper cups, and shoved my phone in my pocket.

Chey greeted me with obligatory air kisses. I rescued one of the three cups he held, and we took the elevator to the top-level suites. The phone weighted my pocket, but I wanted more information before speaking to Nash.

"I'm worried about Van," said Chey. "I just spoke to Lili. She said he threatened to leave the picture, but Mr. Zhao talked him back into directing."

"What do you think happened to Mr. Vorling?" I said. "It wasn't a car accident. The nurse said a fight, but a fight with whom? Jeff Johnson again?"

"I thought that was just an argument." Chey glanced at me, then stared at the cups he gripped in both hands. "Vorling's got debts. He's only tied to the picture as director. No producer credits. He's got no cha-ching for backing."

"I heard. Do you think this fight was related to gambling?"

"I hope not. This so-called accident makes me wonder who he owes."

"Do you mean the Lees?"

"I imagined somebody more local. Break your kneecaps kind of stuff. When you're an addict, you get sucked into some weird shit." He gave me a sidelong glance. "Maybe he got into a poker game with some hillbillies."

"This is Black Pine, not Arkansas," I said defensively, then sucked in a breath. "Is he gambling here? It's illegal in Georgia."

"There are Indian casinos just north of here." He studied me. "What about the Lees? What did you mean?"

I still wasn't sure about the Lees and they were funding the picture that could be Chey's (latest) breakout performance. I couldn't throw him off his A-game. "I heard Vorling's directing *Unlucky 18* as a favor to them. The Lees own casinos in Macau where he gambles. Do you know why Vorling argued with Lili's boyfriend?"

Chey shrugged. "Something happened at the studio. Not on set, but Johnson was nosing around the offices. Then Johnson accused him of something."

"That's weird, right?"

"Yeah, but the fault is with Lili." He rolled his eyes. "She's giving Johnson a lot of access for a boyfriend."

"Is she or is he just taking advantage?"

"Good question."

The elevator doors slid open. In the hall, housekeeping pushed a cart. We moved toward Vorling's suite, switching our conversation to everyday chitchat. The maids had paused in their duties to watch us. Chey tossed them his winning smile. We pressed the bell on Vorling's door, and he opened it for Chey.

Vorling looked like he'd been run over by a truck. One with fat tires and a big engine.

"We wanted to see if you needed anything," I said. "And to talk."

Vorling nodded curtly and waved us inside. Taking the hot

tea Chey handed him, he hobbled toward the couch and lowered himself, wincing. I exchanged raised brows with Chey.

"Van," said Chey. "I met Maizie in rehab. She understands where I'm coming from when I say I think you need to get professional help."

"The hospital has given me what I need." Vorling shook his head. "I've got to work."

"You're no good to the film if your mind is somewhere else," said Chey. "Especially if you're thinking about where to find a game or if you're chasing your losses. Believe me, I get it. The painkillers will mess with your head, too. Take some time, while you're healing anyway, and get some help."

Sighing, Vorling stared at his hands in his lap. "I'll take a few days off, then I will return."

"Do you want to talk to my sponsor? No judgment. He's a great guy—"

Vorling cut him off with a wave of his hand. "I will be fine. I just need some rest."

I studied him while he sipped his tea. He didn't just look battered, Vorling seemed mentally beaten.

"Who hurt you?" I asked. "We'll keep it confidential. And I can get you protection. I know a local police detective who—"

"No police."

"Sure, Van," said Chey, giving me a look. "Maizie just wants you to feel safe."

"What about my partner?" I said. "Nash is a great bodyguard, and he's good at keeping his mouth shut. And because we work for Vicki—"

"Vicki Albright?" Vorling spat. "Get out."

I felt the blood rush from my cheeks. "What did she do?"

"Maizie," said Chey. "We had different addictions. Maybe it's better for me to stay with Van. You go on. I've got this."

"What's Vicki doing?" I persisted. "Did someone threaten you?"

Vorling turned his head and stared at the other side of the room.

I reluctantly rose, casting Chey an apologetic look. "Mr. Vorling, I'm sorry to cause you more distress, but I need to know what's going on. Vicki's my mother."

"I'm sorry to hear it," he said. "Very unfortunate for you. For that reason alone, get out."

THIRTY-NINE
#GARYCOOPERING

INSIDE THE ELEVATOR, I called Nash. "What did the federal agent say?"

"They're going to speak to a more international branch of the government about the Lees. To determine what connections they might have."

I sucked in a breath. "CIA? Vicki's going to be on a spook list?"

"He didn't say CIA. They're not suspected terrorists. Just suspected crooks. Right?"

"Oh God, it keeps getting worse," I moaned. "I just left Van Vorling's room. He hates my mother. And me by proxy."

"He just needs to get to know you," said Nash gently. "Don't feel bad."

"What does that mean?"

"You sounded— Never mind."

"I thought someone beat Vorling up and now I know it. Chey thinks it's related to gambling, and it could be. But I'm worried someone was hired to bust his kneecaps."

"For what purpose?"

"He threatened to quit *Unlucky 18*."

"I thought that was because someone busted his kneecaps."

"The timeline is as vague as the reason he was pummeled."

"Don't guess. Only make inferences from facts."

"Last night Vicki was desperate to get to the hospital to speak to Vorling," I said. "To convince him not to quit the film for Lili's sake. In the middle of the night, which made no sense."

"You're surmising Vicki heard Vorling was quitting, hired someone to scare him into sticking with the movie, then went to the hospital to make certain he did just that. Am I hearing this right?"

I chewed my thumbnail, considering. It did sound a little too *Goodfellas* for Vicki.

"You're reading too much into this," he said slowly. "We don't even know there's an organized crime connection. Maybe you're making these links because—"

"I'm not jealous of Lili," I cried. "I don't miss Vicki helicoptering all over my career. I just wished she'd shown me the kind of affection she does that fish."

I sucked in a breath and mentally face-palmed. *Slow your roll, Maizie.* Of all the times to trip.

"Okay, then," Nash drawled. "I'm going to reflect on some other motives for Vorling's accident and get back to you later."

"Sounds good," I said in my cheeriest imitation of a sane person. "Enjoy."

Getting off the elevator, I shoved my hands in the pockets of my puffy coat and focused on not focusing on my mother. At the front door, I remembered Misty wasn't waiting. I circled back into the lobby, parking my boots before the fire, and dialed up ye olde Uber. My neck prickled. I glanced over my shoulder. Didn't see anyone I recognized. I shrugged off the feeling and thought about my plans for bugging the Peanut Mansion.

My skin crawled again. I tapped the camera app on my phone, set it to selfie-mode, and held it an angle to capture the room behind me. Clusters of people passed, chatting with each other. At the end of the lobby, a figure stood in the corner, then darted into the bar. Too quick and too far away, I couldn't catch a good picture. My instincts prodded me into hurrying toward the bar.

Inside, a sizable crowd lunched on high-top tables. A few people loitered at the bar. I walked through, self-conscious and feeling silly. My fuzzy snapshot revealed someone with dark hair and a dark coat. Half the people in the bar fit that description. I exited out on the other side of the lobby and circled around to the front door.

Under the portico, I huddled against the chill and checked my phone for the status of my ride. A silver sedan pulled up. Leaving the motor running, the driver hopped out and came around to open the passenger door. "Ms. Albright?"

"You're Juan?" I studied the driver, a young guy with a neck tattoo and light brown beard.

The kid yanked his ski cap lower over his dishwater blonde hair. "Yeah."

"Hang on." I looked at my phone. "You're not a gray Toyota. This is a gray Nissan."

"Wife's car," said the man. "Mine's in for repairs."

"You have a wife?" I backed up a step. "Not that I'm judging, but I don't see a ring."

He glanced at his hand and shrugged. "I cheat so I take it off. Go on, get in."

Could you trust an honest cheater? "Look, I'll still pay for the ride, but I'm not comfortable—"

"You're Ms. Albright, right? I don't got all day." His voice dropped into a growl, "Just get in the car."

Darting forward, he grabbed my elbow. I twisted out of his grip. My lips parted to scream and he opened his jacket, showing me his holstered gun. I choked off my scream.

"Don't be stupid. I'm not messing around."

"But—" How could I get mugged in front of Black Pine's premier guest facilities?

A car motored to the sidewalk. I glanced over my shoulder. A gray Toyota. Juan. Here to give me a ride, not knowing I could possibly get him killed.

"I'll get in," I said. "Let me tell the Uber to move on."

"I'll tell him. You get in."

I ducked inside and poised on the passenger seat. Not-Juan slammed the door shut and moved around the front of the car. He wasn't going to tell Juan to move on. Which was good as I didn't want Juan to get shot.

Not-Juan rounded the front of the car. Someone hollered. I looked out the back window. Juan had gotten out of his car to yell at Not-Juan.

"That's my ride," called Juan. "What are you doing?"

Oh, shiz. Juan was going to get himself shot. And this was why Nash was always harping on me to carry my .38.

I popped the door and hopped out of the car. "Juan, it's okay. I'll still pay you."

"I came all the way from the other side of town."

"She said she'd still pay you," said Not-Juan. "Chill. Easy money."

"It's the principle of the thing," said Juan. "Why'd she order a ride if she's not going to take it? It's rude, man."

"Dude, don't mess with me," said not-Juan.

"Don't mess with him, Juan," I pleaded. "Just get out of here. Report me. That would be good."

"Shut up," said not-Juan. "Get back in the car."

"Is he harassing you, lady?" said Juan. "Is this a domestic situation? Are you in trouble?"

I bobbed my head, then shook it. "Juan, I wouldn't tick this guy off."

Juan cocked his head. "He's carrying?"

I glanced behind me. Not-Juan had eased his jacket open, standing with his hands on his hips like we were reenacting *High Noon*. "Shiplap."

"Juan. Go," I said. "I'll be fine."

"No, ma'am. I was raised right. I'm not abandoning you." Juan unzipped his coat, exposing his shoulder holster.

"That's against Uber policy," said Not-Juan.

"Hard to enforce what they don't know," said Juan. "Ma'am, get into my car."

I hesitated. Juan was Gary Coopering. Not-Juan was doing a good imitation of Frank Miller and not backing down. I'd have to out-Gary Cooper Juan's Gary Cooper.

Putting my back to Not-Juan, I faced Juan and made the international sign for phone and 9-1-1 against my puffy coat. "I appreciate your help. I'll be fine." I exaggerated the widening of my eyes and glanced at the hotel, hoping he'd get my hint. "You're getting a five-star from me, that's for sure."

Juan watched my hand signal, then shook his head. "No, ma'am. Not letting you get in that car."

"Hells." I looked to the sky for help. A handgun blasted behind me. I spun around. Not-Juan had ducked behind the car, his handgun pointing toward Juan.

"Lady, get down," yelled Juan. "Get out of the way."

I swiveled around. Gripping his arm, Juan dropped behind the door of his car.

"This is Black Pine Resort," I screamed. "Where's the valet?"

FORTY
#HOLDINGOUTFORAHERO

I SANK onto the curb and backed against the running car. A siren screamed in the distance. Someone had reported the gunshot. Where was everyone? I glanced over my shoulder, searching for a doorman or valet. Concierge. I'd even take a bartender. Wasn't anyone in Black Pine Resort interested in helping us?

Another shot rang out.

"Juan?" I called.

"Not me."

"Are you okay?"

"I'm fine. Ma'am, please stay down and get away from the damn car."

I peeped through the passenger window. Not-Juan scuttled to the driver-side door and yanked it open. Juan was right. Time to move. I crab-walked toward the closest pillar. Ducked behind it and dialed Detective Ian Mowry.

"Shooting at Black Pine Resort in front of the hotel," I said when he answered. "My Uber driver, Juan, was shot."

"Not shot," yelled Juan. "Lady, get over here."

The Nissan's engine roared and the tires squealed on the pavement.

"Juan's got some kind of white knight complex," I said. "And Not-Juan is getting away."

"Maizie?" said Mowry. "The 10-72? That's your shooting?"

"Very likely considering this is Black Pine. I hear sirens. Someone's on their way. Just giving you more info." I rose and ran toward the front doors. A crowd stood in front of the glass watching. The front doors wouldn't open. "Shooter is a young male. Light brown hair. Beard. Neck tattoo. Beanie. Driving an older gray Nissan. Let me get the license—" I squinted at the car, but a black cloud plumed from the exhaust, obscuring the plate. "Shizzles, he needs an oil change or something."

"Maizie, just get to cover," shouted Mowry.

"He's getting away," I crept to the door. "Someone knew I was here. I want to know who and why they wanted to pick me up."

"We'll get him," said Mowry. "Just stay put. Calm down. Let me see what I hear on the radio."

"I feel calm for a witness to a shootout."

"Wasn't a shootout," said Juan, walking over to me. "Please note I didn't shoot back."

"I've got you covered, Juan." I returned my mouth to the phone. "Ian, Juan's a hero. Please tell the reporting officer that he may be armed but he didn't do anything. And he will lay his piece down."

"Hang on, Maizie," said Mowry.

I waved at the onlookers. Made the international sign to unlock the doors. They waved back and shook their heads.

"They won't want you coming inside and disrupting the guests," said Juan.

"I'm not the one with the gun." Juan and I stared at the crowd. They stared back through the locked front doors.

"I blame the valet," said Juan. "They're supposed to be out here helping the guests. If the valet had talked to your boyfriend first, this wouldn't have happened."

"He wasn't my boyfriend. I have no idea who he was."

"Sounds like the incident is over," said Mowry, back on the

line. "Resort security called it in. They're coming around to meet you. Do you need me there, hon'?"

"I think we're good."

Juan bounced on his toes, glancing from the door to the parking lot. I patted his arm. "Security is coming around to meet us."

Juan returned my smile with a nervous grin.

"Where's Nash?" said Mowry.

"Florida. He'll be back soon. When I had you check into Vorling's accident, did I tell you we were involved in a murder down there—" I looked at Juan.

He'd blanched. The bouncing had turned to a backward creeping.

"Lord, Maizie," said Mowry.

"Not involved-involved. Nash is working with Clearwater police. I'll call you back, Ian." I shoved my phone in my pocket. "It's okay, Juan. I'm a private investigator."

"You should've told me when I was willing to take a bullet for you."

"That's so sweet." I reached to hug him. The stiffness and immovability of his body made it difficult. I gave him a quick pat and pulled back. "I'm sorry Juan. By the time, I figured out the guy wasn't Juan, you were in danger. I wanted to protect you."

"Protect me?" Juan reared back. "With what?"

"Quick wits?"

Juan gave me a look. "Why is someone trying to kidnap you?"

"Good question." I had no idea who sent Not-Juan. But he knew my name. Actually, only my last name. I bit my lip. "Kind of weird he kept calling me Ms. Albright, right?"

"I can't say. I've never been involved in something like this before."

"I mean, most people call me Maizie. Except for Mr. Nash and he calls me Miss Albright."

"I don't know him. I also don't know you."

"But people do call Vicki, my mother, Ms. Albright."

"I don't know her either." Juan folded his arms over his chest. "Lady, what are you trying to say? That dude was trying to kidnap your mother and got you instead?"

"Oh, God. Vicki had a brunch meeting here. And Misty had to drive the Lees. Maybe that car was for Vicki." I searched the crowd in the doorway for Vicki. "I don't see her. Juan, this is bad. Really bad."

I pressed her number and received an auto-text she was in a meeting. I tapped my phone again to redial. After the second auto-text, and third redial, she picked up.

"Do you not understand the meaning of those texts, Maizie? I'm in a meeting. I mean, collaboration. Has someone died?"

"No," I whispered and slipped the phone back in my pocket. "That was her, Juan. She hung up on me. But it means she's fine."

"Don't cry, ma'am." Juan patted my arm. "Your mother is okay. Maybe he just wanted to kill you, after all."

FORTY-ONE
#SURPRISENOTSURPRISE

IF YOU'VE NEVER GIVEN witness testimony to a shooting — particularly when you're not just an innocent bystander and you're also a witness to a murder in another state — be prepared for the questioning to take a great chunk out of your day. I felt so bad for Juan that I paid for pretend rides to make up for his lost afternoon's income.

Black Pine Police had caught Not-Juan and learned — surprise, not surprise — he was an "independent contractor" with loose ties to "organized crime." Not-Juan didn't specialize either. If your money was good, he'd take it. And do whatever.

Not-Juan was easygoing like that.

He also had no idea which Albright he was meant to take to an abandoned garage.

Ian Mowry had pulled me aside after the official questioning. "Ms. Albright could very well mean *you*. This isn't the first time someone's tried to kill you. The career you've chosen is full of lunatics."

"Nash is not a lunatic," I'd said.

"I was talking about clients. Although the man has issues. I tried to warn you." He waved aside the statement at my blush.

"Why don't you work for DeerNose? Corporate and retail investigations is a growing field."

"My father and I aren't speaking." I stared at my shoes. It'd only been a few days since I'd seen Remi and I missed her like a phantom limb. "And anyway, I have a job."

"At least keep a low profile at Boomer's until we find out who the perp's working for."

"I'm living at Vicki's now."

"Maizie, is that a good idea? You thought the guy was trying to kidnap your mother. Not only does she deny it, but she also refuses to have us check on her. We can only send a cruiser to make rounds."

"Exactly why I need to be there, Ian."

Ian had turned a mottled scarlet, opened his mouth, shut it, and opened it again. To say goodbye.

I couldn't leave Vicki alone. Not even at a house filled with people. Including one who might have sent someone to abduct us. Or murder us. Or just bust our kneecaps.

None of those outlooks looked good. I promised Ian I would take my friends home with me. Which pleased him. Although, I wasn't so sure if I should introduce more people to the lunatics.

After the police finished questioning us, Juan drove me to LA HAIR. Then told me he hoped we'd never meet again. I had a feeling I was now on Uber's Do Not Pick Up list, much like the DNR listing I faced with rental companies.

"We're packed and ready to go. I am so excited to stay at the Peanut Mansion," said Rhonda, waving me to the reception desk. "I know you said we'll be helping you do surveillance. But I might take a few snaps. I'll show you the pictures, as a show of good intention. I'm not there to paparazzo your movie stars. The pics will mainly be for my blog."

"You have a blog?"

Rhonda's gaze traveled to the other side of the room and back to me. "Just a personal account of my friendship with a previous TV A-lister and B-movie star."

I rubbed my temples. "Anything that will get me in trouble at my next court date?"

"Oh no," Rhonda breathed. "Besides, what could be worse than what got you in trouble in the first place? Mostly, it's pics of your hair and nails. I cross-post to LA HAIR's social media."

My stomach cramped. Too weary to argue, I nodded and schlepped to the chairs lining the wall. Some days were longer than others. I'd almost gotten an Uber driver shot. My mother might be consorting with criminals. Life was short and friends too few to worry about some bad pictures floating around the web. Besides how many followers could Rhonda have?

Okay, I didn't want to know the answer to that. A Pomeranian had 28 million Instagram followers.

I crashed on a chair with a two-month-old copy of *Us* and waited for my friends' shift to finish. I thought of lost time and lost people. And of not telling Nash an armed stranger had tried to ride-share me to an abandoned garage.

He'd take that worse than Detective Mowry.

Speaking of people who wouldn't take things well, I dialed Vicki to let her know I was bringing friends home. As my show of good intention. And to let her housekeeper know there'd be two more for dinner.

"A slumber party?" said Vicki. "Aren't you a little old?"

"Not a slumber party," I said. "My friends are staying with me. You know, because I was almost abducted…"

"I won't have your *friends* playing fan girls to Lili and Stanley. Or the Lees. They're staying here for the anonymity."

"I thought it was so you could keep tabs on them."

"Make sure your friends keep to themselves. And no making smoothies in your bedroom. The stains don't come out of the linens."

"I was nine."

"I doubt stain removal technology has changed much in twenty years."

"I'm not…never mind." I swallowed my anger. Too spent to

go through a quick therapy checklist, I focused on the case. "Vicki, I visited Van Vorling. He seemed particularly upset with you."

"I can't imagine why. The odious man."

"Wait. What? He was beaten up yesterday and you're calling him odious today?"

"He was in an *accident*."

"I know about his gambling. And I know why he agreed to direct this movie."

"Because it's an amazing script with an incredible cast?" Vicki pushed a breath out. "Stop listening to rumors. The man has issues, yes. But believe me, gambling is the least of his problems."

"What's his first problem, Vicki? That he might die if he doesn't stick with the movie?"

Rhonda had stopped sweeping to stare at me. Tiffany's head popped around the corner.

"What are you talking about?" said Vicki.

"What did you do?" My fingers cramped, and I relaxed my grip on the phone. "What did you say to make him he hate you this much?"

She huffed. "I reminded him of some of the particulars in his contract. And what breaking the contract would mean."

OMG. Did she witness the busting of his kneecaps? Did she order the heavy like that Texas cheer mom? Was not-Juan her newest flunkey?

No, she'd make him dress better.

"What would it mean?" I whispered. "If Vorling broke his contract? What did you tell him?"

"I simply told him I had a certain attorney on retainer. One famous for going after powerful men in Hollywood."

"Wait." I took a minute to process the non-*Godfather* moment I expected but didn't experience. "What?"

"I realize Van's European and living in Asia to boot, but how can he miss those headlines? I mean, really, Maizie. It's one thing for a director to get close to their actors. They need that emotional connection to lay a foundation of trust. But making a pass at Lili? I will not have it. I must protect my dau—client."

I relaxed the grip on the phone. And took a moment to deconstruct the conversation I'd just had. Without focusing on Vicki's last sentence.

Where Vicki had almost, accidentally, Freudian-slipped out, "daughter."

My insides softened like all my organs had been made of Jello molds. Poor Vicki. She did miss—

"Do you know I had to speak to the police for an hour?" Her voice sharpened to something akin to an ice pick. Each word stabbed at my Jello-mold heart. "Really, Maizie. Do I need this drama with everything else going on? No, I do not. For once in your life, grow up."

"What?" I barked and blinked away the red spots dancing in my eyes.

Shiztastic, the whole seeing red wasn't just a saying. But I didn't have a temper. I was good-natured. All my therapists said so. I placed a finger on my neck to measure my pulse. Took a deep breath. And pretended she hadn't blown off the attempted abduction like she had the ninja attack in her office.

"The hired driver might have been sent for you," I scrambled to push past her defenses. "He's facing an attempted kidnapping charge. Possibly attempted murder for the weapons discharge. Juan and I would say he had malicious intent, at the very least."

"You should've used your criminal justice degree for law school. A waste of education in this current pursuit."

"Are you hearing what I'm saying?" I held in the scream I felt building. "Someone might want to kill you."

"That's not what the police said. It's a lot more likely they wanted to kill you because of your employment. It seems private investigations is rife with paranoid psychotics and sociopaths."

"Makes sense. I work for you." I hung up.

FORTY-TWO
#DOORBELLDITCHING

I GAVE the girls a house tour. As we toured, we affixed doorbell cameras behind vents, on molding, and in potted plants. The cameras would help me watch for fake-Uber drivers and ninjas. It would also help me keep an eye on Vicki.

I was struggling to find a higher purpose for her protection. Other than evidence to say, "I told you so."

Rhonda and Tiffany took turns acting as a lookout while I used the cordless screwdriver to zip open vent panels and angle a camera inside. It was a lot easier to stick the cameras to the walls, but random doorbells on walls seemed like a giveaway to our spy efforts.

"This would be so much easier if I could use the security already installed in this house." I grunted. Wobbled. Righted myself.

"You okay?" Tiffany called from my shoulders. Her toes hooked behind my armpits, the little points digging into my flesh worse than any bra.

"Just hurry." I held her legs as she rose from her squat to reach the upper molding outside the office.

"I forgot to peel off the hanging strip doohickey," said Tiffany. "I'm trying to get as high as I can."

"I'm going to lose my balance." I teetered sideways. Tiffany clamped an arm around my head. I tipped in the other direction. Then slammed against the wall. An "oomph" resounded above me. We panted against the wall, staring across the balcony. Picturing the fifteen-foot drop to the parquet below. Or worse, into the aquarium. With Charles.

At least that's what I was thinking. I couldn't speak for Tiffany. But I could feel the breath whooshing from her and stirring static into my hair.

"Do y'all need some mat talk?" called Rhonda from the corner of the hallway. "You can do it, Tiffany."

"Rhonda," I hissed. "Stop shouting. We're trying to install these on the QT."

"I forget. Y'all were reminding me of my short time as a cheerleader. If you were stronger, Maizie, I could easily stick those doorbells on the ceiling. I'm twice as tall as Tiffany."

"Twice as heavy, too," muttered Tiffany.

"What was that?" Rhonda swung around to pierce Tiffany with a look.

"We can't all be flyers," said Tiffany.

"We're about to fly off this landing if we're not careful," I said between pants. "Get it stuck so we can go."

"You're vibrating," said Tiffany.

"It's called shaking."

"No, I think it's your phone." She rose, slapped the doorbell to the wall, and slapped my head. "Down, girl."

I teetered into the office. Rhonda helped Tiffany clamber off my shoulders. We collapsed on the floor. I checked my phone. "It's Nash. I better take this. He might have news about the investigation on Xi's death."

"Don't you sound all *Law & Order*," said Rhonda. "We'll just mosey around this room. Where I might take some pictures."

I waved her on. "I'm at Vicki's," I said into the phone. "With Rhonda and Tiffany."

"Not in the pokey, then?" said the growl that answered.

"I guess Ian called you."

"I thought Detective Mowry might lock you up rather than release you." Nash pulled in a breath. "I'm letting that go. For now. Glad no one was hurt."

I smiled. "Thank y—"

"I'm talking about Vicki and what I'd like to do to her. She refused police protection? What the hell?"

I held the phone away from my ear, waiting for his rant to finish. The girls looked over at me. Even Tiffany's eyes rounded at the language blasting from the phone. His words ebbed and fizzled, I returned the phone back to my ear.

"I think you broke the wifi," I said. "I can't get bars in this house. You're fading."

"Okay, I'm done," he said. "Sorry about that. But Miss Albright. Maizie. Vicki is wading in too deep. The optics on this are not good."

"What did the police learn? Is it the Lees?"

"There is no real evidence the Lees are tied to organized crime. But there are associates of theirs who are. Thanks to the murder, the Fed's forensic accountants are auditing the funding of *Unlucky 18*. They're looking for dirty money in the Lees' books. So far, nothing's shown up."

"Okay." I clutched at my Ksubi hoodie and forced a swallow around the golf ball lodged in my throat.

"It gets worse."

"Worse?" I squeaked. "How?"

"The state department's involved. China's government is rumbling about actors not paying their taxes. In China, it's called 'yin-yang contracts.' One contract states a significantly smaller salary than the real amount. I guess underreporting income is common over there, especially with the booming economy. And China wants to make an example of people in the limelight who are making more than what the communists believe is their fair share."

"What does that have to do with Master Xi? He didn't pay his taxes?"

"No. From what the Feds say, Xi's always toed the party line. But he is tied to Lili Liang. And they think China's been watching her income pretty closely. It looks like she's showing intent to emigrate, what with the American boyfriend and *Unlucky 18*."

"Do you think Master Xi's death was part of a government conspiracy? In Julia Pinkerton, there was an episode—"

"Miss Albright, this isn't a TV episode. Reality check, please."

"Right." I blew out a breath. "Everything with this case reminds me of movies. So what's the connection between Lili's taxes and Xi?"

"They still don't know. Maybe nothing. There's a lot of red tape within the government. And white-collar forensics takes forever. The case has stalled here otherwise."

"Wouldn't the Chinese government worry about the Lees' money more than Lili's salary?"

"I'm sure they want everyone to pay their taxes, even alleged criminals." He paused. "But if there's corruption, they might look the other way. I don't know how it works over there. I don't know if I want to know."

"Don't forget, we found all those bugs in Lili's trailer and the Peanut Mansion. Do you think it wasn't Jeff? It was a government spy?"

"I can't stop thinking about those bugs. For another reason. I'm wondering if they've been replaced."

I lowered my voice, "They're watching us?" I pinched my thumb and blew out three quick breaths. He didn't know I'd planned on watching everyone, too.

"Don't worry." His tone had gentled. "The police are working this. I wish I was there. You probably need one of those hugs."

"I wish you were, too," I whispered. I glanced at the girls. They were pretending to examine *The Black Rose* poster. "Am I putting my friends in jeopardy?"

"I don't think so. If it's someone in the house, they're not going to make a move there. Pardon my French, but you don't shit where you eat. It's why they hired that guy to pick you up."

The golf ball feeling in my throat released.

"I didn't stay at the hotel," Nash continued. "It was weird."

"The hotel was weird?"

"No, sleeping in a place like that…without…alone. As a guy."

"That's so sweet."

"I'm staying with Lamar's retired cop buddy, Joe. I keep thinking about—" The line fuzzed out again. "—business."

"I lost you again."

"Not important." He cleared his throat. "Listen, the investigation is moving north. As soon as the Clearwater detective gets clearance, he's coming to Black Pine. The Feds have already moved in. Mowry talked to one of them."

"That's nice," I snapped. "It was good to know they had my back today when Juan and I were shot at."

"You were shot at?" Nash thundered.

I guess Ian hadn't told him that much. "This connection is bad. I should go." Before he began another four-letter rant. "Tell Joe I said, hi."

IN OUR LEGGINGS AND SWEATSHIRTS, the girls and I sat cross-legged on my bed. We each watched a laptop. Screen windows readied for each doorbell.

"If we see anything suspicious, we'll call Detective Mowry." I looked up from my laptop to Tiffany's. All was quiet on the guest wing front. Rhonda scoped out the first floor.

"If I see anything suspicious, I'm heading to that safe room," said Tiffany. "Y'all can open the door for the police."

Rhonda reached for the popcorn. "I'm not worried. If it stays this quiet, I'm going to work on my blog."

"You know, everything is tied to Lili and Vicki," I said. "I can't believe this has anything to do with the Chinese IRS."

"I'm not feeling great about staying here, to be honest," said Tiffany, looking up from her bowl of ice cream. "Vicki made us eat dinner with the help. Are you sure she won't try to off us while we sleep?"

"I'm sorry about that. You probably had a better dinner than I did with the Lees. Lili and Stanley went to Atlanta with Mr. Zhao to meet with a PR firm. Through a translator, Vicki and the Lees talked about Charles the whole time." I wrinkled my nose. "I'd much rather eat with the help. And would have if I wasn't spying on Vicki."

"I like that Misty," said Rhonda. "She's funny."

I sighed.

"I just got an alert. Something's going on at the kitchen door," said Rhonda. Tiffany and I rose onto our knees to peer at Rhonda's screen. "This is so exciting."

"That's the housekeeper," I said. "What's she doing?"

"She's handing a package to someone at the door."

"It looks like a bag of groceries."

"Betcha she's selling quality meat to a dealer." Tiffany snorted. "Black market groceries."

"Should I report her?"

"Do you want the housekeeper to die?" said Rhonda. "We have no idea what makes Vicki wig out."

"I can't believe we're talking about my mother like this."

"You started it," said Rhonda.

"Vicki used to nannycam all the staff." I pointed at the screen. "This is why."

"Whoa," cried Rhonda, sliding off the bed. "You're okay with her spying on the help?"

"Dude." Tiffany waved her spoon. "Not cool."

"She's stealing. That's not cool." I logged the housekeeper and time, then caught a flash in the corner of my eye. I turned back to my laptop. "Hang on. What's going on in the foyer? No, that's just Charles watching me."

"He can't see you through the doorbell cam," said Tiffany. "And he's just a fish."

"Let me go back." I tapped on the keyboard to rewind. "Never mind. Just Lili, Jeff, and Stanley returning. And Mr. Zhao. You've got guest hall, can you follow them?"

"This is the most boring surveillance I've ever done," said Rhonda.

"Most surveillance is boring," I said, writing down the time, place, and people in my notebook. "And if you look away for a second, that's when something happens. Murphy's law."

"Kind of like you just did now," said Tiffany. "Someone else was in our hall."

I turned back. "Frigtastic. Who was that?"

"Dunno," said Tiffany.

"Hells. I'll rewind."

"I've got an alert, too." Rhonda climbed back on the bed. "Oh wait, just the housekeeper again. Now she's letting someone in."

"Who was that?" I glanced at her screen, then back to mine. "Shiz, I've got to rewind again."

"Party at Lili's," said Tiffany. "Everyone but Stanley Wu went to her room. The assistant, too."

"What about the Lees? Remember to write down their movement with the time." I squinted at the screen. "I wish the hallways were brighter. It's hard to see who this is."

"And the vent doesn't help." Rhonda looked over my shoulder.

"I couldn't risk putting a camera on the molding by Vicki's room. She'd notice it." I gnawed my lip, tapped on my computer, and penciled a question mark on the log.

"Can't you enhance the image?"

"These are doorbell cams. We can't enhance the image."

"Once on *CSI*, they enlarged the image so they could see a person reflected in another person's eyeball."

I looked at Rhonda. "Does that even sound remotely possible to you?"

She shrugged. "They made it seem remotely possible, isn't that what counts?"

"Man, got another alert," said Tiffany. "I've got to switch screens. Crap, a bunch left her room and I missed it."

"Someone's in our hallway. Look at the alert." Rhonda elbowed me.

"Wait, that's Jeff Johnson. Is he…waving?"

"That dude's staring at your camera," said Rhonda. "Can he reach it?"

"Let me see," said Tiffany. "Oh, man. He can totally see us. Not see us, see us. But he knows we're watching."

"What's he doing?" I said. "Something on his phone?"

The screen blacked.

We looked at each other. I tapped on the keyboard. The image had frozen in the viewer.

"Check your cameras. Hurry." I tapped to switch windows. "Oh, shiz."

"Nothing," said Tiffany, looking up from her screen.

"I think the wifi went out," said Rhonda. "Did he do that?"

The room went dark.

"And there goes the electric," said Tiffany. "Now's a good time to head to the panic room. Except I'm not sharing it with your mom. Perfect opportunity for her to off me."

"Shiplap, shiplap, shiplap."

FORTY-THREE
#ICKYTHUMP

I SET my phone to flashlight mode and slid from the bed. "I've got to go out there."

"Wait." Rhonda hopped down and grabbed my arm. "Do you hear something?"

"A thud," said Tiffany. "Something hit the wall."

"This is the worst horror movie I've ever been in," squealed Rhonda and clapped a hand over her mouth. Darting to the bed, she grabbed a pillow and squeezed it against her stomach.

A series of muffled pops sounded from somewhere in the house. A splash followed. We simultaneously cocked our heads. Padded thumping grew faint, like footsteps running down the hall.

"What was that?" I said. "Charles? If someone messes with Charles, Vicki will kill them. Oh God, Vicki was right. Someone was trying to shoot her fish."

"Lawd," moaned Rhonda. "That fish *is* out to get you."

"What if he jumped out?" I squeaked. "I don't want to touch him."

"Don't shine your flashlight on your neck, Maizie. Those chins are freaking me out."

"Someone left," said Tiffany. "Their car backfired."

Rhonda bobbed her head. "I definitely heard a door closing. And running. Maybe they stole the fish."

"No," I said. "Those were gunshots. Nash said they might have used a suppressor the last time."

"In the movies, you can't hear a silencer." Rhonda squeezed her pillow. "It couldn't be gunshots. They'd be louder. Or quieter."

"The movies are fake," I hissed. "A suppressor only dulls the sound. That was a silencer. I should see what happened. Call Nash. No, wait. He's in Florida. Call Mowry."

Tiffany waved her phone. "No bars and no wifi. This place is a tomb."

I had placed my friends in jeopardy. To protect Vicki. Who wasn't protecting her guests under the guise of protecting their privacy. The red spots returned, dancing in my eyes.

"This is what happens when you live in a giant bomb shelter and someone cuts your power," I seethed. Holding the phone over the gym bag, I searched for a real flashlight. "Bleeping Jeff Johnson. Now I've got to go out in the dark and check on my mother. Who knows who's in her room and who's on her ship list. Why didn't I go to Nash's and get my .38? Shiz's sake."

"Ship list?" said Tiffany.

"Shit list," said Rhonda. "Too many years on TV watching her mouth."

I pulled on my shoes and grabbed the Maglite. "Stay here and lock the forking doors. Hells, Vicki. If she had the flipping alarms online, we could push a fracking button."

"One of these days, Vicki's gonna push her too far. All that therapy out the window," whispered Rhonda. "She's gonna sound like she's got Tourette's."

"Today might just be the day," muttered Tiffany.

I RAN down the hall and pounded on Vicki's door.

"Who is it?" said a man's voice.

My heart battered my chest and leaped into my throat. In my mind, a million memories of Vicki ran together in crazed patterns that shattered with a "pop, pop, pop" of a silencer.

"Who are you?" I blurted. "Where's Vicki?"

The door cracked open and Master Kevin peeped out. "Maizie? Do you know what's going on?"

"Where's Vicki?" My neck grew cold. My feet felt hot. I took both as bad signs. "What are you doing in there?"

"Maizie, why is the power out? There's no storm," called Vicki. "Why haven't the generators started? Lydia is not answering her phone."

I pushed past Kevin, into Vicki's room. "Someone cut the power and wifi. You need to go to the safe room."

"Why?" she said.

"That's what it's for," I shrieked. "Safety."

"What about Lili? Stanley? Oh Lord, the Lees?"

"I'm going to check on them now. I came here first."

"Your first thought should be for our guests. The captain goes down with the ship. If I go to the panic room, they need to come with me."

One of the guests might have shot another guest. I pulled in a long breath through my nose and counted to five. "Vicki." My voice sounded strangled. I let out the breath. "Do you really want to go down with this ship? If you recall, someone thought I was you and tried to shoot me."

"If you're going to be like that. Let me get my things." She padded away.

"You don't need—" I called. "Whatever. Hurry it up."

"Can I speak to you for a minute?" said Kevin.

"Not now." I glowered at him. "Where were you five minutes ago?"

"Here. With Vicki."

I didn't know if I could trust him. But I had to trust someone. "I guess she'd corroborate that. The panic room's through her closet. The biggest closet. Can you find it?"

"What little faith you have in me."

I lowered my voice. "I don't know who else may be in this house, but Jeff Johnson cut the power."

"Lili's boyfriend?" Kevin pulled in a long breath. "It can't be him."

"Why doesn't anyone believe me about him?" I held in a frustrated scream. "Didn't you hear that gun? After the lights went out?"

"Gun?" His voice faltered. "No, we were arguing. Are you sure?"

"I'm going to check it out."

"Maizie, that's not safe. Come with us." He placed a hand on my arm.

I stared at the hand, then looked up at him. "I can handle myself. You have no idea what my life's been like recently. It's taking a lot for me to trust you with Vicki."

He jerked his hand away. "I'm shocked at you. After all our years together. To treat your teacher with such disrespect."

"I'm not twelve anymore, Kevin. And you're no longer my teacher. I don't know you or why you're really here." I looked in his eyes and felt the chink in my armor. I'd loved him like a father at one point. At the moment, I needed to feel like I had some family who I could count on. "Just keep her safe. Whatever she's done, she's still my mother."

I FLED to the guest wing staircase, pausing to look out over the foyer balcony. The front door was ajar.

Shiztastic.

I ignored the door to bound up the stairs. A small group congregated in the hall. I shined my flashlight on the group, counting three heads. The Lees were likely in their room. Kevin was with Vicki. That left Jeff Johnson and Mr. Zhao among the missing.

Low in my belly, my anxiety tightened and burbled.

"What happened?" I said.

"Such melodrama," said Stanley. "Positively enthralling. I came out in the hall to witness the spectacle myself."

"What spectacle?"

Lili groaned. "A stupid fight. Between Jeff and Zhao. I'm so humiliated."

"Quite the show of machismo," said Stanley.

"Fight with..." I trailed off, waiting for the mention of gunshots.

"To the untrained eye, it looked like a mixture of Wing Chun, some jiu-jitsu, and dirty street fighting. But I leave it to the experts. Shiyu? Lili? What do you say?"

"Stop it, Stanley," fumed Lili. "It's bad enough without your awful jokes."

"No one had a gun?" I said. "I thought I heard gunshots."

"They were so loud, someone could have shot a gun off, I suppose," said Stanley. "Right, that's it for me. I need my beauty sleep. Long day at the studio tomorrow. We have rehearsals, Lili. Van insists he's ready and wants to begin."

"Where is Jeff and Mr. Zhao?"

"When we appeared and let our presence be known, Mr. Zhao stormed off to his hotel. Jeff took off a moment later, to cool his heels, I suppose."

The lights flickered. We blinked in the bright light.

Lili groaned. "I'm so sorry, Maizie. I'll pay for the damage."

A side table had been demolished. The wallpaper torn. A vase lay on the floor, water puddling beneath it. The vase's forsythia branches had been trampled and scattered. A painting hung sideways. And one doorbell camera lay on the carpet. I picked it up and shoved it inside the front pocket of my hoodie.

"Don't worry about that now," I said. "Just explain what happened."

"I'm not exactly sure," said Lili. "We returned from Atlanta with Zhou. While Jeff went to work out, I showered. During that time, they got in a fight and the lights went out. Or the lights went out and they fought. I was drying my hair when we lost power."

"Mr. Zhao behaves badly," said Shiyu. "I'm shocked he would lose his self-control."

"It's been tense between them," I said. "That must be uncomfortable for you, Lili."

She rolled her eyes. "It's ridiculous."

"I should check on the Lees," I murmured and stepped around the broken furniture. Mulling over the timeline of events, I moved down the hall. I knocked lightly on the door to the Lees' room. A robed woman answered the door. The translator from dinner. She bobbed a bow and smiled.

"Did you need something?" said Jen.

"Do I have the right room? I'm checking on the Lees."

"They're sleeping," said Jen. "Jet lag, you know."

"You weren't disturbed by the…commotion?"

"I was watching Netflix on my iPad with my headphones. Did something happen?"

I raised a brow. "The wifi and electricity went out."

"I download my shows," she said. "I didn't notice the power. But I had the lights off."

"Are you're sure the Lees are in there?"

She nodded. "Vicki insisted I sleep on their couch in case they need anything. Usually, I go to corporate events to translate, but this gig pays well. I don't mind the couch."

"Good." I backed from the door. "Enjoy your show."

I stalked down the hall. The three had gone to their respective rooms. I knocked on Lili's door. Shiyu answered.

"Has Lili heard from Jeff Johnson? Do you know where he went?"

She shook her head. "How are the Lees?"

"Fine," I said. "The translator answered. She said they slept through it all."

"They don't need to be bothered about such childishness."

Lili called from behind the pocket doors.

Shiyu hunched her shoulders. "I should see what she needs."

"Listen, when Jeff returns, can you pay attention to the time he arrives? Let me know tomorrow?" After she nodded, I continued, "And one other thing. Did you notice when the fight began exactly?"

"The time? No. I heard them and opened my door."

"There was still power then. If you saw them."

"For a minute, yes."

Then why did Jeff Johnson appear in my doorbell camera just before the wifi and power went out?

FORTY-FOUR
#CRUSHINGIT

I RETURNED to my room and rapped our secret knock. Tiffany answered. They'd shifted the laptops to the loveseat in front of the flatscreen. And dragged the blankets from the bed onto the couch.

"We're watching *Sporting Love*," said Rhonda. "Giulio's very good, you know."

"And we're watching you on the laptop," said Tiffany. "What was the hubbub in the hallway?"

"A fight between Mr. Zhao and Jeff Johnson caused some of our guests to leave their rooms. No one but us heard the gunshots. Not even Kevin and Vicki. Are we sure we heard them?"

"I think so?" said Rhonda.

"I could have been right about the car backfiring," said Tiffany.

"At least I didn't find anyone with a bullet in them. Yet. Jeff and Mr. Zhou left the scene. And Kevin Yuan is with Vicki in the panic room." I blew out a frustrated breath. "I forgot to give them the all-clear."

"You also forgot to check on the help," said Rhonda. "The kitchen was busy tonight, too."

"First, I want to check the doorbell camera timestamp from when we saw Jeff Johnson. Something doesn't add up." I grabbed my laptop from the bed and pulled up the earlier footage. "Look at this. When I check the time, it's earlier than what I recorded in my notebook."

"How does that work?" Rhonda cocked her head then snapped her fingers. "I saw this on *Ocean's 8*. He made a video loop."

"It's in every heist movie since *Speed*. But it wasn't a reality until recently." I gritted my teeth. "That bleeping blugger."

"You need better curse words," said Tiffany. "Can he hack into the doorbell cams?"

"Of course, he can. He has access to Vicki's wifi. Zhou said Jeff's an IT something-or-other. It's relatively easy to hack anyway. Then he created some sort of time lag. It probably reset when he cut the wifi. If it was him."

"He looks guilty. Check out the face." Rhonda peered over my shoulder. "He's so cute."

"Not cute. Don't go there." I shut the laptop. "This is totally my fault. If I'd encrypted the transmission from the laptop to the cameras, he couldn't have gotten in. Jeff wasn't in Atlanta with Lili, Stanley, and Zhou. He spied on us while we were sticking up the cameras."

Rhonda shuddered. "Creepy."

"We're doing the same thing, Rhon," said Tiffany.

"This is going in my blog," she muttered.

I flashed Rhonda a look. "No blogging until after the police have arrested Xi's murderer."

"That could take years," she wailed.

"Thanks a lot." I glanced between the surveillance log and the time stamp. "It's not a lot of time. Thirty minutes. I'll have to assume he did it to all the cameras online."

I slumped. Then jerked upright. "I've got to check on everybody else. Stay here."

"We'll keep an eye from here." Rhonda saluted. "Watch out for that housekeeper. She's dealing in black market meat."

"And she let someone in the house." I rubbed the bridge of my nose. "Shiplap."

IN MY HEAD, I triaged the remaining people in the Peanut Mansion and placed the housekeeper as greater importance over Vicki. Vicki was safe in the panic room, after all. I trusted Kevin. Pretty much. And a part of me (Not a small part. Most of my parts.) cheered at prioritizing the help over Vicki. It felt empowering.

Also enabling, but I'd deal with that later.

I bounded down the grand staircase and eyed the fish tank, remembering the splash. Also a low priority. But one side felt damp. Charles swam into view, muscling his way through a school of neon tetras. Then he ate two.

"That's just rude." I glared at him, then considered the splash I'd heard. "Were you trying to tell me something, boy? Did somebody shoot somebody else and you were trying to warn us?"

My mother was literally making me crazy. I was recreating *Lassie* with a fish.

I scooted across the parquet to shut the front door. Then considered the splintered wood and dust on the parquet.

Shiztastic.

"You've got to be kidding me." Another bullet lodged in the door. I eyed the hole and splintered wood. Began to search for more holes. Checked the parquet for blood. Or new wood. And holes. Combed the entryway walls.

One bullet. Again. And buried too deep to know if it was the same kind of bullet.

I called Nash.

Hung up.

Dialed Mowry.

Hung up.

Pressed Nash's name.

"Did you just call?" His voice sounded distant. In the background, a cheer roared and his phone jostled.

"Where are you?"

"Sarasota. The Braves are playing the Cardinals. Ninth inning. Long game. It's a close one, too."

Irritation cold-cocked me like a bracken-filled wave after a wipeout. "You're at a baseball game?"

"I know," he said excitedly. "The Braves, even. I rarely see them in Atlanta. Lamar's going to be so jealous. What's going on there?"

"Oh, just another bullet in the door," I said snidely. "And someone cut the power and internet for a bit. Maybe to shoot at the door. Or a person. Or a fish. Who knows? It's like a funhouse run by Hitler. No, Stalin. No, Mussolini."

I was running out of totalitarian dictators. I couldn't remember if there was a dictator who didn't seem to care if their daughter had almost taken a bullet for them.

"I'm detecting some hostility," said Nash carefully. "Which isn't your usual parlance. Do you want to walk me backward from the shooting at the door bit?"

I explained the evening's course of events — Minus the doorbell cameras. I wasn't in the mood for that lecture. — ending with the bullet in the door.

"How many shots did you hear?"

"I'm not sure. Possibly three."

"And only one bullet in the door?"

"The door was open. Maybe they shot out the door." I opened the door, stepped out, and searched the porch. "It's too dark. I can't find anything. Notice, the alarm didn't go off when I opened it."

I began a rant on the kind of people who had million-dollar security features but didn't use them. And stopped. I was stealing from Nash's script.

The other end of the line had quieted. Not just because Nash wasn't talking. No beer and hotdog crowd, either.

"Hello?" I squeaked. "Are you there?"

"Darlin'." Nash's voice surged through the receiver, deep and gentle. "I'm coming home as soon as I can get a flight. Police be damned."

My shoulders caved, my knees wobbled, and I slumped to the floor. "I'm a strong woman."

"I know you are."

"I can handle this."

"I know you can. I wouldn't be at the baseball game where — dammit, sounds like the Cardinals just got a hit. Sumbitch." He cleared his throat. "Anyway, I wouldn't have sent you back if I didn't think you can handle things up there. I'd rather have you here with me."

"You would?"

"Maizie," he growled. "The hotel room? And my plans for you. In it."

"Right." I bit my lip.

"I'm not great at, well — Let me start again. When I was with Jolene…no, just—"

I winced at the name of his (evil) ex-wife. I hoped he had winced, too.

"Honestly, Maizie, you drove me bonkers. In the beginning. With your— Okay, that sounds…"

There was that word again. Bonkers? But his deep voice and (semi) romantic words caressed my soul. Cooled my feverish mood. Lapped at my raw nerves like the lake setting on my meditation app. I clenched the phone to my ear, greedy for more.

"But certain women get under my skin. I have to watch myself. It's like a rash." He cut himself off. "Dammit, that sounds worse. Lord help me, I'm bad at this."

He was super bad at this. "Nash? Are you trying to explain your feelings for me?"

"Yes, dammit. I have feelings for you. Strong feelings. I'm

trying to be cautious. With us. You're too…important to me to ruin this. I'd do the ruining. Not you. Ruin what we have." He paused. "I don't mean the business."

"You mean our relationship. Our personal relationship."

"Yes," he exploded. "Our relationship. Why you want one with me, in a million years I will never understand. I can't offer you—"

"You offer me you," I said quickly. "That's all I want."

"But if I spend one more day with that woman, I might throttle her. What she does to you. What she's doing to you. I know she's your mother. And the thing with your dad? I understand why he doesn't like me, but to kick you out of your home?"

"I'm sure he'd like you if you weren't working for Vicki. Or if I wasn't working for Vicki. I'm not entirely sure of his point, but then I'm usually not. Which is frustrating." My dampened shriek came out as a bark. "He's exasperating. She's infuriating. Is this a delayed reaction to their divorce? Is that a thing? It's been twenty years."

"Hon'. It's your anger that's getting to me. You should hear yourself, Maizie. This isn't you. You're a happy person. You're sunny and warm and bright. You care about people. You smell good. And look amazing. And you make me relax when I'm so damn tense all the time." He exhaled a breath. "You're like…Florida."

My skin grew hot. The knot in my stomach eased, releasing butterflies. They danced in my gut then fluttered under my skin. I felt prickly and dizzy.

And happy.

"Maizie? Are you crying? Don't cry, hon'. I'm sorry. I know I'm terrible at this stuff," he stumbled over his words. His drawl disappeared as he rushed to explain. "I thought you needed to hear how I feel. You sounded so…crazy isn't the right word, but kind of crazy. And if I were there, you'd need a hug or something. But I'm not there. And I'm sorry."

"That was perfect," I whispered. "It was so you. You crushed it."

"Alright then," his voice deepened and surged.

"And I think you should stay in Florida a little while longer."

"Wha— why?"

"Because I have to take care of my mother. And I need you to have the strength and serenity you're feeling right now. Really I need it. What you just told me? Better than all the therapy I've ever had combined."

I blew out a breath. "Only one of us can be tense. And right now, it has to be me."

FORTY-FIVE
#FRESHMEAT

NASH and I debated whether to call the police. No crime had occurred. We knew what the owner (Vicki) of the house would do (refuse and deny). Jeff Johnson's plans — whatever they were — must have been thwarted. He'd disappeared. Again. The police would likely handle the fight and firearm discharge as a domestic disturbance, bringing further embarrassment to Lili. With her fame and the movie's hype, the press would pick up on it. We'd have a media circus that would quickly morph into an international carnival. And we had no idea what that might trigger for the Lees.

Maybe nothing as we still didn't know of their involvement, other than producers.

That was my take.

"It might mess with the Fed's investigation," said Nash. "And the last thing they'd want is to lose the chance to bust an organized crime ring over a 10-16. If the Lees pull up stakes…"

"*Unlucky 18* would lose their funding. It might ruin the careers for Chey, Stanley, and Lili. Or at least, kill their big break. Then there are thousands of jobs contracted for an action picture. That'd put a crazy amount of people out of work."

"I was going to say, the Feds would lose the big fish and all the minnows swimming with them. Not to mention, justice for Xiáng Xi." He sighed. "I think we lost."

"It's not over," I pleaded. "I'll figure out what happened tonight. If it's the same gun that shot the door again, it's a major link in the evidence chain, right?"

"I meant the Braves. I'm sitting in the rental car and everyone's pouring out of the stadium, looking unhappy." His voice cheered. "But I got to see them. That was nice."

"I could get some prints off the door handle with tape or something."

"Don't worry about prints. Too many people have used the door. But I like the way you think."

Nash had such a bad run of luck lately, he needed Florida.

Such a bad run of luck since meeting me. My gaze moved to the upper landing leading to Vicki's wing.

"I need to speak to Lydia, the housekeeper, and see what she knows. She's also doing some dubious stuff, probably unrelated. I'm unsure if I should bust her or use it as blackmail. According to Tiffany and Rhonda, social etiquette leans toward blackmail."

"Miss Albright, as investigators, we don't blackmail people," said Nash. "But if you have compromising information on Lydia, there's no law saying you can't suggest your knowledge of said information. That can be helpfully intimidating."

LYDIA EXPOSED herself without any pressure (or blackmail) from me. When I knocked on her door, a man answered. Partially clothed.

Mostly not clothed.

He opened the door, thinking I was Lydia.

Super glad I'm not Lydia.

Turned out, Lydia had a gentleman caller. The grocery bag she'd handed him earlier had been filled with leftovers. He had returned to show his thanks. Apparently. Lydia had neither seen nor heard anything (due to the subsequent enthralling passion) and had been quite surprised when the lights went out.

She had turned on the generator — restoring power — and called the electric company. The electric company had restored the real power. In doing so, they discovered their server had been hacked and the grid shut down. Or at least the section covering the Peanut Mansion. One thousand apologies (with promised firmware updates and a security audit) later, all's well that ends well.

For the power.

I checked (and locked) the back doors, the downstairs rooms, and the garage. Confident Jeff Johnson wasn't about, I climbed up the back staircase and took another trip down the guest wing hall. Cleaned up the mess left by the male contingent of the love triangle. Listened at doors. Looked in empty rooms. Waved at the lone doorbell cam for Tiffany and Rhonda's benefit.

Yes, I was procrastinating. On purpose. Letting Vicki stew.

On the second floor, Vicki's office was locked. After my ninja attack, she promised to secure her rooms. I took it as a good sign and continued on my way. I shlepped down the hall and knocked on Vicki's room. Found her door unlocked and the front room empty. In the bedroom, I slipped into the appropriate closet and located the almost hidden door. I pressed the code in the wall panel designed to look like a shoe shelf, and the door swung open. Revealing the cozy room inside. And the people in it.

Blinking, I stumbled back. Gagged. Covering my mouth, I fumbled my way out of the closets and into her bathroom. Threw up. Leaned over her sink. Ran cold water over my wrists. Splashed my face.

And thought I'd never recover.

FORTY-SIX
#WENEEDTOTALKABOUTKEVIN

I STUMBLED back to my room and tapped the secret knock. Yawning, Rhonda let me inside.

"Do we have to keep watching the doorbells?" She peered at me, then grabbed my chin. "Damn, girl. You don't look so good. What happened?"

"Can't. Even."

"Tiff," called Rhonda. "Something happened."

Tiffany strolled in, toothbrush hanging from her mouth. "Wha?"

"Maizie's all pale and acting funny." Rhonda scrunched her nose. "Paler than usual. Look at her, she's like a ghost. Ghostier, anyway."

I collapsed on the loveseat and lowered my head to my knees. "I don't want to talk about it."

Tiffany yanked the toothbrush from her mouth. "Where was Maizie? Were you watching the doorbells?"

"She was all over," said Rhonda. "Literally everywhere. Just poking around. No skeletons or bodies or ninjas showed up."

I sat up, glad to have something else to talk about. "Someone shot the door again. If you walk out of the office to the balcony, you have a direct line across the foyer to the door. They hide the gun in Vicki's office. Hellz, I should've checked when we were in there earlier."

"Why would someone want to shoot the door?" Tiffany held up her hand. "Amend that. Who went out the door and could have been shot?"

"After the fight broke up, Mr. Zhao left for his hotel. Jeff Johnson followed a short time later. I'm sure he took the Makarov with him." I hopped up from the loveseat to pace, glad to have something easier to think about. Like attempted murder.

"We should check—" Rhonda stopped. "Without power or wifi, we've got no video. Damn. But the bullet hit the door, so Jeff Johnson didn't allegedly shoot Mr. Zhao in the foyer. Maybe you'll get lucky and find out Jeff tried to shoot him again."

"Not so lucky for Mr. Zhao," said Tiffany.

"Why didn't I think of this before? I need to call Mr. Zhao. Make sure he's okay." I glanced up from my phone. "I'm asking the resort to buzz his room."

"I'm glad to hear about the door," said Rhonda. "The way you looked, I thought you saw somebody shot. Oh, damn, you went all white again. Sit down."

I waved her away but lowered myself to the loveseat. On the phone, the ringing flipped to voicemail. I bit my lip and left a message for Zhao to call me. "He's not answering. And I don't have his mobile number. I should go out to the resort and see if he showed. If not, I'll have to call the police."

Tiffany and Rhonda glanced at each other.

"It's been a crazy night and you don't look so good," said Rhonda. "You should rest."

A knock sounded on the door. Rhonda shrieked. Tiffany spun around, jabbing her toothbrush in the air. Groaning, I rose from the loveseat and shuffled to the door.

"Tiff, look at Maizie," muttered Rhonda. "She's ghosty again."

"Don't worry. This will be Kevin Yuan." Unlocking the door, I disciplined my feelings. Thought about which character could assist me through the upcoming conversation.

Shiplap. I couldn't do this as anyone but me.

I opened the door.

Kevin placed a hand inside the doorjamb. "We need to talk. About your mother. And what you saw."

I shook my head. "I don't want to talk about it."

"Please, Maizie." Kevin stepped inside and closed the door. "I need you to speak to me."

"It's not my business. And I don't want to make it my business." I squeezed my arms across my chest. "There's too much going on now for this kind of drama."

"It's not meant to be drama. We never told you, but when you were doing *Kung Fu Kate*, your mother and I—"

"Stop." I placed my hands over my ears. Felt my stomach bubble up. Moved my hands over my belly. Then my mouth.

"Just stop," I mumbled through my fingers.

"I'll close the door to the bedroom," said Tiffany. "But we'll be on the other side if you need us."

"We will?" said Rhonda.

"No, stay here," I said. "I need you here."

"Sweetheart," pleaded Kevin. "I'm sorry you had to—"

"Nope," I barked. "Don't even."

"Why?" His gentle voice grated on my raw nerves. "You're an adult. We're all adults."

"She's engaged," I blurted. "To Giulio. Doesn't anyone care about him?"

"He's in a bachelor competition," said Tiffany. "I don't think even Giulio cares."

"Well, I care. I was engaged to him, too. I take engagements seriously. Why doesn't anyone else?"

"Not making a lot of sense," muttered Rhonda. "But at least you got your color back. The little you had."

"You know, Vicki might be in real danger?" I ranted. "Or she might be putting others in danger? Look at her house of horrors. Her door's been shot twice. And while someone's shooting up the house, she's doing," I waved my hand, "with you. As if. Please."

Kevin cocked his head. "Aren't you overreacting?"

"Maybe. Maybe not. I thought I knew her. God knows I've had enough therapy to try to understand her. But I don't think I do. I've been defending her. I've been trying to protect her. But I think…seeing that…" I scrutinized the ceiling for help. "I think she finally broke me."

"Honey, I know she's changed," Kevin sighed. "In the beginning, she had principles I admired. Mainly about protecting you in the industry. Your career was taking off and truthfully, she was more focused on the business than us. There's a hardness in her now. I saw it coming. It's why we split up. We didn't end well."

I rubbed my chest, trying to massage out the ache. "That's why I didn't see you again?"

"She thought it best if we severed ties completely. We fought about it a lot. Believe me. I loved you, Maizie. You were like a daughter to me. But she chose to not reveal our relationship to you, and I had to respect that."

Kevin dropped his chin, sighed, and looked up. "When Vicki asked me to come to Black Pine and coach Lili, I wanted to say no, but couldn't. It's been painful."

Rhonda yanked Tiffany onto the loveseat and passed her the popcorn.

I swiped at trickling tears then rubbed at my eyes. "She deprived me of my father. Then she deprived me of you. Why am I helping her? Why does our relationship have to be so torturous?"

"This was the reason I didn't want to tell you what I suspected of the Lees. I hoped to counsel her, get her to see reason. Protect you from her bad decisions. She wouldn't listen to me. I threatened her with telling you about our past."

"That's why she's so skittish around you? But why doesn't she want me to know? What could it matter now?"

His shoulders lifted and collapsed. "I can't answer your questions. I couldn't fifteen years ago and I can't now."

"I know why," my voice rose in anger. "Because she's afraid of ceding any kind of control. Not even to you. She would rather be alone than share any sort of power."

"That's very harsh," said Kevin.

"OMG." A harsher reality backhanded me like a teenage girl in a catfight. "Vicki wanted me to think she was completely devoted to me. When she obviously so wasn't if she was sneaking around with you. Who knows how many other men were hidden from me?"

"This is better than *Real Housewives*," muttered Rhonda.

"A lot better than *Sporting Love*, that's for sure," said Tiffany.

"Honey, I know this is hard to hear, but—"

My hand shot up to stop Kevin. "Did she ask you to come before Master Xi left?"

He shifted his eyes away from me and swallowed.

"I already figured it out, Kevin. You couldn't have dropped all your students and contracts and moved here in less than a week."

"I can't help myself, but I love her, Maizie," said Kevin. "God help me. And I think she loves me, too. In her own way. We were…making up when you found us."

I swallowed and tasted bile. This discovery felt bitter and small. And wicked.

"If Vicki is involved with the Lees, like you think, she could have ordered a hit on Master Xi." I stared at Kevin. "She could have murdered Xiáng Xi. For you."

"Girl, I'm sorry," whispered Rhonda. "But damn, this is getting good."

FORTY-SEVEN
#CROUCHINGTIGER

I HAD to get out of the house. And I needed to check on Mr. Zhou. A man's life was satisfyingly more important than my mother's melodrama. The girls agreed to watch the cameras. Kevin agreed to watch Vicki. Everyone agreed to lock their doors.

I drove Tiffany's car to Black Pine Resort, praying Mr. Zhou hadn't been shot and fallen into a topiary where he'd lay until morning. I also prayed Jeff Johnson wasn't the nutjob I feared and a perfectly reasonable explanation would explain the newest bullet in the door.

I was still waiting for an explanation for the last bullet.

At the front desk, I waited while the attendant called Zhou's room. When he didn't answer, I explained my fears. And who he was in relation to the film. And who I was. With a helping of borrowed attitude from Julia Pinkerton and Vicki to create a cold-hearted character I'd often seen pushing around desk clerks.

I accompanied the manager and bellhop to Zhou's room. Surprisingly, not a top-floor suite like Vorling's and Chey's. They knocked politely and, with no answer, louder. I gnawed on my thumbnail.

As the door swung open, Zhou stumbled forth in an open robe and boxers, swearing in Chinese. His lean, muscular body bore tattoos and evidence of the fight with Jeff Johnson. Faint red marks on his chest and legs, a purpling on his cheek, a cut lip. And a wicked cut on his collar bone, grubby with dried blood.

"Is it a fire?" he said to the manager. They explained while he glowered.

After apologies made by the staff, I pushed forward. "I was worried about you. After what happened at the house."

His dark eyes roved from the hotel staff to me. He nodded at them. I walked inside, and he shut the door.

"It's late. I have meetings tomorrow." The burning scent of alcohol wafted from his skin. He'd been drowning his sorrows after a defeating match with his rival. "Did Lili send you?"

I coughed, taking a step back. "Do you need a doctor?"

"This?" He pointed to his cheek and forced a curt laugh. "It's nothing."

"I heard gunshots in the house. And I thought..." I lifted my chin. "You might have been shot. The front door had been left open."

His eyes narrowed. "Gunshots? You must be mistaken."

"There's evidence. In the door. Did he try to shoot you?"

"It wasn't me." His face tightened. "I don't know anything about this."

We appraised each other for a long moment. I had the feeling he told the truth yet knew another version. Or at least guessed at it. I'd run into another wall of sticky diplomacy issues.

I knew why he hated Jeff Johnson. He must know about the Lees' connections. If the financial backing from the movie came from illegitimate means, the Lees wouldn't tell the associate producer. And he wouldn't ask. He'd already warned me about Vicki's relationship with them.

"Did Master Xi know my mother had asked Kevin Yuan to replace him?" The words burst from me. "Was he afraid of her?"

Zhou stared at me, then laughed.

"Xiáng Xi was not afraid of Vicki Albright," he said. "Someone like Shifu Xi scared of her?"

"She asked Kevin Yuan to coach Lili. Before Master Xi left."

"I see." He pulled out the desk chair, motioned me to it, and collapsed in the side chair near it. With the robe hanging open, the bruises exposed, and his large frame sprawled wide, the civil businessman had disappeared replaced by someone who appeared brutish. Dangerous.

I shivered.

"You think Vicki Albright forced Xiáng Xi to leave. Lied about his disappearance?" His brooding eyes pierced me. "Had him killed?"

When put so bluntly, what kind of daughter was I to think this of Vicki? Sure, she had lied to me. Stolen from me. And manipulated me. But this? It was like scraping all the good toppings off a bagel and still facing calories and carbs.

But still wanting the bagel.

"I'm not sure." I worried my lip. Then stopped. Mr. Zhou struck me as someone who'd note nervous habits as tells. "Does Vicki seem like a woman who'd do something like that?"

He shrugged. "I've learned not to be surprised by what people say or do. I look at motives. Why would she want Xiáng Xi out of the way?"

To give a lucrative and life-changing job to an old lover? To gift a Trojan Horse to Lili? To prove to the Lees her loyalty? To cement a new eco-system of alliances for building her empire?

People did demented things for love. Insane things for power and money. My criminal justice classes had taught me that. It wasn't just sociopathic behavior. Jealousy, greed, desperation, and pride drove criminal acts. A slow erosion of ethics and principles didn't help.

Vicki was crazy like a fox. But was Vicki this kind of crazy?

"She doesn't have a reason to murder him. It's a horrible thing to think about her."

"I believe you can do better than that." Zhou leaned

forward and clasped his hands. "I don't come from the same background as Lili, Stanley, or even the Lees. I grew up very poor. I was lucky to be a man where I came from. I struggled to rise above the poverty we faced in our city. And during that time, people I trusted and knew — even family — did things *too horrible* for me to think about. But it happened. I moved on."

My stomach cramped.

Zhou's gaze penetrated me. "You are a private investigator. You must care about the truth, right?"

I nodded.

"You should let this go, then. Some truths are *too horrible* to digest." He gazed pointedly at my stomach, where I'd unconsciously clamped my hands. "As for the gunshots in your mother's house. This troubles me greatly. It is not safe for Lili. I'm going to move her tomorrow."

I opened and shut my mouth. Vicki was going to kill me. But he was right. The Peanut Mansion wasn't safe. "What about everyone else? Your producers? Your costar, Stanley?"

"Haven't my motives been obvious?" He gave me a sad smile. "I only care about Lili."

I WEPT in the parking lot. Despite my original hesitation, I called Mowry, reported the fight between Zhou and Johnson and hinted at Johnson's disappearance. Without mentioning the weapon discharge.

I was still protecting Vicki. Why, I wasn't sure.

"Johnson's more than likely nursing his wounds," said Mowry. "He'll get over it."

"Keep an eye out for him, just in case," I said. "I don't trust him."

I drove back to Vicki's. I felt too groggy to reflect on what Mr. Zhou had said. Only his laser-focused zeal for protecting Lili penetrated my exhaustion. I needed that kind of discipline. I was too emotional about everything. Too wrapped in my feelings to do this case any justice.

What case, anyway? We'd found Xiáng Xi. Too late. I'd failed Lili. Now I was left with random door shootings and botched attempts on my life that might be meant for Vicki.

At least I had insisted on handling that myself so Nash could enjoy himself for once.

I parked Tiffany's car outside the garage, used the codes to enter the back door (finding them on thanks to Lydia), and schlepped into the mudroom. Heard Kevin arguing with Vicki in the kitchen. And hoofed it toward the backstairs.

Anything to avoid parents fighting.

Before reaching the second-floor landing, I heard a noise and paused. The grand staircase from the foyer met on the same landing, leading to the short flight to the guest wing. Below me, I could hear Vicki's rebuttal to the debate in the kitchen. I tuned my ears away from her dry tones, trying to determine from where the sound had emanated. A splash caught my ear. I relaxed. Just Charles. I was too tense.

Although I still didn't know where Jeff Johnson had gone.

I began my climb and stopped on the landing. I'd heard it again. Not quite a creak. I turned toward the gallery but moved back to glance up the stairs. No moving shadows. I hurried across the balcony. The hall beyond stretched before me, dark and ominous. The hall sconces had been turned off. I glanced up to wave at the doorbell cam.

No doorbell cam.

Before I could turn, a force struck my middle back, knocking out my breath. Grabbed my right arm. Bent it backward. Wheezing, I swung my body around. Swept my leg beneath theirs. They jumped, taking my arm with them. I crashed to the ground, pulling them with me. The attacker rolled. A knife flashed, pulled from the recesses of their garments.

They wore a sparring helmet with a spandex mask beneath. A chest protector covered their loose fitted gi. Dark rubber soled shoes and dark gloves concealed their hands and feet. Their crouch hid their size. Their stance showed they knew what to do with the knife. They didn't need the protection. It was a disguise. I was severely outmatched.

"Who are you?" I croaked.

They lunged. I coiled and lurched backward. Slammed into the wall. Pushed up. Staggered right. When they leapt, I stepped left and kicked out. The knife sliced. I heard the tear. Felt the sting on my thigh. And moved into their attack, anyway, shifting my weight to the left. An old *Kung Fu Kate* move.

My punch to their helmet did nothing to hurt them, but their head jerked back, exposing their neck. With my curled fingers, I hit their throat with the side of my open hand. Tiger Claw strike. Spun to the side and ran for my door. Banged on it. Looked back.

The masked intruder had disappeared.

FORTY-EIGHT
#CLUEREVISITED

IF BREAKFAST HAD BEEN A MOVIE, it would have been billed as *Brideshead Revisited* meets *Clue*. We acted as nothing had happened. Except for Stanley, who hooted softly at Zhou's black-eyed appearance. And Tiffany and Rhonda, who, with wide-eyed wonder, kept their mouths shut.

Mostly.

"What in the hell is this," muttered Tiffany, pointing at the congee on the buffet.

"Rice porridge," I said. "It's good. Savory. Like grits. Or oatmeal."

"Rice grits," said Rhonda. "I like that. Where's the cheese?"

Across the table, Lili and Shiyu kept their eyes on an iPad, murmuring softly. Zhou sat on the far end, pretending to read script notes while sipping coffee. Stanley cheerfully regaled us with Far East entertainment news. The Lees ate in their room (my guess).

The Lees had a *Wizard of Oz* vibe. For all my suspicions about them, I rarely saw them. Vicki had given them the proverbial curtain to hide behind. Whether she did that on purpose, I still wasn't sure.

I watched everyone, trying to surmise who my masked

assailant had been. I also pretended my thigh didn't have a deep cut that ached like a rotten tooth. I masked my limp by wearing my Gianvito Rossi motorcycle boots. Also by wearing them with R13's zebra print skinny jeans and Velvet Underground t-shirt.

Wardrobe can be magic like that.

But wardrobe worked both ways, as I learned the previous night from the masked intruder. Retrospectively, I believed the body armor had been taken from Kevin's uniform stash in the gym. Today, cashmere turtlenecks were popular with all the guests. A northwestern wind attacked Black Pine and old stone mansions weren't known for their warmth. They also hid marks to the neck.

Jeff Johnson didn't appear. But Vicki swept in, wearing Ralph Lauren and smelling of Armani Beauty. Kevin closely followed. Wearing Adidas. And a smile.

It seemed like they'd made up again.

I shuddered.

Motioning him into the hall, I made him follow me into the sitting room. Far from the maddening crowd. And walls with all their ears.

"Someone attacked me after my visit with Mr. Zhou," I whispered.

Kevin sucked in air through his teeth. "Where? Here or the resort? You have a bad history with both."

"Here. They jumped me in the hallway." I explained their costume and technique. "They were waiting for me. Prepared. Someone knew I had left the house."

"Are you hurt?"

"No, I used Tiger Claw strike to their throat and escaped."

He smiled. "I'm glad to see you have retained some of the skills I have taught you."

"Listen, after speaking to Mr. Zhou, I'm even more worried about Vicki's involvement with the Lees."

"I think she may suspect their criminal associations, but she doesn't want to know if their money is dirty. Vicki believes if she has no knowledge, then she is innocent of any wrongdoing. And she needs their backing for future capital as an associate producer." Kevin grimaced. "It's not a good character trait."

How did he miss her other not-so-good character traits? Love was blind, yadda. But still.

"You should tell her Zhou won't let Lili do business with her if she's involved with the Lees."

Floorboards sang outside the dining room. I pulled Kevin farther into the living room.

"Here's why I'm worried," I whispered. "Even if she doesn't think she has a connection to Xi's murder, in passing she might have mentioned wanting you as a coach for Lili. She talked you up and mentioned all the big names and movies you've worked on. And to get rid of Xi, they might have ordered a hit or something."

"God, I hope not." Kevin's expression crumpled. "How could they do something like that? Why not just fire him?"

"I can only guess at the workings of criminal minds. But the fact remains Xi was professionally killed. Or at least that's what the Clearwater police say. And the FBI is investigating, too."

Kevin rubbed his temples. "FBI? God."

"Maybe the CIA, as well." I shrugged. "Who knows." Probably not, but it didn't hurt to put the pressure on Vicki. "If you're serious, you need to know what you're getting yourself into."

"I'm glad I'm here to help. I will take care of your mother." He bowed.

I shuddered and scrunched my nose.

Kevin's eyes rolled. "Grow up, Maizie."

WE WALKED BACK to the dining room. Zhou's gaze followed me to my seat. His bruises were more evident today, including one on his throat. I tried to remember if I'd seen that mark the night before. Because of his open robe and boxers, I'd concentrated on keeping my eyes on his face.

Rhonda elbowed me. "Who's the hot guy" she whispered, pointing to Zhou beneath the table.

I pressed my lips together and cut my head in a quick shake.

"Lili," said Zhou. "Your suite at the resort will be ready this afternoon. And Shiyu, I have secured a room next door for you as well."

"What?" Lili looked up from her iPad. "How dare—"

"It has been brought to my attention someone fired a gun last night after I left."

Vicki sucked in air so hard her nostrils almost stuck together. "Maizie," she gasped, trying to exhale and speak at the same time. "May I speak to you for a moment. Now."

I firmed my lips and cut my head to the left.

"Oh, my goodness," said Stanley. "This takes the cake. My first American gunfight. No one was hurt though, I take it?"

Zhou stared at me.

I unstuck my lips. I'd scoured the front porch and the front walk before breakfast. No bullets and no dead bodies in the topiary. "Not that we're aware of. But—"

"Jeff is missing," cried Lili. "There were gunshots and Jeff hasn't returned."

Possibly because he was the one with the Makarov, but I didn't feel it polite to bring it up at breakfast. Also, I didn't have any evidence Jeff had been the shooter.

But I also hadn't any evidence he'd been shot. "There's a bullet in the front door. That's all I've found."

"It's been there for a week," said Vicki. "Mr. Zhou, Lili is perfectly safe here."

"A second bullet," I said. "Your door is riddled. In more ways than one."

"This is your fault, Zhou," said Lili. "Your jealousy is ruining this film."

"We're in preproduction, Lili," said Zhou. "Early days for a film to be ruined. Did you ask Mr. Johnson about the studio's accusations of corporate espionage." It wasn't a question. Did he have evidence that Johnson was a corporate spy? Or was he just messing with Lili?

"Jeff said he didn't do that," said Lili.

"And you believed him. Despite his background in technology."

"Of course, I believed him." She angled her chin away from him. "I'm not leaving. I'm very comfortable here."

"No thanks to you," muttered Vicki to me.

I returned her dagger stare.

"Ms. Albright, is Shifu Xi's room still available?" said Zhou. "I understand you had a different room readied for Master Yuan while Shifu Xi was still here."

Vicki's lips parted and closed. She'd been caught, but I had given Zhou the means to set the trap. I wasn't sure how I felt about that.

She sniffed. "Yes, Mr. Xi's room is still available."

"May I stay there? You may bill me. I do not find your home a safe place for my actors. The least I can do is stay nearby to protect them."

"I feel better already," said Stanley.

"I'm Lili's manager," said Vicki. "I'd never put her in harm's way. We're very safe here. My God, the Lees are staying here. If they feel fine, why wouldn't you?"

"You're being ridiculous, Zhou." Shiyu's words hissed through gritted teeth. "Enough already."

"Stalk much?" muttered Tiffany, plunging her spoon into the congee.

"He's protecting his actors, Tiff," whispered Rhonda. "Very romantic. Gentlemanly. And that black eye is hot."

"You're psychotic," said Tiffany.

"What are they doing here?" said Vicki, looking pointedly at my friends.

"Those are my guests." My voice rose.

"Everyone needs to calm down," said Kevin. In a steady voice, he spoke quickly in Chinese. Lili's burning cheeks faded to a rosy pink. Shiyu's eyes narrowed, but she nodded. Stanley laughed. Zhou's dark eyes gleamed.

"We will compromise," said Kevin. "I am giving my room to Maizie, and I will stay with Vicki. Maizie's an investigator. She can keep an eye on Vicki's guests. Mr. Zhou can stay in Shifu Xi's old room. Then he will feel better. And we will inform Mr. Johnson when he returns."

"He'll turn up," said Zhou. "He always does."

Shiyu glared at him.

"What was so funny?" I said to Kevin.

He blushed. "Just an old Chinese saying. Never mind."

I narrowed my eyes. Likely an old Chinese saying about which bed he preferred to sleep in. I knew the bed I wanted.

My own. With its cushy pillows and fluffy duvet.

Zhou stood. "Chey and the others will meet us at the studio. There are more changes to the script, but Vorling will explain at rehearsal. Master Yuan, I expect you're needed at the studio, too. The Lees want to watch the rehearsal, so I will accompany them."

Lili waited for him to leave before rising. "He is so high-handed."

"Zhou's a producer," said Stanley. "Why would you expect any different? His job is to order everyone around."

"But he also needs to follow orders," said Shiyu darkly. "Not just his heart."

FORTY-NINE
#DEATHANDTAXES

VICKI and her guests had gone to the studio. Tiffany and Rhonda left for work. For once the Peanut Mansion was empty. Except for the staff. I tried not to think of them as not counting, but I still tended to forget.

I popped the laptops and opened the windows for the doorbell cameras. Took out my trusty notepad. Prepared to look for suspicious intruders and to think. For what reason would someone want to attack me from going to my bedroom? No one but Vicki and the staff had known Tiffany and Rhonda had spent the night. Not until we appeared at breakfast, anyway. Therefore, they must have thought I couldn't be rescued.

Better question. Who had known I'd gone to Mr. Zhou's and returned? Other than Tiffany, Rhonda, Kevin, and possibly Vicki.

And Mr. Zhou.

Could Jeff Johnson have been watching Zhou and seen me? But why would he want to attack me? Why would anyone want to attack me?

Unless it had something do with Vicki. Maybe her purchase of the Peanut Mansion had inspired someone to ransom me.

A sharp knock rapped my door. I held in a shriek and slapped a hand over my heart to shove it back in place. No doorbell camera in our hall yet. I hadn't wanted to drag a ladder onto the gallery walk where the staff would see me. I leaned over the computer, searching for the screen to the foyer.

"Miss Albright? Are you in there?"

"Nash?" I knocked the computer aside, lunged, and fell off the bed. Scrambling to my feet, I lurched across the room and flung open the door.

He stepped inside, filling the room with his presence. A flannel shirt hung open to expose the Aerosmith t-shirt stretched over his muscular chest. He was gorgeously tan, and his shoulders had lost their usual rigidity.

I felt a little envious he could naturally achieve a color that would take me several appointments in a spray booth. His loose-limbed stance also made me jealous. I had a crick in my neck due to the pain in my neck, aka Vicki.

Nash ran a hand across his chin and his polar blue eyes sparked. "You're a sight for sore eyes." He grinned, flexing the dimple and scar. "Those are some pants."

I automatically glanced at the zebra stripes and quickly set my gaze back, drinking in all his wonderfulness. "What are you doing here?"

"There have been some developments. But before we get into that, it's freezing up here. How about I warm you up?"

I vaulted toward him and he caught me, laughing. I slid my hands inside the flannel and ran them along his back. Clung to his shoulders. And rested my cheek against his hard chest. He wrapped his arms around me and pressed me until I fit snugly against him.

"This looks a lot like our hotel room," he murmured into my hair. "Except the view is lake instead of ocean."

"It feels like a hotel. Has room service, too." I looked up.

His eyes were on the bed. "It's hard to imagine living like this. You didn't live like this with Boomer, did you?"

"No, it was more…normal."

His eyes were still glued to the bed.

"Nash, does it bother you that much?"

"Bother me?" He looked down. His eyes had darkened, like melted polar caps. Either through irritation at the grandiosity of my living situation or through a more personal, biological global warming. "Who's here? Anyone?"

"Just the staff. They've all gone to the studio."

"Good." He relaxed his arms and cupped my face in his hands, threading his fingers into my hair. "I've been wanting to do this for a long time."

He kissed me, long and slow. Taking his time. Patiently and thoroughly. I rose onto my toes. My fingers spread across the wide expanse of his shoulders, digging into the hard flesh through his t-shirt. He smelled like Nash but also like the sun and ocean. An intoxicating fragrance. It made me want to burrow into him. To have that scent on myself.

He drew back, his large hands still cradling my face. "You're so beautiful."

I smiled. "You must have good news."

"I don't want to talk yet." His lips crashed against mine and his thumbs caressed my cheeks. His hands dropped to my shoulders, then skimmed my sides. Wrapped around my back to land on my other set of cheeks and pulled me against him.

My own version of global warming was happening. Seismic activity caused by volcanic rumblings in my core.

His mouth trailed from my lips to my ear and down my neck. His hands roamed and returned. Frustratingly so. Nash gazed at me like he was trying to decide whether to cash in on his winning lottery ticket or save it for a rainy day.

"This place is very much like a hotel," I gasped. I didn't want the familial ownership of this house to come between us. I'd yearned for this moment, not just because of my feelings for him. Or physical attraction. I wanted that ultimate connection. To cement those feelings tangibly. To overcome all his gentlemanly conditions (I suspected) he'd made to protect me. Because of who he thought I was.

He wanted me to carry concealed, but Nash also wanted me safe from himself— in Snow White's glass-topped coffin. Until our world was perfect with acceptable housing and whatever else he deemed appropriate.

Didn't he get that the way our luck ran, we'd never have perfect?

For all my talk of serial engagements, I grew up in another world. Maybe it was different in Black Pine, but swiping right was the norm in my old zip code. My friends mocked my serial monogamy as PR moves. Relationship-wise, I hadn't been trendy, but I understood the norm.

Beyoncé's ring be damned, I wanted the norm. Right now. Like crazy.

A firestorm of emotions rushed through me. My hands snaked from his shoulders. I slid one up his chest and slipped the other around his waist. I pressed my hips against his, satisfied with the slack-jawed look it produced. Walking backward, I pulled him with me. Toward the bed.

"Why are you limping?" he panted.

"I'm not limping. I'm just excited."

"You're limping." He halted, forcing me to stop. "What did you do?"

"I thought we weren't talking yet." I yanked on him. "Come on."

He cocked his head. "Your right leg? Is it your ankle?"

Shizzles. Why had I taken off the boots? "I'm fine. I'm good. More than good—"

Nash bent to sweep me up in his arms and carried me to the bed. He gently set me on the edge and stepped back to gaze at me.

I sighed. This was our moment. The police and FBI were handling Xi's murder. Someone might want to kill me. Or Vicki. Or possibly they just hated her door. But all that could wait. My heart pounded and the tiny butterflies bouncing inside my stomach grew larger, dancing under my skin.

"It's not your ankle. You winced when I picked you up," he said. With more than a hint of accusation in his voice. "What aren't you telling me?"

I flopped back on the bed. "I give up." I sat up. "No, I don't. If I tell you, can we pick up where we stopped? I was greeted by another ninja, but it's all good. For now. At this moment. Okay, let's begin."

I drew myself onto my knees and leaned forward, arching my back and tilting my head up. Eager to be kissed.

Nothing happened.

Possibly I was a little too eager.

"I'm sorry. It was wrong of me to start something. I couldn't help myself. You just looked so good and I missed you." He crossed his arms. "Maizie, I've got to tell you something."

Shiplap.

Nash sat next to me on the bed. "Remember what I told you about the yin-yang contracts in China? How they're hunting tax dodgers?"

I nodded.

"The Feds pulled an email from Xi's phone. He had photographs of two contracts for Lili's last movie. One showing she made $1.6 million. The other stated her making $7.8 million. It looks like the recipient used a VPN to mask the email's IP address. But the Feds think the person was in the U.S. They can find the buried IP address. It's just a matter of time."

"Master Xi reported Lili? Why would he do that? I thought he was close to Lili."

"I don't know. Someone had to have helped him set up in Florida, so maybe he was paid off."

"Obviously, I'm not for cheating on taxes, but what the hey? Xi took payment for turning in a friend for tax dodging?" I drew myself up. "I can't believe it. He had a great job—"

"We don't know how he felt about the job. Or Lili." Nash smiled but his eyes didn't warm. "Not everyone has the same loyalty as you. If it makes you feel any better, the feds thinks

Xiáng Xi was patriotic. Maybe he was convinced it was the right thing to do."

"Thanks to her teacher, Lili's in tax trouble." I sucked in a breath. "Hells, if she's busted, will they revoke her visa and not let her do this movie? Do you think she'll be slapped with more than a fine? This could ruin her."

Nash took my hand and squeezed it. "I think with this information coming to light, there's a much bigger problem than revoking her visa."

A series of hurried knocks rapped on my door. I slid off the bed and approached the locked door.

"Miss Albright?" said Lydia. I opened the door for the housekeeper.

"Ms. Albright needs you in the foyer. Immediately. She says she doesn't care what you're wearing and to…" Lydia pulled in a breath. "'Get your ass in front of her, pronto.' I'm sorry, but I was supposed to direct quote her."

Shiplap. Lili was now the prime suspect in Xi's murder.

FIFTY
#FORFORK'SSAKE

WE HURRIED DOWN THE HALL, across the gallery, and rushed down the stairs. Below us, Kevin had his arm wrapped around Vicki. More to restrain than comfort her, it seemed. I'd never seen her angrier. Her beautiful skin was flushed and her green eyes glittered. Her fists clenched, and she leaned slightly forward in her Prada pumps.

Nash hesitated, then moved around me, and halted on the stairs. When I tried to move around him, he blocked me.

"You," shouted Vicki.

The front door opened and the rest of the *Unlucky 18* circus walked in. Including the director and producers. Just in time to see the spectacle.

Sucktastic.

Vicki trembled, and Kevin tightened his grip on her. "Do you know what you've done?"

All eyes moved from Vicki to me. Even Stanley didn't smile.

I had a pretty good idea of what she was going to say. But for some reason, my mouth uttered "what" without my brain stopping it.

Nash cast me a glance over his shoulder. His eyebrows lowered and he shook his head.

"Lili has been arrested," said Vicki. "The Lees are going back to China. I hope you're happy."

It didn't even remotely come close to making me happy. But I had the sense of mind to keep that thought to myself.

"You were supposed to figure out who killed Shifu Xi. And guess what Sherlock, it wasn't Lili."

Of course, Lili had the best and only motive we'd found. But sensibly, I also kept that to myself.

"Who called the police? Was it you?" She pointed at Nash.

"Vicki, we had to call the police," I said. "He was murdered."

"But federal agents? Really? You have gone too far."

"Xiáng Xi's a foreign citizen," said Nash calmly. "That's a federal matter."

Vicki's chest heaved. For a nanosecond, I feared she was going to code blue in the foyer. Then I realized it was from the exertion of trying to pull from Kevin's grip.

I backed up a step.

She glanced behind her, suddenly realizing the onlookers. Sipped in a breath to compose herself. "You're fired."

"What?" I said. "I'm fired?"

"No," she said. "Mr. Nash is fired. You'll be working for Annie Cox. She's affiliated with Georgia Association of Private whatever, so she can mentor you."

"Who?" Wait. "The woman at the office yesterday? I thought she was a potential client."

Nash stiffened.

"He's out. Annie's in."

"What the—" A stream of words I'd never uttered — or at least not since getting a Disney contract — launched from my mouth. "You set us up. You were waiting for a reason to fire Nash. You—"

The guests edged toward the living room, murmuring small apologies. Reaching the doorway, they rushed through. A splash from the reef tank told me I'd also offended Charles.

Nash turned around to face me. His face registered a mixture of shock, fear, sympathy, and perhaps a teeny bit of pride. Mostly astonishment and concern. "It's okay, Maizie. I knew this was coming." He winked. "Why do you think I was enjoying Florida so much?"

I sucked in air faster than I could expel it. Nash placed a hand on my shoulder and my breath slowed. Felt a piece of myself — the part that had hoped Vicki's bailout would actually help Nash get back on his feet and return to his old office — crumble into dust. Knowing that dust would be swept by servants and not Vicki herself, I cast my fury to the blonde in Ralph Lauren.

"You know something about this murder," I shouted. "That's why you have bullets in your doors, people trying to kidnap us, and attack me. Yet you haven't blinked an eye except to tell me not to call the police."

"Don't be ridiculous." She raised her chin but glanced sideways at Kevin. "I just know Lili didn't do it."

"Of course, Lili couldn't murder Shifu Xi. He was killed by a professional," I seethed, ignoring the tightening grip on my shoulder. "Unless you know she hired someone to do it. Like maybe her boyfriend? Jeff Johnson, along with everyone else, was in Florida the day of the murder. Quite convenient how everyone was in the same freaking city as the victim."

"Miss Albright. You are speaking out of turn," Nash muttered. "The information from the authorities is not for the public."

I ignored Nash. "I know why Lili's in trouble. And I think you do, too. It's called tax evasion."

"I know nothing of the sort." Vicki jerked out of Kevin's grasp and stalked toward the living room where her guests hovered. "Lunch will be served in thirty minutes."

"I quit," I screamed. "Daddy was right. We were 'fool-idiots' to allow you to bail us out. I'd rather flip burgers than work for you."

The words seemed to bounce off the wood and stone. Charles swam circles in the center of the tank.

Nash squeezed my shoulder and firmed his mouth. "You can't give up on the mentoring out of anger, Maizie. This will blow over. I'll get another job and we can...Just don't do this for me."

"This isn't for you," I said. "This is for me. She's done this to me my whole life and now she's gone too far. She's criminally negligent for fork's sake."

"You need a job. You're on probation."

"I'll work for DeerNose. And I'll move back to the cabin." Approaching Daddy, hat-in-hand, would require me to consume a king-sized plate of crow. But I was in an "anything is better than this" kind of mood. If Tiffany and Rhonda were right, Vicki might follow me to my next company and buy them out. She couldn't do that at DeerNose. "If he doesn't hire me, I do like burgers, so slinging hash might work, too."

Nash dropped his hand, bolted down the stairs, and flew across the foyer. He slammed an arm across the doorway, barring Vicki's exit. "You need to apologize to your daughter. You will regret it if you don't. Mark my words."

"The only thing I'm going to mark is your employee termination checklist." She narrowed her eyes. "Maizie used to be a sweet, amiable, tender-hearted young woman. Until she began working with you. Am I really to blame? After all, we've been together her whole life. Bad mother or not, I haven't treated her much differently than I'm doing now."

He dropped his arm.

"I thought you might want to think about that."

FIFTY-ONE
#HIDDENDRAGON

NASH HELPED ME PACK. Then assisted me in taking down the doorbell cameras. Thankfully, he didn't remark on that impropriety. My constant tears and sniffling presumably kept his thoughts to himself. He was never much of a talker, but I was glad of it for once.

Outside, he placed the suitcases on the sidewalk near his truck. He ran his hands up and down my arms, then dropped them to his sides. "You might be right about Lili, although you shouldn't have said it for everyone to hear."

"I know. That was stupid." Tears bit my eyes and I began to sob. Again. "But what will you do, Nash?"

"Don't worry about me." He shrugged. "I probably needed this kind of kick in the ass."

I stared at him through tear-filmed eyes. "She's been horrible to you. I'll never forgive her."

"Maizie, don't say that." He pulled me against him and tightened his arms around me. "It'll hurt you more than her. Having that kind of hate in your heart darkens your soul. I know this personally, and maybe it's what's been happening to you. Vicki's right. You're tender-hearted and sweet. At least, until you met me."

"What?" I looked up. "You're wrong and she's wrong. Vicki only said that to get under your skin."

He traced a tear down my cheek. "You can't blame her for pointing out the obvious. I've never liked her. I haven't kept those feelings to myself. I forced you between us. She's your mother, not just our boss. And dammit, I should've kept my mouth shut because it's hurt you. But I'm too big of a cocky sumbitch to swallow my damn pride. This isn't the first time pride has gotten in my way, darlin'."

I bit my lip and shook my head. Tears bounced off my cheeks and splattered my puffy coat.

"I'm no good. I don't know why you don't see it. Parents always see through me. Your friends see through me."

"Lamar is my friend and he loves you."

"Lamar pretty much raised me. And he'd tell you the same thing." Nash sighed. "I'm a fool to think I could make this work. I've got nothing, Maizie. Absolutely nothing to offer you. I keep trying to tell you this. Look what I've done to your career."

"You've had bad luck since meeting me. This isn't your fault. It's mine."

"Honey," he sighed. "My bad luck didn't start with you."

"We'll make our own luck," I said. "You said you'll get a job. And I'll get a job. That's what people do."

"But you're not just people," said Nash. "You're Maizie Albright. And you deserve a hell of a lot more than me."

His gaze drifted behind me. A car motored up the drive and stopped behind his truck. He waved and pointed at the suitcases.

"What are you doing?" I clutched his arm.

Misty hopped out and began loading my suitcases into the Escalade.

"Misty's taking you to the cabin." He ran a hand over his head and squeezed his eyes shut. When he opened them, he avoided looking at me. "Don't worry about Vicki. Until the Feds figure out who Lili hired to kill Xi, the Black Pine police will keep an eye on her. On you, too. I'm sure Mowry won't mind that job."

"Nash, don't do this." I hated the desperation in my voice. My throat caught. "I love you. Why are you doing this?"

"Just give yourself some time, then go see her. Don't take too long, though. Like ripping off a Band-Aid. Just get it done fast. And then you'll start to feel better."

"What are you talking about?"

"Making up with your mother." He glanced at me, then sprinted toward his truck.

FIFTY-TWO
#DRESSEDFORSUCCESS

IN THE BACK of the Escalade, I bruised my thumb from pinching. Despite it not stopping my tears. Or the gut-wrenching sobs that forced Misty to turn on the heavy-metal station again. To top it off, the cut in my thigh ached from taking down doorbell cameras and the blood had seeped through my bandage to stain my zebra-print skinny jeans.

At the cabin, I threw away the jeans and put on a pair of sweatpants and slippers for my meeting with Daddy. As much as I loved R13, I didn't care. The jeans reminded me of Nash, and I couldn't stand to look at them. And he'd only seen them once. I'd have to purge my wardrobe, which would leave me with my old clubbing outfits and red carpet attire. Which left room for shopping.

The fact that I didn't even want to shop made me realize how sideways my life had gone.

I shuffled to the wood-paneled (and dead animal) attired office. I felt a kinship with the animals, although I only felt dead inside. At his desk, Daddy waved me to a chair.

"Your sister has been a mess since you left," he said. "She claims you were bringing her back a hermit crab. That is a very bad idea."

"I told Remi I wasn't allowed to bring a crab on the airplane. I brought her a stuffed Mickey."

"Thank the Lord for small favors. I'm not comfortable empathizing with a hermit crab." He opened a binder and skimmed his thumb down a list. "Now, what can I do for you?"

Without preamble, I gave him a modified version of an explanation and apology. I left off the scene where my heart had been run over by an Escalade. "Neither of us are working for Vicki now."

"Good to hear." He kept his eyes on the open binder before him. "Nash was a fine security specialist. I used him to vet clients and investigate a few thefts. Hope he gets on good at another outfit. He's better than working for your mother."

"But he's not good enough for me?" I said, not bothering to remove the bitter from my voice. Bitter would be an important component in my new role as a rejected, broken-hearted loser and former doorbell camera installer.

"I wouldn't put it that way. But I couldn't see him having the financial wherewithal to handle you." Daddy gazed up over his readers. "And don't give me that malarky about being an independent woman. He's got a terrible credit rating which affects your score if you did hitch."

"Nash is a southern gentleman. That goes beyond credit ratings."

Daddy stared at me. "What in the hell is a southern gentleman?"

"Never mind. You offered me a job and I need a job. Does the offer still stand?"

"I'll set up an interview with HR. I hope you know how to dress for one."

I flinched. "I made *Vanity Fair*'s best-dressed list several years running."

"And I am the designer and founder of a clothing company that has made the Fortune 1000 list several years running."

"Do that many people want overalls that smell like deer pee?"

"I'd advise you not to ask questions like that in your interview." He pushed back in his chair. "Are you even aware of all the other apparel we design and manufacture?"

To be honest, I had never wanted to ask. In case of the expectations. Like wearing something that smelled like deer pee. More so, because I never wanted to hurt Daddy's feelings by wrinkling my nose.

"I think I need a primer," I said.

He beamed. Daddy loved nothing better than mansplaining. "You know, I always thought you got your love of fashion from me. The crazy fashion sense must be from your mother."

I felt my brow furrow with confusion. I had a feeling there were going to be many opportunities for furrowing my brow in the future.

But better brow-furrowing than crying.

I pinched my thumb and used my best craft skills to act my way into hunting apparel interest. It would be good practice for when the numbness wore off and I had to act like I hadn't just lost all my hopes and dreams for the future.

Not just for my career as a PI, but for the man I loved and was convinced still loved me, too.

BACK IN MY OLD BED, the night dragged on. Nash hadn't called. That wreaked havoc on my imagination. The memory of screaming obscenities at Vicki had left me humiliated and ashamed (more so for doing it in front of all the *Unlucky 18* cast and crew). My upcoming interview with DeerNose Human Resources played with my nerves. And then there was Remi.

Sleeping with a six-year-old was a sure guarantee of no sleep.

To disabuse myself of my other anxiety-producing thoughts, I pondered the notion that Xi had been guided to Florida by the person who had received the photographs of Lili's double contracts. Previously, I had thought the Clearwater connection had been merely the coincidence caused by the popularity of the beach destination. After spending the night ruminating over it, I felt this government-connected agent had set Xi up.

Or more likely, set Lili up.

If something happened to Xi, the person with the greatest motive to off him — Lili — would be in the vicinity. If true, this agent had known not only the Lees had a condo in Clearwater, but that Lili and her entourage would be brunching at said condo.

Someone close to Lili had framed her and possibly killed Xi. He was no longer needed, after all. A disgraced actress with a dodgy alibi was an easy scapegoat for murder.

Who was the actual culprit? Jeff Johnson topped my list, but I had no evidence or motive.

I rose from the bed, snuck to my childhood desk, and turned on a lamp. When it appeared I hadn't woken Remi, I pulled out a notebook and made a pro and con list for Jeff as number one suspect.

Zhao said Jeff had hidden the bugging devices and accused him of corporate espionage. But Zhao was also in love with Lili, so he was an unreliable source. Both pro and con.

Nobody seemed to like Jeff, including me and Xi. Excluding the woman who was currently in jail and might have been framed. I couldn't decide if either counted and moved on.

Jeff disappeared and reappeared with alarming consistency. Yet Lili had wanted me to find him after he'd only been gone a day. Lili had known something might happen to both men because of her. She'd been surprised when I'd said we'd initially found Xi alive. Later she'd been frantic about the gunshots and Jeff missing.

Stanley had said Lili hadn't necessarily wanted help finding Xi and Jeff. He thought she wanted me to help her. Lili must have suspected betrayal by someone close to her. I still wasn't sure if it was Jeff.

I also wasn't sure if it wasn't.

AT THE BREAK OF DAWN, I peeled Remi's arm off my face and her foot out of my armpit. Rose and showered. Donned a Burberry fawn-print skirt (Burberry could also do camouflage) with coordinating pumps. Then picked up the DeerNose blazer I'd borrowed from Carol Lynn (surprisingly un-scented) and slipped it over my blouse.

It'd been a while since I'd worn anything but jeans and sneakers to work. The act of dressing up for work depressed me. I really had changed.

I picked up my phone. My dead phone.

I'd left the charging cord at Vicki's and forgotten to ask Carol Lynn if they had an extra. I ran into the kitchen and plugged it into the charging station. Choked down a biscuit sandwich and checked my messages. One from Giulio. Three from the girls.

None from Nash.

None from Vicki.

I listened to Tiffany and Rhonda's semi-comforting messages — "you're better off" and "I knew Vicki would trigger you" and "can I post pictures of the Peanut Mansion because I already did" — and played Giulio's.

"Darling, I'm just calling to say I am sorry to hear about the unfortunate incident. I understand you're available. I have won out over most of my competitors, but there's always the very small chance I can lose. In that case, I will call you in a few days. *Ciao.*"

Unfortunately, erasing a message didn't have the same impact of hanging up.

I recharged my phone, asked Carol Lynn if I could borrow her minivan. I was two hours early for my interview, wanting my phone charger, and disturbed by my musings during the night. I turned around at the gate, drove through town, and up the mountain road to the Peanut Mansion. Parked and marched up the steps and into the house.

Which was not locked. Again.

In the foyer, I studied my gorgeous Burberry pumps and fought the rage building inside of me. Looked up. And spotted Jeff Johnson.

Floating in the coral reef tank.

FIFTY-THREE
#NOTACORONER

I RUSHED FORWARD, clamping a hand against my scream.

Jeff Johnson lay face up in the water, floating near the top of the tank. Charles circled him and bumped against the body with his nose.

"Do. Not. Eat. Him," I shouted.

I ran for the stairway. Bolted up the stairs and across the gallery. I stopped above the aquarium. Jeff Johnson was dead. Not by drowning. He wasn't bloated and blue. Killed by the bullet lodged in his head. Just like Master Xi. Jeff had been shot and fell in the tank. Or was dumped there. He wasn't bleeding. Yet his limbs hung loosely, not stiffened with rigor mortis. But perhaps that was due to the water.

Why had we spent so much time talking about fly larvae in Forensic Anthropology at Cal State Long Beach? I could have used more rigor examples.

Okay, Maizie, you don't need to establish time of death, because number one, you're not a coroner. Number two, you're in shock and trying to distract yourself.

And number three, Jeff wore the same clothing from the night he disappeared. After his fight with Zhou. Either he'd been in hiding all this time, or he never left the house because someone murdered him on the gallery. With a pistol.

I spun around. The office door had been locked yesterday. Not so today.

Because it no longer held a body. Did it hold a gun?

I slipped into the office and ran to the desk. Felt beneath. No gun. The Velcro was gone, too.

The killer could still be in the house. With a gun.

I sprinted toward Vicki's room and banged on the door. The door swung open.

"Vicki?" I called, hurrying through the suite. No Vicki. No Kevin.

I yanked open the closet door. Moved the shoe boxes and tapped in the code to the panic room. The door swung open.

No Vicki. No Kevin.

The edges of panic, held back by my activity, began to close in. I stood in the closet, sucking in air, unable to think.

Maizie, you're hyperventilating. Claustrophobia isn't helping the situation. Get out of the closet.

I lunged out the door. Took in a deep breath of bedroom air and tasted Beautiful. Vicki had been here recently. I hunted through the room and found her Birkin sitting on the escritoire. Wallet, phone, iPad, makeup bag, and scheduler packed tidily inside.

Shiplap.

Okay, think. She's in the house somewhere. Possibly, no one had gone into the foyer yet and the killer had recently left Jeff as a calling card. Perhaps the killer didn't want to murder anyone else. It was early. Breakfast would be served later. I wouldn't think a hitman would stick around to eat breakfast.

But I should find Vicki. Check to make sure she's safe. In case…

The memory of bullet holes in Jeff and Xi caused me to double over. I clutched my stomach and forced myself upright. I had to find Vicki.

Kitchen.

Did Vicki ever go in the kitchen?

Gym.

I dashed for the door and slammed my shoulder into the frame in my rush.

Right. Phone. Call the police.

I pulled my phone from the blazer pocket and touched the screen. Nothing. I clicked the power button. Shook it.

"Shiplap," I screamed.

Shoving my dead phone back in my pocket, I jogged toward the stairs. I peered up the steps toward the guest floor, debated, and flew down the backstairs. Took a left toward the gym. The lights were off. I slapped them on. Peeked into the dressing room, the sauna, and showers. Bounded out of the gym. And fell against the wall, panting.

Maybe everyone was murdered.

There's a dark thought.

Phone. I needed a phone.

Kitchen.

Lord, help me, I hoped I wasn't playing Clue for real.

FIFTY-FOUR
#NOTTWIDDLINGTHUMBS

IN THE KITCHEN, I found Lydia. Limping toward her, I fell into her arms and cried. A dangerous choice. She was cooking bacon and still held an egg.

"What's all this?" said Lydia. "Break up with your boyfriend?"

"Well, yes, actually." I stopped myself from going down that road. "Phone. Does the kitchen have a phone?"

"Miss Vicki declined to put in a house phone. She said they're passé," said Lydia. "I tell you what's not passé. Calling workmen and what not, which she expects me to do. We dickered over that detail, I tell you."

Fabulous. "Where's everyone? Vicki, particularly."

"Let's see." She cracked the egg into a bowl and picked up another. "The Lees left yesterday. Good riddance, if I had anything to say about it. I couldn't keep up with the trays for the translator, Jen. Constantly wanting room service. Did you ever hear of such—"

"I don't mean to rush you, Miss Lydia, but there's a bit of an emergency. Anyone home besides you?"

"Stanley and Kevin already left for the studio. I made them breakfast sandwiches to go. I like that Stanley. Always going on about my cooking—"

"Lovely, lovely man. Kevin, too. And how about Vicki?"

"She doesn't eat breakfast." Lydia cracked another egg. Not much to say about Vicki. "You know who's a good eater? Shiyu. She'll be down, but with sweet Lili in jail— Did you hear about that? Oh, my stars, you could have hit me with a brick—"

"Yep, all caught up on gossip." Obviously, Lydia hadn't heard my screaming yesterday. "Anyone else home?"

"There's a new man. A Mr. Zhou. Quiet type but very nice. Always compliments my cooking." She cracked another egg. "Misty's not here yet. Nor the girl who helps with the cleaning. Yard man's come and gone already. Who else?"

"Vicki. Where's Vicki?"

"She doesn't eat breakfast, remember?" When I nodded, she paused. "You want to know where she is?"

Nod. Nod. Nod.

"I believe she's going to visit Lili. Should be down shortly. Maybe catch her when Misty drives up."

"Miss Lydia, you need to leave. Call the girl who does the cleaning and go to brunch together. I'll pay. Sound good?"

"Brunch." She snorted. "What do you think I'm doing after I finish cooking everyone's breakfast? Twiddling my thumbs?"

"Miss Lydia, you need to leave this house right now." She opened her mouth to argue, but I continued. "There's a dead man in the coral reef tank. I need a phone to call the police."

Her face paled and eyes widened three times their normal size. I shoved Lydia onto a chair and pushed her head between her knees.

"Bacon." Lydia gulped air and sat up. Turned off the bacon. Fluttered her hands above the eggs.

"Time to go."

"But the eggs." She glanced at the stove. "And that bacon needs to be taken out."

"I'll put the eggs in the fridge. I'll take care of the bacon. Please, Lydia. You need to go now."

"Miss Vicki does not like a messy kitchen. I should do a quick wipe down, at least."

I didn't want to tell her Miss Vicki could be dead. I couldn't say the words. Instead, I handed her twenty dollars. "For your brunch. I promise, I won't leave the kitchen a mess."

I hustled her to the door. On the way, we retrieved her coat, her purse, the shopping list, and garbage. I felt like asking for my twenty dollars back.

"And Miss Lydia, as soon as you're off the property, please call the police. 9-1-1. Tell them what I told you." I paused, thinking about Lydia's delivery. "Only the part about the man in the tank."

I needed to check on the remaining guests. A hitman could be hiding in the house.

Having caught my breath, I ran up the backstairs to the third floor. And stopped. I shouldn't assume Jeff Johnson had been killed by a hitman. The execution had been the same as Master Xi's murder, but Lamar had said the Makarov was accurate. The killer didn't have to be a sharpshooter.

Most likely the killer was someone who stayed in the house.

I needed to be careful. But I also needed to find Vicki, Shiyu, and Zhou in case it was someone else. Perhaps they had an early morning collaboration. I knocked on Shiyu's door first. She didn't answer. I tested the lock. Hustled to Lili's room and knocked. No answer. Locked. Ran to Zhou's room.

Also, no answer.

I rattled the knob. Pulled out my wallet and took out my Albright Security credit card. A gold card meant for work expenses. Vicki had said, "And Maizie, expenses doesn't mean lunch." But she hadn't said anything about not using the card for breaking and entering. I leaned against the door. Slid the card between the door and jamb and began to wiggle. Jiggled the handle. The door opened.

Now was not the time to rant about how anyone with

wikiHow knowledge could break into a room inside a house with million-dollar security features.

Zhou's room — Master Xi's old Green Room — was tidy and unencumbered with personal effects. Also unencumbered with bodies or weapons.

Thankfully.

I shut his door and broke into Shiyu's room.

No bodies here either. However, in terms of tidiness, the similarities ended. Her bed wasn't made, and the clothes lay on chairs and the bed. But more in a "I'm in a hurry because of my schedule" way, rather than in a "total slob" or "I murdered someone and need to get the heck out of Dodge" way. I crossed the room to the bathroom and knocked. No running water. I opened and peeked.

No dead bodies. Also, no live people.

Panic fluttered in my chest. There were many rooms in this house to explore. But Vicki, Shiyu, and Zhou should be in their rooms at this hour. Their absence implied a different story.

What would Nash do?

The thought made me wince but also honed my senses.

Let the police search the entire house. They'd be here soon.

But I wasn't leaving until the police arrived or I found Vicki. Whichever came first.

I moved through the room, examining Shiyu's things while trying not to disturb anything for the police. Scripts were piled by her nightstand. Her iPad charged on the escritoire. A quick tap caused the screen to light up, previewing her notifications. Today's schedule, unread messages, and the weather appeared before the screen darkened. All in Chinese.

Disappointing. Not that I expected her Reminders notification to show, "Six a.m., hide in the laundry room." I turned to study the messy room. Folded my arms.

The tossed clothes appeared distinctly piled and chaotic at the same time. No separation between whites and darks, dry cleaning and permanent press. The laundry basket was empty and so were half of the hangers in her closet. Almost like Shiyu had been in the middle of a Maria Kondo tidying experiment, piling sparked and unsparked joy.

Not that I knew Shiyu well, but it seemed odd. Especially for a temporary living situation.

I slipped my hand inside the first pile, wiggling and patting. With Jeff Johnson in the fish tank and everyone missing, I didn't want to disturb anything crucial. In the middle of the second pile, I felt something hard amongst the cushioning. I carefully lifted the clothes on top, set them aside, and stared at a Uniqlo down-filled coat. Patted it again. With a sock covering my hand, I unzipped the jacket and peeled back the front panels.

A computer lay inside. If I remembered correctly, Xi's laptop.

Shiplap.

FIFTY-FIVE
#FINALISTFORWORSTDETECTIVE

I LEFT the puffy coat open with the computer exposed. Not wanting to further disturb Shiyu's room, I moved to Zhou's. I sat on his small loveseat and forced myself to think instead of react. The police would be here soon.

If Shiyu had Xi's computer, she or Lili must have figured out he'd turned Lili in for the yin-yang contracts. Possibly, Lili had asked Shiyu to hold the laptop. Maybe stealing the computer and phone had triggered Xi into running.

Or he had run, abandoning the laptop so he'd remained untraceable. They'd found it in his room. Knew why Xi had run. Hid the computer and phone in Vicki's office. And hired a private investigator (me) to search for him. Therefore, they could tell the hitman where to find him.

I led them right to Xi. Me and my stupid saltwater taffy clue.

A new ball of agony slogged around my stomach and rolled up my throat. My skin prickled. Dots danced before my eyes. But not the red spots this time. Just the normal pinpricks that occurred before passing out from stress.

I collapsed over my knees and shoved my head between them. Took a cleansing Ujjayi breath, opened my eyes, and spied the corner of something beneath the loveseat. I drug the thick paper from beneath the green damask flounce. A photo of Xi and Lili. Forgotten by Xi and missed by the maid. It appeared to have been taken after practice or a match. Both wore traditional gi. They'd been captured high-fiving and smiling. Lili's long hair was pulled back in a ponytail. Even from the side, the photo revealed the adoration on her face. His, too.

Lili had seemed sincere when she'd asked me to look for Xi. Sincere and worried. Later, I'd thought she'd been acting. Then I'd thought Lili had been framed by Jeff. Finding him in the tank changed my mind. Finding this photo changed my mind again.

Gah.

Once more, I won the worst-private-investigator-of-all-time award. I constantly made decisions based on little evidence. I'd done it in this case and previous cases, allowing my emotions to lead me down rabbit trails and waste time.

I also adulted badly. I'd put my friends in danger. I'd disappointed Daddy by working for Vicki (and now missing my interview). Put Remi through the stress of fighting with our father. Damaged a new relationship with Kevin because my feelings had been hurt. I'd thought he liked and cared about me for me. Not because he'd been sleeping with my mother.

That was how a child thought. I was an adult. I'd liked and cared about Kevin back then. For that reason, my feelings for Kevin shouldn't change now. Despite his questionable taste in women.

And poor Nash. I'd done everything in my power to manipulate him into hiring me and seduce him into loving me. Then destroyed his business and broke his heart.

Most especially, I failed Vicki. She was a huge pain in my butt, but I'd left her when she needed me the most.

I'd make up for all of it. Hopefully.

Leaving my preconceptions on the loveseat with Master Xi's photo, I tore out of his bedroom. I had more rooms to inspect. Starting with Lili's. Using my Albright Security gold card, I listened at the door, then broke into her room. Quietly closed her door and hugged the wall. Took my time to listen for movement in the bedroom area. In the sitting area, everything looked like I'd last seen it. Tea service in the side cabinet. The framed photo of Lili and Jeff on the table near the couch.

Lili had loved him, too. She wouldn't have wanted Jeff killed.

But I couldn't shake the thought he seemed like an imposter. There had to be a reason for his death.

Facts only, Miss Albright. The laptop was in Shiyu's room. The laptop implicated her. She appeared loyal and introverted, almost skittish, but it meant nothing. She never kowtowed to Zhou. Shiyu knew kung fu but downplayed it. She could have attacked me.

She'd refused to shake my right hand and forced me to use my left, which was weird. I'd seen her wince using that hand. Like it was bruised. Lamar had said the Makarov's recoil made his hand feel broken. Shiyu had also been in Clearwater the day of Xi's murder. I never asked if she'd brunched with the Lees. She could have accompanied Lili, left, and returned. Shiyu had the means and opportunity.

The flash of sunglasses I'd seen when the driver had spoken to Xi's exotic dancer friend…

I gasped. I had presumed sunglasses because we were in Florida. It'd been regular glasses. Shiyu's glasses.

Hopping from the loveseat, I began to pace. What about motive?

Retribution for Xi's betrayal.

But did she like working for Lili that much?

A lunatic might turn to homicide. Shiyu didn't seem erratic enough to be a lunatic. Unless she was sociopathic. As a sociopath, she was extremely high-functioning. All business. Like Christian Bale's character in *American Psycho*.

In that case, I'd find more bodies.

Shuddering, I moved toward Lili's bedroom, placed my ear against the pocket doors, and slid them open. No dead bodies, thank goodness. Vicki's housecleaner had made the bed and tidied. Even if the guest currently resided in jail, the bedroom had been readied for her return.

For Vicki's sake, I hoped Lili was cleared of any crimes and misdeeds.

Assuming Vicki was still alive.

I couldn't go there.

Hurrying back to the living room, I thought about my next move. The floor creaked outside the door. Goosebumps broke on my skin and a chill climbed my neck. I placed my ear against the door. Someone was in the hall. It couldn't be law enforcement. The police would call out, announcing their presence. Looking for me and the others. I'd been listening for them.

Not for the sound of scurrying.

I cracked Lili's door and peered into the hall. At the far end, Shiyu moved toward the Lees' suite. I waited until she slipped through their door. I scurried out of Lili's room and down the hall. A sliver of light shone beneath their door. I pressed my ear against it. Heard the faint sounds of movement. Then Shiyu spoke. In Chinese.

Someone was in the room with her.

Or she was on the phone.

Nash had once read me an article about RF Capture technology developed at MIT. It could detect motion through walls using wifi signals. Very handy for cases like this. Zhou's spoon worked well, too. I had neither, so I kept my ear to the door.

If I'd found the laptop hiding in Zhou's room, I'd have been less surprised. Zhou had good motives for murder. He'd already beaten up Vorling for Lili's honor. He hated Jeff. Revenge on Lili's behalf would fit for the murder of Xi. Zhou had been angry after the fight with Jeff. An hour or two after seeing him at the resort, he'd still given me shivers. Zhou could have waited, shot Jeff on the gallery, and hid his body in the office until he had a chance to toss it in the fish tank.

Although the water burial didn't make much sense. Black Pine Lake would have been a much better choice for hiding a body. What kind of statement did the aquarium make? A threat to Vicki, possibly. Like the horse head in *The Godfather*.

I'd returned to my movie-mob theories. But Xiáng Xi had chosen the alias of Tang Lung in *The Way of the Dragon*. The mob had been after Tang's family. Lili was Xi's family. But unlike Bruce Lee's Tang Lung, Xi had fled instead of fought. And he had betrayed Lili by exposing her double contracts.

Zhou loved Lili. But Shiyu had the laptop.

My attention drew back to the Lees' suite. Shiyu's rapid-fire discourse had ended. The bang of wood-on-wood marked the slamming of the pocket doors. I heard more speaking, but fainter than before. A lower rumble this time. Then a woman's scream.

Vicki's.

FIFTY-SIX
#HOWITDOESN'TEND

I SLOWLY ROTATED the door handle, expecting the Lees' door to be locked. It wasn't. The police hadn't arrived. And Vicki was inside. My mother needed me.

I could feel my heart hammering in the back of my neck. My clamped teeth made my mouth ache. I wiggled my jaw, then forced myself to shake out my limbs. Tilted my head toward each shoulder. Rotated my shoulders back. The moves made me think of Bruce Lee again, preparing for battle. Or the tough guys cracking their knuckles before a fight.

Tension was a killer on your joints. Before a match, you'd warm-up. In a movie fight, the villain didn't let you stretch first.

I pulled the door open and slipped inside. Moved to the wall and shimmied to the corner closest to the pocket doors. Inside the bedroom, footsteps marked someone pacing. They were thinking. Or angry. Something rustled and the footsteps stopped. Shiyu's angry voice barked a few words in Chinese.

"This is never going to work," snapped Vicki. "And I've seen enough movies to know how it ends."

"Shut up," said Shiyu. "I need to think. You're such an idiot."

I drew back against the wall to analyze the words. Totally not what I was expecting. I didn't know what I was expecting.

Maybe it shouldn't surprise me. But if her life was in danger, pleading for her life seemed more apropos. With an appeal for a phone call, perhaps. Last words. Possibly an apology to her daughter.

Okay, Maizie, get real. She may be facing death, but she's still Vicki. Focus.

"You're unreasonable," said Zhou, confirming my suspicions of the low rumble I'd heard earlier.

"You can't control your anger. And now we have this."

I wished Shiyu could be more specific. What was "this?" As I had told Remi many a time, you didn't get the whole story when you eavesdropped.

Right, focus.

"I will confess," said Zhou. "Johnson has ruined everything. It's too late anyway."

Hold the phone. Johnson?

"What's too late?" said Vicki. "Too late for Lili? I understand the government will hold her accountable, but Fan B—"

"Fan was detained by the authorities for four months, paid a hefty fine, and was essentially blacklisted in China," growled Zhou. "And her manager was arrested. Luckily for that actress, she and her family were loyal members of the party. But she was still used as a warning."

"How could I be arrested?" gasped Vicki. "This happened before I signed Lili. I thought she was immigrating."

My eyes narrowed. Had Vicki been abducted, or was she in on this?

I'd placed my life on the line for a woman who'd been complicit in murder.

The red dots danced in my vision. Blowing air from my nose, I pushed away from the wall. The pocket doors rattled. I jumped back against the wall.

Shiyu spat out words in Chinese.

"I don't care about any of that," said Zhou.

"Obviously," said Shiyu. "It ends with you."

Behind the door, someone whimpered. My chest tightened. Vicki didn't whimper. Why was she whimpering?

Did it end with Zhou? Or Vicki? What was ending?

The faint strains of sniffling turned to quiet sobs.

My eyes smarted. And my skin felt prickly. Shizzles, I had to do something. Was Shiyu armed? Was Zhou? I couldn't tell if they were working together.

I'd never heard Vicki cry before.

I forgave her. Everything.

A noise in the hallway drew my attention. Shouting. The police. I sighed but shook out my limbs again. There could be a showdown. Vicki could be killed. I had to prepare to protect her.

For a fight, *Kung Fu Kate* relied on martial arts. *Julia Pinkerton* used household items (Guns were deemed too violent and a bad example for teenagers). If Shiyu had done the compliance hold on me, my chances against Shiyu were better if I imitated Julia Pinkerton. My eyes skimmed the room, seeking a weapon. Tea kettle. Vase. Orchid. Where was a fire extinguisher or a letter opener when I needed one?

Readying myself, I yanked off the camo blazer and leaned over to kick off my pumps. Remi was right. The heels could be handy. Handier than an orchid anyway.

The shouting grew louder. And more personal.

"Maizie," shouted Nash. "Where are you?"

What in the fork was Nash doing here? And where was the police?

The pocket doors slid open. I grasped a stiletto in my left hand and recoiled against the wall. Moved my weight to the ball of my left foot. Shiyu stormed out of the bedroom, leaving the doors partially open. Without glancing back, she stalked to the hall door.

I rushed to attack her with my shoe. She stopped and pivoted. Slid to the side. I compensated and leaped. I wasn't going to kung fu battle. I wanted to take her out and down. We thudded to the floor. She bucked below me. I spread my arms and legs, trying to use dead weight to keep her down. Her arms snaked around and punched my back and kidneys. Her legs squirmed beneath me, sliding out to grapple mine.

Raising my hand, I slammed the sole of the shoe against her nose. Burberry made a well-constructed shoe. Her eyes squeezed shut and face scrunched. I pressed the heel against her throat.

"Don't move," I said. "Your throat is tender. And this is a four-inch stiletto."

"Get off her," said Zhou.

I glanced over my shoulder. "She killed Xi and Jeff."

"Shiyu's doing her job. I'm the one who made the mistake."

"It's true," said Shiyu.

My head whipped back to look at her. Her eyes were open. Tears glimmered at the corners, but her reddened nose told me it was pain, not sorrow.

"Zhou's an idiot," continued Shiyu. "Why push Jeff into the tank? To teach Vicki a lesson? Stupid."

"I hate him," said Zhou. "I wasn't going to do it. It just happened."

"Even more stupid," said Shiyu. "And lazy."

"But who killed Jeff and Xi? Zhou?"

"Zhou put the Lees in jeopardy," said Shiyu.

"Jeff Johnson put the Lees in jeopardy," shouted Zhou.

"Shiyu, do you work for the Lees?" I was confused all over again. "Not for Lili?"

Shiyu's eyes narrowed. Not at me. Her gaze had moved to the ceiling. "I handled it. You made it worse."

She spoke to Zhou, ignoring me. I still couldn't get anyone to answer my questions. So frustrating.

"I'll make it right," he said. "I have no choice now anyway."

"Get off of me." Shiyu swept her hand at the shoe, knocking it out of my hand. She rolled over, dumping me on the ground, and sprang to her feet.

So much for my awesome fight moves.

"Vicki?" I called, scrambling up. "Are you all right?"

"She's fine for now," said Zhou. He looked at Shiyu. "Take care of it."

Shiyu reached under her shirt, unclipped a holster, and drew out a pistol.

I held my breath, my brain buzzing with regrets. This couldn't be how it ended.

"I'm sorry," I called to Vicki. "I love you, Mom."

Shiyu rolled her eyes, pivoted, and grasped the door handle.

This wasn't how it ended. At least not for me.

"Watch it, Nash," I screamed. "Shiyu's got a gun."

FIFTY-SEVEN
#BUTIDIDN'TSHOOTTHEDEPUTY

SHIYU SLIPPED OUT THE DOOR, tossing me a look of contempt. My body tensed, trying to ascertain what would happen in the hall. I felt afraid to breathe. I also had to pee. Nerves. My attention drew to Zhou. He stood before the bedroom. Holding a gun. Watching me. Guarding what lay behind the pocket doors.

Vicki.

I moved forward. Stopped. Pivoted.

Nash.

"Which one?" whispered Zhou. The question was meant to be snide and it stung.

The gangster tattoos made sense. Zhou was no more a producer than Chili Palmer in *Get Shorty*. I liked Chili as a character. Zhou was no Chili Palmer. Zhou was just a thug trying to be a movie guy for Lili.

"Which one what?" I said.

"Which one will you try to save. You won't succeed, but you'll try. You see everything in terms of identity. That is why you're conflicted."

"I—" Dammit. I hated philosophical villains. "Just open the door so I can see if Vicki's okay."

Zhou shrugged, stepped to the side, and slid the door open.

Vicki sat on the edge of the bed, her head and shoulders bowed. She glanced toward me. Mascara smeared. Her nose pink.

I'd never seen her makeup smudged let alone raccooned.

She gasped. "Maizie? I thought I heard you. What—"

A gunshot rang from the hallway.

Clenching my fists, I stared up at the ceiling. "Nash?" I shouted.

My nerves spasmed at the silence that followed. I dropped my gaze, picked up my shoe, and threw it at Zhou. He held out a hand to block the shoe.

I ran forward, slamming into him with my hands and pushing to spring back. He staggered backward. I slid my left foot forward. Raised my right knee. Aimed for his groin. As Zhou doubled forward, I threw my right elbow at his face, slamming it against his nose. His hand fumbled with the gun's grip. I grabbed his face and pressed my thumbs in his eyes. Ripped the gun from his hand. Jumped into the bedroom and slammed the pocket doors closed.

I couldn't perform real kung fu. But I could do a pushup, climb a stair, pull my seat belt, and test a melon. Self-defense moves Kevin had taught me along with stage fighting.

The element of surprise helped. A lot.

"Bathroom," I said. "Go."

"Maizie," said Vicki.

"Go. Now. Lock the door. If anyone tries to break in, take the lid of the toilet tank and swing it at them. Hard."

Her jaw dropped. I pointed. She hopped from the bed and ran to the bathroom. I pivoted and opened the pocket doors. Zhou was gone and the door to the hall stood open.

"Nash," I called. "I'm armed. Vicki's safe. I'm armed and coming for you."

I paused in the doorway.

"Not to kill you," I added. "I mean, I'm coming to save you."

I crept down the hall. The silence was worse than the gunshots. Almost.

At the end of the hall, a long shadow darkened the floor. The lights in the stairwell had been turned off, but the dim glow from the foyer betrayed the lurker. I slipped to the same side and flattened against the wall. The figure hid near the short flight leading to the landing where the two main staircases converged with the gallery.

The only exit off the floor.

Shiplap.

Behind me, something metallic rattled.

Double shiz.

My pulse thudded in my ears. I gripped the pistol in both hands. Pointed it toward the floor in front of me. Slid the safety off. Swiveled slowly so I could see in both directions without turning my body. I planted my feet and focused on slowing my breathing. Steadying my movements. Lessons from my father. Meant for deer hunting, but I'd use what I had. I wasn't going to use it on a deer, that was for sure.

Across the hall, the door to Zhou's room stood ajar. Just a sliver. Enough for someone to peek into the hall. I wondered about weapons. Remembered the Velcro under the desk. But that was probably for Shiyu to hide her gun. Zhao had moved from the hotel. He could have hidden an armory in his room. Like an amateur, I didn't check. Too busy deciding if Shiyu was the only culprit.

I had so much to learn.

The shadow down the hall stirred.

I swallowed. If I moved, the shadow would see me. But I was also in a direct line of fire from Zhou's room. I glanced down the hall to the Lees' suite. At least I knew Vicki was safe.

I'd chosen her over Nash.

Not thinking about that now.

I concentrated on the two figures in the hall. An icy chill crept up my feet and legs. My breath moved in short pants. I fought to quiet my movements. The house felt preternaturally still. Small ticks and groans from the walls and the low whoosh of the furnace broke the silence. The pistol in my hand terrified me. I was scared to shoot it. Scared the recoil would hurt me. Scared it would hurt someone else.

Zhou's door creaked and the crack widened. The tip of a revolver touched the door frame. I wanted to shrink to the floor. Curl up in a ball. A ball with bulletproof coating. Instead, I cautiously swung my arms up. Locked my elbows, relaxed them a tiny bit, and looked down the sight. Slid my finger onto the trigger. Aimed the sight at the space between the door and frame. And waited.

The shadow moved. The door banged open. I sucked in a breath and let it out. Nash stepped into the doorway and gunfire blasted down the hall. He stepped back. The wood splintered where his head had been. A muffled bang punched the air. The door slammed against the wall. I rotated right and squeezed the trigger. The shadow disappeared. Something thudded. Splashing emanated from the foyer.

I'd shot Charles.

I shook my head. No. But I might have shot a person. And I'd almost shot Nash.

My breathing sped up. I lowered my arms. Yanked them up again. But they shook and I couldn't straighten them. I had to pee and I wanted to throw up. And I was still standing in a hallway where two killers might lurk.

"Nash," I whispered. I glanced down the hall, looking for the shadow. Dashed toward his door sideways, keeping my arms locked and gun pointed in front of me.

Before I reached him, he eased into the doorway. Eyes on the stairwell, he stepped out. With one arm, he pointed his .38 toward the landing. The other snaked out, grabbed my waist, and hauled me inside.

"Miss Albright," he panted. "Glad to see you're finally carrying your .38."

I stared at Zhou's gun in my hand. A revolver. Not a Makarov. No wonder my hand didn't feel broken. The pistol had been Shiyu's. She'd killed Xi and Jeff Johnson.

"I thought it was going to hurt," I said. "But I didn't think. I just fired."

"Self-preservation. You operated on instinct and muscle memory."

"This is not my gun. It's not pink."

"Whose piece is it?"

"Zhou's. I took it from him."

"Atta girl."

Spots danced in my sight. My brow furrowed and lips tightened. I drew back my right hand and slapped him. Hard enough to lose his tan for a beat.

Nash stood a moment, blinking. He hauled me against his body and kissed the top of my head. "It'll be okay," he murmured, his arms tightening around me. "You're going to be okay."

The familiarity calmed me. I hadn't realized how hard I'd been shaking.

"I think I shot somebody." Somewhere deep inside, I felt a wail bubble up, ready to burst. I suppressed it. Packed it down. Tromped on it. "And you seem happy about it."

"I'm happy you protected yourself. Happy you're not hurt. Happy you didn't shoot me." He dropped his arms and stepped back. "Stay here."

I grabbed his shirt. "Wait, where are the police? Lydia was supposed to call them."

He shook his head. "She didn't make it out of the garage."

"What?" The word exploded from my chest, surprising me. "They killed Lydia? They shot the help?"

His brow puckered. "Yes?"

"You wait here," I spat the words. "Zhou's may be unarmed. But I'm going to kill Shiyu."

He grasped my shoulder. "No, you're not."

Tears bit my eyes. "I shot at her once. I'll shoot her again."

"No."

"They killed the housekeeper. Lydia was supposed to go to brunch. On me."

He slipped the revolver from my hand, flipped the safety, and slid it inside his shoulder holster. "They're gangsters. They work for the Lees. It's what they do. Clean up messes."

"They," my voice trembled and caught, "took my mother and planned to kill her."

He folded me into his body. Wrapping me tightly. I couldn't move. I didn't want to move.

Nash spoke into my hair. "The federal agent told me Jeff Johnson sold the yin-yang contract information to China. Jeff told Xi who the Lees really were. Scared him. Jeff convinced Xi he'd help him defect if Xi could get photos of the contracts. You were right, Jeff was a spy. He was recruited when he studied overseas as a college student."

Frat boy smirk. "Jeff knew the Lees had a condo in Clearwater, didn't he?"

"Yes."

"Why Lili? She's going to be heartbroken."

His hand smoothed my hair and kneaded my neck. "Miss Liang's been looking at Hollywood and fishing for an American boyfriend. She wasn't paying her taxes and willing to let crooks finance her film. Do the math."

I pressed my forehead against his chest. "But she's so talented."

"Shortcuts don't always work."

"What if Shiyu and Zhou get away?"

"I called the police when I arrived and found Lydia," he said. "When I heard about Jeff, I came to get your mother. Take her somewhere safe. I didn't think you'd be here."

I looked up at him. "You were going to save my mother?"

He nodded. "Where is Vicki?"

"In the Lees' bathroom. I told her, if anyone tries to break in, hit them with the toilet tank lid."

He clutched me tighter, his body trembled, and he buried his face in my hair.

"Are you laughing?"

"I'll go to Vicki now." He released me, unclipped his holster, and handed me the .38. "They're still out there, so stay alert. But don't shoot the police. They don't like that."

"I'm going with you."

"Then *you're* opening the bathroom door."

FIFTY-EIGHT
#18CALIBER

IN THE DISTANCE, sirens blared, but they sounded too far off to protect us. Nash eased into the doorway, revolver gripped in both hands and angled toward the ground. He studied the stairwell, glanced toward the other end of the hall, and nodded.

I slipped behind him, my hands clasping Zhou's gun and my brain flashing through every *Julia Pinkerton* season finale. I held my arms out, careful to keep the .38 pointed toward the floor. Ran toward the Lees' room in a semi-crouch.

At the entrance, I peered inside. Satisfied they hadn't returned, I pivoted to see down the hall. Positioned myself to cover Nash. Somewhere in the house, a door opened and shut. I shivered, already anxious for the search the police would have to conduct. I forced my brain to stay present and squelched my body's trembling. Nash glanced back. I nodded. His long legs loped toward the Lees' suite.

On the landing, shadows moved and converged. A large figure appeared, framed in the passage by the faint light of the stairway.

Zhou.

He raised his arms. His hands gripped something. Had to be a weapon. I screamed. Nash glanced back, swiveled, and aimed.

Checking myself, I fixed the sight on Zhou and blew out my breath, readied my finger on the trigger.

Zhou collapsed accompanied by a series of gunshots.

Not from us.

Nash still stood with his feet planted and arms raised, ready to fire. He cocked his head. Glanced back at me. Laid his .38 on the ground and motioned for me to do the same.

"Put down your weapons," shouted a male voice. "Law enforcement. Hands where we can see them."

Another figure appeared in the stairwell. Then two more. They slunk around the sides of the walls.

Placing my hands on my head, I moved out of the doorway and stood next to Nash. The shadowy figures leaned over Zhou. Another moved through the entrance and into the light of the hallway.

Misty.

"Boy howdy," said Misty. "You know how to throw a party. You two okay?"

"Misty, what are you doing here?" My arms slithered off my head and trembled at my side.

"She's a Fed," said Nash. "Found out yesterday when I met with the agent from Florida. They'd been watching this house because of the Lees. That's why everything came together so quickly."

"Misty's an FBI plant?" Not a very good one, IMHO. "I told you about the bullet in the doorway."

"And no crime was committed, but I logged it." She shrugged. "Zhou let off a gun at a party, I'm guessing. Probably Jeff Johnson had just gone out the door. Mr. Zhou has a temper."

"You shot Zhou."

"Better him than you." She smirked then sobered "He had his weapon pointed at you."

"What weapon?" I said.

"Looked like a pistol. Hopefully the murder weapon. Makes our job easier."

"Where's Shiyu?"

"Found her tied up in the office."

"Shiyu killed Xi and Jeff Johnson. She's faking. The Makarov is her weapon." I pointed to the .38 on the floor behind me. "That's Zhou's. He said he was going to make it right. He must have heard the sirens. He was on a suicide mission. He loved Lili and had failed her."

"He also failed his bosses. If he was on a suicide mission, Zhou would have killed you first. And whoever else is here," said Misty. "Then he would have turned his weapon on us, so we'd shoot him. Shiyu's story would have only worked if there were no witnesses. He didn't realize we were here yet. We entered the house before the local police arrived. "

Zhou would have killed us. All of us. He only cared about Lili. I bit down on my lip hard. Pinched my thumb.

Nash glanced at me, then slung an arm around my shoulders. "Come on. Let's rescue Vicki from the bathroom."

VICKI and I sat on the Lees' bed, blankets draped over our shoulders. Our testimony taken and questions answered. For now. Nash had chosen a chair in the front room and refused the blanket.

"You ordered the sweep for bugs in Lili's trailer," I said. "You knew someone could be spying on her."

"Lili's request. I thought she was being quirky." Vicki had fixed her makeup and hair in the bathroom. She'd also fixed her nerves. "Misty was an excellent driver. What am I going to do now?"

I did a quick emotional check. No sense of hurt or abandonment. Just irritation. Mild at best. I could handle irritation.

"Honestly," said Vicki. "All of this could have been handled better if Misty had just collaborated with me. If I had known the Lees were crooks, I would have worked harder to find more appropriate funding for *Unlucky 18*. Now production's halted and everyone's out of a job. Lili will have to return to China."

The spots in my eyes were closer to pink than red. Progress.

"Stick with Lili, Vicki," I said. "She's going to need a friend. But she broke the law in her country and will have to deal with the consequences. When that's done, she'll have to rebuild her life and career. It would help Lili to know that you're waiting."

"If they let her out of the country again."

"Give her hope. She's been through a lot of betrayals even if she's criminally negligent," I said. "And so have you."

"I'm not criminally negligent."

That was for the law to decide. But Vicki needed to feel grounded again. I was no longer a child. I could help my mother in a new way. With my emotional support. "I mean you've been through a lot. You have someone waiting for you, too. Kevin loves you. And he'll want to help Lili. He believes in her talent and he has strong political feelings about her situation."

She arched her neck to study the ceiling. "Yes. Assisting political dissidents has always been popular. We'll have to play down the tax evasion angle—"

"Kevin won't do it for the PR. And you shouldn't either."

"Really, Maizie."

"Just trust him. He came here for you. Working with Lili and *Unlucky 18* was a bonus for him, but he dropped everything to help *you*."

Her cheeks flushed.

A good sign. Keeping Kevin out of the spotlight meant her feelings for him were real. "Kevin knows enough people that you can find new producers for *Unlucky 18*. He wants to see the film succeed. It's a good opportunity for you, too. You need real insiders, not just wannabe film backers like the Lees. You're a strong negotiator and a good schmoozer. You can do this."

"A motion picture associate producer," she whispered.

"If you make it happen quickly enough, Chey and Stanley

will still have a chance to shine. And the crew won't be out of work."

"Stanley's extremely talented. And so is Chey. I always said he had star potential."

My internal eyeballs rolled. "But you'll give Kevin a chance, right? Not just in business. But personally. I'd love to have him around. Permanently."

Her head whipped to the side. She stared at me. "Permanently?"

"He's good for you. He gets you." I placed my hand on hers. "I love you, Vicki. But I've got to live my own life. I give you my blessings for a lot of success in your career. But I'd like to see you happy in your home life. As you might have noticed, careers can crash in a millisecond."

"I love you, too, Maizie." She patted my hand. "I guess I've been overzealous in trying to keep you close. You're all I have that's truly important. It's why I want the best for you."

My eyes prickled and skin flushed. Joy gave a better adrenaline rush than any drug.

"And I'd like you to partner with me," she continued. "You'd make a good life coach. I could use an advisor. Perhaps all that therapy you had worked better than I thought."

The rush had fizzled, but the joyful impact remained. "There's only one career for me. And I still have a lot to learn. A. Lot. But I look forward to growing into the role."

"I still think it's a bad idea. Look at all this violence. And your wardrobe? Burberry with camo? Really, Maizie." She slid her hand out from under mine. "Tell Mr. Nash I'd like to speak to him about Annie."

Hope swelled in my chest. "You're not firing him?"

"I'm sure we can work something out."

I jumped from the bed and dashed through the sitting area door. "Nash, did you hear any of that?"

He nodded. Stood. Closed the pocket doors.

"I'm not going to do it." His look was long and patient.

Painfully so. "It's time for me to move on, Maizie. You know I don't like mixing business and personal. I can't focus, and in this business, you can't get away with that. Look what happened. I missed a lot of important details because, frankly, you make my thoughts cloudy. I checked out this Annie Cox and she's got a good rep. She'll be a fine mentor for you."

A million thoughts crashed inside my head, all ending with the word, "No."

"Nash?" called Misty from the doorway. "We could use you out here. Maizie, you and Vicki are free to go. Tell her she can pack some things, but this house will be closed off for a while."

"But." I reached for Nash's hand, then dropped my arm.

"I'll call you." He pulled me into a quick hug. "It'll be okay. Take care of your mom."

FIFTY-NINE
#SHUTUPANDKISSME

THE SAVORY SCENT of chicken fried steak permeated the kitchen once again. Pies were made. Sweet tea stirred. Carol Lynn bustled about, humming. Remi had ordered the dogs outside (supposedly) and left her Daisy in the garage (allegedly). Daddy swore to be on his best behavior, but he had locked himself in his office to "get his head in the game."

Whatever it took. Their last meeting had been at my court date with Judge Ellis. Hopefully this time, it would play more like *Irreconcilable Differences* than *Clash of the Titans*.

I wore Saint Laurent again. This time a satin tie blouse with skinny jeans and leather platform sandals. Completely opaque. Chunky heel, no stilettos. The girls had given me a fabulous blowout and my nails were on point. And when I answered the door, I got an eyebrow raise and nod. From Vicki. I also received a kiss and a hug. And a takedown.

From Kevin.

Love my stepdad. Or soon-to-be stepdad, I hoped. But we would have to talk about the whole *Pink Panther* surprise attack-thing. I might have broken my tailbone.

"This is why you should wear flat-soled shoes, Maizie," said Kevin, holding out a hand to help me up. "You never know when someone might sweep your feet. You can't land well in heels."

Remi nodded. "You could crush some things pretty good with those heels, though."

"That one," I pointed to Remi. "Is not allowed to learn any kung fu. She's already dangerous."

At Remi's pout, Kevin winked. "I'll talk to your father."

"Vicki," rumbled a voice from the hall. Daddy tromped into the foyer. He wore camo but unscented. The print detailed his slacks, jacket, and a tie. His beard looked freshly trimmed, too.

"Boomer." Vicki nodded. "Lovely little place you have here. Cozy." She caught my daggered look. "It's very nice. Very you. And your daughter is delightful."

Daddy's gaze moved beyond Vicki. "Remington Marie," he growled.

"I'm trying to take Kevin down like he did to Maizie." Remi had wrapped her legs around Kevin's waist and jerked on his neck. "He's super strong. I bet he could fight a bear."

"Nice to meet you, Boomer." Kevin walked forward and held out his hand. Remi hung from the extended arm. "Your daughter would make an excellent wushu student. But I might recommend Tai Chi for her. Not only is it defense training, it's also meditative."

Boomer stroked his beard and smiled. "Let me get you a beer."

Before Vicki could roll her eyes, I shot her another look. "We also have wine."

"Boone's Farm?" she muttered.

"Clos du Val. Daddy has an excellent cellar."

The doorbell chimed. "Go on," I said. "I'll get it."

I waited until Boomer had led the group into the kitchen. Sipped small breaths, stilled the frantic beating of my heart, and opened the door.

Not what I was expecting. Giulio Belloni with his arm wrapped around a beautiful woman. Her caramel locks fell across her shoulders in perfect ombre waves. They wore matching Armani.

"*Ciao*, darling." He leaned forward to give me a double cheek air kiss that ended on my lips. "Meet Giselle. My fiancé. Didn't you hear, darling? I won *Sporting Love*. Won't you congratulate me?"

"I'll congratulate you both," I said, holding out my hand.

Giselle stared at my hand. "I'm, like, not into handshakes. Uh, germs, you know."

"Sorry." I slipped my hand back. "But on the show, weren't you with multiple men…you know forget it. Congratulations."

"Isn't it fabulous, darling?" Giulio beamed. "We'll be on the cover of *People* this week."

"Fabulous." I glanced over my shoulder. "Giulio, Vicki's here. Have you told her yet?"

"Of course, she's my manager."

I quelled the questions in my mind. I'd never understand his explanation anyway. No better than I did Vicki's. Some mysteries were best left unsolved. "Do you want to meet Kevin Yuan? He and Vicki renewed their relationship recently. We're having a family dinner tonight. Join us. Carol Lynn made enough for an army."

"Sounds fabulous, darling. I've always wanted to see this *casa padronale*. This cabin is interesting, Giselle, yes?"

"I told you, English only, Giulio." Giselle pouted. "I don't speak Spanish."

I pointed toward the kitchen and said a quick prayer Daddy wouldn't kill me for inviting them.

The doorbell rang again. I whirled around and yanked on the handle. Nash stood in the entrance. A fresh-scented breeze, promising spring, blew through the door. He held plastic-wrapped tulips in one hand. A paper bag in the other.

He handed me the tulips. "These are for Carol Lynn."

"Very nice," I said, trying to hide the confusion in my voice. "She'll love them."

"Boomer invited me."

"He told me. But why?"

"We had a conversation." Nash ran a hand over his head and stepped inside. I shut the door. "A job interview, too. He asked me to head up his security team."

"Oh." Disappointment flooded me faster than San Fernando Valley after a Pacific storm.

"Not what you expected, I know. But it's a solid job that pays well. Holidays and health insurance."

I nodded. "All good things."

"It's not sexy. Or interesting. I worked in retail before. It's mostly busting skimmers and shoplifters. But it's stable."

"Sexy can be overrated." I filed that nugget about his work history for later. "I have some bad news for you. Vicki's also here. With Kevin. As a business dinner, it'll be awkward. For you. If you want to back out now…"

"Boomer told me it's a family dinner. Your idea."

I sighed. "Yes, I'm trying to create some stability of my own. But seriously, I know how you feel about family dinners. If you don't want to stay…"

"I want to stay. If you'll have me." He held out the paper bag. "These are for you. I came here to ask for your forgiveness."

I unrolled the scrunched top and breathed in the sweet scent of fried dough. "Dixie Kreme donuts." The perfect gift. From whom I thought was the perfect man.

"Lamar misses you." Nash folded his arms over his chest. "I miss you. More than I can put in words. I guess I could have found a Hallmark card that explained it better…" He shook his head. "What I'm trying to say is, I want to work at DeerNose for you."

"But I don't want you to work at DeerNose."

His shoulders sagged. "I want to be a better man. For you."

"But I want you to be you. For you." I frowned. Did that make sense? "I don't want you to give up your career for me. I ruined your business. It wouldn't be fair for you to work for my father."

"I already worked for your mother."

"And look how that turned out," I snapped.

He pinched the bridge of his nose and worked his jaw. "What I'm trying to say, Miss Albright. Maizie. *Dear*. Is that I'm willing to work for your father. Have a stable job which pays well and has health insurance and holidays. So I can get out of debt and buy a house. And give you more than donuts. Why don't you understand this?"

"I like donuts." I fisted my hands on my hips. "A lot."

"I know you do," he thundered. "That's why I brought them."

"You do you." I jerked my chin up. "I'll do me."

"What does that mean?"

"It means we're different. I accept that now. And you should accept it, too. But you're wrong about what you think I want because of how I grew up."

"I'm wrong?" His hands clenched his biceps. His brow furrowed and his jaw hardened. "Financial stability is important. I talked to your dad. He got it. Why don't you?"

"Because you're both men?"

"Why is this so hard?" He stared at the ceiling, then dropped his gaze to me. The ice blue eyes narrowed. "Dammit. Maizie Marlin Spayberry Albright, I love you. I want to be with you. And I'm just trying to do right by you."

"Well, dammit, Wyatt Nash, I love you, too." I crossed my arms. "But I told you that. And you left me anyway."

"For your own good. Until I could clean up my act."

"Why don't I get a say in what's good for me or not?"

He stopped pacing and swung around to face me. "Do you want me to leave? I'll leave."

"No." I secretly pinched my thumb behind my back. "I want you to apologize."

"I'm sorry."

"And promise when your debts are paid off, you'll decide on

a position based on your future career goals. Not on how many donuts you can buy me."

His eyebrows lowered and eyes glinted. He opened his mouth.

I held up a finger. "It's important. I need to buy my own donuts. And a car. And, as soon as the probation officer okays it, my own place."

His shoulders relaxed. "I promise."

"And promise to never make a decision about our relationship without discussing it with me. We decide together."

"I promise," he said quickly. His jaw softened and the indentation between his eyes disappeared.

"I don't want to be mentored by anyone else." I felt my chin wobble. I gritted my teeth. "But I'll do it. For you."

"Don't do it for me. Do it for you." He grinned and the little dimple near his scar popped into view. "You do you. I'll do me."

"But I want the old office back. Nash Security Solutions. And Lamar in the chair. And us." A fat tear slid down my face and stained my satin. "I want us. Not you and me."

He moved forward, capturing me in his arms. His hands slid to my shoulders and he brushed back my hair. "We'll make it a goal. Our goal. But the sign will say Albright and Nash Security Solutions." He paused. "Unless your name changes."

"Like Nash and Nash?" My nerves sang the Hallelujah chorus. Fireworks shot off in my head.

The dimple disappeared. "Something to think about. Later. After the debts are paid off. I want to do things right this time."

I told my nerves to quiet down, but I allowed a few more Roman candles to pop. "You should kiss me now."

He complied. And only stopped when we heard Remi complain.

The End.

(But not really! 18 1/2 DISGUISES is next.)

SIXTY
BONUS CHAPTERS
#CABINFEVERISH &
#SPORTINGSUSPICIONS

ORIGINALLY THIS SCENE happened around Chapter 14. During my revision, I cut out these two short chapters. If you remember, Maizie had learned from her mother that Giulio was competing on a Bachelorette-styled reality show. She left the Peanut Mansion to get Giulio's take on Vicki's strange behavior and to learn what he knew about the gun/bullet situation.

As much as I love Giulio (not as much as he loves himself), it slowed the pacing down. However, it's a fun scene, so I saved it. It doesn't interfere with the arc of the story, so it won't take away from what you just read. It just wasn't necessary.

I hope you enjoy this little edition! :)

Larissa

CHAPTER 14.5 #CABINFEVERISH

———

MASTER KEVIN and Lili were ready for round two in their workout and although I should have stayed to get more information on Master Xi's disappearance, I wanted to find Giulio before he was booted from his bachelor cabin. I felt fairly certain he'd soon be given his rose. Or whatever symbolic gesture they used for a cabin theme.

Roasted chestnuts, perhaps.

I sat in the backseat of the Escalade, allowing Misty to fulfill her chauffeuring dreams. As we zipped down Black Pine Mountain, I called Nash to update him on my plans.

"I found Giulio," I said. "I hope he knows something about what's going on with Vicki. He's on another reality show during the *All is Albright* hiatus. They're filming in Blue Ridge. A *Bachelorette* spinoff called *Sporting Love: Cabin Fever*. I looked it up. Twenty men vie for the hand of one woman by competing in winter sports. The winner has a chance to propose at the next Winter Olympics. Giulio's from northern Italy, so he grew up skiing. I'm sure he'll do well. Despite already being engaged."

"Sounds like hell on earth," said Nash dryly.

"Sounded cold to me. Can I borrow your truck? I can't trust Lucky to drive that far."

"Absolutely you can't drive that toy up to Blue Ridge. I'll meet you at the office."

I sighed. "It might be better to let me go alone. You know how you get around Giulio."

"Giulio Baloney?"

"See? It's Belloni, not Baloney. And that kind of antagonism just makes him worse."

"I was kidding."

I wasn't so sure.

"And Maizie?"

"Yes?"

"I'm still driving you to Blue Ridge."

Hells.

THE *SPORTING LOVE: Cabin Fever* location was secret, but Giulio's assistant gave us the address readily enough. Which meant he was either a terrible assistant or Giulio was bored. Or maybe a bit of both.

In Georgia, Blue Ridge could refer to the mountains, the scenic highway, or the town. It seemed the cabin and shoots were in various locations, so check all of the above. The cabin lay due west although the driving was circuitous, which always happened in the mountains. Nash and I left in sunny, coolish weather. We arrived at a cabin surrounded by snow.

"I didn't dress for this," I said. "I was afraid I'd have to spar with Master Kevin, but he let me off the hook today."

Nash gave me a sidelong, eyeing my leggings. "I agree. You should've covered up more. But not because of the weather. How many men are in this cabin?"

"They started with twenty. I don't know how far into the season they are now."

Nash hopped from his side of the truck and walked around to get my door. I smiled. Always the southern gentleman. Wrapping my arms around my Electric & Rose sweatshirt, I readied for a blast of arctic air. My door swung open and I slid out tentatively.

The air was no cooler here than in Black Pine. Which made sense as we were in the same mountain range and it'd only taken 45 minutes to get here. I dropped my arms from their hug and stepped into a snowy puddle.

"What gives?" I said, shaking the water from my Veja leather sneakers.

"Fake snow." Nash kicked a pile with his boots. "Where are they doing the winter sports? Closest skiing is in North Carolina or Gatlinburg. Both are three or four hours from here."

"Maybe I misunderstood the sporting events."

"Or maybe they're stretching the definition of sports." Nash pointed to an area cleared of trees to the side of the large cabin.

A brightly colored obstacle course had been built. Nash and I trekked to get a better view. Several camera crews were stationed around the course. A stage had been built where a woman perched on a throne, poised on a dais. Muscular men with pageant ribbons crossing their bare chests huddled around a man and woman I took to be directors or producers. I spotted Giulio. His dark hair had been slicked back into a ponytail. His pants appeared tighter than normal.

Quite a feat for Giulio.

"Its like *Ninja Warrior* meets *Wipeout*. But instead of water hazards, they have snow."

"And instead of athletes, it's a bunch of TV-wannabe knuckle-heads." Nash turned toward the parking area. "It looks like they'll be a while. I'm going to wait in the truck."

I tiptoed through the slush to the edge of the obstacle course. Giulio waved. "Maizie, darling. Come meet the cast."

Signaling my consent, I approached the stage. While trying to keep my sneakers from getting soaked, I crept over cables, camera tracks, and piles of melting snow. I climbed the stairs to the stage and found myself surrounded by a large group of McDreamy himbos.

Giulio reached for a hug and circled his arm around my shoulder. He gestured with a hand draped precariously low over my sweatshirt. "My friends, this is Maizie Albright. Surely you know her. She starred in *Julia Pinkerton, Teen Detective* and some terrible tv movies, plus my show, *All is Albright,* until she was arrested and extradited back to Georgia."

"There was no extradition involved—"

"I think I'm too young to remember *Julia Pinkerton,*" said a blond, blue-eyed man. While flexing his muscles. Perhaps involuntarily.

"We look to be the same age," I said. "But that's cool. You were probably into other shows."

He laughed and his teeth glinted in the sunshine. "Can't be. I'm twenty-eight."

"You're actually older than m—"

"Darling," Giulio's Italian accent deepened. "What brings you to my new show?"

"I need to talk to you about some stuff going on at Vicki's."

"Do not mention Vicki," Giulio whispered, then raised his voice. "Your mother, Vicki Albright, the famed celebrity manager?"

Nineteen male heads directed their focus on me.

"What did you say your name was?" said Blondie. "I have a headshot I can sign for you. And a buttshot, if you're more into that. So many fans have talked about my Jacuzzi scene, my assistant made buttshots. Maybe your mom would like one?"

"Yeah, no." My second mental vomit of the day. "I'll pass. But thanks."

"Darling, let me introduce you to Giselle. She's doing such a good job. It's her first television gig, and I've been coaching her quite a bit."

"I bet." This time I had an involuntary muscular spasm. My eyes circling their sockets.

Giulio guided me across the stage toward the beautiful woman still sitting on the throne. Her caramel locks fell across her shoulders in perfect ombre waves. She was shivering in a sleeveless ball gown, but I had to give her credit. She kept her shoulders squared, chin up, and lipstick unsmudged.

"Giselle, meet Maizie. She's fabulous. Maybe you know her work? She was on my show, *All is Albright*—"

"I know Maizie Albright. I'm a huge *Kung Fu Kate* fan," said Giselle. "At least, when I was eight. I loved how after fighting the bad guys, you and your girl posse would kick back in the club-house and make smoothies. I still use some of those smoothie recipes."

I grinned and stepped onto her throne's dais to shake her hands. "Thank you. That's so sweet. It was a fun show."

She frowned. "You're not supposed to be up here."

"Yes, Maizie. You can only kneel on this platform," said Giulio.

"Sorry." I backed off the dais.

"It's okay." Giselle shrugged. "Rules, you know. But you can, like, kneel if you want."

"I'm good." I slid backward a step.

"What have you done since *Kung Fu Kate*?" said Giselle. "To be honest, I'm kind of surprised to see you. I thought, like, you had died or something."

"Died? After *Kung Fu Kate*? I was fourteen when that show ended."

"No? I could've sworn you died."

"No, didn't die. Still here. Won an Emmy at one point, but you know, whatevs. That's in the past."

"Totally in the past." She nodded. "I mean, like, who are you now? I ask myself that question, like every day. It's so important."

"I'm a private investig—"

"It is so wise to do the reality check, Giselle," interrupted Giulio, his accent thickening. "Otherwise…" He lifted his hands with his shoulders. "Tragedy, yes? Like with Maizie. One day she has the Emmy. The next she is facing the prison."

"I don't think I ever really faced prison—"

"It is okay, darling." Giulio gave me a side hug, his eyes on Giselle. "You are so brave. Isn't she brave?"

"So brave." Giselle's eyes narrowed. "Giulio, have they scheduled our hot tub scene yet?"

Giulio's arm dropped from my shoulder. "I am not sure, darling. Maybe you should ask Brenda. She might have scheduled someone else today. Anyway…" Giulio paused. I could almost hear him counting the beats. "I planned to catch up with Maizie this afternoon. Or as long as Maizie can stay."

"But Giulio." Giselle pouted. "We should really do a scene today. Wardrobe has this super cute bikini for me. From the back, it looks like I'm not wearing anything."

"It sounds very naughty." Dropping forward, Giulio kneeled on the dais and took Giselle's hand. "Speak to Brenda, *amore mio*. It is the only way we can be alone."

He rose, slung his arm about my waist, and turned. Glancing over his shoulder, he spoke in his most tragic Italian accent. One I recognized from *All Is Albright*'s pivotal scenes. "I only hope Brenda comes through for us. But if not, it will give me time for Maizie, no?"

He guided me toward the platform's stairs. Before I could clamber down, Giulio took my hand, helping me as if I wasn't an able-bodied woman wearing sneakers.

"Brenda," screamed Giselle. "I need you right now. Someone get me Brenda."

I yanked my hand from his and glared. "Nice acting," I said through my teeth. "You got the gig."

"Thank you, darling." He smiled, dazzling me with his over-whitened teeth. "I find the competition exhilarating."

"Glad I could help," I seethed. "Humiliating me got you a seat in a hot tub."

"Humiliated? No. It is impossible with your talents," Giulio shrugged, feigning ignorance. Another trick I recognized. "You have the many great qualities. I am so sorry if I offended."

"Just give me a heads up next time you use me to advance your bachelor placing, step-dad-to-be."

"Don't be ridiculous. You're way too old for the step-father. Let me apologize properly." He reached for me.

I sidestepped to avoid the fake hug. Another trick I recognized. And suspected he overly enjoyed. "And stop touching me." I swung around and almost smacked into Nash.

"Miss Albright," said Nash.

"Your private dick has followed you to the Cabin of Pleasure," exclaimed Giulio. "How exciting. Would you like to compete with me on Mount Winter Warrior, Detective Nash? I must warn you. I'm quite good at the dodging and climbing."

"I'm sure you are," said Nash. "But no. We want to talk to you about a bullet, a gun, and a missing person."

CHAPTER 15.5 #SPORTINGSUSPICIONS

NASH, Giulio, and I sat in overstuffed leather chairs before a fire crackling in a large stone fireplace. He assured us this was not part of the set but a kind of green room. It had a fully stocked bar and a table catered by Craft Services. Happy to relive my craft service days, I drank cocoa and nibbled on home-made cookies. Giulio had a Peroni. Nash refused all offers, including the *Cabin Fever*-branded bottle of water that he looked at with such disdain, I thought it might spontaneously leak.

"Of course I don't own the gun. And Vicki?" Giulio shrugged. "Who knows? I have been gone for three weeks while we're on hiatus. I don't know what she does in that time."

"You haven't talked to her for three weeks?" I said. "She's your fiancee."

"She understands my need for concentration. When I'm working, I'm absorbed in the role. I can not break character."

"Your character is you scamming on a woman," said Nash. "How hard is that to muster?"

Giulio lifted his chin. "I take my work very seriously. And this is not like the average reality competition show. They bring in the new man all the time. You have to work very hard to stay at the Cabin of Pleasure."

"Please stop calling it that," I said. "It's really hard to enjoy a cookie when you want to puke."

"How was Vicki last time you spoke to her?" said Nash. "Did she seem different? Act differently?"

"In maybe a worse way?" I said. "And have you seen the new fish tank?"

Giulio leaned back in his armchair, taking his time to sip the Peroni and pretend to think. "She's different, yes. Nervous, no?"

I squinted at him over my cookie. "You think she's acting

nervous? How?" I'd not seen Vicki nervous. Or if I had, it was before I had any solid acting gigs, back when we first moved to LA. It's hard to remember your mother before she was your manager.

Nash shifted next to me and I glanced at him. He had his investigator game-face on. Impassively regarding Giulio but looking a little scary while doing so.

"Vicki, she is the confident woman. But lately..." Giulio shrugged and set his Peroni down, consciously building suspense for his monologue. "I don't know. She is working very hard to impress this foreign production company. The Asian money has mostly dried up, you know. It's not like it was ten years ago. New laws in China or something prevents them from financing US movies like they were."

"Why is Vicki trying to get in with a Chinese film production company?" I leaned forward. "That's quite a leap from celebrity management to movie producing."

"She's a producer for *All is Albright*. And for your horrible TV movies."

"They weren't all horri—"

Nash cleared his throat.

"Anyway," I continued. "Jumping from cable TV to film is a big leap. I thought she had Lili Liang staying at the house because Vicki's hoping to get Lili to sign with her as an American agent."

"That, too." Giulio studied his manicure. "Vicki is always— how do you call it?—hustling." He looked up and fixed me with a hard stare. "More so now than ever."

"Why now?"

"She desires fingers in all the pots." Giulio gave me the slow blink and pursed his lips. "To cover her eggs. She does not make the same mistake twice."

"Come again?" said Nash.

"Giulio has some difficulty with American idioms," I said. When it suited him. "I think what Giulio is trying to say is Vicki had banked on moving me from a TV star into a film star and I blew that dream for her. So now she's diversifying. Which is incredibly hard to do."

"Not when you have financial backers," said Nash. "So this foreign investment opportunity is making her nervous?"

"*Sì.*" Giulio picked up his Peroni and took a delicate sip. "It is better that I'm here in the Cabin of Pleasure and away from that stress."

"Probably," I said. "But it still doesn't explain the possible gun in her desk. Or the bullet hole in her door. And why she may be lying about it."

"Or the missing Chinese man," said Nash.

"I have no idea, darlings," said Giulio. "Your guess is as good as mine. I have been working very hard to win the hand of Giselle, so I haven't met any of the *Unlucky 18* guests. Perhaps there was a party that got a little wild…"

"Have you heard about any wild parties?"

"I've told you I haven't spoken to her, but you know Vicki. She will show her guests the good time. Vicki's very good at intuitively understanding what someone really desires and obliging them." He smirked.

I dropped my cookie and my appetite. "Are you and Vicki still engaged?"

"Who knows? We wait and see how I do here, then make our decision."

"Based on which relationship offers the best PR opportunity."

"Of course, darling." Giulio's teeth gleamed. "That is what I like best about your *madre*. She's always thinking of what is best for my career."

"She's always thinking about what's best, that's for sure," I muttered. "But I don't know if it's your career she has in mind."

MOVIES AND TV SHOWS MENTIONED

Alice in Wonderland
America Ninja Warrior
American Psycho
And Then There Were None
Brideshead Revisited
Bugsy
Casino
Clash of the Titans
Clue
Crazy Rich Asians
Downtown Abbey
Get Shorty
Goodfellas
Gosford Park
High Noon
Irreconcilable Differences
James Bond films
Julia Pinkerton, Teen Detective
Kung Fu Kate
Lassie
Law & Order

The Maltese Falcon
Minority Report
Mission Impossible
Monty Python (flesh wound)
Mr. And Mrs. Smith
Nancy Drew
Narcos
Oceans 8
Once Upon a Mattress
Real Housewives
Rebecca
Scooby Doo
Shawshank Redemption
Speed
Sporting Love
Supercop
The Bachelorette
The Black Rose
The Godfather
The Karate Kid
The Lady From Shanghai
The Pink Panther
The Positively True Adventures of the Alleged Texas Cheerleader-Murdering Mom
The Proposal
The Sopranos
The Way of the Dragon
The Wizard of Oz
White Knights
Wipeout

LARISSA'S SERIES

15 MINUTES

16 MILLIMETERS

NC-17

A VIEW TO A CHILL

17.5 CARTRIDGES IN A PEAR TREE

18 CALIBER

18 1/2 DISGUISES

19 CRIMINALS

20 CARATS

21 GUNS

"Child star and hilarious hot mess Maizie Albright trades Hollywood for the backwoods of Georgia and pure delight ensues. Maizie's my new favorite escape from reality."

GRETCHEN ARCHER, *USA TODAY* BESTSELLING AUTHOR

Ex-teen TV and reality star, Maizie Albright, returns home to Black Pine, Georgia, determined to start a new career as a private investigator, modeled after her childhood starring role as "Julie Pinkerton, Teen Detective." Unfortunately, Maizie's chosen mentor, Wyatt Nash of Nash Security Solutions, is not a willing teacher, and her learning curve includes becoming her own person after spending life under the thumb of managers, directors, and producers, particularly her stage-monster mother.

FINLEY GOODHART CRIME CAPERS

"As fun as it is moving and at times heartbreaking, never the more so when the final page comes and readers are only left wanting more."

CYNTHIA CHOW, *KING'S RIVER LIFE MAGAZINE*

THE PIG'N A POKE (prequel)

THE CUPID CAPER

Ex-con Finley Goodhart finds her criminal past — and criminal ex-boyfriend — useful in catching crooks. Can she make up for her past by helping victims double-cross their swindlers? More importantly, can she convince Lex that going straight is the best (and most challenging) hustle of all?

ABOUT THE AUTHOR

Wall Street Journal bestselling and award-winning author, Larissa Reinhart writes humorous mysteries and romantic comedies including the critically acclaimed Maizie Albright Star Detective, Cherry Tucker Mystery, and Finley Goodhart Crime Caper series. Her works have been chosen as book club picks by *Woman's World Magazine* and *Hot Mystery Reviews*.

Larissa's family and dog, Biscuit, had been living in Japan, but once again call Georgia home. See them on HGTV's *House Hunters International* "Living for the Weekend in Nagoya" episode. Visit her website, <u>LarissaReinhart.com</u>, join her VIP Readers' Group, and get a free short Finley Goodhart story.

facebook.com/larissareinhartwriter

instagram.com/larissareinhart

bookbub.com/authors/larissa-reinhart

goodreads.com/LarissaReinhart

pinterest.com/LarissaReinhart

amazon.com/stores/Larissa-Reinhart/author/B008EME5MA